"Long-buried secrets cause tension and emotion to run high."

—*The Old Book Barn Gazette*

"A story of forgiveness and personal redemption . . . [from] the prolific Michaels."

—*Booklist*

NO PLACE LIKE HOME

"Uniquely charming . . . bursting with humor . . . this warmhearted confection is as soothing as a cup of hot cocoa."

—*Publishers Weekly*

THE REAL DEAL

"Exciting contemporary romantic suspense. . . . The exhilarating suspense plot is filled with twists. . . . Will appeal to fans of Nora Roberts and Jayne Ann Krentz."

—*Thebestreviews.com*

"If you are seeking a story of passion, suspense, and intrigue . . . *The Real Deal* is the perfect choice."

—*Romance Reviews Today*

LATE BLOOMER

"Michaels does what she does best [in *Late Bloomer*]. . . . Entertaining, action-packed . . . fun to read . . . engaging romantic suspense."

—*The Midwest Book Review*

"Heartwarming . . . *Late Bloomer* is nothing short of wonderful. You won't want to put it down."

—*Winter Haven News Chief (FL)*

Books by Fern Michaels

The Marriage Game
Hey, Good Looking
The Nosy Neighbor
Pretty Woman
Family Blessings
The Real Deal
Crown Jewel
Trading Places
Late Bloomer
No Place Like Home
The Delta Ladies
Wild Honey

THE
MARRIAGE
GAME

FERN MICHAELS

POCKET STAR BOOKS
New York   London   Toronto   Sydney

Pocket Star Books
A Division of Simon & Schuster, Inc.
1230 Avenue of the Americas
New York, NY 10020

This book is a work of fiction. Names, characters, places, and incidents are products of the author's imagination or are used fictitiously. Any resemblance to actual events or locales or persons, living or dead, is entirely coincidental.

This Pocket Star Books paperback edition June 2011

POCKET STAR BOOKS and colophon are registered trademarks of Simon & Schuster, Inc.

For information regarding special discounts for bulk purchases, please contact Simon & Schuster Special Sales at 1-866-506-1949 or business@simonandschuster.com.

The Simon & Schuster Speakers Bureau can bring authors to your live event. For more information or to book an event contact the Simon & Schuster Speakers Bureau at 1-866-248-3049 or visit our website at www.simonspeakers.com.

Cover design by Lisa Litwack; front cover photographs: woman © Herman Estevez; flowers © Getty Images; dog © superstock.

Manufactured in the United States of America

10   9   8   7   6   5   4   3   2   1

ISBN 978-1-4516-4835-5
ISBN 978-1-4165-3943-8 (ebook)

Once in a while a special person enters your life whom you want to acknowledge. For me, John Stephens is that special person. Thank you, John, for all you do for me.

F. M.

THE
MARRIAGE
GAME

Prologue

Samantha Rainford, just hours away from her thirtieth birthday and forty-eight hours away from being served with divorce papers, looked around the tiny apartment she'd lived in for the last five years. It was tiny but cozy and comfortable. For the most part, all she did was sleep here. Every piece of furniture had been chosen with care. Every knickknack meaningful. Even the plants had been chosen with regard to light and temperature. Translated it meant she was a home-and-hearth kind of gal. So much so that her husband of three weeks had just served divorce papers on her.

Sometimes life was a bitch.

Sam took another look around the tiny apartment. She'd sold off the furniture, the knickknacks, and even her luscious plants to the new tenant who was moving in tomorrow, at which point she would move into the condo she'd been in the process of buying when she'd been caught up in a whirlwind romance with Douglas Cosmo Rainford, III.

Samantha gathered up her coat, her purse, and the carry-on that contained what she referred to as her "life," and made her way through the living room to the front door, where her bags waited for her. She shoved them one by one out into the hallway. The manager would have them in the garage waiting to be loaded into her BMW by the time she took the elevator to the garage. Then she would take them to her new condo a mile away in Alexandria, Virginia. The condo was a spacious, two-bedroom, two-bath, up-and-down condo that she'd furnished in two days' time. It even had a fireplace, the main reason she'd bought the condo in the first place. The fireplace was part of her nesting home-and-hearth personality. The kitchen had new appliances and ample counter space. She could hardly wait to cook her first dinner and mess up the place. Best of all, she had an unlisted telephone number that she'd given out to only a select few, including her closest friend Sara, otherwise known as Slick, who was a super, glossy, high-fashion model, her employer, and, of course, the bank where she had her checking and savings accounts. In addition to those accounts, she had several CDs that she'd taken out with her modest inheritance from her grandmother years before and all the savings bonds she'd gotten as gifts during her lifetime. She was definitely solvent.

An hour later Sam was lugging her bags into her new home. The minute the bags were in her spacious living room, she locked the door and danced around the room, clapping her hands in glee. It was all hers. No one could cross the threshold unless she invited them in. All hers. She started to cry then because it wasn't supposed to happen like this. She was supposed to start her new life with her new husband, not alone in a condo just three weeks after her honeymoon.

She swiped at her eyes with the sleeve of her shirt as she looked at her watch through tear-filled eyes. She had one hour till her appointment with Douglas's attorney. What *that* was all about, she had no clue. The call had come in yesterday, just an hour after she'd been served with divorce papers, *inviting* her to the offices of Prizzi, Prizzi, Prizzi, and Prizzi.

She thought about blowing off the Prizzi law firm but decided to keep the appointment so that when she returned to her new nest, her past would be just that, her past. Her lawyer could handle the divorce, and she would simply move on. She needed time to grieve, to cry and sob, to stomp her feet and get down and ugly. The honeymoon must have been some kind of test that she failed. How crazy was *that*?

The honeymoon was everything a honeymoon was supposed to be. She'd loved every minute on the exotic island. Loved the togetherness, loved making love on the beach under the stars. Loved hearing her new husband whisper sweet words of undying love in her ears.

She had every right to expect that she would return home and have a normal marriage. Instead, she'd returned home to be served with divorce papers. Even a stupid person could figure out the divorce papers had to have been drawn up and filed while they were still on their honeymoon.

Sam looked around for her purse and car keys. The little mirror by the front door showed her that her eyes were red and puffy. As if she cared. Minutes later she was on her way.

As she maneuvered the BMW up and down the streets, she wondered what this particular summons was all about. Something to sign undoubtedly. She'd called an attorney who was a client of the accounting firm where she worked to represent her, but he'd been out of the office taking a deposition. His secretary said she would have him return her call later in the day.

She was on K Street with two blocks to go. She found a vacant spot, parked, buttoned her coat against the cold wind, and moved toward the entrance to the building that housed the Prizzi law firm. She signed in, showed her ID, and headed for the elevator that would take her to the eighteenth floor.

The law firm was one of the most prestigious firms in the DC area, befitting Douglas Rainford, III, who liked to say he measured everything in life by dollar signs and beauty. "I have an appointment with Mr. Prizzi. Is it one, two, three, or four? Prizzi I mean," Sam asked.

The receptionist looked up at Sam with a blank expression before she looked down at her appointment book. "Which one?" Sam prompted as she looked around the shiny, marble lobby with the expensive furniture and luscious green plants. She looked down at her watch. "I'm in a hurry," she said coolly.

"Isn't everyone?" the receptionist responded just as coolly.

"Yes, but I'll leave if Mr. Prizzi doesn't see me in the next . . . three minutes," Sam said, her eyes glued to her watch. *What am I doing here? I never should have come. My lawyer can handle things.*

The phone console buzzed. The receptionist listened attentively. She hung up the phone, and said, "Mr. Prizzi will see you now. Go through the door on the right. Mr. Prizzi's office is the third door on the right."

Sam unbuttoned her coat as she walked through the open door and down the hall. She took a second to look at the nameplate on the door. Emmett Prizzi. The worm. Number Four in the pecking order of Prizzi brothers. Smallest office off the long hallway, one tiny window, no secretary. It could only mean one thing, Emmett Prizzi was the runt of the litter. She felt insulted.

Emmett Prizzi was a smallish man, thin and wiry. He wore large, thick glasses that magnified his eyes and seemed to engulf his thin face. He didn't bother putting his jacket on, nor did he bother to stand up to greet her. A worm. She felt more insulted. Without waiting to be asked, she sat down across from his desk. She felt bold and aggressive. She also felt wounded and sad, but this worm didn't need to know that. She wished she'd put on some makeup. "I don't have much time, Mr. Prizzi, so let's get right to the point." That's when she saw the folder on his desk. Even though it was upside down, she knew it was the prenuptial agreement she'd signed before she married Douglas. She waited.

The attorney was just about to speak when a knock sounded on the door and it opened almost immediately. A secretary handed over a sheaf of papers, which the attorney ignored.

Emmett Prizzi shuffled the papers in a folder that had her name on the flap. Sam saw a blue check work its way out of the folder. The lawyer picked it up and waved it around, then wet his lips as he tried to decide what he was going to say. Sam lost her patience. "Yes?"

The lawyer took a deep breath. "Your husband said I was to give you this check and to tell you he's sorry things didn't work out. The check is for five thousand dollars as per the prenuptial agreement. As you know, if you and Douglas had remained married after the five years stipulated, you were to get ten million dollars. Since that isn't going to happen, this is your payoff." He slid the check across the desk. Sam looked down at the blue check and wanted to cry. Five thousand dollars for a three-week honeymoon. The man she'd married, the man she'd thought she loved, certainly moved at the speed of light. She made no move to pick it up because she was too busy fighting the tears that threatened to roll down her cheeks. She leaned back in the leather chair and forced a laugh that sounded hysterical to her own ears.

"I don't find this a laughing matter, Mrs. Rainford," the worm squeaked. Another paper slid across the desk. "All you have to do is sign the release, and the check is yours."

Sam laughed again as she stood up. She started to fasten her coat. All she could think about was the new cozy condo she was going to return to. She was going to cook a wonderful dinner, build a fire, and settle in with a good book. She didn't know if that would be before or after she cried her eyes out.

"I don't want it. I don't need it. Is there anything else, Mr. Prizzi?"

"You have to take it," the lawyer sputtered.

"No. No, I don't have to take it. I'm not signing anything either. From here on in, you can talk to my attorney."

The lawyer snorted. "That's what the second Mrs. Rainford said. It didn't get her very far."

The second Mrs. Rainford. Surely she'd heard wrong. She shrugged. "Ask me if I care."

"That's exactly what the third Mrs. Rainford said. In the end she *did* care."

The third Mrs. Rainford. That had to mean she was the *fourth* Mrs. Rainford. She had to get out of here *immediately* so she could think about what she'd just heard. She was almost to the door, the lawyer following her, when she turned, and said, "What did the *first* Mrs. Rainford say?"

Prizzi started to sputter again. "She said she didn't give a good rat's ass what her husband wanted, and she would take him to the cleaners. Of course, that didn't happen."

Sam opened the door and sailed through. Douglas had had three other wives he hadn't seen fit to tell her about. Prizzi caught up with her at the elevator. Up close and personal, he still looked like a skinny worm. He reached out to touch her arm. Sam jerked away. "You have to sign the paper or you don't get the check, Mrs. Rainford. The bank in the lobby is giving a free blender if you open a new account," he said.

Sam pierced him with one scathing look before she stepped into the elevator. "I have a blender, Mr. Prizzi. Tell Mr. Rainford he can just kiss my ass."

Hysterical laughter bubbled out of Sam's mouth as she rode the elevator to the first floor of the office building. She dabbed at her eyes, not caring if anyone saw her or not.

Three ex-wives. Three!

Forty-five minutes later, just as Sam was fitting her key into the lock of her new home, her cell phone rang. She clicked it on, jiggling her shoulder bag and the key. "Slick! Wait, wait, I can barely hear you. Let me get inside. What's wrong, you sound terrible. Then again, you're half a world away. You're not half a world away? You're at Reagan National? Of course you can come here. Wait, I'm not in the old apartment. I moved into my new condo today. You have the address. You're crying, Slick. Get a cab, and I'll have the coffee on."

Sam shrugged out of her coat and hung it in the closet. Her best friend in the whole world was coming to visit, and she was crying. Slick never cried. Never. Ever. Crying made the eyes puff, something no model could allow to happen. Something must have happened in her love life, and she was coming home to lick her wounds. They'd curl up by the fire and cry together, then talk it to death. At least with Slick here, she wouldn't have to think about Douglas and his three ex-wives and getting dumped the day after her honeymoon.

In her bedroom, which was painted a delicate peach color, Sam shed her business suit and pulled on a navy sweat suit and heavy wool socks. She turned up the heat as she made her way to the kitchen to prepare her first dinner in her new abode. Stew and homemade bread. Perfect for a cold, blustery November day.

Don't think, don't think, she cautioned herself as she dredged the meat in flour, then browned it. In minutes she had the vegetables chopped and the stew set to simmer. The bread machine took an additional few minutes. She was proud of her pantry and stocked refrigerator and freezer. *Don't think about Douglas and the three wives that came before you. Don't think, period.*

All the dinner preparations had been taken care of with an economy of motion, the way Sam did everything. The oven was on, but it hadn't yet reached the temperature required to bake the frozen blueberry pie compliments of Mrs. Smith. While she waited, she made her first pot of coffee in her new coffeepot. It was a bright cherry red machine.

Done. Sam smacked her hands together. *Three wives and I never had a clue. Don't think about it. It's over and done with. Think about Slick and whatever her problem is.*

This was the perfect warm, cozy place for Slick and herself to lick their wounds. Sam looked around the kitchen. She'd taken pains with it, hanging ferns and settling potted plants in colorful clay pots in the corners of the counters. The maple table and chairs by the bow window were inviting, allowing for a full view of the garden outside. It looked barren now, but in the spring and summer it would be beautiful. She did love the color red, and all the accent pieces in the cozy kitchen reflected that love. She couldn't wait to have her morning coffee and frozen bagel right here in the morning.

Sam slid the blueberry pie into the oven, set the timer, and moved on to the living room, where she built a fire. Douglas was divorcing her after a three-week whirlwind courtship, a justice-of-the-peace wedding, and a three-week honeymoon. What did that say about her? What were the three Rainford wives that came before her like? *Why did Douglas divorce them? More to the point, why did he marry me?* she wondered.

Sam stared into the fire, looking for the answers to her

questions, finding nothing that would satisfy her. She turned around, savoring the tantalizing smells wafting in from the kitchen. There was nothing like the smell of baking bread to remind her of the times she spent at her grandmother's when she was a little girl. Thursday was always bread-baking day. Of course her grandmother hadn't had a bread machine. She did it the old-fashioned way. Everything Grandma had done, she'd done the old-fashioned way. She'd hung clothes on the line outdoors, ironed her sheets and pillowcases. She'd stretched her curtains on a contraption that was a killer on the fingers. She'd canned vegetables, made her own root beer, and kept a fully stocked root cellar. She was gone now, having died, Sam thought, of a broken heart soon after Grandpa had died after a long illness.

One of these days she was going to return to Pennsylvania, and the old house with the big front porch that her grandmother had left to her. But not yet. She simply wasn't ready to bear those old ghosts. She paid the nominal taxes every year, paid the neighbors to mow the lawn in the summer and shovel the snow in the winter.

Sam almost jumped out of her skin when the doorbell rang. It was a five-note chime. She ran to the door and threw it open. "Slick!"

"Oh, Sam! Thanks for letting me come here. God, it's cold out here!" Sam stepped aside for the taxi driver to carry in Slick's bags.

"Oh, it smells *sooooo* good. And that fire is great. Can I sleep in front of it? Let's have a sleepover the way we used to do in college." Slick gave Sam a quick hug, then wiped the tears from her eyes. "They fired me, Sam. Sheer Delight fired me! They replaced me with a nineteen-year-old girl whose legs go all the way up to her neck. She's Scandinavian and weighs ninety-three pounds. Just like that they fired me! Do you believe that? I was so upset I packed up when the shoot was over and for two months I ate my way across Europe. I put on eighteen pounds. What do you think of *that*!" She burst into tears, not caring if her eyes got puffy or red. "My whole life is over!"

Sam waited until Slick paid the driver, then led her over to the deep comfortable sofa in front of the fire. "What I think is you look wonderful! You don't look like a plank of wood. Your bones aren't showing. You look *healthy*, Slick. Your life is not over, it's just beginning. I'll get us some coffee. Then we'll talk."

"Four sugars and cream," Slick said.

"What happened to black coffee?"

"I left black coffee with the Scandinavian. By the way, her name is Grette." Slick started to cry again.

It was midnight when Slick finally asked the question Sam dreaded. "What are you going to do now, Sam?"

"I'm going to work for the FBI after all. I was going to sign on, but then I met Douglas, and everything changed. They gave me ninety days to make up my mind. They've been actively recruiting for the past few months. Want to join up?"

"Hell, yes. It's got to be better than strutting down a runway throwing my hips and pelvis out of joint."

"Then we'll sign you up tomorrow," Sam said.

Chapter 1

Eight Months Later

Special Agent Jim Yakum approached Sam on her way back to the room she shared with Slick. "Hold on, Rainford."

Sam turned, a feeling of dread settling over her. She stopped in midstride and waited, knowing full well what was coming. She bit down on her lower lip, her hands clenched into tight fists at her side. She wanted to cry, she really did. No one out of her class of thirty-two had worked harder, struggled more, and now here was Special Agent Yakum to tell her it had all been in vain. She was a washout. A wannabe FBI agent. She would never be called a *fibbie*. The bottom line was she couldn't cut it.

The FBI agent shuffled his feet, looking over her

head, then around the hall to make sure they weren't overheard. "Look, Rainford, I just wanted to give you a heads-up. There's no other way to say this other than to say it. You didn't make it. I'm sorry." Sam knew they weren't just words. Yakum *was* sorry. Special Agent Yakum was one of the good guys. At least in her eyes.

God, she wanted to cry so bad, to stamp her feet and just pitch a fit. She knew she couldn't do any of those things. She squared her shoulders and struggled for a sickly smile. "I know." She absolutely refused to ask if she was the only one who didn't make it.

The agent shrugged. "It was your lack of upper body strength, Rainford. If it's any consolation to you, Hawkins didn't make it either." Hawkins was a six-foot-two, 180-pound hunk of a guy who was so good-looking he made your eyes water. The agent continued, "Nine others, not including you and Hawkins, washed out. A total of eleven washouts for this class."

Sam turned and started down the hall. Yakum was still with her. "I guess that means you want me to leave *now*."

"That's your call, Rainford. I can walk you out to your car and that way you can avoid any . . ."

"Embarrassment? You're thinking I'd rather slink out than walk out with my head up, is that it? Maybe the others will slink out, but I'll go out the way I came in. I'll walk out on my own, thank you very much," Sam said, a catch in her throat. The hot tears were pricking her eyelids. She had to get to the room she shared with Slick.

She wondered if Slick made it. She almost asked but knew the words would come out all garbled. Big girls didn't cry. Especially big girls who wanted to be FBI agents.

They were at the door to her room. A hateful room, with stainless-steel this and stainless-steel that. She had one suitcase to pack. Ten minutes tops. She turned to the agent and said, "Thanks for the heads-up. I know you didn't have to do that."

"You worked hard, Rainford. Sometimes life just isn't fair. Good luck." Yakum held out a big, beefy paw. Sam shook his hand. "See ya around."

"Yeah, see ya around," Sam responded. Like she was ever going to see this big galoot anywhere.

Sam opened the door to see Slick sitting on her bunk, her packed bag at her feet. "What took you so long?"

"Yakum gave me the bad news. You washed out, too! I thought . . ."

Slick wiggled her fingers. "Not strong enough for rapid fire on an Uzi. I heard Hawkins washed out. Now that's a mind-bender right there. C'mon, Sam, pack up and let's head for Flip's. I could use a drink. If you cry, I'll smack you, Sam. Accept it, we weren't good enough. I can live with that, and so can you. We can cry in our beer at Flip's. Not here. Wait, wait, wait! I have an idea." She ran to the closet and yanked out a scarlet spandex dress and tossed it to Sam. She had her own suitcase open within seconds. Five minutes later, she'd shed her jeans and donned skimpy thong underwear and a black push-up bra. "We're going out of here in style, baby, and I don't want to hear another word! That means makeup and hairstyle. Fifteen minutes and we're both runway material. Now, goddamn it, Sam, move!"

Sam moved.

Fifteen minutes later both women looked at their reflections in the stainless-steel mirrors fastened to the closet doors. Sam gasped. "We look like *sluts*!"

Slick waved her hand airily. "There are sluts, and there are *sluts*!"

In spite of herself, Sam laughed. "Should we call down to have someone take our bags?"

Slick took a second appraising look at herself in the mirror. Satisfied, she turned to Sam. "I say we leave the damn bags. I don't want any reminders of this place, and I don't think you do either. Take the makeup, though. Now, aren't you glad I insisted we bring these outfits? The first rule in modeling is always be prepared."

"Oh, yeah," Sam drawled. "I hope I don't kill myself in these three-inch heels. The first thing I'm going to do is take a gardenia-scented bubble bath when I get home to get the stink of this place off me. Are we really leaving our bags?"

"Yeah, let them paw through our cotton underwear and have wet dreams while they're doing it. Is the bath before or after Flip's?"

"After."

Slick's hand was on the doorknob. The time was four-thirty in the afternoon. Within seconds the hall would be full of agents and their classmates. Slick cupped her hands under her breasts, gave a little push, tugged the spandex down over her ass, and marched out to the hall. She turned to Sam, and hissed, "Strut, baby! I showed you how to do it, now make me proud of you. Head back, and push out that pelvis. Don't look at anyone and follow me."

Catcalls, whistles, and lewd comments followed them down the hall and out to the main concourse. A group of Marine officers stopped in their tracks, giving Sam and Slick stunned looks and raised eyebrows. Slick slowed, twirled her beaded purse before she wagged her finger under the officers' noses. Sam winked, and said, "Your loss, boys!"

The wannabes sailed through the door unaware of the surveillance cameras aimed at them. The women high-fived each other as they walked toward the parking lot and Sam's car.

"Last chance, home or Flip's?" Slick asked.

"Flip's. You drive, Slick. I want to make some calls. I think we should have a party at Flip's."

"Oooh, I like the way that sounds. Who are we inviting?"

"The first, second, and third Mrs. Rainford! My divorce was finalized yesterday. I think it's time to compare notes. I used the FBI data bank to get their numbers, and I have full profiles on them. Hell, I even tried to do one on my ex. You won't believe what I found out about that guy. He doesn't exist. What do you think of that?"

Slick's jaw dropped. "You married someone who doesn't exist! How can that be? If you found the other . . . ah . . . wives, why can't you find him? Did you get copies of the marriage licenses? You must have done something wrong, Sam. The FBI had files on *everyone*, and I do mean everyone." She nibbled on a nail before she said, "What are you going to do?"

"Well, his identity is so secret that it can only be accessed by those with top secret security clearance. I'll figure out some way to find out who Douglas Rainford really is. That's a project for tomorrow."

Slick slipped the car into gear. "Shouldn't we . . . you know, do something . . . say something, you know, meaningful as we depart? Maybe something profound. How about a single-digit salute?"

"We made our statement in these outfits, Slick. You wanna yell, Semper Fi or something like that to all those gung ho Marines out there, go for it! The gardenia bubble bath can wait. Head for Flip's."

Slick lowered her window, her left hand hanging out while she steered with her right hand. The minute they roared through the gates, Quantico behind them, she offered up her single-digit salute. The cameraman off in the distance caught the salute in midair with his zoom lens. Women always had such interesting conversations. He laughed as he imagined the look on his superior's face when he showed him the pictures and let him listen to the audiotapes.

*   *   *

Flip's was your regulation DC bar, with lots of mahogany and polished brass. By five forty-five the bar would be full of politicos, Pentagon workers, secretaries, and Hill staffers, most, if not all, on the make. Happy hour was from six to seven, and Flip turned out a good table, meaning wings, chips, salsa, and pizza rolls. Friday nights were a madhouse; it was when Flip served all-you-can-eat shrimp. Free, of course. The place hummed and bustled, and if you were lucky enough to get a table, you hung on to it for the night. Unless, of course, you got lucky and headed home for an early evening with a member of the opposite sex. On more than one occasion, the occupants of the table took a gratuity of twenty or so bucks from someone waiting for a table, enough to pay for the drinks before departing. It was DC, the land of power brokers and spin artists.

"These shoes are killing me," Sam said as she moved through the revolving door. They were early enough that a table was available in the rear of the room, far enough away from the brass-and-mahogany bar that a person could actually hear what his or her companion was saying. The bar tables were high enough and round enough that five stools could fit comfortably. Each woman slid onto a stool, then looked at each other before they burst out laughing.

The man who was tailing the two women was Poke Donovan. His real name was Peter but he'd been christened Poke a lifetime ago because he always carried a poke on his back, a canvas bag with the tools of his trade. He settled himself at the far end of the bar, the end closest to them. He ordered a Heineken he intended to nurse for a while as he settled down to wait. He found himself a little chagrined that the two women hadn't noticed him following them. So much for the FBI surveillance course they'd taken.

Poke eyed the red-hot wings Flip's was known for. Certain his quarry wasn't going anywhere, he walked over to the buffet and loaded up a plate that he carried back to his seat at the bar. The women were drinking margaritas by the pitcher. Before he dived into the wings, he pulled out his BlackBerry and clicked it on. Two messages from the boss. **Check in. Details please.** His own return emails were just as succinct. **On target. Too soon for details.** He settled back to devour the wings.

He saw the first, the second, and the third Mrs. Rainford walk past the section of the bar where he was sitting. Lookers, all three of them. Definitely on a par with the two at the bar table. A miniature listening device in his ear enabled him to eat and listen to the conversation among the five women.

"Kayla Rainford. The first Mrs. Rainford," the redhead said, offering her hand to Slick and Sam.

"Olivia Rainford. The second Mrs. Rainford," the blonde said. She shook hands all around.

"Zoe Rainford. The third Mrs. Rainford," a blackhaired woman with eyes just as dark said.

"I'm the fourth Mrs. Rainford. Call me Sam. My divorce was finalized yesterday," Sam said. "Please, sit down. Have a drink. This little party is on me."

The women looked at Slick. "I'm Sara, but my friends call me Slick, and I don't belong to your little club. I'm just a friend of Sam's." She poured from the pitcher and signaled the waitress for another.

Sam eyed the beautiful women and wondered what in the world had possessed her to initiate this meeting. Maybe it was washing out of the FBI. Maybe it was the signed divorce papers. Maybe she just wanted to know how the three women had gone on with their lives after Douglas divorced them. Maybe a lot of things.

"We need to make a toast," Slick said. "I say we make it to new beginnings and to womanhood."

The women raised their glasses and drained them. Slick poured again.

And they're on their way, the man at the bar thought. He headed back to the buffet and filled his plate again. He was back on his barstool as the women started to explain their relationships with Douglas Rainford, III.

"I guess I'll start, since I was the first. At least I think I was the first," Kayla said. "Douglas used to come to see me dance. I'm an exotic dancer." Sam raised her eyebrows. "Okay, I'm a belly dancer. I have muscles in my stomach that are like steel. My *real* job is working as an architect. I just dance three nights a week. I make more money dancing than I do at my real job. Douglas swept me off my feet," she said, with a dreamy look in her eyes.

"His money dazzled me, I admit it. The honeymoon was fantastic. He divorced me three weeks after the honeymoon. I walked away with five grand. One of the Prizzis called me into the office and served the papers on me right there. I have to tell you, it was a hell of a honeymoon. I had stars in my eyes the whole time. And the bait of the ten million down the road didn't hurt either. That's my story."

"Mine is pretty much the same," Olivia began. "Three weeks after the honeymoon, he gave me my walking papers courtesy of the Prizzi law firm. I didn't see it coming either. I took my five thousand dollars and walked off into the night. I have to agree with Kayla, the honeymoon was out of this world. Nothing ever measured up to it. I can't deny he was a hell of a lover."

"I don't have anything to add to that," Zoe continued. "My own experience was identical. I think Mr. Douglas Rainford, III, is a honeymoon junkie. It's obvious now that Douglas is not husband material. I blew my five grand in one day. I don't even remember what I spent it on." Zoe's voice turned dreamy-sounding, her eyes glazing over. "I guess I more or less feel like you all do, but I have to tell you, I have one outstanding, mind-blowing memory I will never forget."

The others looked at Zoe, their eyes angry at what they didn't know. "Share," they said in unison.

"Well, the second-to-the-last day of our honeymoon, we took a walk around the resort, which by the way was so private you could run around naked and no one would see you. It started to rain. It was a warm rain. Douglas kissed me and one thing led to another and then we were on the ground making love on a bed of gardenia petals. Buck naked, I might add. There were gardenia bushes all around us. The scent was so heady. I never wanted the moment to end, and Douglas didn't either. He picked a gardenia and stuck it between my breasts. It was a perfect gardenia. He said I was just as perfect as the flower. I . . . ah . . . still have it. The gardenia, I mean. Douglas said he would love me forever and ever. I said the same thing. He smiled and kissed me. It was all just so perfect.

"Then the son of a bitch divorced me. End of my story. What about you, Samantha?" Zoe asked.

"My deal was pretty much the same. I got dumped after the honeymoon. I didn't take the five thousand, though. He broke my heart."

Olivia's dark eyes glowed as she leaned across the table. "There's four of us here. Between us, we should be able to come up with a plan to get our ten million bucks. I think we all earned it."

Slick refilled their glasses.

"I'm sure we can find some sleazy lawyer who can file a class action suit. Too bad there's only four of us."

"Not true," Sam said. She leaned across the table and explained what she'd found out by using the FBI database. "There are four more besides us. I didn't have time to run checks on them, though."

Slick gasped, her eyes wild at Sam's declaration.

"Four more!" the women exclaimed in unison.

"Damn. I planned on putting that ten million dollars in my pension fund," Zoe said. "He has to pay for breaking my heart."

"Lawyers get most of it, you know. I know that because I'm a bean counter, and I crunch numbers. You know what, ladies, it's doable." Sam couldn't believe she was saying what she was saying.

Slick whistled between her teeth to be heard over the decibel level in the bar. She waggled the empty pitcher. A fresh one was brought almost immediately. She poured generously, slopping over the tabletop. No one seemed to mind as they raised their glasses in yet another toast.

The conversation turned to lawyers and who knew whom. The man at the bar listened in awe as Douglas Rainford, III's, future and financial demise were discussed. His gut told him they would prevail. His face turned hot as the conversation grew raunchier and more off-color. He started to pity Douglas Rainford, III.

It was ten o'clock when Poke heard Sam Rainford call a car service after she invited all the women back to her condo to spend the night so that they could further plot and scheme. He couldn't help but wonder if any of them would remember anything in the morning. They'd consumed six pitchers of margaritas. The bartender looked at him pointedly, so he ordered another Heineken.

Surely they would make a stop at the ladies' room on their way out. Or, they'd go one by one. He needed to contact his boss for further instruction. He yanked his BlackBerry out of his jacket pocket. Another message. **Check in.** He did. His message was simple. **They're sloshed. Scratch original plan. Have better one.**

He almost missed Sam when she tottered toward the bathroom. He slapped bills down on the bar and followed her. He stepped out of the way to allow Slick to enter the restroom behind Sam. He leaned against the wall and waited. He argued with himself about approaching them or waiting till morning. Before he could make up his mind, Sam and Slick exited the restroom, their spike-heeled shoes in hand. He was about to speak to them when the first, second, and third Rainford wives appeared out of nowhere.

His chance to speak to Sam and Slick evaporated. He walked to the door and left the bar. Morning would be time enough.

Outside, Poke stood to the side out of the rain that had started to fall. The night was warm, perfect July weather. He watched as the five women piled into the Lincoln Town Car. All of them were carrying their shoes and laughing as they tumbled over one another. Just to be sure the women made no other stops along the way, he followed them home at a discreet distance.

He hated sleeping in his car, but his boss would kill him if he allowed the two women to get away from him.

They were wily enough to pull a fast one. For all he knew, they had been on to him the whole time. He'd learned a long time ago never, under any circumstances, to underestimate a woman and her capabilities.

He didn't settle down for the long night until he was certain the women were inside and the lights went out. Only then did he sigh with relief. He pulled out his BlackBerry and typed in a message. **I'm on top of it. Stay tuned.**

Poke was an expert at sleeping with one eye open. He was an expert at so many things that sometimes he surprised himself. A sound he hadn't heard in years jerked him upright. He looked down at the glowing numerals on his watch. Five o'clock. The sound he heard was a milkman banging his metal crates. This was a new one on him. He thought everybody bought their milk in supermarkets or Quick Checks, which just proved that in his line of business you learned something new every day.

This was the part of his job he hated. Waking up, having to go to the bathroom, wrinkled clothes, a scummy mouth, and stubble on his face. He turned on the car engine and headed for the nearest Mobil station, a few blocks away. He felt certain nothing was going to happen while he was gone. It wasn't even light out yet.

Poke Donovan looked like an overripe pumpkin, round body, skinny neck, and narrow head. He also had a photographic memory and a mind like a steel trap. He wore glasses he didn't need. He thought the glasses made him look benevolent, but in reality they made him look even scarier than he did without them.

Poke longed for a shower. It was how he liked to start his day. Steaming hot, then freezing cold, followed by a cup of freshly ground coffee. Not one cup but three. It was his morning ritual. Except on occasions such as this one.

Ten minutes to revitalize himself, and he was back at Sam Rainford's condo. It was just starting to get light out. The milkman was gone. At the end of the cul-de-sac, a man in a jogging suit ran with a golden retriever. The streetlights were still on, casting everything in gray-and-lavender shadows. Poke got out of the car, reached in for his briefcase, then locked the door. The man with the dog was watching him. Maybe they had a Neighborhood Watch or something. He waved airily as he made his way toward Sam's condo. He had a lockpick in his hand, but with the neighbor watching him, he was wary of using it. He pretended to ring the bell as his chubby fingers worked the pick. Two seconds later the lock clicked, and he was inside.

Poke knew where everything was. He'd been there earlier to get the layout should he ever have to come inside without being invited. He took a minute to look around before he headed for the second floor and the bedroom that belonged to Sam Rainford. He made no sound as he climbed the stairs. He waited in the narrow hallway for a few seconds to see if anyone was moving.

The only thing he could hear was the sound of the golden retriever barking in the cul-de-sac outside.

Back downstairs, Poke walked to the kitchen, his gaze taking in everything. It took him five minutes to find the coffee and fill the pot with water and grounds. They would have to drink it black with sugar unless Sam had powdered milk. The refrigerator held nothing but bottled water, a bottle of wine, three bottles of beer, and two shriveled-up apples that were about to disintegrate.

Minutes later, he was back on the second floor checking the other rooms to see where the other women were sleeping. They were going to figure in his plans, too. Faint dawnlight was creeping through the shutters in Sam's bedroom. He tiptoed over to Sam's bed, aware that he was stepping on the scarlet spandex dress she had worn the evening before. It looked like she was wearing green plaid pajamas. He leaned over and cupped his hand against her mouth. She jerked and started to thrash about on the bed. "Shhh, I'm not here to hurt you. I just want you to come down to the kitchen to talk to me. I already made coffee. If you scream or make a sound, I *will* hurt you. Blink your eyes twice to show me you understand what I just said." Sam blinked twice, her eyes full of terror. "Good. I'm here to offer you and Slick jobs. Like I said, I don't want to hurt you. Relax, and I will show you something." Poke stepped back and turned, just far enough so that Sam could see the gun in his shoulder holster. With his free hand he pulled out a small leather folder and whisked it open. A gold shield glowed. A second later it was back in his breast pocket.

It was getting lighter out, and the bedroom wasn't so dim and dark. "I'm going to take my hand off your mouth. If you make one sound, I will hurt you. Blink if you understand." Sam blinked. "Good. Now, I want you to get up, go into Slick's room, and bring her here. Be very careful what you say. The three of us will go downstairs, have some coffee, and I'll tell you why I'm here. Now, move! I've never been known for my patience."

Her heart thundering in her chest, her mind racing, Sam bolted to the room next door, where she shook Slick's shoulder. She whispered in her ear before she backed out of the room. The pumpkin man backed up and headed down the steps, Sam right behind him. Outside, the golden retriever was howling.

In the cozy kitchen, Poke motioned for Sam to sit, then did the same thing when Slick walked in, her hair standing on end. She was dressed in a knee-length sleep shirt that said SWEET DREAMS on the front.

Poke poured coffee. The women eyed him warily, their hands cupped around their respective mugs.

"Believe it or not, ladies, I'm here to make your day!"

Chapter Two

Poke drained the coffee in his cup before he spoke to his wary audience. "I'm Poke Donovan and I'm here to make you both an offer of employment with a very select organization. You were both chosen because you washed out of the FBI Academy. We monitored you for the entire sixteen weeks you were at the Academy. We feel you were shortchanged, hence the offer. Should you wish to join us, you will sign a contract for four years. The first year will consist of training where you will *unlearn* everything you *think* you learned at the Academy. You will be trained by professionals, professionals unlike the instructors at the Academy. After your year of training, you will, as a team, conduct *missions*. Should you wash out, you will return to this life with a sizable bonus for your time. The salary for your training year is fifty-five thousand. You will earn every penny of it."

"What's the name of the organization you represent?" Sam asked carefully.

"All in good time. This is not a good time." Poke opened his backpack and withdrew two folders. He handed one to Slick and one to Sam. He watched their outraged expressions as they flipped through the pages.

"How . . . how did you . . . get our records from the FBI?" Slick demanded as she slammed the folder shut.

Instead of answering her, Poke reached into his backpack again and pulled out the photographs he'd taken yesterday. Both women gasped. It was Sam who said, "How did you get onto the Marine base to take these shots?"

Poke shrugged.

"Let me see that badge you showed me upstairs," Sam said defiantly.

"All in good time. I need your answer now. I'm prepared to give you ten days to wind up your affairs, at which point you will be taken to your new place of employment."

"This is way too vague for me," Slick said. "I need more details. What exactly will we be doing? What kind of training are you talking about? Are we going to be agents of the government? Why do we have to unlearn what we were taught at the Academy?"

"You were given pussycat training at the Academy. As I said, you will be retrained by professionals. As in professional mercenaries, professional assassins," Poke said, stretching the truth a bit. "You will do what you're told to do with no questions asked. You're going to be trained to be mercenaries, vigilantes if you prefer. *For the good guys.* Our organization is on no one's radar screen, government or otherwise. In fact, we don't exist. You as individuals will also cease to exist. That means you have to give up your plan to bring a class action suit against your ex-husband, Mrs. Rainford. You will have to sell this condominium, your car, close out your bank accounts. You will leave no trail that can be followed."

Sam's mind raced. "No. I can't give up this place. It's my home. I haven't even had a chance to enjoy it yet. My car is new. I'll never get back what I paid for it. If we close out our bank accounts, where do we put our funds? Fifty-five thousand a year isn't exactly a fortune. I can make that much during tax season and take the other eight months off. No."

Slick looked at the pumpkin, and said, "I'm with her." She got up to pour herself another cup of coffee. She added coffee to Sam's cup but ignored him.

Poke turned around, looked at the empty pot, then cleaned it out, added fresh water and grounds. He stared at both women with unblinking intensity. Sam moved uneasily on her chair. Slick looked up at the silk plant hanging over the kitchen sink.

"So, you're content being FBI washouts and wannabes. You're willing to accept the Academy's decision that you aren't fit material to be FBI agents."

"I don't think that's a fair summary," Sam mumbled.

"I agree with Sam," Slick said. "We didn't cut it, it's

that simple. Where will we be going for the year in question if we agree to your proposition?"

"A place that's not on any map. That's all I'm at liberty to tell you at this point. This is your chance to do something meaningful for your country. To redeem yourselves. To be true Americans." Donovan's voice rang like a politician's on the eve of an election.

Slick sipped at her coffee. It was almost cold. "How big is the training class?" she asked.

"Six," Poke said.

"Six?" Sam queried. "Who are the other four? Yeah, yeah, you aren't at liberty to tell us that either. Do you just snatch FBI rejects, or are you open to recruiting other people?"

"Normally, we go with the rejects from the Academy. Because . . . because the men and women who apply to the FBI want to make a difference in law enforcement. Recruiting off the street for the most part didn't work. But we never closed that door. If promising potential recruits come along, we don't turn them away. I'm not going to try and fool you. It's dangerous work, and you could get killed. You have to decide if being a good American is worth all that I'm telling you." His voice still sounded like a politician's. Sam knew if there was a baby nearby, he would have kissed it for effect.

Slick gnawed at a hangnail on her thumb. "Do we get a gun and a shield?" she asked inanely. "They said I had weak fingers."

"Of course you get a gun and a shield, but not till

your training is completed. This is not a Mickey Mouse operation, Slick."

Sam knew she was waffling. "What if it doesn't work out? I won't have a place to come back to. I don't like that part of your proposal."

"We can make arrangements. We always try to work with our trainees if we feel they have potential. All your questions will be answered when we arrive at our destination. We haven't had anyone wimp out if that's your next question." Poke filled his coffee cup. He picked up the portable phone and walked to the doorway. "This might be a good time for you two ladies to discuss my proposal. I can give you ten minutes, then I have to leave. I would be remiss if I didn't tell you the decision you make today will be life-altering. Keep that in mind, ladies. And don't forget for one minute that you will be doing your country an immense service."

"Oh, God!" Sam said, the minute the door to the dining room closed behind Donovan. "What should we do, Slick? Do you think this is one of those covert operation organizations? The kind the agents at the Academy whispered about. An organization that doesn't exist, that isn't on anyone's radar screen. Now, that's pretty scary if you want my opinion. How the hell did he get those pictures and our records? Not to mention he's been here before, in this house. He made us coffee in my very own house, and he was in my bedroom for God's sake. This is freaking me out, Slick."

"Ten days to wrap up our lives. That's what he said. I

liked that six-person training class. Four of *them* and two of *us*. That's the part that doesn't appeal to me. How about if we even up the odds and ask him to take on the three Rainford wives. Assuming they would want to do something like this. Personally, I think they'll jump at the chance. You can tell they all work out. They looked in damn good shape to me. What do you think, Sam?"

"Look, let's not kid ourselves. This *invitation* is a way for us to prove maybe, just maybe, we can cut it. I for one am never going to forget our exit from the Academy. We left there knowing we weren't good enough. We washed out. No matter how you look at it, those we left behind at the Academy are now referring to us as wannabes. If what this guy is saying is true, I think we owe it to ourselves to give it a chance. If we're lucky, we might ace the training. I'm damn well sick and tired of being a failure. As for the others, they look to me like they're ripe for an adventure. And they are in excellent shape. Donovan said it's better that the others weren't trained by the FBI like we were. I guess it means they'll be easier to mold and shape into what his organization wants."

"I guess it's a go then?"

Sam grimaced. "A belly dancer, a cartoon artist, and a female plumber as secret agents. Who would have thought the plumbing business was a six-figure-income job," she added as an afterthought.

Slick leaned across the table. She dropped her voice

to a low whisper. "I don't know about you, Sam, but I'm thinking our lives are going to be . . . to be different if we don't agree to this. As in maybe dead. I think I might make a good mercenary. For the *good guys* of course. Let's do it, Sam. If we don't like the training program, it's just a year out of our lives. It will be something to tell our grandchildren. And like the man said, we'll be doing something great for America in the bargain."

Sam looked at her best friend. Today Slick was nothing like she'd been when she'd gone off to Europe on her last modeling job. The gauntness was gone, her skin had a healthy glow to it. She'd put on twenty pounds, and she looked good. She even slouched, something she'd never done in the past. She was in such good shape, not just physically but mentally as well, that it was mind-boggling. If a supermodel aced the physical training the Academy demanded, why couldn't the three Rainford wives do the same thing? Maybe it wasn't such a cockamamie idea after all.

A washout, a wannabe. Did she want to go through the rest of her life with those tags hanging over her head? No, she did not. She also didn't want to go through the rest of her life being known as a number cruncher or a bean counter. But did she want to tell her children and her grandchildren she'd been a mercenary? *But that's okay, kiddies, I did it for the good guys. I was just being a good American.*

"If we go along with this and actually start to lead that secret life, we'll never meet anyone, never get married and have kids. We'll be old maids. We'll be like that ship with no home port. You know what I'm talking about, the one that sailed day and night and could never claim a home. We have to think about that, Slick. There won't be any children or grandchildren to tell our story to."

Slick ran her fingers through her hair. "I love this kitchen, Sam. It's easy to see you put a lot of work and thought into it. I know you'd miss it terribly, and we'd be crazy if we agreed to do this, but I still think we should. The guy said no one has *wimped* out. Maybe we aren't the rejects the FBI said we were. Maybe he's right, and we were trained wrong. Maybe, just maybe, some of those agents teaching us were right and the FBI doesn't really want women agents. I bet they have a secret quota just to keep it all on the up and up. And we both know those sensitivity classes sucked. Remember that second class where one of the guys pinched your ass after the class was over. They had no respect for women. None at all."

"All right, all right, you talked me into it," Sam said. "I have such a headache. I don't know when I ever drank as much as I drank last night. Never, that's when. Should we go talk to him or what? He said ten minutes. Are the ten minutes up yet?"

"I wasn't looking at the clock, Sam. Let's just sit here and wait. Do female plumbers really make six figures a year?"

"Zoe said she did. She said she wears these cute little outfits with lots of skin showing. Picture someone like that unclogging your kitchen drain? She probably has helpers to do the dirty work. Like some *man*."

"I never thought of that. Yeah, a man to do the un-clogging, and all she does is show up to collect the bill. She has a French manicure for whatever that's worth. But if she does earn that much, why would she give it up to make half that amount?"

Sam shrugged. "Maybe like us, she has something to prove and she wants to serve her country," she said, her eyes wild at the thought of what she was committing herself to.

Upstairs, the other three Rainford wives sat huddled in a nest of blankets and comforters. They looked up at the round man, their eyes full of awe, shock, and disbelief at what he was suggesting.

"Let me make sure I have this straight. You're offering the three of us jobs that pay fifty-five thousand dollars a year. We'll be good Americans if we take you up on your offer. We get a gun to shoot the bad guys. We're going to live somewhere for a whole year and train to become mer-cenaries. We're going to a place you can't pinpoint for us right now because it isn't on any map. You want us to work for an organization that is so secret, no one knows about it. After said training, we receive a bonus and owe you four years of work. Three, actually, since the training year is subtracted. It's a dangerous job, and our lives could be put in jeopardy. For all intents and purposes we will drop off the face of the earth. In other words, the minute we agree, we cease to be who we are. Right?" the belly dancer asked.

Poke Donovan smiled. "That about sums it up, Mrs. Rainford."

Kayla showed her pearly whites. "Okay, count me in." She sounded like she was agreeing to go to the grocery store for a friend. "But," she said cheerily, "I think you need to sweeten this deal a tad." She looked around at the others to see their heads bobbing in agreement.

Donovan clenched his teeth. "My superiors do not negotiate."

"Well then, I guess you should be on your way," Olivia said.

"All right, all right, I'll listen. What exactly would sweeten the deal?"

"More money," Zoe said. "Like *exactly* what I was earning in the private sector."

"Six-hundred-thread-count sheets and Egyptian cotton towels. I personally like pink ones," Olivia said.

"My CD collection," Kayla said.

Sam shrugged. "All of the above."

"Wait here. I have to make a phone call."

The women high-fived one another.

Donovan returned and shook his head. "Absolutely not."

"Yeah, well, let me show you to the door, *Mister* Donovan," Sam said, pushing the pumpkin toward the door.

"Okay, okay. My superior said we can meet your demands."

"You weasel!" Sam screeched. "Why didn't you just okay it when we told you what we wanted?"

"There are procedures. Chain of command. I do not have authority to authorize such silliness. I was just doing my job. So, do we have a deal or not?"

The women nodded. Donovan held out his hand. The women ignored him.

"Well then, ladies, that finishes our business. Get dressed and meet me downstairs. I'll have coffee ready for you," Donovan said generously.

Outside the bedroom Poke palmed his BlackBerry and typed in a short message. **All five cats are in the cradle.** He hummed under his breath as he made his way downstairs. He headed straight for the coffeepot. As it was empty, he made himself at home and prepared a fresh pot.

Poke congratulated himself on the deal he'd just made. Little did the women know he had been authorized to give them whatever they wanted, no matter how outrageous their demands.

At this point whenever he was making a deal he always made a bet with himself. Would the recruits ace the year on the mountain or wouldn't they? He bet yes. These five women were unlike any he had recruited to date. Yes, they would make it. He felt proud of himself.

"Nothing like making yourself at home," Sam sniped as she entered the kitchen.

"I'm not a male chauvinist, Mrs. Rainford. I never expect a woman to wait on me. Whatever I can do myself, I do."

Sam looked at the round man over the rim of her coffee cup.

"You all made a very wise decision." He nodded at the four other women who filed into the kitchen.

The kitchen table wasn't big enough for all six of them to sit comfortably. Sam and Slick moved over to the window seat that overlooked a summer garden full of colorful flowers. They waited while Donovan poured coffee for the women. Then they waited while he took his sweet time gathering official-looking contracts from his backpack.

When Donovan handed Sam the contract, she read it word for word, then read it a second time. Satisfied that she was indeed signing her life away, she held out her hand for the pen Donovan held toward her. She scribbled her name. Slick was next, followed by the belly dancer. The plumber and the cartoonist followed suit.

Donovan stacked the contracts neatly before he shoved them into the backpack. He offered up a jaunty salute, thanked them for the coffee, and headed for the door. Then he stopped. "You are not to discuss anything that transpired in this house today. Someone from the organization will be in touch. You'll all be receiving daily overnight packets. Do exactly what they say and things will work out smoothly. You have ten days to get your lives settled. You can expect a special overnight package with the final details on the ninth day. It's been a pleasure talking with all of you. Good-bye."

"Wait a minute. What about mail forwarding?" Slick asked.

"That goes under the heading of taking care of things. That's another way of saying you won't be receiving any mail where you will be residing." And without another word, Poke Donovan left the condo.

The five women stared at one another. No one seemed willing to break the silence.

Sam played with the collar of her pajama top. "I'm sorry I can't offer you breakfast. I can call us a cab, and we can go to Mulligan's. We all have to pick up our cars anyway. We also need to talk. What do you say?" Sam said.

The first three Rainford wives agreed. Sam and Slick sprinted upstairs, where they brushed their teeth and donned jeans and T-shirts. They were back downstairs in less than fifteen minutes.

"I called the taxi company. The cab's waiting. I think we should go to Flip's first so we can all pick up our cars. We can meet up at Mulligan's afterward. Is that okay with everyone?" Olivia asked.

It was.

The women piled into the cab. Sam hadn't bothered to lock her front door. What was the point?

Mulligan's was a local breakfast and lunch establishment that had been on the corner of Lotus and Sizemore Streets forever. Some people referred to it as a cafe. Others just called it Mulligan's. It opened at five in the morning and closed promptly at two thirty in the afternoon. The elder Mulligans made fresh bread daily. Mrs. Mulligan made her own strawberry-peach preserves, which the establishment was known for. They were known for other things, too, like the fresh eggs that were brought in daily from the farm in McLean where the Mulligans lived. Their milk and cream, which also was from the farm, was so fresh that the cream was yellow and sweet, the perfect complement to the fresh-ground coffee. The line for take-out coffee and cinnamon rolls had its own cash register. Most days the line of people waiting for a table, even on rainy, snowy days, circled around the block.

Sam was stunned when they all piled into the restaurant and were ushered to a table capable of seating five people. Then she looked at her watch. The rush hour was over.

A huge stainless-steel pot of coffee and a crystal pitcher of fresh orange juice were brought almost immediately to the table.

The women gave their orders to the young waitress, whose name tag said she was a Mulligan, Carol. They ordered the same thing all around, two eggs, extra crisp bacon, and a platter of the thick, Texas-style toast with fresh butter. A round bowl of the strawberry-peach jam followed. From past experience, Sam knew the bowl would be empty when they were done eating.

Slick tapped her fingers on the blue-and-white-checkered tablecloth. "Is there anyone here who doesn't think we're all nuts?" No one responded.

"Stop and think, what's a year out of our lives?" Kayla said in a voice that wasn't as blasé as it had been earlier. "We're women. Women can do anything they set their minds to."

"I wish I knew where it is we're going. No one will know our whereabouts. That scares me. Maybe we should . . . you know, leave a message in our safe-deposit boxes or something," Olivia said.

"I'm just starting to live, and he said we could die. I don't want to die. My business is growing by leaps and bounds. I finally found good people to do the grunt work. Why did we sign those damn contracts?" Zoe complained.

"The spirit of adventure, maybe," Slick said. "He'd already signed you up before we could suggest he consider the three of you. I'm starting to think it was his game plan all along. Think about it for a minute and tell me I'm wrong. Do any of you know anything at all about law enforcement?" The three Rainford wives shook their heads.

"I know what a mercenary is," Olivia muttered. "But I never thought I was going to go into training to become one. I think . . . it's one of those kill-or-be-killed things. I really don't know if I'm capable of killing anyone."

Sam's head shot up. "Think of Douglas Rainford, III, and see if you still feel that way."

Olivia laughed. "That makes me feel a lot better. Him I could kill without blinking."

After much banter back and forth, it was confirmed that they all, including Slick, had second thoughts.

The women looked at one another. Olivia spoke first. "Why are we doing this again?"

"To get over our respective divorces," Kayla said firmly. "Sam said she was going to come up with a plan to get Douglas for dumping us and reneging on the ten-million-dollar payment. And for the adventure of it all. It's a year out of our lives. There is every possibility that this might be the niche in our lives that will work for us. I'd like to get my hands around some bad-ass dude's neck and wreak havoc. In our mundane lives we could never do that and get away with it. When the year is over, we'll be kick-ass mercenaries and able to take on that jerk Douglas. That's how I'm looking at it. What about the rest of you?"

Kayla got hoots of pleasure, raised fists, and a little catcalling. She had her answer.

"Here comes breakfast," Sam said. "Let's not talk about this anymore until we're done eating."

They ate like truck drivers who'd been on the road for twenty-four straight hours. The coffeepot was empty, as was the juice pitcher. Zoe swirled the last of the strawberry-peach jam out of the bowl with her finger and licked it. Slick and Olivia fought over the last piece of toast. They ended up breaking it in two pieces. Their plates were clean.

"I bet you five bucks that guy sitting over there with the *Washington Post* is one of *them*," Kayla said. "Don't look now, though. I bet they have some kind of device that enables them to hear every word we're saying. How else did that guy know about Flip's and the stuff we were talking about? Like suing Douglas. Maybe I was cut out for this stuff after all." She whipped a slip of paper and a pen out of her purse and proceeded to scribble a message. When Kayla was sure the women had read the message, she pointed to Zoe.

Zoe picked up the gauntlet and ran with it. The sexual confessions that followed were explicit enough to burn a high-priced madam's ears. All lies of course.

Sam watched the man with the *Washington Post* out of the corner of her eye. From the color of his face and ears, he was hearing something he hadn't expected. Then she did what Kayla had done. She scribbled a message and slid it toward Slick. "Let's take him and see what happens. Just you and me." Slick nodded as she passed the note across the table. The three Rainford wives smiled.

It was so quick and sly, the few patrons left in the cafe had no idea what went down. They were just five women converging on a male customer, laughing and tweaking his chin as they led him outside.

Within seconds, Sam had the man's gun, and Slick had his credentials. Still laughing and giggling, the Rainford wives led the man to the parking lot and their four cars.

Sam looked around the parking lot to make sure no one was watching. Satisfied, she hissed, "Who is he?"

"His license says his name is Avery Mateo. This," she said, flipping open the slender folder, "says he works for AT&T. My ass," she said succinctly. "Well, lookie here." Slick plucked a small button out of the man's ear. "He has a license to carry the gun."

Sam shoved the heavy gun into her purse, but not before she crunched the small listening device under her foot. "Put him in the car. One of you take off your panty hose and tie one of his ankles to one of his wrists. Then you sit on him, Zoe. If he twitches, squash him. Follow me back to my house," she ordered.

"Oooh, this is *soooo* exciting," Kayla said.

"You can't get away with this," the man said coldly. "This is kidnapping."

"Shut up," Olivia said as she hiked up her skirt and stripped off her panty hose. "I hate people who spy on me and my friends. That means the person is usually up to no good." Within seconds she had the eavesdropper trussed like a Christmas turkey.

The ride back to Sam's condo was short. The women parked their cars, then circled their trussed-up trophy. They half dragged and half carried him up the three short steps to the front door and shoved him inside. Huffing and puffing, they followed Sam's orders to take him out to the small deck off the living room, where they sat him in a chair and tied one arm and one leg to the deck railing, again on Sam's orders.

The women trooped inside and closed the sliding door. They all moved out of sight into the kitchen, where Slick filled a pitcher with water, a wicked gleam in her eyes. As one, the women understood exactly what she had in mind. They laughed.

"This is way too cool," the cute little plumber said.

They were into it, there was no doubt about it. They had worked as a team, and that was the main thing, Sam thought, as they trooped behind her and out to the deck.

"You must be thirsty, Avery," Sam cooed. "Slick, do the honors."

The trussed-up man knew exactly what was happening. "I'm not thirsty," he cried.

"Oh, it talks!" Olivia said. "Sure you are. Thirsty, I mean. Now drink, or I'll pierce your nose."

The man's eyebrows shot upward. He took a sip from the twelve-ounce glass of water.

"C'mon, bottoms up," Olivia insisted, "or we'll be here all day. Drink it, or I'll call in a tattoo artist friend of mine to do a nude on your neck . . . after I pierce your nose. Attaboy. I do love a man who knows when to do what he's told," Olivia purred as she poured out a second glass of water.

The women waited until Mateo gulped down the second full glass of water. With the coffee he'd consumed at the restaurant, Sam figured his bladder would start giving him a problem within minutes.

"So let's hear it, Avery Mateo. Tell us what it's like to

work for AT&T. What's your boss's name? What are your hours? What's with the gizmo in your ear, and why were you listening to our conversation? Who sent you to spy on us? Talk fast."

"A job's a job. Working for AT&T is just like working for Coca-Cola. You make seventy grand a year and do what you're told."

Sam dropped to her haunches. She looked Mateo in the eye. "We're going to give you that one, but from here on in, we ask, you answer. You got that? Olivia, call your friend and have him come over here ASAP. With the tools of his trade." The man groaned as Slick handed him a third glass of water.

"You're beyond evil," the man blustered. "I'm not going to forget this."

"Yep, we're all that and more. Guess who's trussed up and guzzling water! Slick, get your camcorder! I'm thinking we might want to preserve this and add it to our résumés if things don't work out."

Mateo guzzled the water, his face beading with sweat.

"Is this guy part camel or what?" Zoe grumbled. "Thirty-six ounces of water is the equivalent of three beers. Plus the coffee he had earlier. What will we do if his bladder bursts? Even I know your brain can explode or swell or something if you don't . . . you know, pee."

No one answered her.

Sam, still on her haunches, stared at the man in front of her. "Let's start over. Who do you work for?"

"Okay, okay. Poke Donovan."

"And who does Poke Donovan work for?"

"I don't know. It's a chain of command."

Sam digested this information. "Who signs your paycheck? That seventy grand a year you earn?" She could see Slick with her camcorder focusing on both of them.

"I have no clue. I never see a check. Direct deposit," he sneered.

"What does your W2 say? Don't even think about telling me you don't know. Is the tattoo artist here yet, Slick?"

"Any minute now, Sam. Oh, I think I hear his car." She handed the camcorder to Zoe as she ran inside to open the front door.

"All right. Listen, I have to go to the bathroom," Mateo said, squirming in the deck chair.

"I bet you do but not yet. And you didn't answer my question. I won't ask twice."

"It's just a bunch of initials. I swear, I don't remember. Something like XYZ or YZX. Yeah, yeah, I think it's YZX. Now can I go to the bathroom?"

"No," Sam replied.

"No!" the man shouted. "You said I could go if I told you what you wanted to know. I told you."

"I lied. I need more information. What does Donovan want with us? Who does he report to?"

"I don't know who he reports to. I told you, it's a chain of command. He just said I was to listen to all of you and take notes. That's all I did."

"Does Donovan have an office?"

"If he does, I don't know where it is. We do all our business on the phone or through email. I'm telling you the truth."

Hearing a commotion behind her, Sam turned to see Slick with a man who was tattooed from his neck to his fingers. He was also the sorriest-looking individual she'd ever seen. She knew she would have to disinfect the deck after he left. She heard Olivia tell the man to set up shop. Sam looked at Mateo and shrugged.

"Where's this place we're going in ten days?"

"I-don't-know!"

"Do you have a BlackBerry?"

The man wilted. Sam reached over and checked all his jacket pockets. There it was. "You have a message. Actually, you have two messages. Tell me how this works. But before you tell me that, what do you do if you need to meet with Donovan?"

"I tell him I need to meet him, and we arrange a meeting, usually someplace public."

"You're lying. I can smell a lie a mile away." Sam turned to Olivia, her eyes questioning.

"He's ready to go as soon as we pick out a picture. I like this one," she said, holding up a nude picture of a woman with monster breasts. "Barry said this one is his most popular and most expensive. Five hundred big ones."

"Sold," Sam said smartly. "Our guest needs another glass of water."

"I know how to work that thing," Kayla said, pointing

to the BlackBerry. "In my line of business it was a necessity. What do you want to know?"

"I want to read the messages, and I'd like to know if he saves them. See if you can find a message that indicates a meeting, either coming in or going out. Wait, what do the two new messages say?"

"The messages are identical. It just says, **Update** on each one," Kayla said.

"Okay. Send a reply. Too busy. Need to meet. Any luck on retrieving old messages?"

"Not yet. Oh, wait, here's one. Donovan initiated it. No location. It just says, **Same place.**"

"Where's the place, Mateo?" Sam barked.

"Crystal City underground. The pretzel stand," the bound man responded immediately, his eyes on the tattoo artist.

"Drink the water, Mr. Mateo."

"Oh, God, I can't. Please let me go to the bathroom. I was just doing my damn job. This is torture."

"We don't take kindly to people spying on us. You spied, Mr. Mateo. You aren't going anywhere until we say so. You aren't going to the bathroom either."

Sam leaped to her feet and motioned to the others to follow her into the house, leaving the tattoo artist with Mateo. She headed straight for the front door and outside. "Bugs," she said.

"You have bugs?" Zoe squealed.

"Surveillance bugs," Slick said, disgust ringing in her voice. She looked at Sam, her eyes full of questions.

"I say we take Donovan out, too. We can do it. He sure as hell isn't expecting anything like this. We got Mateo. How hard could it be to take him down, that little pumpkin of a man? There's five of us and one of him. Let's show him what we're made of."

"Sugar and spice and everything nice." The cartoonist giggled.

"Try guts, steel nerves, and superior intelligence. Toss in female intuition, womanly wiles, Mateo's gun, his BlackBerry, and I'd say that makes us the CIC. Translated that means we're the cats in charge. Doncha love it?" Sam said, an evil look in her eyes.

"Email coming in," Kayla said, excitement ringing in her voice. Her voice was disappointed when she said, "It just says, **two o'clock.**"

Slick looked at Sam. "Don't respond. Turn it off now. The meeting place must be the pretzel stand in Crystal City. Olivia, do you think your friend Barry is capable of babysitting our guest?"

"For money, he'll do anything. I'll go talk to him."

Olivia was back within minutes. "Barry said he'll stay with him *and* he'll *pretend* to give him a tattoo. For six hundred bucks." The women could barely hear her whispered voice, but her gleeful look told them all they needed to know.

At precisely seven minutes past two o'clock, the women formed a baby brigade, with strollers the mall provided and dolls purchased from K-B toys. Sam held a plastic diaper bag. The gun inside she jabbed into his ribs. "Gotcha covered, Donovan," she hissed. "Now walk out nicely and nothing will happen. You screw up, and the same thing that happened to Mateo is going to happen to you, but you'll get the tattoo on that plump cheek of yours. You following me here?" The round little man nodded. "In case you're wondering why we're doing this, it's because we had a business deal. You stacked the deck, Mr. Donovan. You spied on us. You're still spying on us. We don't like that, do we, girls?" Four heads wagged a negative.

The minute they pushed the roly-poly little man into the backseat of Sam's car, Zoe ripped off her panty hose. Her voice rang with belligerence when she found she couldn't get the little man's ankle up to his wrist. Frustrated, she yanked at his ankle and tied it to the door handle. "He's not going anywhere," she said triumphantly. When she slammed the door, Donovan's face slammed into the back of the front seat. She shrugged. "Take it away," she bellowed.

The parade of cars peeled out of the parking lot.

"What the hell do you think you're doing?" their "guest" blustered.

"Wrong question. We already did it," Slick said. "Now shut up. From here on in, we ask the questions, and you answer them. If you screw with us, you'll be sporting a naked lady on that fat cheek of yours, and I will personally pierce your tongue. Think about that, *you spy!*"

"It's part of the deal," Donovan said. Sam thought he sounded pitiful.

"I told you to shut up."

Donovan clamped his lips shut as he struggled to get comfortable.

"Slick, see if he has a BlackBerry. If he does, take it," Sam ordered.

Slick unbuckled her seat belt, squirmed around until she was on her knees facing the backseat. She pawed through his pockets, taking everything she could find. She reached for the briefcase and tossed it on the front seat.

"How's *this* for a Mickey Mouse operation?" Sam snarled.

Donovan ignored the question.

Slick clapped her hands together. "Oh, goodie, we're home. Bet you can't wait to get that tattoo, huh, *Mr.* Donovan?"

The yuppie neighborhood was empty of people. Still, the women surrounded Donovan and did a repeat of their trek with Mateo. They led him out to the deck, where Mateo and the tattoo artist waited. Sam blinked at the very big, very obvious tattoo on Mateo's neck. Slick gasped. Olivia met her gaze and mouthed the word, *decal*. Barry, the tattoo artist, was smiling from ear to ear as he admired his phony handiwork. Donovan would have fainted if Zoe and Olivia hadn't been holding him up by his arms.

"Tie him to the other side of the railing so that his back is to Mateo," Sam ordered. "I think you underestimated what we learned at the Academy. Actually, your mistake was thinking we were fools. You're going to spill your guts or suffer the consequences. Did you really believe any of us would go off with you under the conditions you laid out? Well, did you?"

"Yes," came the muffled reply.

Sam glared at him. "Big mistake."

"Barry, do you have a Mickey Mouse pattern?" Slick asked. "A really colorful one."

The artist stroked his straggly beard, wondering what was going down in this nice little slice of suburbia. "Yep. Got all the cartoon characters."

The women huddled and whispered. "Okay," Olivia said. "We'd like you to put it on his . . ."

The artist grinned. "It's gonna hurt. Do you think the dough boy can handle it?"

"You must have us confused with someone who cares if it hurts or not. Just do it," Sam snapped.

"I just love this mercenary stuff," Kayla enthused. "Do we get to watch?"

"Absolutely," Sam said.

Chapter Three

The five women piled through the front door of Sam's condo and huddled on the front steps, all of them talking at the same time. "Do we change our minds?" "Are we really going to let Barry . . ." "What are we doing here?" "We signed the contracts . . ." and on and on they went until Sam held her hand up for a time-out.

"Hold it, hold it. Look, we won this little bout, but"—she looked at Slick—"I'm thinking it was just a little too easy. It could all be a setup to see how we'd react as a team. Think about it. For the moment, we're in control. I think it's safe to say both those guys are a little nervous. The blazing question at the moment is what are we going to do now? We have the little guy's briefcase and our signed contracts. We can tear them up or let them stand and honor them. For what it's worth, I think we should honor the contracts and go through with it. No one forced us to sign on. I gave my word. But. I want more answers. What about the rest of you?"

Kayla slapped Donovan's BlackBerry from the palm of one hand to the other. "I don't like the idea that no one knows where we're going. It's not that I have a husband or a lover, but I do have a half brother and some really close friends and distant relatives. What if I die in some godforsaken place, and no one ever knows? I don't have a fortune in money or anything, but I don't like the idea that I have to give up what I do have. I also want to be able to access my funds. I want to know that if I come back, I have something to come back to. Giving up a year is okay, I can handle that. I don't think I can give up my cell phone, though. Call me selfish, but it's my lifeline to the outside world. I also want to know exactly where the hell we're going."

Zoe and Olivia concurred. Slick nodded in agreement.

Sam tugged at the waistband of her jeans, settling it more comfortably over her hips. "Okay, let's put the squeeze on Mr. Donovan and see what he's made of."

Back on the outside deck, Sam almost laughed. She didn't think she'd ever seen two more miserable human beings in her life. The tattoo artist was singing and swaying from side to side. Sam decided he was as high as a kite from the looks of his glazed eyes. "Slick, fill the water pitcher. Mr. Donovan can use the same glass as

Mr. Mateo. We aren't going to worry about germs at this point."

The women clustered around Donovan and stared down at him. It was a humiliating experience for anyone to find himself in.

Sam inched her foot close to Donovan. She looked down at him. "We can do this the easy way or the hard way. Bear in mind that we have your briefcase and your BlackBerry. Mateo," she said, jerking her head in the other direction, "says he works for you. Who do you work for?"

"It's a chain of command," Donovan said miserably.

"Names. Give me names. I want you to talk, and I don't want you to hold anything back. The artist over there looks to me like he's been sniffing something. I don't know too much about tattoos, but I tend to think you'd need a steady hand, especially when working on a . . . *delicate* part of the anatomy. If you're willing to take your chances, it's okay with us. None of us have had a laugh for a while. Your call, Mr. Donovan."

Slick held out the twelve-ounce glass of water. "Drink it all." Donovan knocked the glass out of her hand. Olivia grabbed a hank of Donovan's hair, jerking his head backward. Slick filled the glass again and handed it to him. "The next time it will be *hot* coffee."

"What the hell do you want from me?" Donovan said, gagging as he struggled to drink all the water in the glass.

The tattoo artist was on the railing, his arms outstretched as he giggled and made faces at the two men. Mateo hid his face in the crook of his arm. Donovan turned as white as the shirt he was wearing.

Slick filled the glass with water. "Who do you work for? We want a name."

"For Christ's sake, Donovan, tell them. I quit, you bastard. You said this gig was a piece of cake. Does this look like frigging cake to you? Well, does it? You said they were just a bunch of stupid women. Washouts and wannabes, that's what you said. You want to get your private parts tattooed, it's fine with me. I just want out of here. I'm going to have to get surgery to have this ugly thing removed from my neck. If they don't kill you, I will."

"Shut up, Mateo," Donovan snarled. Slick dumped the rest of the water from the pitcher over his head. He squealed like a scalded cat.

The tattoo artist hopped off the railing to squat in front of Donovan. "So, man, why you fighting the chicks? Give it up already, man. I am so totally ready to start working on you."

Sam kicked the chair Donovan was sitting in. "Just a bunch of stupid women, huh? I think you might be a little mixed up as to who is stupid and who isn't. Give me a name. *Now*."

"Pappy," Donovan gasped.

"Pappy who? Who is Pappy?" Sam demanded.

"He's the guy who operates everything. I only know him as Pappy. He's the only contact I have besides

Mateo and a few other men who do exactly what Mateo does. I told you, it's a chain of command. That's all I know."

"Well, guess what, Mr. Donovan, that isn't enough. Where does this Pappy hang his hat? Can we call him?"

"Someone named Pappy is on the BlackBerry," Kayla volunteered. "We can email him. The last message Donovan sent says that the cats are all in the cradle. I think that's some kind of mercenaryspeak."

Sam winced. She dropped to her haunches so she was eyeball-to-eyeball with Donovan. "What do you think will happen if we send another email saying the cats fell out of the cradle?" Donovan's eyes rolled back in his head. "I'm waiting," she singsonged.

"I'll probably get fired. If you didn't want to sign up, why did you do it? I didn't twist your arm. Tear up the contracts, untie us, and this whole thing never happened."

Sam laughed. "And you think we're stupid enough to believe that? Yeah, I guess you are that stupid. Drink up, Mr. Donovan."

"Are we ready yet?" the tattoo artist queried.

"Not yet, sweetie. Soon, though," Olivia trilled.

"Okayyyy."

"Where is the place you planned on taking us? The one that isn't on any map," Sam asked.

"In the mountains."

"That's too vague. Clarify please," Sam said, tapping him none too gently on the arm.

"Big Pine Mountain. It's the second-highest mountain in North Carolina."

"What's there?" Sam queried.

"Everything."

Zoe yanked at his hair. "That's vague, too. Don't make that mistake again. Now answer the question. Spell out what *everything* means."

Slick handed Donovan a glass of water. "Drink it before you answer the question."

"I can't. I'll puke."

"Ask me if I care. Drink!" Slick said. "By the way, the first thing you learn at the Academy is you never give up your gun. We just took yours and the one that yahoo over there had. And you had the gall to say we're just a bunch of stupid women! Now drink up!" Donovan drank the water.

"Oh, man, tell these pretty chicks what they want to know," the tattoo artist said. "I got a business to run, and people are probably standing in line waiting for me and my ink. Come on, spill your guts, man. Can't you see they got you by the short hairs, man?"

The last of the summer sun was gone. Dark clouds scudded across the sky. Somewhere in the distance a roll of thunder could be heard. Donovan and Mateo heard it, too.

"You were going to explain what *everything* meant," Zoe prodded.

"It's a fortresslike compound where Pappy trains his . . . people. Everything is state-of-the-art. Accommodations are first-class. It's beyond anything the FBI or the CIA could even think of. Think NORAD in the Cheyenne Mountains in Colorado. It's on a par with that. The only way in or out is by helicopter."

Slick blinked. They'd heard tales of NORAD at the Academy. "Who funds an operation like that?" she asked.

"I don't know. I don't think Pappy knows either. I told you, it's a chain of command. Need to know, that kind of thing. Whoever it is must have an unlimited supply of money. Pappy gives me an order, and I follow it or delegate like I did with Mateo. That's all I can tell you. Now can I go to the bathroom?"

"No," Sam said. "Tell me where you planted the bugs in the house, and I might change my mind."

Donovan couldn't wait to spit out the locations. Slick raced into the house and came back with the three listening devices.

"Now can I go to the bathroom?" Donovan pleaded.

"No," Sam said.

"Lying bitch," Donovan moaned.

Sam motioned for the others to follow her through the house and outside again to the front steps, where the women eyed her expectantly.

Sam looked off into the distance. It would rain soon. "I don't think we're going to get too much more out of Donovan. Let's see what happens when we send an email to Pappy. Say all the cats fell out of the cradle. I want to see what the response is. Slick, go on my computer and see what you can find out about Big Pine Mountain and NORAD. If he's telling us the truth, an operation like this would need virtually unlimited funds. Like some kind of secret government operation. Who else do you know who has unlimited funds? No one, that's who."

Kayla typed in the message. She shrugged. A return message surfaced almost instantaneously. "He wants an explanation." She shoved the BlackBerry under Sam's nose.

"Send this message: Change of heart. They want explicit details, or it's dead in the water." Kayla punched in the message.

They waited. They discussed the rain that was about to start falling.

"I love thunderstorms," Zoe said. "What are we going to do with those two guys?"

Sam looked at the blank screen on the BlackBerry in Kayla's hand. "I think we should move them to the garage but not until they get a good soaking. I'm sure they have a phone number to call for emergencies. Once they give it up, we'll make a decision."

"That jerk has to pay for the stupid women crack," Olivia snarled. The others agreed.

The BlackBerry came to life. Kayla read the message. "It says to offer more money but *nada* on the details."

"Send this message. Not interested. Specific details. Exceptional women, not a stupid one in the bunch. The best so far."

They all laughed as Kayla typed the message.

The return message was short, just two words. **Instructions stand.**

"Okay, that's enough fooling around. Give me that thing," Sam said. She typed furiously. **No, the instructions do not stand. It's a new ball game. Your people are trussed up like Christmas turkeys. We even have their guns. Imagine five stupid women managing to do something like that. We want details, specific details on your operation, or our deal is off.** Sam signed her name and pressed SEND. "Where's Donovan's cell phone?"

Kayla ran into the house and brought it to Sam just as the phone buzzed to life. Sam's fist shot in the air. She flicked the power switch to ON, and said, "This is Sam Rainford, and I'm not taking any messages at the moment. Call me in an hour." She clicked the power to OFF. She looked at the others and said, "I did that because I want to see what Slick comes up with on Big Pine Mountain before we actually talk. He was just checking to see if the message on the BlackBerry was legit. Let's have a look at our guests. It's starting to rain. We certainly don't want to be inhospitable now, do we?"

Business taken care of, the first three Rainford wives departed for their respective homes, promising to return by seven with dinner in hand. Donovan and Mateo were in the garage. The BlackBerry and the cell phone were off. Sam wanted "Pappy" to sweat.

"Your turn, Sam. I'll hold the fort while you shower and change. I'll keep busy on the Net to see what else, if anything, I can come up with," Slick said.

Thirty minutes later, both women sat on Sam's bed hugging their knees. "What now, coach?" Slick asked as she finger-combed her wet hair. "We can't keep those two guys in the garage forever. You look kinda funny, Sam. What's really bothering you?"

Sam plucked at a corner of her bedspread, her eyes lowered. "It's this whole thing, I guess. I wasn't prepared to like my predecessors, but I do. Finding out there were three more Rainford wives kind of blew me out of the water. I must have really crappy judgment, Slick. I fell for that *schmuck*. I really did love him in the beginning, and it isn't easy to turn off feelings like that. If I used that kind of judgment in my personal life, maybe the FBI was right to wash me out."

"You're talking apples and oranges, Sam. With Douglas you were dealing with your emotions. That's allowed, Sam. That's normal. The Academy, that's a different thing entirely. You washed out because of your lack of upper-body strength. You didn't make poor judgment calls during those sixteen weeks at Quantico.

"In addition, Sam, everything you've done and said since Donovan approached us has been perfect. That leads me to think that what's bothering you is Douglas. Douglas you can deal with at any time. In fact, the more time that goes by, the clearer your head will be. You don't want to do anything rash while you're still feeling bruised and battered. Married eight times! That's really over the top."

"What do you suppose he saw in the . . . the others?" Sam asked carefully.

Slick eyed her best friend. "Well, Kayla is an exotic dancer, a belly dancer to be precise. I'd say he got off on the sexual movements. Olivia as a cartoonist probably tickled his funny bone. She's also easy on the eye. Zoe, I'm not sure. I'm thinking maybe he thought it was cool that she was a plumber. Hell, maybe she fixed his pipes. Or cleaned out his drains." Slick laughed.

"And me?" Sam asked hesitantly.

Slick untangled her legs, her arms flapping. "This is just my opinion, but I think he saw the home and hearth in you. The warmth and the caring. You aren't like the other three. Let's face it, Sam, you were always a homebody. You're also levelheaded. The other three are kind of flighty. You, my good friend, are grounded.

"Please tell me you don't still love him because if you do, I'm pulling out. This caper is never going to work if you're hung up on him and his first three wives."

Sam looked over at the bedside clock with its bright red numerals. They had half an hour until the others returned. "Rest easy, Slick. I knew I made a mistake when I married him. No, I don't love him. Call it lust or infatuation. I can separate my job from my personal life. Trust me on that."

"Okay, I trust you, and I believe you. Do you think Donovan told us the truth when he told you where the bugs were? He said there were only three. I did comb this place from one end to the other and only found three. Which brings me back to my earlier question. How long are we going to hold those two guys prisoners?"

" 'Guests.' Refer to them as 'guests,' Slick. I think we should continue to entertain them until after I talk to Pappy. What do you think?"

"I think you should call this 'Pappy' now, before the others get back. Do you know what you're going to say?"

"I don't think it's one of those things you can rehearse. I'll wing it. I guess I'll just hit the REDIAL button. Five bucks says he picks up on the first ring."

"That's a sucker bet," Slick replied with a grin. "Take a deep breath. Slow and easy. You're in the catbird seat. I think the mysterious Pappy knows it, too."

Sam took a deep breath at the same time as she hit caller ID and dialed the number that appeared. She held up her thumb to show that Pappy had picked up on the first ring. "This is Samantha Rainford. Since the rules have changed, tell me what you can do for me."

"What would you like me to do, Samantha?"

"Nah, nah, don't ask questions, Pappy. I want answers. We're going to play my game. I asked you a question. Be a man and answer it. What you say now will help me make my final decision. I speak for the others, by the way."

The voice that responded was smooth as silk, yet husky-sounding. "Fair enough. I imagine you're balking at the secrecy. It's necessary. We'll deal with your respective properties from our end. Your bank accounts and credit cards will also be taken care of. When—and if—you agree to join us, you will receive a packet explaining how your holdings are being protected. Yes, you will be leaving your little world, but you *will* be able to go back to it at some point. That point will depend on you. I've just upped the deadline. The day after tomorrow, I want all of you at Dulles Airport promptly at noon. Bring your personal papers and bank cards with you as well as your signed contracts. Each person is allowed one duffel bag. No more than a hundred pounds, so choose what you bring wisely. We will provide you with all the essentials. You will be briefed within an hour of your arrival. Is there anything else you want to know?"

"Yes. Whom do you represent?"

"That will be discussed at your briefing."

Sam looked at Slick and shrugged. "What if we don't cut it? What happens to us then?"

"That won't happen, Samantha. We know what we're doing. You were chosen carefully. You just proved I didn't make a mistake. I didn't think the person was born yet who could take Donovan. I'm impressed. You can let him and his associate go now."

"Yeah, right. They go free when I'm good and ready to let them loose and not one minute sooner."

"What will you gain by keeping them prisoner, Samantha?"

Sam thought about the question. "Let's just call it female power for the moment. Donovan referred to us as stupid females. I didn't like that assessment; neither did the others."

"I guess I can understand that. Okay, you can keep them." There was a hint of laughter in the voice. Sam noticed it and grinned to herself.

Sam clicked the OFF button. She repeated the entire conversation to Slick, who listened with rapt attention. Her only comment was, "One duffel bag!"

The doorbell rang. Both women leaped off the bed and raced downstairs. Sam opened the door to admit the girls and their Chinese dinner. She fished in one of the bags and withdrew two fortune cookies, which she carried to the garage. She tossed one to each man. "Dinner! By the way, Pappy said I could keep you both. Tsk, tsk." She slammed the garage door behind her.

Sam sat down at the table to join the women. Slick was repeating the telephone conversation Sam had with Pappy. "Day after tomorrow. High noon at Dulles Airport. One duffel bag each, weighing no more than a hundred pounds."

"I have that much stuff in my bathroom," Kayla grumbled.

"I take that much stuff for an overnighter," Olivia said.

"That's impossible. What about accessories? I need two bags just for shoes and purses," Zoe snapped.

Sam dug into her chow mein. "It's called sucking up. We suck up, or we stay here. Your call, ladies."

The women ate in silence as they pondered her last statement. By the time they got to the lichee nuts, they were all in agreement. They had another round of Chinese beer before they decided to call it a night with the promise to touch base prior to meeting up at Dulles Airport in two days' time.

"We need to decide what we're going to do with those two guys," Slick said.

"I say we strip them naked and turn them loose. Let the cops pick them up," Olivia said. "Should we take a vote?"

"Hell, no. Let's just do it," Zoe said, getting up from her chair.

Both men groaned when Sam opened the kitchen door leading to the garage. Slick looked at the pitiful-looking men and laughed. "Cut them loose," she said to Kayla, who was holding a wicked-looking pair of scissors.

"Zoe, strip Mateo down. Olivia, peel off Donovan's clothes."

The women made a production of holding their noses as they tried not to laugh.

"Okay, gentlemen, you're free to go. What, you don't want to leave now?" Sam demanded, outrage ringing in her voice. She pressed the remote on the wall and opened the overhead garage door. "Push them outside, ladies!"

As soon as the men were outside, Sam slammed the button that sent the garage door crashing to the concrete. She dusted her hands dramatically as she led the way back into the house. "I'll get rid of their clothes tomorrow and hose down the garage. So much for stupid women!"

The women high-fived each other as they cleaned up the dinner table.

An hour later, Sam and Slick headed for the second floor, the doors locked, the security system armed.

"Sleep tight, Sam!"

"You, too, Slick!"

Sam brushed her teeth and was in bed within seconds. She closed her eyes and was asleep instantly. She knew there would be no dreams or nightmares about Douglas Cosmo Rainford, III.

Chapter Four

It was a perfect July day, warm, sunny, with a blue sky full of cotton-candy clouds. Sam couldn't help but wonder what it would be like in the North Carolina mountains. Would the sky look the same, would the air be cleaner and fresher? Of course it would. She held her face up to the sun, relishing the warmth. She felt cold, possibly from apprehension. She struggled to shift her emotions into the neutral zone as she watched her colleagues chattering like magpies in the small private waiting room at Dulles. She knew they were viewing the future as some grand adventure. In her own mind she wasn't sure how she saw it.

A smile tugged at the corners of Sam's mouth as she looked at the outfits the women were wearing. Slick, always the model, was dressed in a long, silk sheath printed with colorful flowers. Her hair was slicked back, the ends just long enough to lick her neck. Kayla wore lime-colored capris with a matching cropped top that showed off her pierced belly button. Olivia wore skinny jeans that looked like they were painted on and a tank top so tight across her chest that her breasts looked like a bridge. Zoe wore a mini sundress with spaghetti straps and no bra. She herself wore a khaki pant suit with a white tee underneath. Miss Preppy herself, Miss Girl Scout Leader. Suddenly, she felt stupid. The feeling lasted all of five seconds when she saw a woman striding toward them.

Their contact. Sam sucked in her breath.

She was tall, shapely. She looked like she'd just stepped from some boardroom. Her hair was glossy brown and arranged into a pristine knot at the back of her head. She wore sensible, professional-looking heels with a lightweight powder blue suit. She also looked extremely efficient, with a sharp, keen gaze that seemed to take in everything all at once.

"Ms. Rainford?"

Four of the women stepped forward. The contact looked confused. Sam clarified the names and waited.

The contact shrugged, as though to indicate she'd seen and heard it all, and this little glitch was nothing to get upset about. She didn't extend her hand in greeting. "I'm Marsha Fielding. I'm here to escort you to the helicopter. If you'll follow me, please. Step lively, ladies, the pilot doesn't like to be kept waiting. Don't leave anything behind."

"I think we need a porter, someone to take these bags," Kayla said, looking around as though hoping one would materialize out of thin air.

Marsha Fielding pierced them all with one steely-eyed look. "No, Ms. Rainford, we do *not* need a porter. Now, pick up your bag and follow me."

Sam did her best not to laugh, as the women in their high heels struggled with the hundred-pound duffel bags. Slick was the first to remove her backless, strapless shoes. Muttering and mumbling under their breath, the other women followed suit. Fielding looked approvingly at Sam's loafers.

When they were outside again, the sun was just as bright, just as warm. The clouds were just as puffy, the sky possibly a shade bluer. A beautiful day.

They saw it then, their mode of transportation, and it was scary-looking. To Sam it looked like a giant black bird with a rotor on its back. She'd never been this close to a helicopter before. In fact the only times she'd ever seen one were on TV or in the movies.

Bent over with the weight of her duffel, Kayla was sputtering in what sounded like five different languages. What Sam got out of it was, "This is so unfair. I'm not a pack mule."

"You are now," Fielding said. "It goes with the territory. Get used to it."

Someone who looked like a mechanic appeared from behind a piled-high luggage dolly. He handed Fielding a clipboard. She read it carefully before she scrawled her name and handed the clipboard back to the mechanic. She stepped back to a military-looking Jeep that had just roared to a screeching stop. Sam watched as Fielding climbed in and waved. Then she was gone.

Suddenly the urge to turn tail and run was so strong that Sam actually took one step backward. She called herself a *wuss* and other assorted names before she turned around to board the helicopter. Slick reached for her arm. It was all she needed. It was too late to back out. Besides, Sam reminded herself, she'd never been a quitter.

There was nothing even remotely luxurious or comfortable about the interior of the helicopter. Plain and simple, it was a mode of transportation. No food or drinks would be served. The seats were cramped and uncomfortable. The others were struggling with their blow-dried hairdos as wind rushed through the open door. After they all donned sound-deadening headsets, the rotors roared to life with a steady *twump, twump* that Sam hoped would lull her to sleep in short order.

And then they were airborne.

Sam smiled when she saw her colleagues—that was how she had come to think of them. Even with her khaki jacket she was cold. Wishing for a warmer outfit, she settled back, closed her eyes, and allowed her mind to race.

Thinking about Douglas wasn't going to get her anywhere, but she did it every time she shifted into what

she called her neutral zone. She'd been a fool. Everyone, at some point in her life, was entitled to make foolish decisions and choices. Douglas had been a colossal
mistake. How weird that she could actually like her predecessors. She should be raging with jealousy, but she
wasn't. In fact, she actually liked all of them. Maybe at
some point in the future the four of them could collab-
orate and write a book titled, *The Honeymoon Junkie*. Of
course that meant she'd have to track down the other
four Rainford wives to make it authentic. She did feel
pleased with herself that she hadn't taken his five thousand dollars. He was probably, right then, right that very
minute, courting soon-to-be Wife Number 9.

Sooner or later, probably later, she and the others
would come up with a plan to get back at Douglas for
his shameless treatment of them. There was nothing
like a scorned woman to fuel a plan. So what if Douglas
was one of the richest men in the country, a fact she
couldn't confirm or deny because she could find no
trace that he actually existed? For all she knew he could
be a pauper who lived off credit cards. So what? She
knew in her gut that Douglas would never, ever, expect
his ex-wives to meet. Especially under the present circumstances.

That was enough thinking about her ex-husband.

At last she actually slept. She woke when Slick
shook her.

"We're going down. Look! That must be the place
we're going," Slick yelled to be heard over the sound of

the helicopter. Sam craned her neck and gasped. How in the world had the place been built on the mountain? She could see buildings, houses, the helipad, and something that looked like a training area. Acres and miles of habitation. What she couldn't see were roads of any kind. As the helicopter banked and turned, an Olympic-sized pool came into view, its water azure blue. She blinked when she saw horses grazing in a small pasture next to a barn with a red tile roof.

They were lower by then, at the tree line, making it possible to see another helicopter on the pad, this one newer-looking, sleeker somehow. Then she saw something that jerked her upright—a cable car and pulley, the car itself at rest inside some sort of structure. She tried to comprehend the amount of money it would take to construct what she was seeing.

They were on the ground, the sound of the rotors deafening.

Sam was the first one off the copter, her hair flying backward as she ducked and ran to a grassy patch of lawn at the edge of the pad. This time she did laugh when the others came barreling after her, their gelled, moussed hair standing straight in the air when they removed their headsets. She smoothed her own curly locks, feeling almost normal.

"Okay, do we just stand here, or is there a welcoming committee or what?" Kayla asked, hugging her arms to her chest. "I'm never going to be warm again. Look, my feet are blue!"

The sudden silence was deafening. The pilot tossed out the five duffel bags before he hopped out of the copter. "Help yourselves, ladies," he said.

Grumbling under their breaths, the women marched over to their respective bags and picked them up.

They heard the golf cart before they saw it. Sam gawked, while the others openly stared at the handsome man and vicious dog that looked like a wild wolf sitting next to him.

"Welcome to Big Pine Mountain! Follow me."

And that was their welcome greeting. No more, no less.

Sam knew a sharp retort of some sort was about to erupt from one or the other of the group. She squelched them all with a stern look and a shake of the head. They followed the golf cart in a straggly line, pulling up short when it ground to a halt in front of a long, low building with a sign on the front door that read, OMEGA THREE.

The man whose name they still didn't know said, "This is where your team will reside. You have an hour to unpack. Alpha," he said pointing to the huge, vicious dog, "will stay here and escort you to the conference building in exactly one hour. Do not be late. The last member of your team will be arriving shortly."

The women stared at the cart as it rocketed across the compound. No one said a word as they gave the big dog a wide berth.

Omega Three was a comfortable building. There was a sitting room with a huge fieldstone fireplace with what looked like a cord of wood piled up on the hearth. The furniture—three chairs and two couches—was covered in a brown plaid fabric. Area rugs were scattered on the pine floor.

There was a minikitchen complete with refrigerator, microwave, washer, and dryer. Beyond the kitchen was a bath with three stall showers, two bathtubs, and a triple vanity. Beyond the oversize bathroom was a barracks-style bedroom, with four windows with slatted blinds but no curtains, six beds with a footlocker at the end of each bed. Towels, blankets, and pillows were piled neatly on the beds. Everything was drab olive in color.

It wasn't the Ritz.

The others seemed to be waiting to see what Sam would do. When she opened her footlocker, they opened theirs. Sam unpacked. Slick did the same. The other three Rainford wives dumped their duffel bags inside the footlockers but not before they removed their makeup kits and slammed the lids.

"Done," Olivia said airily as she led the way back to the bathroom, where the three women picked out places on the vanity to display their war paint. Sam and Slick made their beds, bounced a quarter on each of them to make sure the covers were tight enough. Satisfied, they walked over to the long sofa that could accommodate six comfortably and sat down.

A flurry of movement let them know the others were making their beds. When they were done, Sam and Slick both laughed. Loudly.

"What! What! I haven't made a bed in years. I'm just going to sleep in it and mess it up," Zoe snarled. "I didn't come here to learn how to make beds." The first two Mrs. Rainfords concurred.

"You might want to rethink the bed making," Slick said. "And the footlockers. You might have to do some extra sit-ups, laps in the pool, whatever. Rest assured, it will be strenuous. I think you should start off by obeying the rules."

More grumbling. The duffel bags were dumped willy-nilly into the footlockers. The beds took on a whole new look as sheets were scrunched at the corners and the lopsided blankets were tugged and stretched.

The knock on the door startled all of them. The women looked at one another. "Maybe it's our last teammate," Slick said.

Olivia opened the door. A tall man with a broad chest and a duffel bag stepped into the room. "Eric Hawkins," he said. "I'm a member of Omega Three."

"Hawkins!" Sam and Slick said in unison, shock ringing in their voices.

"Slick! Sam! What the hell!" He looked around at the others. "What the hell is wrong with this picture? Five women, one guy. Oh, no. No, no, no!"

"Yes, yes, yes," Sam said. "What's the matter, Hawkins, you afraid of us women?"

"There must be some mistake. Isn't it girls versus boys? I don't get it."

"What I don't get is how the hell did you get here?

When and where were you recruited? Do you know anything about this place?" Sam demanded.

"I was sitting in a bar with a couple of guys, and this little man came up to me and said he needed to talk to me about the FBI. I was just too pissed off at the FBI to listen to what he had to say. Did I also say I was drunk as a skunk? I was. The guy actually drove me home to my apartment, and when I woke up the next morning, he was in the kitchen. He offered to make me a cocktail guaranteed to get rid of the Queen Mother of all hangovers. I took him up on it. Then he made me another offer. He knew everything about me, even that I was a tighty whitie opposed to a boxer guy. I was ripe to be recruited. I signed on, and here I am.

"As to what I know about this place, I know squat, but here I am."

Sam nodded.

Slick eyed the good-looking guy standing in the middle of the living room. At the FBI Academy he'd done his best to help her with the firearms class. She could hardly believe, considering his size and the breadth of his chest, that he'd washed out for the same reason Sam had—lack of upper-body strength. "I wouldn't make an issue of being the only man in this group, Hawkins. Hey, what could be nicer than five women and one guy," Slick said, hoping to ward off what might turn into something ugly.

"I'd be willing to bet five bucks one of the other teams has five guys and one woman," Sam said.

Kayla, Olivia, and Zoe ogled the man standing in front of them. Sam correctly translated the look to mean Hawkins was prey, and they were the predators. God help Eric Hawkins.

"Your bed is in there," Slick said, jerking her head in the direction of the barrackslike bedroom. "You aren't going to like the arrangement, but you better get over it in a hurry. We have eighteen minutes until it's time to go to the orientation building, wherever the hell that is. The dog is supposed to lead the way. The guy who met us said we shouldn't be late."

Hawkins moved at the speed of light. He was back in sixteen minutes with two minutes to spare. They exited the Omega Three building as a group. The huge dog looked at them, seeming to take a head count before he started off.

"That is no true German shepherd if that's what you're thinking," Hawkins said. "He's part wolf. I know everything there is to know about dogs, and when I tell you that dog is part wolf, I want you to believe me. Translated, that means the dog is loyal to one person only, and that's his master."

"Is that supposed to scare us?" Slick asked.

"A dog like that scares the piss out of me, Slick. They don't play by the same rules dogs play by. Think about this place, and it figures," Hawkins said in a serious, ominous voice.

Sam, minus her khaki jacket, sniffed the air. It was pure and clean, heady with the scent of evergreens. It reminded her of the Christmas season. This was another world, and she hoped and prayed she could conquer it. Her shoulders started to twitch when she remembered Donovan telling her Big Pine Mountain was the second highest mountain in North Carolina. What bothered her more than anything was that the only way off the mountain was by helicopter or cable car. She knew in her gut that if any of them tried to leave via the forest, the vicious dog that was part wolf would be sent to bring them back. She shivered in the bright sunshine.

The dog stopped in front of a long, low building that was constructed of pine logs. It had a sturdy front door, a skinny porch, and wraparound louvered windows. The sign over the door read ORIENTATION. The dog barked once, then once again. The parade halted. No one moved until the door to the building was opened by the man who'd driven the golf cart. He motioned them inside to what looked like a classroom. Most of the seats were already full. Sam counted eighteen people. With her five roommates and herself, it came to four teams of six.

The room looked just like a college classroom minus the charts and blackboards. The wooden chairs with wide arms for writing and books were comfortable. What surprised her more than anything was that there was no chatter.

Whoever the man standing in front of them was, he was mouthwateringly handsome in sharply creased khakis and a matching shirt rolled to the elbows. He was brown from the sun, with gray eyes the color of a mourning dove. With his crop of unruly-looking dark curly hair, he could have passed for Greek, Spanish, or possibly Jewish. He looked exceptionally tall standing on a raised dais. Sam put him at six-three or -four. Strong chin that jutted out with unbelievable dimples when he smiled. His teeth were magnificent.

Sam jerked herself to awareness. What difference did it make what the guy looked like? What she wanted to know was who and what he was and how he would relate to her in the year she would be there. Sitting next to her, Hawkins cleared his throat as if to say, let's get on with it. Those in front of her seemed to be fidgeting and squirming in their seats. Obviously, everyone's patience was wearing thin.

The man stepped down from the dais and started to pace in front of the room as he talked. "My name is Kollar Havapopulas. Everyone calls me Pappy." He walked over to one end of room, where a stack of bright yellow folders waited. He picked them up and carried them back to the front of the room. "When I call your name, stand up so we can all see who you are. Tell me which team you belong to."

Pappy! The guy on the BlackBerry! Double damn. Who was it that said Pappy was high up in the chain of command? Probably Poke. Then again maybe it was Mateo. Hmmm. So, her first assessment was right. He was Greek. Sam's heart kicked up an extra beat as she listened to the roll being called. The man didn't acknowledge any of them as he called their names. He didn't blink or nod or smile. When she heard her name, she stood up and stared directly at him. A devil perched itself on her shoulder. She winked, as if to to say, yes, I'm the one who gave you and Donovan a run for your money. He looked startled, she had to give him that. She sat down, her heart beating trip-hammer fast inside her chest.

The introductions over, Pappy carried the yellow folders back to the table under the far window. He stared outside for a few seconds before he returned to the class. He wondered which one had communicated with him over the BlackBerry.

"Before we get under way, I want to tell you that in your quarters you will find a packet with your name on it. It will explain how we've taken care of your properties, your banking needs, and any special requests you might have made. You will also find cell phones. In order to make a call, the phone has to be activated by the communications room. You can, of course, call any of us here on the mountain. Any call you wish to make to somewhere off the mountain will be monitored with a five-second delay in case you try to . . . outsmart us. We bounce the calls off a satellite so they can't be traced. Any questions?"

There were none. "When you leave this room, you'll go directly to the company store, where you will be outfitted with suitable gear. At the moment, it's summer gear. At the end of September it will be full winter gear. It gets cold up here in the winter, and we do get a lot of snow. No civilian attire is allowed after today. Tomorrow is a day off. You will find an itinerary with your packet. A full schedule. All times will be Zulu, but we'll get to that later. It takes a little getting used to." He looked around to see if there were any grumblings, and when his steely glance was met with silence, he continued.

"We are on no one's radar screen. This operation is funded by a private consortium in the interests of justice and the American way. We do what other people can't or won't do because of rules and regulations. Do we break the law? Yes, sometimes we do so in the interests of justice. We pick up where the judicial system fails. Do we get caught? No, we do not. The reason we don't get caught is because we train our people not to get caught. It's that simple. Now, if you screw up and somehow manage to get caught, you're on your own. I want you all to think about that. I also want you to think about this. You belong to a team. You have to look out for one another and protect your teammates, the way you protect yourself. You are only as good as your teammates. There is no room here for pettiness, egos, or pecking order. Each team will pick a leader, purely to streamline the communication process, and that's the person I will deal with. There will be no sensitivity-training classes. I won't humiliate any of you by starting one. We're all equal here; it makes no difference if you're a man or a woman. I'd like to see a show of hands on this one. Do you read me, ladies and gentlemen?"

Twenty-four hands shot in the air.

"Good."

"This organization is referred to as AFJ. That's it. It's easy to remember. It stands for Americans for Justice."

"In other words, vigilantes," a man's voice said from the front of the room.

"If you like that word, use it. I prefer the word *operative*."

The same devil that perched on Sam's shoulder earlier moved to her other shoulder. Her voice was loud and strong when she said, "What about *mercenary*? Isn't that what we're here for, or did I miss something?"

"*Mercenary* is good if you like that term, but you have to earn that title. Call yourself whatever you like. I still prefer the word *operative*." Pappy smiled, his strong white teeth glistening against his exceptionally suntanned skin.

The devil was still perched on Sam's shoulder. "It's not a question of whatever we like. I want this clarified right now. Are you going to train us to be mercenaries? For the good guys, of course. I don't have a problem with the term. When questions like this are answered outright in the beginning, there's no room later for misunderstandings, or anything ugly cropping up. In the real world down below this mountain it's simply called covering your ass. If we aren't on any radar screen, and this organization can abandon us at will, I think we have every right to know every single nit-picking detail."

"You're big on words and details, is that it, Rainford?" The bronzed man sounded frustrated.

He remembered her name. "Damn straight, *Mr.* Havapopulas." The loud murmurings from the others sounded like they were in agreement with Sam's statements. "If there's even the remotest possibility I'm going to be hung out to dry, I want a fighting chance before I get off the ground. You haven't mentioned any kind of confidentiality agreement, so if we do . . . *get caught* . . . how do we explain all this?" Sam said, waving her arms about to indicate the elaborate compound. "Suppose we do get caught and we tell people about this place. Assuming you and your people abandon us."

"If you adhere to the rules, do what you're told, work as a team, that's not going to happen. That I can guarantee. If it does happen, you will have no one to blame but yourself and your team members. We haven't lost an operative yet, and we've been an organization for over ten years. I'm sorry I can't give you personal testimonials, so you will have to take my word for it."

The same devil was still dancing on Sam's shoulders. She bristled as her jaw set in a grim line. "I don't find that reassuring enough, *Mr.* Havapopulas. I have no desire to spend time in a federal slammer. I know how the system works."

"Yeah, I know how it works, too," Hawkins said loudly. More murmurings could be heard from the others.

Havapopulas held his cool until things quieted down. He directed his comments to Sam, whose neck and face were pink with heat at being the center of attention. "Then what are you doing here? What would be your suggestion, Rainford?"

"Some kind of parachute to assure a safe landing. If we're unfortunate enough to get caught," Sam said succinctly. "You'll have to excuse me if I don't find any comfort in what you've said so far. Mr. Donovan and Mr. Mateo come to mind. Considering my washout status at the FBI, taking them down was like taking candy from a baby."

The murmurings grew louder, the two front rows sounding like they were more on Sam's side than on the side of the man standing in front of them. *This whole thing is a mistake, a big mistake,* Sam thought.

Havapopulas's dove gray eyes grew steely as he eyed Sam. He looked like he was weighing his next words. "I was hoping I wouldn't have to say this in front of an audience, but you're leaving me no other choice, Rainford. Donovan set you up. He clued in Mateo. We wanted to see how you'd react. You came through magnificently, I might add, confirming that our faith in you wasn't misplaced."

The heat in Sam's neck climbed to her cheeks. For one intense minute she almost believed him. She looked across at the others sitting in her row. All four women were shaking their heads.

Olivia was on her feet in a heartbeat. "Setup my

foot! We took them, pure and simple." Kayla, Slick, and Zoe jumped to their feet, too, then Hawkins, team player that he was. Sam remained in her seat for another second.

"No, we weren't set up. Your man was asleep at the switch. Admit it, and we stay. Stick with your story, and we're outta here," Sam said.

The man called Pappy clenched his jaw so hard it looked like it was going to crack. His eyes were cold and hard, like slivers of ice. "How about this, we discuss the parachute before training begins. Let's get through the orientation and go on from there. I promise to work with you."

Sam nodded, and the others sat down.

"Good going, Rainford," Hawkins whispered in her ear. "I'm glad you're on my side."

Somehow, some way, Sam knew she was going to pay for her comments. She felt cold, all the way to her toes.

Chapter Five

Sam leaned back in her chair, aware suddenly that the tone of the orientation had changed. She wondered if anyone besides herself was aware of it. A second later, Hawkins gave her a gentle nudge. Obviously, he, too, was aware of the change. She nudged back. Out of the corner of her eye she could see Slick staring straight ahead. Kayla was nibbling on her thumbnail. Olivia was busy taking off her ring and putting it back on. Zoe was pleating and unpleating the material of her skimpy sundress.

Havapopulas continued speaking, explaining mealtimes, where the dining hall was located, reveille, classrooms, where the outdoor training grounds were. He talked about the pool, the vegetable garden, the sewage system, the forest, the horses, the barns, and on and on. The even monotone of his voice was lulling Sam into a state of sleepiness.

Two hours passed before Havapopulas called a halt, saying they were on their own for the next thirty-two hours. The exit routine was that of a graduation ceremony as the first row left first, followed by Team Two, then Sam's team, with Team Four bringing up the rear. Teams One, Two, and Four separated, leaving Sam and her team standing alone outside the orientation building.

"Let's go for a walk, guys," Sam said. "This is just a guess on my part, but I think all the buildings are bugged, so let's agree now that we don't talk about anything important unless we're outside. What do you think, Hawkins? By the way, thanks for the support earlier."

Hawkins jammed his hands into his pockets. He looked at the women, a frown building on his face. "Look, I admit when I washed out I was bummed. I was ripe to be recruited for this organization. I'm assuming you felt the same way. So, we either accept it, or we move on. Yes, the details were sketchy when I was recruited, but what I heard was we would be working for the good guys. Not the bad guys. My recruiter was big on saying it was all on a need-to-know basis. I accepted that, too. But, I don't like the part about no backup if things go awry on a mission. Something needs to be put in place for such a situation. Just because it has never happened before doesn't mean it can't happen. There's a first time for everything."

Slick jumped when a pinecone fell from one of the

monster trees and hit her smack on the head. She laughed. "My official christening," she said, picking up the prickly pinecone that was as big as a baseball but weighed no more than an ounce or two.

"My opinion, for whatever it's worth, is that the three of us would have made good FBI agents. We had the basics and aside from Slick's thumb strength and Sam and I not being able to scale the wall, we have the edge over just about everyone who was in that room, assuming the others are FBI or CIA rejects," Hawkins said.

Kayla tugged at her cropped top, and said, "The classes are small, so we'll get individual attention. Remember in school when there were thirty kids to a class and you tended to get lost. We're green as grass, but we can learn," she said confidently. "I know how to be a team player. I think the rest of you feel the same way."

Olivia fiddled with the ring on her finger. Her voice was stubborn-sounding when she said, "We should make a game plan on our own, just the six of us, in case things go awry at some point in time. We don't have to do it right now, but we need to put something in place. I think we'll all sleep better if we do."

Team Three was outside the company store when Zoe led the little group over to a wooden bench under a pungent pine tree. Slick took the initiative and checked out the bench for listening devices in anticipation of Zoe's saying something that wasn't for anyone's ears but their own. Hawkins looked up at the tree and shook his head. They all moved off to a clearing to stand in a cluster under the golden sunshine. Though they realized they might be overheard if a long-range listening device was being utilized, sometimes one had to take a chance.

"That bench was put there for a reason," Hawkins said. "So, what were you going to say, Zoe?"

"Just that I called my brother from a phone booth before we left and told him I was going away for a while and not to worry. I told him a bit of a fib and said I was doing a government job. Joey didn't ask any questions because he understands confidentiality stuff. So this is what I arranged—if any of us get into trouble, we call him. I'll give you his number, but you have to memorize it. I told him all your names except for you, Hawkins, since I didn't know about you. Not to worry, though, I gave him a code word. It's Buckaroo. We used to have a dog named Buckaroo. He didn't have a tail, and one of his ears was crooked. God, how I loved that dog. Joey did, too. When Buckaroo died, we had him cremated. Joey has his ashes." She rattled off a number in Riverside, California. "Joey will help us if . . . if . . . things get out of hand. He's a vice cop."

"Good going, Zoe," Sam said, clapping the third Mrs. Rainford on the shoulder.

"Wait a minute. When they did the background check on you, your brother would have shown up on the radar screen. They have to know about him," Hawkins said.

"No, they don't. Joey's last name is different from mine. He's my mother's second husband's son. He never wanted me to acknowledge him because of his job. He's really a good guy, and he took good care of me when I was growing up. He's fifty," she said, as if that explained everything. "The truth is, he was more like a father than an older brother. No relation. Don't you get it? Like I said, he's not on my radar screen."

Hawkins still looked dubious. "We'll deal with it later," Sam said.

The double trio left the clearing and continued to troop around the massive compound, their eyes growing wider and wider.

"Beaucoup bucks," Slick said. "How many people make up a consortium?"

"I guess as many as needed. People that rich don't have to explain what they do with their money, meaning they could band together and fund an operation like this. I would like to know what kind of missions the previous operatives went on. And the results they achieved. I'm sure Pappy isn't going to give us that information willingly," Sam said.

"Do any of you find it strange that our team is the only one out and walking about?" Olivia asked. No one answered the question, but they did look around to verify Olivia's observation.

"Nice garden," Hawkins said, as they approached the dining hall and the huge garden behind it where pole beans could be seen growing up tall stakes. "My dad used to have a big garden like this. They must have to chopper in food, supplies, and propane. Unless they lied, and there is another way up and down this mountain. Wonder what the food is like?"

"Just like the FBI Academy food, I bet," Slick said. "Okay, let's head back and pick up our gear at the company store. I'd like a nap before dinner."

"Let's do the gear pickup tomorrow," Zoe said. "Right now I'm not in the mood to look at or try on that drab-looking stuff." The others shrugged and headed off for the Omega Three building.

The Omega Three team marched to the dining hall promptly at three minutes to six. Inside, they stood in awe, their jaws dropping. Beautiful draperies swathed the double-hung windows; thick, luxurious carpets covered the floor. A Chippendale sideboard and breakfront were set against two of the walls. The third wall was the entrance to the kitchen, with beautiful swinging doors that matched the breakfront and sideboard. The fourth was comprised of a massive fieldstone fireplace. Beautiful, fresh floral arrangements adorned both the breakfront and sideboard. Delicious smells wafted from the kitchen. The tables, four in total, were covered with fine linen, beautiful crystal, exquisite china, and shimmering silver. A white card to the left of a centerpiece of fresh flowers said the table was reserved for Team Three.

Teams One and Two were already seated, sipping wine. Team Four could be heard coming up the wooden steps to the building. Hawkins led the way to the table. He didn't hold out anyone's chair.

Havapopulas had said dinner for the trainees was from six to seven. Promptly at seven the tables were bussed and reset for the staff, who dined from seven to eight.

Four foreign-looking waiters dressed in sacklike loose clothing served the meal. First came a rich chicken noodle soup along with homemade crusty bread served with what looked like a scoop of freshly churned golden butter. A crisp garden salad with a raisin-pecan vinaigrette dressing was set with impeccable expertise in front of Team Three. They ate with relish, savoring every mouthful.

"Beats the cafeteria at the Academy," Slick said, as the main course of rack of lamb with fresh mint jelly was served. Accompanying the lamb were fresh garden peas that looked like emeralds, tiny glazed carrots, and a mound of spicy mashed potatoes. A basket of fresh bread followed.

No one said a word as they cleaned their plates. The dessert, a banana drenched in a heavy syrup full of crushed pecans and strong Kona coffee, completed the meal.

Somewhere, probably the kitchen, a buzzer sounded. The four waiters appeared with large trays in their hands. Clearly it was time to leave. Team One left, followed by Team Two. Sam led her team out into the early evening, followed by Team Four. They all stood aside as the staff marched up the three steps to the dining hall. Sam counted as the men and women passed them. Kollar

Havapopulas was the last to enter the building. Like the others, he didn't acknowledge the new training class in any way.

"I think I need to walk off that dinner," Slick said.

"Want some company?" Hawkins asked.

"Sure," Slick said.

Sam watched Slick and Hawkins until they were out of sight. Back at the Academy she'd thought there was something going on between the two of them. Something that never managed to get off the ground. It wasn't going to get off the ground on Big Pine either, she thought as she remembered Havapopulas's cold warning at the orientation. Anyone caught fraternizing would be dropped off the mountain. Even the appearance of fraternizing was reason enough to be cashiered.

The four Rainford wives looked at one another. Sam shrugged. "I guess it's a nice hot shower, then bed for me. It's been a long, exhausting day," she said.

Kayla looked around the compound. "The last time I went to bed at eight o'clock, I was six years old. Did we make a mistake in coming here, Sam?" she asked quietly.

"Off the top of my head, I want to say no. But I really don't know, Kayla. What I do know is we have to give it our best shot. C'mon, we're women. We can do anything we set our minds to. I know you all want to talk about Douglas and get even with him. All in good time. This is how I see it. There has to be some very sophisticated computer hardware up here on the mountain. I'd say it's probably better than what the FBI has because this is all privately funded. We'll find a way to access it at some point, then we'll nail old Douglas. We just have to be patient. I'm going to make a promise to you. And it is that I guarantee somehow, some way, I'm going to find that guy, and we'll all get our revenge. It will happen. Let's just concentrate on getting our feet wet here, and we'll get to Douglas in proper order. Remember now, don't talk indoors about anything you don't want anyone else to hear."

"What did you think of Pappy?" Olivia asked.

"He's hot." Kayla grinned.

"I'm in lust already," Zoe said.

"He could put his shoes under my bed anytime," Olivia added, giggling.

"He's a son of a bitch," Sam said as she marched into the house that would be their home for the next year.

"I think that means she thinks he's hot," Kayla observed.

The day after their arrival was boring yet filled with a high level of anxiety for all the members of Team Three. Their issued gear was packed in their footlockers, as civilian dress was still permitted for one last day. Introductions were made by Kollar Havapopulas during a simple lunch of tasty, homemade soup, thick sandwiches, and slices of pie for dessert. As a team, they toured the grounds, inspecting the stables, the various barns, all of the outer buildings, including one that was referred to as the command center, the pool house and the heated pool, and the building that housed four classrooms and a room that held ten computers. All state-of-the-art. The last building at the edge of the compound was the clinic/infirmary, where a huge red cross hung on the door.

Each team was introduced to their academic instructors and their drill sergeants. There were no smiles and no levity at all. There was a NO ENTRY sign over the firearms building and shooting range.

Perhaps the most frightening thing of all was the half acre dog kennel, where six dogs, almost clones of Alpha, were housed. The trainer said they patrolled the grounds at night and at certain periods of the day. The dogs looked mean and angry but nothing compared to Alpha's demeanor. They were told by the trainer that Alpha was the dogs' leader, and that the others, all sired by him, were so attuned to his silent messages that they obeyed him instantly. The trainer went on to explain that if any of the team members stepped over the line, one of the dogs would make them wish they hadn't. "There are certain areas of the compound that are off-limits to everyone but the staff. Ignorance will be no excuse if you tread where you aren't supposed to tread," he said before he walked away.

Hawkins was more impressed with the building called the motor pool, which housed a variety of motorcycles, golf carts, and scooters. For the mountain terrain, of course. "Would you look at that Ducati," Hawkins said, his eyes those of a child on Christmas morning.

The women were busy examining the scooters, the kind driven in Bermuda and the Bahamas, and the golf carts. Everything was painted olive green, even the scooters.

"In the fashion world this color would be referred to as asparagus green or celery green," Slick said. "I whizzed around Europe on motorbikes all the time. They're fun," she said.

Ever practical, Sam said, "I guess they have to airlift in the gasoline. Let's check out the cable car."

"It's off-limits," Hawkins said. "Don't even go there."

"Anyone up for a hike?" Sam asked. Her eyes said it was time to check out the mountain, not just the compound. The others agreed. "Long pants, long sleeves, and sneakers," she ordered, having earlier been voted in as team leader, as they trudged back to their barracks to change.

Always prepared, Sam slipped on a backpack that held a first-aid kit, a water bottle, and some granola bars. She led the way, the others following in a single file.

Just then a golf cart roared around the corner, Alpha sitting at attention next to the driver. Sam and her team pulled up short. Havapopulas stopped on a dime. "Going hiking?" he asked pleasantly.

Sam stared into the silvery eyes and nodded. She didn't know if she was seeing respect or suspicion.

"Okay. Don't go too far, or I'll have to send Alpha to fetch you back. Don't get too tired, tomorrow you start your training. By the way, lights out at nine sharp. Reveille is at four."

Kayla gasped. "Four in the morning!"

Alpha barked sharply as Havapopulas moved the cart forward. He didn't bother to respond. Alpha barked a second time.

Team Three started off. "What's the difference between woods and a forest?" Olivia asked.

"Density, underbrush, the terrain, or the grade would be my guess. I was never a Boy Scout or the outdoor type," Hawkins said.

Sam thought his voice sounded defensive. She whacked at the underbrush with a broken limb she'd picked up when they'd started out. "Don't touch the vines. Some of it is poison ivy and sumac. That stuff," she said, pointing to a tree on her right, "is Virginia creeper."

Sam noticed that Hawkins was more or less partnered with Slick. She was definitely going to have a talk with Slick later on.

As she hacked and whacked, Sam thought about the dark-haired man who would be calling the shots for a whole year. Who was Kollar Havapopulas? More to the point, *what* was he? He had a military bearing. Did that mean he was ex-military? Was he some kind of spook in his own right? *Spook* was a name given to CIA operatives, like *fibby* was the name given to FBI agents. He had to be someone with an impressive background to be in charge of an operation like Big Pine Mountain's.

Sam tripped on a stringy vine that was as tough as steel and went down on one knee, which jarred her thoughts back to the present. She picked herself up and moved forward. In the early days at the FBI academy she remembered hearing tales of a one-man army of some sort. She also remembered that she'd heard the word *Greek* used in the discussions. She wondered if they were one and the same. She stopped and turned around, fixing her gaze on Slick and Hawkins. "Back in the first few weeks at the Academy do either one of you remember hearing a story about a Greek who was some kind of one-man army? A legend in his own time, that kind of thing. I can't remember if someone told me or if I overheard it. My mind must have been on something else because I don't remember any of the details. Did either one of you hear it?"

Slick and Hawkins shook their heads.

Olivia snapped a branch from a sapling. Her eyes looked worried. "What does it mean, Sam? I mean if you're right, and Pappy is that one-man army?"

"I don't know. Probably that he's qualified to run this operation. You have to admit, it's a pretty impressive place, built into a mountain the way it is."

Zoe screamed, a bloodcurdling sound that stopped Team Three in its tracks. "Snake!" she screamed again.

In the time it took the others to stop in their tracks

and turn around, another sound could be heard, a hard wind, a crash of brush, then a black-and-silver streak that landed in front of them. Sam saw a white flash of teeth and the snake—which had to be a foot long and at least two inches thick—sailed through the air minus its head. She almost fainted.

No one moved as they watched the part dog, part wolf, shake his head from side to side before racing off.

"Okayyy, I think that's enough hiking for one day," Slick said, heading off in the same direction the dog had taken. She was trembling from head to toe.

"Was it a poisonous snake?" Kayla asked, her voice shaking.

"Probably. Its head was smaller than its body. I think that means it's poisonous. Maybe it's the other way around. I read that somewhere in a dentist's office. *National Geographic*," Hawkins said in a jittery voice.

As Team Three walked out of the forest, they saw Havapopulas in his golf cart, Alpha sitting next to him. The dog's ears looked like sharp spears as he eyed all six of them.

Sam had no intention of asking the question, but the words tumbled off her lips. "Was the snake poisonous?"

"Yes. Donovan told you about the mountain. Be careful. The next time Alpha might not be close enough to help you." A second later he was gone, the golf cart trundling across the paved compound.

"I hate that guy. I mean I really hate him," Olivia

said vehemently. "I could grow to love that animal, though."

"I could lust after him—Havapopulas, I mean—with very little trouble," Kayla said.

Sam was tempted to tell the others she'd dreamed of him the night before, but she didn't. Suddenly, she felt foolish and wasn't sure why. "Let's go to the dining hall and get some coffee."

"Coffee, hell, I need a stiff drink," Zoe said. "I know, I know, no alcohol on the premises. It's wishful thinking on my part. Does anyone around here smoke? A cigarette would taste real good right now. My nerves are twanging all over the place. Okay, okay, no cigarettes either. I'll take the coffee," she said, stomping off to the dining hall, where coffee was available twenty-four hours a day.

Team Three trooped into the dining hall, sniffing as they went. Tantalizing aromas wafted in from the kitchen; tonight's dinner. Something Italian, hot and spicy.

"Spaghetti," said Hawkins, sniffing like a hound dog.

"Chicken Parmesan," Slick said.

"You're both wrong. Eggplant Parmesan. My mouth is watering already," Olivia said.

"Who cares as long as it's good," Kayla said.

"Boy are you guys going to be disappointed if it's meat loaf with some kind of Italian sauce," Zoe said, pouring coffee into her cup.

Team Three looked at their leader. Sam grinned. "I

think it's spaghetti and meatballs. With crusty Italian bread, mountains of soft, yellow butter, and a crisp garden salad with a raisin-pecan dressing with just a smidgin of balsamic vinegar. I bet there's either fruit or sherbet for dessert. The Parmesan cheese is going to be in the meatballs, and it will be freshly grated at the table. The sauce is going to have a hint, mind you, just a *hint* of basil."

"You sound like you have the inside track on dinner. How do you know all that?" Slick asked suspiciously.

Sam laughed. It was a relief to laugh after the experience with the snake, the wolf-dog, and Havapopulas. "I looked at the menu on the back of the door. I bet you guys didn't even notice it. You really all need to become more observant."

"Smart-ass." Hawkins chuckled.

"Guess that's why we made you the team leader." Sam smirked.

The group settled themselves at one of the tables, coffee cups in hand. Two members from Team One and three members of Team Two were also drinking coffee and chatting.

The conversation was general, hometowns, the weather, dogs, cars, hobbies, and the dinner menu. At best it was boring. Hawkins, who loved to talk, started to share their experience with the snake. The others looked at him, jaws dropping, eyes wide. "That dog is part wolf. Take my word for it." And that was the end of that conversation. The others turned away. Hawkins shrugged.

Team Three drank their coffee in silence, each busy with his or her own thoughts. Everyone came to attention when the Greek marched into the dining hall, Alpha at his side. He poured coffee into a mug he'd brought with him. He looked around, smiled, waved, and marched back outside.

Sam's heart kicked up a beat. Was he checking up on them? Wherever his *lair* was, one would think he'd have his own private coffeepot. He was definitely checking up on them. Most definitely.

Sam wished she had someone to compare the Greek to, but she didn't. She'd never come across anyone as muscular, as good-looking, or as cold as Kollar Havapopulas. Not even Douglas Cosmo Rainford, III. DCR, as she thought of Douglas these days, couldn't hold a candle to the Greek Adonis. She felt herself frowning. Didn't Adonis have blond hair? She had to stop thinking about the man and get on an even keel. She gulped the last of the hot coffee and stood up. The others followed her.

Tomorrow was another day.

Chapter Six

"Dress up time!" Zoe shouted as she paraded through the barracks in her combat boots, socks, olive green shorts with matching tee shirt. "Ta da!"

"These damn boots are heavier than ski boots," Kayla mumbled as she clomped across the hardwood floor.

Hawkins guffawed good-naturedly, aware of how spiffy he looked in his matching attire. He could have posed for *Esquire*, *Town and Country*, or any number of magazines, and he knew it.

Sam and Slick were used to the combat boots and the heavy socks. They'd both had their share of blisters, some of the scars still remaining on their heels and toes.

"These are just perfect for kicking butt," Olivia trilled, her eyes on Hawkins.

"All right, children, stop complaining. Get your books and let's go. You know what the Greek said about tardiness," Sam reminded them, leading the way outside and across the compound to the building with the sign overhead that read SCHOOL. She felt like she was in the first grade again as she made her way up the steps.

They were on time, with ninety seconds to spare.

It was a pleasant room as far as schoolrooms went, certainly more comfortable and friendly to the eye than the one at the FBI Academy. Instead of hard wooden chairs, there were seven club chairs set in a circle with a huge, round, wooden table in the center. The lighting was subdued but more than efficient, meaning there was no glare on the textbooks. A long table held a huge stainless-steel coffeepot with bright yellow cups arranged on a matching tray. Luscious green plants hung from the beams while tall, thick banana plants graced the corners. The floors were hardwood and shined to a high polish. Even their combat boots didn't mark up the superb finish.

Team Three settled themselves. The coffee would have to wait for the ten-minute break on the hour.

The ethics instructor, who would also be their instructor on white-collar crime, introduced himself, shook hands all around. "Call me Don. We're pretty informal around here," he said.

Don Harmon was a prissy-looking little man with wire-rim glasses and a receding hairline. His rich, early-summer tan gave his thinness a healthy appearance. Behind the wire-rimmed glasses the instructor's eyes were shrewd.

Team Three settled into their chairs to listen and learn.

At eleven o'clock, the academic portion of their training would end, and they would spend an hour at the firing range, followed by lunch, which lasted thirty minutes. Thirty minutes of free time for personal needs came on the heels of lunch, which was lean and full of protein.

A six-mile hike with a twenty-five-pound backpack was scheduled for one o'clock, after which there would be time in the pool. From four thirty until ten minutes to six a class on behavioral science was scheduled. Then came dinner and a ninety-minute class on operational skills that rounded out the day. Study time or homework followed showers, then it was lights out.

Kayla summed up the day by saying, "This sucks!" The others agreed, as they gingerly removed their boots to care for their raw, blistered feet.

Sam fought to keep her eyes open even though she was in bed. She waited, willing her eyes to stare at the ceiling. The moment she was certain the others were asleep, she crept from her bed, opened her footlocker, and removed the weights she needed to use to build up her upper-body strength. She was stunned to see Hawkins in the living room doing the same thing she planned on doing. She grinned tiredly. No words were necessary.

Hawkins, like her, was more than aware that at the end of the week they'd be given a physical-training test.

The tests focused on handcuffing, control holds, searching subjects, weapon retention, disarming techniques, grappling, and boxing. The physical training tests would be given every seven weeks thereafter.

Forty minutes into the weight lifting, Hawkins collapsed on a chair. He looked at Sam and the grim, determined expression on her face. And the pain. "No pain, no gain, eh?"

"Something like that," Sam said. She collapsed alongside him. "I don't want to fail again, Hawkins."

"Listen, Sam. We didn't fail. We just weren't good enough. I don't know if we're good enough this time either. I don't think there's a rule here that we can't scale the wall at night. Maybe we could practice together after everyone goes to bed. We can encourage each other. I know it's going to cut down on our sleep time, but to my way of thinking, this is when we should do it, now at the beginning before the training intensifies. Thirty minutes of weights and forty minutes on the wall. What do you say?"

Sam thought about it as her breathing returned to normal. Could she survive on seventy minutes' less sleep? Well, there was only one way to find out. "Yeah, sure. But, do we wait until after the test at the end of the week to see just how weak we are, or do we start tomorrow night?"

"Your call, Sam. I'm okay with whatever you want to do."

"Let's eat the humiliating pill and wait till after the

first test. That way we'll know how hard we have to work. I'm going to bed, Hawkins. See you in the morning. Listen, as your team leader I feel I have to say something to you. Cool it with Slick. I'd hate to see you two get bounced for a little bedsheet bingo. It's not worth it, Hawkins."

Hawkins blushed, but then gave a curt nod. "Okay. Gotcha. Night, Sam."

"Night, Hawkins."

Five seconds later, Sam was sound asleep, her dreams full of huge black walls that were insurmountable.

Outside, Pappy Havapopulas patrolled the compound, with Alpha at his side. Inside the Omega Three building he could see shadows moving about. He stopped to watch, knowing exactly what he was seeing.

Pappy finished his rounds before Alpha nudged him in the direction of the bench where he always took a last break before turning in for the night. This was the time he let his mind drift as he smoked one of the two cigarettes he allowed himself each day. It was treat time for Alpha for a day well done. He stroked the big dog's head before he handed over the chlorophyll chew.

Pappy blew a perfect smoke ring. He watched it circle Alpha's head like a halo. He smiled.

Twenty-four new recruits. Some of them sassy, some of them arrogant, some of them dumb as dirt. Then there were some he rooted for, cheered for silently, like Sam Rainford and Eric Hawkins. A sound of mirth escaped his lips when he thought about how Rainford and her cohorts had taken Donovan. Something he didn't think was possible. He mentally reviewed her file. Blessed with a phenomenal memory, he had it down pat, all sixteen pages. Right then he thought he knew Samantha Rainford better than she knew herself. The only thing he didn't understand was her marriage to Douglas Cosmo Rainford, III. *That* simply didn't add up. He wondered how she would react to living on the mountain for a whole year. He'd bet this entire mountain she would be included among the one out of three who would adapt. He also knew that, when the year was up, he would have, at best, four agents who made the cut. The others would be set loose to go on their way. None of them would look back. Samantha Rainford would be one of the four. He felt it in his gut. There was a downside to that happening. He would have to ride her hard to make sure she didn't waffle. He didn't think that would happen, but when it came to women, he was the first to admit, he knew nothing. Alpha knew more about women than he did.

Pappy blew one last perfect smoke ring before he stubbed out his cigarette. He picked it up and stuffed it in his pocket. Alpha finished his chew at the same moment. They were so in sync, man and dog, that sometimes it boggled Pappy's mind. He bent over and whispered in the big dog's ear, "I want you to take care of *her*, Alpha." The big dog tossed his head as though to say, I already know that. Pappy grinned in the darkness.

Alpha moved to the center of the compound and waited for his nightly signal. The moment Pappy's index finger shot forward, Alpha streaked off to release the guard dogs that would patrol the compound until dawn.

This was the moment when Pappy allowed his shoulders to sag as he made his way back to his quarters, the weight of his responsibility heavy on him. Sometimes, he wondered if he'd ever leave the mountain again. It had been his choice to come here, his choice not to leave in the ten years since he'd arrived. Sometimes he missed the world below the mountain, but only sometimes. There was no place for him down there. Not any longer.

Once, a long time ago, he'd been on a first-name basis with two different presidents. Once he was the man the government called on to do things no other man could do. He was so good at what he did he had a trunkful of hardware. Medals for this, medals for that. Then, when the unthinkable had happened and his deep cover had been compromised, his very own government disavowed him, and he'd been hung out to dry. But he had known going in that that might happen someday. He wasn't bitter. He'd had his days of being in the sun and being known as the best of the best. Presidents still sent him Christmas cards with personal messages inside. He'd licked his wounds and moved on to try to make sense of what had happened to him. In time, he accepted it because he'd had no other choice, but it didn't make it any easier. What he'd never been able to accept was Adrian's death several years later. Adrian had been his partner and the love of his life. Samantha Rainford looked so much like her it was hard to believe Adrian hadn't come back from the dead. While he'd been grieving over his loss, the consortium he now worked for had approached him through a high-level White House staffer and brought him to the mountain. He'd accepted their proposal and never left.

He knew every tree, every stone, every little creek and puddle on the thousand-acre mountain. He could close his eyes and bring up any patch of clear forest, every trickle of water. He could pinpoint the exact spot where he'd killed snakes and wild animals. It was the only way he was able to handle his grief. And suddenly he was right back where he had been ten years ago emotionally. The pain of his loss was so raw, so brutal, he felt light-headed.

Pappy stripped down and pulled on pajama bottoms before he brushed his teeth. He should send Samantha Rainford away, he thought as he climbed between the sheets. Before it was too late. He rolled over. It was no mistake that his bed was positioned under the window that had a full view of the compound. He blinked, then blinked again when he saw Alpha sitting on the top step of the building that housed Team Three. He knew the big dog would sit there all night and not leave until it was time to lead the pack of patrol dogs back to their kennel.

He slept only because he was too tired and weary to do anything else.

Sam woke with a headache that grew more fierce as she looked outside. Her first summer rain on the mountain. The only problem was, it wasn't the kind of summer rain one liked to walk through with a boyfriend. Nor was it the kind of summer rain that was warm with remembrances of childhood. This was a hard downpour, and, according to the thermometer by the front door, it was only sixty-five degrees outside.

Sam brushed her teeth and gulped four Advil before she showered and dressed. Today was her first physical-training test, and she was dreading it. She wondered if Hawkins felt the same way she did. The rest of the team had aced the training segment they'd taken part in during the week. She hadn't. Neither had Hawkins.

Sam reached for her AFJ-issued poncho and headed for the dining hall. She knew from her days at the Academy that she should eat lightly. Fruit and toast. She probably should forgo the coffee but knew she wouldn't. The headache was lessening a little. She prayed it would be gone before it was her time to perform. That's how she thought of it. She would be performing.

Sam's mood was dark when she blasted through the door to the dining hall. She was stunned to see Hawkins sitting at their table eating breakfast. She hadn't even noticed that he wasn't in his bed in the barracks.

The coffee smelled wonderful. The toast was warm

and had already been buttered just the way she liked it. She spread strawberry jam on it and carried her plate to the table. She eyed the slice of melon. Potassium. One of these days she was going to ask who the dietitian was who made out the menus. Not only was the food wonderful, it was nutritious. Vitamins, Centrum to be precise, were always served with breakfast. Since arriving, she'd taken one in the morning and one at night. She didn't know if that was good or bad, and she didn't care. She knew Hawkins did the same thing because she saw him popping the vitamins.

Hawkins stopped eating long enough to mutter, "Morning, Sam. You ready for this?"

"I guess so. I could do without the rain, though. The rope is going to be slippery."

"Yeah," Hawkins said morosely.

The other members of Team Three trooped into the dining hall. None of them looked cheery. *Rain can do that to a person*, Sam thought.

Sam listened as the team talked about the fifteen-point score necessary to pass the PT test. At least one point had to be scored in each of the five events out of a possible fifty required to pass each physical training test. They had to do pull-ups, sit-ups, push-ups, a 120-yard shuttle run, then the two-mile run. The moment the team completed the PT test, they had to pass the DT test as well. Defensive tactics included boxing, handcuffing, control holds, searching subjects, grappling, weapon retention, and disarming techniques.

With the rain, it was a given that everyone's timing would be off. Sam shivered under the wet poncho and looked around. Everyone at the table had removed theirs. Dumb, dumb, and dumb. First she hadn't even noticed that Hawkins was missing, and now she was eating breakfast in a poncho. Irritably, she pulled it over her head. Then she winced at the puddle she'd left on the floor. Slick rushed forward with wads of paper napkins to dry up the rainwater.

Today there was no seven o'clock breakfast for the staff. They'd breakfasted at five o'clock and were already out in the field waiting for the teams to show up.

At ten minutes before six, Hawkins stood up and pulled on his poncho. "Showtime!"

Sam noticed they were the second team to arrive. The moment Teams One and Four arrived, Havapopulas brought his whistle to his mouth. The teams separated and followed their instructors. During the next hour each member of the team passed the push-ups, sit-ups, and pull-ups. The 120-yard shuttle run was no problem. The teams split up and started off on the two-mile run. In future tests and trials the duration of the test would increase; the two-mile run would go to three, five, seven, then ten miles. Endurance was the name of the game when it came to the PT and DT tests.

When they were over, with everyone passing, Sam was proved right that their timing was off. Allowances for the rain had been made earlier.

Pappy stood under an awning that had been erected

the previous night. He was the scorekeeper. He was more than a little pleased with the results he was seeing for all four teams after only one week, especially considering the foul weather. He knew it would be a different story when they moved down to the second and third plateaus. Those recruits with no law enforcement background had trouble all week with disarming techniques, control holds, and the real killer—grappling. He knew that Samantha would excel in everything but the grappling and the climb.

Pappy felt like cursing the weather for throwing off the timing. In dry, sunny weather, grappling and scaling the fifty-foot wall was a challenge. In rain and mud, it was a nightmare. He donned his poncho and moved off.

Sam moved carefully down to the next plateau, where everything but the scaling and grappling on the great wall would take place. She was soaked to the skin, her clothes cleaving to her body, her hair plastered to her head. Her feet were numb from the blisters and raw skin rubbing inside the combat boots. She was tired and wondered if it showed. Well, she couldn't worry about that, and she shouldn't be worrying about Havapopulas and his scorecard either, but she was.

The hours wore on until the last event loomed. Sam would be the eleventh recruit to attack the wall. By then the wall would be slick with mud, as would the rope. She'd be lucky if she managed a two-handed pull-up. She took her place in line, pleased to see that none of those going ahead of her had as yet scaled the wall. Why didn't that Greek jerk call this off? It was an impossible feat, and he knew it full well. Humiliation was the answer. She knew because that had been the answer back at the Academy. There was no reason to believe it would be any different on AFJ's mountain.

Sam's feet burned with pain. She had never learned how to step outside of the pain the way the instructors advised her back at the Academy. Pain was pain. When it was her turn to attack the wall, she moved forward, knowing what was expected of her, her eyes glinting with anger and determination. What she wasn't prepared for was Havapopulas's cutting words. "Okay, Rainford, show us what the FBI failed to teach you." His tone said it all. She wanted to cry. She was at the foot of the wall. It looked as high as the sky as rain pelted her. Her booted feet screamed with pain as she sought for toeholds and proceeded to attempt the climb. She was four toeholds up, her hands reaching for handholds, when she slipped and landed in a puddle of mud and rainwater. Cringing with shame and humiliation, she struggled to her feet.

"Do it again! This time pretend you know what you're doing, Rainford," Pappy shouted to be heard over the rain.

"Screw you, you military reject," Sam muttered as she sought a toehold on the wall. She started to climb.

"Say again, Rainford, I can't hear you," Pappy shouted again.

"I said, screw you, you military reject!" Sam shouted

so loudly she thought she damaged her vocal cords. And
then she slipped and was in the mud again.

"Time's up. You got zip in points. Go to the rope.
Let's see some muscle this time. You academy wimps
are all alike. That was pussycat training. This is the
real thing. Move your ass, Rainford, or are you waiting
for a bus?"

Something snapped in Sam when she realized the
man was making this personal. He hadn't said a word to
any of the others, and they'd fared worse than she. She
wanted to chew iron and spew rust, right on his spit-and-
polish boots. She grabbed the slimy rope, hauling herself forward. She was a quarter of the way up the rope,
her hands raw, when she passed the muddy part; the rest
of the rope was clean but wet. That had to mean she was
farther up the rope than any of the others had gone. She
continued to climb, cursing under her breath, using
every dirty word she'd ever learned. Then the skin on the
palms of her hands split open and blood smeared the
rope. She did her best to work the rope between her fingers, but the strength just wasn't there. She slipped and
slid down the rope to land in the mud again. Her teammates rushed to help her, congratulating her excitedly,
when Pappy blew his whistle, signaling them to back off.
They did.

"You have three more minutes, Rainford. Move!"

Sam turned around until she saw him standing
under his nice, dry, green-striped awning. She brought
up her middle finger before she marched off. She

would have succeeded if not for Alpha, who blocked her way.

"Insubordination, Rainford. Drop and give me fifty."

Sam's middle finger shot upward a second time. Couldn't the man see she was half-dead? Alpha barked. Sam sat down and let the rain pour over her.

"I gave you an order, Rainford!"

If I cry, he wins. If I die here in the rain and mud, he wins. If I do the fifty push-ups, I win.

She was back to the dirty words again to spur her on. Later, if she didn't die, she'd go to the chapel and ask God to forgive her. While she was there she'd pray for God to strike Havapopulas dead in his tracks. Now that was a perfect oxymoron.

Sam could hear him counting. She was up to twenty-one and still moving. She was beyond pain now as she forced her body to do what was expected. She heard him call out thirty-seven. For the life of her she couldn't subtract the two numbers to hear how many more she had to do. The next number she heard was forty-eight. She heard something else. Cheers. Not just from her own team but from the other teams as well. Then she heard the magic number. She should fall on her face in the mud and never, ever get up. That's what they expected her to do. Instead, she somehow managed to get to her feet. She wobbled off, knowing she would kick the wolf-dog if he stood in front of her. Instead, Alpha stepped out of the way.

Pappy watched Sam walk across the plateau. For one

wild moment, he wanted to run after her, to apologize. He felt lower than a snake's belly and knew the members of his staff were aware something out of the ordinary was going on. The recruits wore vicious looks, and he knew that in their eyes, he'd stepped over the line, and they didn't understand what was going on either. None of them would meet his gaze. He waited until all four teams were out of sight before he dismissed his staff. He whistled for Alpha, who joined him under the tent. The big dog was soaking wet. Pappy needed to dry him off. He needed to dry himself off, too. What he really needed was a good dose of absolution followed by a stiff drink.

Maybe the rain would cleanse him to some degree. Then again, maybe it wouldn't. He bit down on his lip when he remembered Sam's defiant reaction to his command. And then he laughed because he'd done exactly the same thing a hundred years ago when he'd undergone his own training.

She's the one. He could feel it in every pore of his body.

Chapter Seven

It was the end of August, and the heat and humidity of the Carolinas had made their way to the mountain. Everyone had a sheen of sweat on their bodies as they trooped to the firing range. Team Three had the highest marksmanship scores of all four teams. Sam was the only one on the four teams to have a perfect score.

Out of the corner of her eye Sam could see Pappy standing off to the side, the ever-present scorecard in his hands. He wore aviator sunglasses and a baseball cap with the bill in the back. She'd seen the stitching earlier signifying he was a Chicago Cubs fan. Personally, she thought the Cubs were a bunch of slugs on the field. She'd played softball all four years of college and could whack the ball better than some of the players on Chicago's National League team.

In the weeks since the PT and DT tests, and her recovery, she'd yet to have a word with him. She knew he watched her like the proverbial hawk. At times it unnerved her. At other times, he was invisible to her. Just then, though, she needed to pretend he was invisible. It was her turn at the range. She stood straight, both hands clasped on the SIG Sauer provided by AFJ. There was almost something seductive about the curve of the trigger mechanism. She didn't blink, and she didn't twitch. What she did was paste a mental picture of Pappy on the target. She fired six consecutive shots and ripped his imagined face to shreds. All shots were dead center. Her team let out a proud whoop of pleasure.

Zoe and Olivia tied for second place, Hawkins and Kayla for third, and Slick came in last.

Sam removed the protective ear gear and moved off to the rifle range. Again she made a perfect score. More whoops of pleasure. Hawkins came in second, with the other three Rainford wives coming in third. Again, Slick was last.

Two hours later, the teams split up. They cleaned their guns while sitting on the ground. This was when Pappy did his stroll and handed out the scores. Sam didn't even bother to look up.

"Good work, Rainford," Pappy said, dropping her score sheet on the ground when she made no effort to take it from him. Suddenly she looked up at the tall man hovering over her. The others stopped what they were doing. "It's easy when you can put a face to the target," she said coldly.

Her team started to babble in the hopes of warding off a verbal confrontation of some kind between their leader and the man who operated the camp.

"I belong to the NRA," Kayla said. "They offer great health insurance to their members."

"These guns would be nice if they came in colors," Zoe said. "I think I'd pick lavender. Stainless steel is so cold and deadly."

"That's the point," Slick said sarcastically.

Striving to keep Pappy occupied, Olivia looked up at him and said, "I think the Cubs stink."

Sam laughed. It was a pure sound of pleasure. It was also a great put-down and too good to let pass. She continued to work at her SIG Sauer.

Hawkins opted to take the high road and remained mute, but a grin stretched across his lips.

Pappy walked away, aware that six pairs of eyes were boring into his back. None of them had forgiven him for what they perceived he'd done to their leader. To date, all four teams were proving to be a pain in the ass. The following day, he decided, would tell a different story. They would all be preparing for the next round of PT and DT testing, after which was Paintball Day—where there were no rules or regulations. It was also known as Last Man Standing. The players, including the entire staff, would be divided into three teams. Teams One and Three, teams Two and Four. The staff made up their own team. It was a drill they did four times a year.

Just the day before, the results of previous paintball drills had been posted in the dining hall next to the menu. In ten years of paintballing, the staff had won twenty-seven of the forty games. After the game, there would be a barbecue and socializing. Even beer. They were all looking forward to it, especially Sam.

Team Three watched silently as Pappy walked away.

Sam folded her score sheet and shoved it into her pocket. She looked at her team, and said, "Are any of you picking up on anything around here? I'm sensing a certain anxiety. I can't explain it any better than that. Something is pending. I don't think that it has anything to do with us, though. I just have this eerie feeling."

"There was a lot of scurrying around earlier," Slick volunteered. "We're without a helicopter if that means anything. The workhorse," she said, referring to the helicopter they rode in on, "brought tons of supplies yesterday. Today the other one is gone. That's never happened before. At least since we've been here."

"The cable car is still here. They were working on the shrubbery and clearing away debris from last week's heavy rain," Zoe said. "That means we aren't totally cut off from the outside world."

"Maybe company is coming. And," Hawkins said dramatically, "I'll bet you my boots it's a night visit. After lights out."

"That's a sucker bet," Sam said thoughtfully. "I for one would like to know who's coming to the party."

"Oooh," Kayla said shivering. "This is exciting. Are

we going to pretend we're at summer camp and do the old spy routine and cause mayhem and disorder?"

Hawkins looked at her with disgust. "With all those vicious dogs patrolling the grounds? I-don't-think-so."

Sam's eyes narrowed. It brought another question to her mind. Why was it that she and Hawkins were never bothered by the dogs on their nightly workouts at the wall? They both knew the dogs were out there, stalking, watching but never coming close to the wall. On more than one occasion she'd seen Alpha's yellow eyes watching her from the perimeter of the wall, but he'd never interfered. That alone was not only puzzling but scary.

"It really is none of our business who comes and who goes around here," Hawkins said.

"To be informed is to be knowledgeable," Sam said, getting to her feet. "We still have forty minutes till our next class. I'm going for a swim."

Pappy strode into the kitchen to snatch some cookies to go with his cup of coffee. His steel gray eyes softened when he smiled at the man chopping vegetables. "How's it going, Pop?"

"Good, son. Real good. I've been busy planning my menu for your late-night guests. Not too heavy and not too light, right?"

Pappy laughed. "Right. She had a perfect score, Pop. She as much as told me my face was on the target. She shredded it to hell and back. That woman hates my guts. She won't even look at me. Alpha *likes* her. Do you believe that?"

The old man with the magnificent culinary skills looked at his son. "Yes, I can understand that. I watch her from the kitchen window when she's eating. You're vulnerable when you eat because you relax. I think I like her myself."

Pappy looked at his father, wondering if he'd done the right thing by bringing the old man to the mountain. At the time the government had turned its back on him, he'd had to decide whether to bring his father with him or put him in the Witness Protection Program. Once his father understood what was going on, he'd gladly agreed to join him. Still, he must get lonely from time to time even though he played chess on a regular basis with some of the other employees. He rode every day, and, in nice weather, he'd swim his laps in the pool. Television, thanks to their satellite dish, was another good old friend. He was a movie buff and could recite the dialogue from *Zorba the Greek* verbatim.

"You lonely up here, Pop?"

"Sometimes. Not often, Kollar. I'm content. Your mother would have loved this mountain, and she'd never want to leave it. Are you nervous about having guests?"

"No, not really. Something's going on, but until they arrive, I don't have a clue. That's always the way it is, you know that." The guests his father was referring to were the five members of the consortium Pappy worked for. Something was brewing somewhere, something they wanted taken care of; otherwise, they wouldn't be coming.

His father stopped long enough to sip at his ouzo, something he refused to give up. Pappy made sure there was a never-ending supply. It was the least he could do for his father.

This man whom he loved more than life was getting old, seventy-four. Still, he had a full head of hair that was half-gray, half-black, and he liked to brag that he had all his teeth except for one. He was stocky and barrel-chested, with arms like tree trunks and hands so big they seemed to dwarf his arms. Those strong arms and hands had taken care of Kollar from the time he was a baby. Gentle arms and hands. Still, they could sting on one's bottom as Pappy had found out on more than one occasion when he was growing up.

Kyros Havapopulas had been in law enforcement during his early and middle years. When he retired, he opened a Greek restaurant and would still be in San Francisco running it if his son hadn't whisked him away in the dead of night.

"Should we make a wager on the paintball game to-morrow?" the old man asked.

"You know the staff is going to win, Pop. What's the point of betting?"

"I think this year it might be a little different. I'll bet a hundred dollars on Teams One and Three. Of course I mean no disrespect," Kyros said slyly.

Pappy felt chagrined. Things were changing right in

front of his very eyes. First his dog, now his father. "You're on." He stalked from the stainless-steel kitchen. He would have huffed and puffed, but that would have made him look like a . . . he couldn't come up with the right word, so he just grimaced, turned his baseball cap around, and headed off to his office.

He heard the laughter coming from the pool area. He sauntered over just in time to see Samantha Rainford lift off the diving board and hit the water. He sucked in his breath and moved on. He knew exactly what she would look like in a string bikini because she looked so much like Adrian, who had refused to wear the one-piece navy blue Speedo all the trainees wore. Not that she'd ever been a trainee here on the mountain but . . . he let the thought drift away. Adrian had been a law unto herself. The best of the best. In the field, in the office, *in bed. And that will be enough of that,* he told himself as he stomped his way to his office.

Sam held a whispered conversation with her team prior to going to dinner. "You might think I'm off the wall with what I'm going to tell you, but if nothing else, I have good gut instincts. Maybe it was mine, Slick's, and Hawkins's stint at the FBI, or maybe it is just woman's intuition. Whatever it is, I want you to listen. The three of us think something is going to happen tonight. Maybe visitors are coming here to the mountain. If we're right, the staff isn't going to want us to see anything. I want you to think about that. Again, this is just our opinion, but we did learn a thing or two at the Academy. Instincts are something you learn to pay attention to. The three of us think the kitchen staff is going to put something either in our food or the coffee so that we sleep soundly tonight. Having said that, it's up to each of you what you eat or drink."

The other three Rainford wives looked at the three ex-FBI students curiously.

"Won't they notice if we don't eat or drink?" Zoe asked.

"Probably," Hawkins said. "I don't think there's much they can do with the lamb chops and baked potato that's on the menu. The mint jelly and carrots are something else. I'd pass on the salad and salad dressing. Ask for an unopened bottle of soda pop and forgo the coffee. Or let them pour it but don't drink it. Sam's going to cut out early pleading a headache. I'm going to leave when dessert comes out. Slick will stay with the rest of you and just pretend to drink the coffee. We're probably being paranoid, but that's an agent's life. Paranoia pays off in the end. Okay, let's go inside. We need to map out a strategy for the paintball game tomorrow. We can talk while we eat."

It was Slick who outlined the plan for winning the paintball game. The others burst out laughing. They continued to giggle, and occasionally a loud guffaw could be heard erupting from Hawkins's lips. The other trainees watched them nervously. Even those in the kitchen could hear the mirth. At one point, Kyros felt compelled to punch the intercom to report to his son.

"Let's face it, none of us have a prayer of winning. The staff has done this forty times and won most of the games. They have the edge because they know the forest, and we don't. A map isn't really going to help us. I also think there's going to be a last-minute change of plans. We aren't going to double up the teams. It's going to be each team defending itself. If you look at that scorecard posted on the door, every year it's six teams instead of three. I think he's going to switch up at the last second," Hawkins said.

"Eric came out on top in our analytical class at the Academy. I think we should go with what he's saying and prepare for that eventuality," Sam said. "It really isn't going to make that much difference to us. In fact, I think it's better if it's team versus team versus the staff. We know our strengths and our weaknesses. The others are a question mark. Guys, I'd like us to win," Sam said.

The first three Rainford wives looked at their leader. Confidence rang in Olivia's voice when she said, "Then we'll win!"

Kayla turned off the jamming device inside the little transistor in her pocket, compliments of her cop brother. Knowing that their duffel bags would be checked, she'd concealed it on her person, banking on there being no body searches. She smiled at everyone. She looked sharply at Sam to indicate it was time for her headache to appear. A second later Sam offered up her apology and left the dining hall.

Crossing the compound, she noticed Pappy and two

of the instructors heading her way. Her eyes swiveled to take in everything at one time. She had two choices. She could simply walk past them, making no eye contact, which would appear strange, or she could break into a hard run and head for the bushes, where she would pretend to be sick. She opted for the latter, knowing the men wouldn't follow her. Who wanted to see a woman throw up her dinner?

Sooner or later she was going to have to figure out why she was letting the Greek get under her skin. Yes, he thought he was almighty, but the instructors at the Academy were the same way. Mean, lean, and hard. No one at the Academy had turned it into something personal, though. Either you cut it, or you didn't. Maybe knowing she'd married Douglas like the others and had been dumped made him think less of her. Maybe he hated women, her in particular. And then there was the real *biggie*. She'd turned the tables on him, stood up to him in front of the others. Then again, maybe the man was attracted to her. The thought was so ludicrous she started to laugh and couldn't stop.

Inside the barracks she let her mind wander back to the PT and DT tests. All four teams had been given three days to tend to their feet. Just when the blisters had crusted over, on the fourth day, Pappy had called a night march. Everyone had shown up except for two women and one man from each of the other three teams. On the sixth day, the helicopter had lifted off before dawn, and although no explanations were given, and no one asked questions, everyone knew those recruits had washed out.

Sam kicked off her boots to rub cocoa butter on her still-tender feet. She followed it up with a menthol rub that made her feet tingle. The first thing she was going to do when she left there was to burn the damn boots. From that point on, she made a promise to herself she'd never wear anything but canvas sandals.

Sam leaned back on one of the chairs and started to think about their game plan. One thing she'd learned at the Academy was always to take the initiative, to be bold, to think quickly, and to consider the consequences but not dwell on them. In other words, as Hawkins said, if it feels right, go for it. This felt so right, so perfect, she was almost certain her team wouldn't fail.

And, this time, it *was* personal.

One by one, the others trickled into the barracks, separating to do what had to be done for the big game the following morning. Sam was proud of all the members of her team. Earlier, she'd had misgivings about her Rainford predecessors, but all three of them had stepped up to the plate. To date no one had hit a home run, but they were definitely in the game. Big-time.

When the lights finally dimmed and went out entirely, it was just Sam and Slick in the sitting area. Sam could feel her nerves bunching into a knot. She knew what was coming, and she dreaded the conversation. She waited.

Slick's voice was nervous-sounding, proof that she didn't want to have this conversation either. "You don't know everything, Sam. What gives you the right to interfere in my personal life?"

"I'm not, Slick. All I did was remind Eric that you were both headed for trouble. I saw what you two were doing. For God's sake, you couldn't keep your hands off each other. If I saw it, so did the others. Maybe this is a lark for you, but it's serious for Eric. He understood when I talked to him. Why are you making such an issue of it? You can't break the rules, Slick."

Slick bit down on her lip. "Why is it okay for you to break them and not me?"

"I assume you're referring to the PT and DT tests. That was a stupid, knee-jerk reaction on my part. I didn't break the rules, it was insubordination. There's a difference. I know there's something else bothering you, so spit it out. Let's clear the air."

"You sure do spend a lot of time with Eric. Do you think I'm stupid, Sam? I hear you when you both go out late at night. I would have followed you, but that damn dog wouldn't let me out of the compound."

"We go to the wall, Slick. We're helping each other. He wants to master that damn wall and rope as much as I do. I failed once, Slick. I don't want to fail again. I'm assuming Eric feels the same way. Some nights we don't say a word to each other. We just work out. Why can't you understand that? I don't have any feelings for Eric.

I am not attracted to him. There's nothing about him that is greasing my engine. I know he feels the same way. He's a nice guy, Slick, and he's perfect for you. Don't blow it now."

Slick's head bobbed up and down. "I guess I'm just insecure. Are you making any progress?"

Sam sighed. "Eric is doing better than I. Slick, I'm so tired. Maybe I'm just one of those people who will never have superb upper-body strength. I can't make it to the top. Ten toe- and handholds on the climb, and I slip. My arms can't hold out. Same thing with the rope. Eric scaled the wall twice. He's on par with me on the rope, though. I hope he succeeds. I don't think I'm going to make it, Slick."

All was forgiven once Slick was reassured that Sam didn't have any romantic designs on Eric Hawkins. "Sure you will. Just don't give up. I'm still exercising my hands and fingers. Yeah, I get discouraged, and I wonder how many times in my life I'll have to use an Uzi. How many times are you going to have to scale a fifty-foot wall and climb a fifty-foot rope? None, that's how many. I even understand the endurance part, I really do. I'm not giving up, and I don't want you to either. Promise me, Sam."

"Okay. Only ten and a half more months to go. How do you think I'll do out there when it's twenty degrees and the rope is frozen?" Sam asked, tongue in cheek.

Slick laughed as she headed for the bedroom. "Good luck tonight."

Sam jumped up to hug her friend. "Night, Slick."

"Night, Sam."

It was a few minutes to midnight when Sam and Hawkins prepared to leave their building. They both noticed that the wolf-dog was gone. They looked at each other in the dim moonlight. Sam started down the steps and backed up immediately when the pack of guard dogs appeared out of the night. She turned around. "Guess we aren't going anywhere this evening. Alpha's services must be needed somewhere else. I think that fact alone confirms our theory that there's company tonight on this mountain. I didn't hear the helicopter, so they must have come up in the cable car. The other possibility is they aren't here yet."

Hawkins moved backward. He sat down on the wooden bench under the front window. "Want a cigarette, Sam?"

Sam shrugged. There was a time back in college when she smoked. Not a lot, but she'd given it up with no trouble. "I didn't know you smoked, Hawkins."

"I don't. I keep a pack handy for some reason. It lasts me a whole year. Sometimes you just need that little crutch. To me, this is one of those times. So, do you want one or not?"

"Nah. I'm going to bed so I can dream about us winning the game tomorrow."

Across the compound, Pappy walked down to the cable car. His guests had arrived. He looked around. The night was dark and secretive, as secretive as his thoughts. The clouds separated momentarily, and a slice of silvery moon could be seen before the cover slid back into place. He wondered if it would rain during the night. Not that it mattered.

It was a quiet night, except for the sound of the crickets and the screech the cable car was making on its ascent. He paced and fired up his second cigarette of the day. He knew he wouldn't enjoy the decadent vice the way he normally did when he was with Alpha, but he did it anyway. Later he would give the big dog his treat.

The car came to a stop. Pappy stood aside until all four of his guests exited the car. Then he stepped forward, his hand extended. The silent greeting over, he started off, the men trailing behind him.

Pappy was pleased to see that his father had set out the buffet in the conference room, which was unusually beautiful in such a rustic setting. The oak table and matching, comfortable club chairs sat in the center of the room. Mountain scenes painted by Kyros hung on the walls in ornate frames. Fragrant, fresh flowers from his father's garden graced one of the sideboards. The carpeting was hunter green, two shades darker than the nubby material on the chairs. Earth-tone draperies were drawn, and soft overhead lighting cast a mellow glow over the entire room. The portable bar in the corner held a silver ice bucket, two brands of scotch, and two brands of Kentucky bourbon.

Pappy made the drinks while the four men filled

their plates with shiitake mushrooms with fresh goat cheese, sushi, tenderloin, and lobster ravioli. Pappy knew all four of the men had hearty appetites. And each liked his whiskey neat with one ice cube.

As the men ate and drank from the fine china and exquisite crystal, they made small talk about the weather, the new training class, his father's garden, and the latest movies.

Pappy knew them almost as well as he knew his own father. He knew how rich they were, to the penny. He also knew where the money came from, where they reported each day, where they lived, and why they were there. Each man was tall, distinguished, immaculately dressed and shod. They were pillars of their communities and their international governments. They were also old. Older than his father. In Pappy's eyes they were vigilantes with an unlimited supply of money and a Rolodex the White House or MI6 would envy. At least one of them had the ear of the president and every politician in the nation's capital.

Normally the consortium met four times a year. This meeting was unscheduled and unexpected. With one member missing, Pappy knew something serious was about to be discussed. He also thought he knew what it was.

It was the tallest man in the Savile Row suit who said the dreaded word aloud. The word *sanction* ricocheted around the room. A unanimous vote on a sanction was nothing to be taken lightly since it meant death to the individual being sanctioned. Pappy waited for further details. They were so simple that they didn't surprise him.

Normally, the men left such details up to Pappy. This time they were unanimous when they said the new class of trainees would take care of the problem as soon as their training was finished. The reason—all other agents were on overload. Time, they said, was not a problem. Nine months wasn't that long to wait.

The man in the Savile Row suit stood up. Business was finished. He looked around for dessert, coffee, and the Havana cigars. They appeared as if by magic.

Another hour passed before it was time for the quartet to board the cable car that would take them to the foot of the mountain.

When the cable car made its descent, Pappy walked to his bench in the compound and lit a third cigarette before he handed Alpha his rawhide chew. He leaned back, closed his eyes, and tried to figure out how he was going to enforce the sanction that had been ordered.

Chapter Eight

Eric Hawkins stared in outright awe at his teammates, knowing he was going where no man had gone before him. Five women were including him as one of their own while they plotted and schemed. If he hadn't been so stunned at being privy to what they planned, he would have cut and run. He knew right at that second that every wild tale he'd ever heard about women was true. He also realized he didn't have a devious bone in his body—unlike the five women who were eyeing him with suspicion.

"What?" Olivia snapped. "Don't tell me you're getting cold feet over our little plan!"

Eric's eyes popped. "Hell, no! I think you women deserve a medal for this little plan of yours. In a million years I never would have thought about such a thing. Look, I want to win this game as much as you do. I think we could all use a win, and it's damn well time we got some respect. I'm also a little sick and tired of hearing the FBI put-downs. You don't have to worry about me holding up my end. By the way, the cable car is gone. The helo came back at dawn. I can't swear to it, but I think it came in around then and left by ten thirty. I know because I went outside to do some limbering-up stretches when I got up. Maybe it means something, and maybe it doesn't."

"That's nice to know," Sam mumbled. She looked down at her watch. "Time for breakfast. Let's make it a quick one so we can get back here to prepare. Slick?"

"We're good to go, Sam. I got up at three thirty and finished a few minutes ago." She started to laugh at what she'd been doing. The others joined in. Even Hawkins.

Breakfast was quick and fast, waffles with the last of the summer blueberries. Team Three was in and out in twenty-three minutes. The staff breakfast hour had been moved back to five o'clock the same way it was the days of the PT and DT tests.

"Wonder why the other teams didn't show up for breakfast?" Slick said, a frown building on her face.

"They're probably inside mapping out their strategy just like we are," Hawkins said, stepping into his one-piece camouflage jumpsuit. He could barely suppress his laughter as the female members of his team donned their respective gear. They held a short, hushed, huddled meeting before they stepped outside. The other teams, along with the staff, were gathering in the com-

pound where a supply of paintball guns, a small mountain of paintballs, and assorted backpacks were dis-
played.

Pappy brought his whistle to his lips and blew a long
steady shrilling sound. Nine members were missing.
The members of Team Three looked at one another.
Hawkins looked smug. It was obvious that the nine missing trainees had been ferried off the mountain via the
helicopter. He loved it when he was right, which wasn't
often with what he considered five know-it-all women.

Pappy issued one more shrill whistle for everyone's
attention. When he had it he said, "We have a change
of plans this morning. As you can see, nine members
from Teams One, Two, and Four have departed the
mountain. They will not be returning. So, instead of
pairing off in teams, the game is going to be wide open.
You can work as a team or work individually." He held
up a map pointing out the different quadrants and the
boundary lines they could traverse. "If you go beyond
the boundaries, you will be disqualified." He handed
out individual maps to each team member. "Take all
the time you need to familiarize yourself with the five-
acre game zone."

Sam was about to open her mouth to ask a question,
but Kayla beat her to it. She made a sweeping motion
with her hands to indicate the other team members.
"We're new to this, we don't know the terrain like you
and your staff. That tells me the deck is stacked. Do you
care to comment?"

"No, I don't," Pappy said shortly.

Bastard, Sam thought as she listened to the other teammates mumble and mutter under their breath.

"This . . . game is about instinct, an unknown environment, tracking, sights, sounds, smells, unfamiliar tools such as the paintball gun and paintballs. There are no rules per se. I don't want to see anyone hit in the face or the head. If you want to call that a rule, then it's a rule. The moment you're hit, make your way to the compound. A member of my staff will shoot off a flare each time a man hits the compound. If I see anyone with two paint smears, that will tell me you didn't obey the order to vacate the forest the moment you were hit. The last man or team standing is the winner, and the award will go to the team the member belongs to or to the entire team. Members of the staff will be monitoring the boundaries marked on the map. Just to be sure there are no mistakes at the end, the boundaries have been spray painted a bright yellow for your benefit. That's another way of saying if you stray, you will pay." This last was said with his gaze on Sam. She glared at him without blinking.

Pappy and his staff handed out the paintball guns, the paintballs, and the small backpacks to hold the paintballs.

Pappy waited till everyone had secured their backpacks and filled their paintball guns. "Head for the forest when I blow the whistle. You have a fifteen-minute head start to settle yourselves into a home base of sorts.

If you prefer to stay together as a team, we accept that, but it is not necessary. I'll shoot a flare when the fifteen minutes are up. That's when the game begins. Last man or team standing wins. Good luck!"

Team Three took off at a brisk run. They were the only members in jumpsuits. Everyone else wore shorts, tank tops, and sneakers. The late-August humidity was raging, but once inside the forest, it would be cooler. As Slick had pointed out, let the swarms of gnats and other assorted bugs attack the others. Besides, she'd giggled, it was the perfect cover for their plan.

Pappy turned his baseball cap backward, something he always did when he was under stress, before he started for the forest. He trotted by rote, his mind busy with other thoughts, mainly the activities of the previous evening. It wasn't sending off the nine recruits that bothered him but the four men who'd arrived in the cable car. His bosses. In the past, he'd always been told *everything* there was to know about a mission. How else could he plan and execute a successful mission if he wasn't privy to every last little detail? This time they wanted to take out one of their own. Why? What had the fifth member of the consortium done that would warrant a sanction? He didn't like the idea that his new training class would be the one to conduct the operation. He understood his bosses' reasoning, but that didn't mean he had to like it, and he damn well didn't like it one little bit.

His watch told him it was time to fire the flare. It shot

high in the air, then spiraled downward, a smoky red, iridescent plume. He dived for cover in the underbrush the moment the flare sizzled in the air.

The game was on.

His gaze ricocheted everywhere in the dim forest, but he didn't move. His ears, however, were tuned to the forest sounds, sounds he'd learned to identify over the years.

Pappy's thoughts were still with his late-night visitors as he crouched in the underbrush. The fifth member of the consortium was famous, wealthy, a real blue blood, and from a family known for its philanthropy. He fit in perfectly with heads of states and power brokers, in Washington and abroad. Was it something as simple as one member pissing off one of the other four? Or was it something more serious, like breaching the secrecy of the mountain? Pappy shook his head. Not possible. He knew that man as well as he knew his other employers—inside and out—because he'd made it his business to know everything there was to know about them.

Pappy switched his thoughts to the departure of the nine recruits. He'd hated to terminate them, but there wasn't an independent thinker in the bunch. What they excelled at was backbiting and ignoring the fact that they were members of a team who had to work together. None of the nine had adapted to life on the mountain. Reason enough for termination. Termination so early in the year had come as a surprise to him; normally, those who couldn't cut it held out till the cold weather set in.

Obviously, Donovan and the others needed a refresher course on recruiting.

A sound to his far left alerted him to the fact that someone was closer than he or she should be. He dived deeper into the shrubbery and waited, his paintball gun at the ready. He saw a head, then an arm holding a gun with red splatters all over it. He took aim and fired.

Pappy heard the muffled, "Damn!" He moved off, slithering on his belly, commando style.

The game was on, and he had the first kill. A few minutes later, a red flare could be seen. Pappy moved into what he called his power mode. He knew if he waited long enough, the other recruits would surface. Ten minutes later, in rapid succession, he fired off two more shots. Within minutes two more flares whipped up and down the tree line. All three hits were from Team One, which didn't say much for them.

Pappy moved to the southeast quadrant, crouching low, so low that he was practically crab walking. He grinned when he saw four more flares go up, one after the other. Seven down, eight recruits remaining. If they were all recruits that had been hit. There was no way for him to know. His eight-member staff, for all he knew, could be cut in half. Team Three was on the ball, and he suspected they had a trick or two up their respective sleeves. What it could be, he had no clue.

While Pappy pondered the question, Team Three was busy stalking two members of Team Four and three members of the staff. Zoe, who had been the point leader, slithered backward and reported to Sam. "I think," she whispered, "the five of them are trying to come up with some kind of game plan. They have to be desperate if they're cozying up to the staff. They don't have any idea we're as close as we are."

Sam nodded as she looked to see two flares hit the pine trees, the smoke like dragons' tails. She was aware that their team was still intact, and they had the power to eliminate five players with one fell swoop.

"You ready?" Hawkins asked as he tried not to laugh.

Kayla, Sam, and Olivia stripped off their flight suits, thanks to Slick's sewing box from her days as a model and the Velcro strips she'd sewn into the suits so they could be removed with one rip of the fabric. Kayla stood in all her belly-dancing glory while Olivia wore her Dallas Cowboy cheerleader's outfit, complete with baton made from a stick and covered with tinfoil. Sam stood nearly naked in her bra and bikini underwear to add more skin to the event.

Sam clapped her hands over her mouth so she wouldn't laugh. "Okay, let's go."

Team Three crab crawled their way through the brush to where the recruits and staff were still trying to come up with a strategy. Zoe, Slick, and Hawkins were elected to do the shooting.

Kayla moved forward, Olivia right behind her, Sam across from her. Slick, Zoe, and Hawkins spread out, their paintball guns ready to fire the moment Kayla, Sam, and Olivia stood up to display their near nakedness.

Olivia jumped up first and yelled at the top of her lungs, "Sis Boom Ba!" as she twirled the homemade baton she'd carried with her, strapped to her leg under the flight suit. Kayla started to gyrate to the tune of some unheard music as she bellowed, "Talk about your Kodak moment!" Sam removed her bra and twirled it with one finger. The startled looks on the recruits' and staff members' faces slowed their reflexes as paint splattered in all directions—all five were hit simultaneously.

"Gotcha!" Sam said exuberantly, as Kayla and Olivia ran back to get their flight suits while she put her bra back on.

Team Three hunkered down in the brush as they waited for the five flares to go off. Then two more flares went off.

Team Three looked at one another. "How many are left?" Slick asked.

Sam shrugged. "I lost track. Wait a minute. Listen."

Sound sailed into the forest as one of the staff members started to recite who had been killed just as two more flares colored the pine trees. More flares went off.

"Okay, we're down to us, Pappy, and one member of his staff. Spread out and be careful."

Pappy grimaced as he made his way through the forest. His gaze went everywhere as he ducked, swiveled, then dropped to the ground. Team Three was still intact, which almost made him proud. He was flat on the ground in a bed of pungent pine needles. The smell was so heady he could almost taste the resin. His hands were sticky and slimy from all the resin on the pine needles around him. He inched backward when he heard a commotion to his left. He rolled to the right, the toes of his boots looking for traction. When he rolled a second time he realized his mistake. His hands grappled for a hold on the slick pine needles and viny undergrowth. Team Three passed him just as another flare went off. That meant he was the only member of the staff still in the game. With that realization, he made his second mistake, and it was a serious one.

Pappy knew exactly where he was and what would happen if he lost his grip on the thick vines he was holding on to. Half his body was over the ledge. If he fell, he would be seriously injured. If he called out, Team Three could pull him to safety. *IF*.

Pappy grappled with the vine he was holding, but the more weight he put on it, the more it rippled across the space where it was growing. Too much slack. He tried wrapping the thick vine around his wrists, but it just kept ripping from the ground to give him yards of slack. The slick resin from the pine needles wasn't helping his handholds; in fact, it was making it worse. *Think, don't be stupid, call out*. The hardest thing to learn in life was which bridge to cross and which bridge to burn. He opened his mouth to shout when he looked upward as a dark shadow crossed his features.

Sam stood a yard away, the paintball gun pointed at his shoulder. "I thought I heard a noise. Were you about to call out? Looks like you could use some help."

"Hell, yes. Get Hawkins to pull me out of here!"

"Why should I call Hawkins? Why don't you ask me? I'm standing right in front of you," Sam asked curiously.

"Because you hate my guts. You're happy to see me in this predicament. It's called getting even."

Sam kicked Pappy's paintball gun out of the way. "Really!" She peered over the embankment. "Oooh, this isn't lookin' good," Sam drawled lazily. "So, do you want me to help you or not?"

"I told you to get Hawkins. That's a goddamn order, Rainford. You don't have the upper-body strength to pull me up."

"Is that a fact?" Sam aimed the paintball gun and fired. The paintball hit Pappy on the shoulder. "It doesn't pay to lose sight of one's mission. Just for the record, this is a pretty silly game. It's for teenagers. Guess you don't want my help, huh?"

Pappy clenched his teeth. "I gave you an order, Rainford. Call Hawkins."

Sam sighed as she shrugged. "Hey, Hawkins, our fearless leader is in need of your help." When there was no response, she looked down at the man hanging on to the vine. "Guess he can't hear me." She dropped to her haunches until she was eyeball-to-eyeball with Pappy. "You got a thing about women, huh. Right now, I'm all you've got. I'm getting kind of tired of this whole thing. I'm going to count to three, then I'm walking away. You want my help, ask for it. One. Two . . ."

"Okay. Help me up, Rainford."

Sam threw her hands in the air. "I don't have a rope. Wait a minute, I have an idea!" She ripped at the flight suit's Velcro fastenings. She stood tall in bikini underwear and lacy bra.

Pappy stared, his eyes almost popping out of his head. "The combat boots make the outfit." He laughed in spite of himself.

Sam twisted the flight suit into a tight, thick rope before she shoved the legs toward Pappy, who grasped them with his right hand, his left secure on the vine. Sam held on to the arms as she dug the heels of her combat boots into the damp bed of pine needles. She used every ounce of strength to pull her tormentor over the top. Twice she slipped, righted herself, and pulled harder. "Damn you, help me here. Give it some muscle, don't make me do it all. Use both hands, you ass!" Sam commanded.

"What, so you can let go!"

"I'm not you, Havapopulas! Now, damn you, let's do it." Sam gave a mighty tug, her upper arms bulging with muscle, her chest rippling, and Pappy was over the top. She took one long look at the man she'd just rescued before she walked away in her underwear. "We're even now," she called over her shoulder.

When Sam walked into the clearing, Pappy behind her, admiring her wiggling derriere, she eyed the recruits and the staff with her head high. "Don't ask!" she said as she clomped her way to the Omega Three building.

Alpha, who was sitting on the steps of the building, threw back his head and howled, an ungodly sound that seemed to reverberate over the mountain. Sam stopped on the top step, looked at the dog, and said, "Shut up, you . . . *you male*!" It might have been her tone or her lack of clothing. Whatever it was, the wolf-dog slunk down the steps and across the compound to where his master stood.

Pappy's hand reached down to fondle the dog's ears. "Yeah, I know," he mumbled.

An hour later, Sam walked out of the shower wrapped in a ratty old robe to see her teammates carrying in a tacky, three-foot-high, silver-plated paintball gun. "It goes with our decor," Slick giggled as she set the trophy on the mantel. "C'mon, Sam, tell us what happened out there."

Sam told them. All of them choked with laughter as they pounded one another on the back. "Chalk one up for Team Three!"

Sam was left alone with Hawkins while the others headed for the showers. "I did it, Hawkins, I pulled him free. He's got to weigh at least 180 pounds. If I can do that, why can't I climb the frigging rope and scale the wall?"

"Because you had your feet working with you would be my guess. You were on solid ground. And you were using your back muscles. Hell, I don't know, Sam. I weigh what Pappy weighs. I'm a guy, and I'm on par with you. How do you think I feel? I'm going to toss out an idea that might help you. When you're climbing the rope and scaling the wall, pretend that your ex-husband is at the top and you get first dibs on him."

Sam's jaw dropped. "Sometimes, Hawkins, you are so smart you boggle my mind. I'll give it a try. On the shooting range it's Pappy's face in the bull's-eye."

Hawkins laughed. "Yeah, I know."

Pappy entered his quarters, Alpha at his side. He looked down at his hands and was surprised to see he was still holding Sam's flight suit. He tossed it on the couch before heading for the shower. His thoughts were chaotic as he turned on the tap. Steaming hot, then ice-cold. Shivering, he stepped out of the glass enclosure fifteen minutes later, wrapped a towel around his middle, and walked back out to the sitting room. He was stunned to see the big dog cradling Sam's flight suit in his paws, his monster body lying half-on and half-off it. He looked up at Pappy and whined.

Pappy dropped to his haunches. "It smells like strawberries, doesn't it? I was *this* close to Sam. I could count the freckles on her nose. She saved me, Alpha. If I'd gone over that edge, I could have broken my neck or my back." He stroked the big dog's head for a long time as he struggled with his memories.

When Alpha finally closed his eyes, Pappy got up, his legs stiff and sore. He was getting too old for this stuff. He walked into his bedroom and straight to the bottom drawer of his dresser. He reached in and brought out a filmy Hermès scarf he'd given Adrian one year on her birthday. She wore it constantly. He brought it up to his cheek, the scent of strawberries faint and sweet. It was time to let it go. His shoulders felt a hundred pounds lighter when he burned the scarf in the fireplace.

When he was dressed, he debated taking the flight suit from Alpha but thought better of the idea. He would lie and tell Sam he'd left it in the forest. Alpha needed it more than Sam needed it. Or was *he* the one who needed it?

Outside in the bright sunshine, he walked to the dining hall. He needed a good strong cup of his father's coffee. Another stupid lie. He *needed* his father.

In the stainless-steel kitchen, Pappy poured himself a cup of coffee. He perched on one of the stools and looked across the workstation at his father. "Aren't you going to ask how it went, Pop?"

"I already know, son. This time around, I think you have a good team. I wasn't sorry to see those nine go. There wasn't one of them that appreciated the excellent food I prepare. They were hamburger and hot dog material." That was how Kyros summed up all the recruits who'd come to the mountain over the years. Sometimes he would be more explicit by saying none of them appreciated goat cheese and most of them didn't know a shiitake mushroom from a toadstool.

Pappy laughed. "I think you're right, Pop. They work as a team. Today proved that. There's no ego there, but they have some kind of agenda that's all their own. I'd give anything to know what it is. It could interfere with our plans here on the mountain."

"Why don't you try asking?" Kyros said slyly. "I see the way you look at the one named Sam. Make it work for you, son. Whatever you do, stop comparing her to Adrian."

"Did you get over Mom, just like that?"

"No. No, I didn't, and that was a mistake on my part. I don't want to see the same thing happen to you that happened to me. Lay it all to rest and move on. I'm thinking, if you play your cards right, you might get another chance at the brass ring."

Pappy eyed his father over his coffee cup. "I'll give it some thought, Pop."

Chapter Nine

The blistering-hot, muggy days of summer had long since given way to autumn and glorious foliage on the mountain. Autumn in turn had slid away to an early winter with almost daily snow flurries.

Other changes had taken place on the mountain, too. Team Two was defunct. Team Four and Team One were referred to as Team Five. Team Five was very competitive as well as combative, with four men and two women making up its complement. The final cut had been made on Halloween, with most of the team members thinking it was some kind of Halloween prank. It wasn't.

It was two days before Thanksgiving when Hawkins banked the fire in the huge fieldstone fireplace before turning in for the night. The last thing he did before heading back to his bed was to check the temperature gauge outside on the miniporch. He whooped and shouted to his teammates. "Hey, come look at this!" The women ran to the front window and gasped. The ground was covered with snow, and the thermometer said it was thirty degrees.

A period of squealing and moaning ensued before the group made its way back to bed. An early-morning fitness run was on their schedule. Lights out had been ten minutes ago. There was more moaning and groaning when Slick said they should get their gear ready before they turned in.

A round of good nights followed as Team Three curled up under the covers. The time was nine forty-five.

Snow fell steadily as the temperature dropped and as Team Three slept.

The compound came alive at two o'clock with floodlights, and a bullhorn demanded that all team members report to the compound in five minutes.

"What the hell . . ." was the general comment as Team Three pulled on their outdoor clothing, zipping and buttoning as they barreled out to the compound. Everyone thanked Slick for the suggestion to ready their clothing before crawling between the covers. They were the first to arrive in the compound. They had to wait a full seven minutes before Team Five arrived, looking like the Keystone Kops. Team Three made no attempt to hide the smug looks on their faces.

Snow continued to fall, as did the temperature.

Pappy stood front and center, dressed in his cold weather gear. "Listen up! We're doing a ninety-minute, ten-mile run starting in two minutes. I'm giving you an extra thirty minutes because of the inclement weather. In case you're wondering why we're doing this, it's to test your stamina. Spinally is our group leader. I'll bring up the rear. If you don't cut it, or if you fall by the wayside, return to camp and you'll be given another chance at five thirty. Two and a half hours from now. You will start from this point, not where you failed. Are we all clear on this? I want a show of hands." When everyone's hand, including Spinally's, shot in the air, Pappy said, "Go!"

It was a torture trek, and they all knew it. Inside the forest, the snow was sparse, but what there was of it was slick on the pine-needle floor of the forest, making it almost impossible to get any kind of traction. The nightmare part of the run was going to be the incline. They were going *up* where it was colder and where there was more snow. Twice, Team Three ran past Spinally, who fell to his knees, losing precious seconds. He never did catch up.

Kayla and Olivia were in the lead, their well-muscled legs pumping furiously. Zoe was even with Sam, who was pacing herself and breathing evenly, a scarf tied around the lower half of her face. Hawkins brought up the rear, but he, too, was pacing himself. Sam knew he had legs like pistons, so she wasn't worried about him, or any of the others for that matter.

"Don't waste time talking," Sam shouted to be heard over the wind and whirling snow. *Stamina my ass*, she thought as she plowed forward. She knew this was a male/female test. There was no doubt in her mind that Team Three was going to win even though Pappy had not said it was a contest. Well, she knew something the other team didn't know. Every single member of Team Three had only 3 percent body fat, which definitely gave them the edge. Now if they could all speak six foreign languages fluently, they could conquer the world. The thought was so funny she started to laugh.

"What's so damn funny, Sam?" Hawkins asked.

Sam broke her own order and explained. "We are so in shape it's scary. Plus, I know something none of you know. The guy named Lukash has hemorrhoids. I was in the infirmary getting some aspirin the other day when he was talking to the nurse. *Bad* hemorrhoids. I can feel him *chafing* as we speak. The tall blonde named Kate has an abscessed tooth. A dentist is coming up today to fix it. Vandameer has flat feet, and Carpenter threw his knee out three days ago."

"How do you know all this stuff, Sam?" Hawkins gasped as he struggled with his footing.

"I make it my business to know what the other side is up to. It's called spying. Isn't that why we're here? To learn how to spy?"

"This might be a stupid question, but without a leader, how do we know we're going in the right direction?" Hawkins gasped again, the frigid air frosting his lungs. "We could be going in circles for all we know. Who's calling the shots here?"

Sam's mind raced. This place was big on leadership, stamina, improvising, and taking charge. With no leader, that had to mean whoever was in the lead was in charge. Sam picked up speed and ran abreast of Kayla. "Do you know where you're going?"

"Hell, no! Up, I guess."

"We don't have a leader. Since you're running first in the lead, the show is yours, Kayla."

"You mean I can do whatever I want? Hot damn!"

"Yep," Sam said.

"Spinally was a Marine platoon leader," Kayla said. "Maybe he'll catch up."

"No way. You're it, Kayla. We've been out here forty minutes. That means it will take us fifty minutes to go back down because we'll be slipping and sliding all the way."

"Okay. On the count of three, I'm going to turn around and head down."

"Sounds like a plan to me," Sam said, as she relayed the information to the other members of her team.

On the count of three, all members of Team Three executed a perfect about-face and headed down. Spinally started to shout as they passed him.

"Hey, chickee baby," Olivia shouted as she playfully cuffed their ex–group leader on the arm as she whizzed past him.

Sam was stunned to see that only Pappy and three members of Team Five remained.

"Get your ass back on the line, Rainford!" Pappy shouted.

"I have to listen to my group leader, and she said we'll make it back to the compound in the ninety minutes allotted. *Your* group leader is back there somewhere," Sam shouted as she waved her arm backward. "In spyspeak, that means he fizzled out. Tough break."

Sam laughed again as she heard Pappy say, "Son of a bitch!" She laughed harder when he slipped in the snow, and a Team Five member toppled over him. By the time both men righted themselves, Team Three was so far ahead, slipping and sliding like greased lightning, there was no way the others could catch up.

Back in the compound, Team Three jogged in place as they waited for the others to make an appearance. Sam wasn't sure, but she rather thought the dropouts were in the dining hall warming themselves by the fireplace.

The moment the stragglers trudged through the snow to the center of the compound, Kayla ripped off a snappy salute and said, "Dismissed."

The unit headed for the dining hall, where a glorious pot of hot chocolate and fat slices of piping-hot buttered cinnamon toast waited for them. As one they wolfed the feast down and went back for seconds.

Sam looked at Kayla, who appeared worried. "He's going to try to bust your chops. Don't let him do it. It's a given that he's going to be *pissy* because he has to go back out again with the ones who didn't make it." Sam chomped down on her third slice of toast just as the door to the dining hall blew open.

Pappy walked over to their table. Kayla squared her shoulders as she prepared herself for a dressing-down. The tall, good-looking man removed his wool cap, revealing tight curls plastered to his head. He ran a hand through them. "You did good out there, Rainford. You took charge. This time I'm going to overlook the fact that we came in three miles short because you made it back in the allotted time. Congratulations! Tomorrow at 0600 we'll correct that little error."

Team Three sat with their mouths hanging open. For a second, Sam forgot to chew. She shrugged. This spy/mercenary stuff was a surprise a minute. She watched as Pappy walked through the swinging door that led into the kitchen. Sighing, she stood up to lead her team back to their quarters. At the door she turned around to the others sitting glumly at their table. "Tough luck, guys."

"Shove it, Rainford," one of the men said.

Sam laughed. Then she said, "*Sit on it, you schmuck.*" Then she laughed again when the heckler turned red as she noticed how he was sitting on his chair, more like on the side of his thigh than on his rear end. "You gotta move past the pain, Lukash," she singsonged. This time the others joined in her laughter.

The second the door closed, Team Five declared war on Team Three.

In the kitchen, Pappy watched the little byplay through the windows on the swinging door. His father's soft laughter made him turn around. "Go on, say it, Pop!"

"I'm just a cook, son. I don't know anything about whatever it is you do outside my kitchen."

Pappy sat down on the stool and laughed. The man sitting across from him was a genius. Years ago he'd taken $25,000 from his savings, another $25,000 from his son's savings, and invested it in a dot-com company. He bailed out with $150 million, before the crash. Then he bought the mountain from the state and leased it for half that amount to the people his son worked for. Yes, sirree, his old man was a genius.

"Make it work for you, son. You might have to show a little humility, but it's a wise man who knows when to step backward and cut his losses. She's just what you want, isn't she? Why can't you accept it? Her team is exceptional. They work in sync. They're tuned to one another. They're giving you a hundred percent. It doesn't get any better than that. You keep riding them, and she's going to call it off. Stop being such a damn robot and be the man I call my son. You'll be ferrying her down the mountain if you don't."

Like he really didn't know what went on beyond his kitchen. "Were you always such a know-it-all, Pop?"

Kyros rattled something off in Greek that made Pappy laugh.

Pappy reached for a hunk of toast and a cup of hot

chocolate. He downed both within seconds. He waved to his father, who watched him leave, deep sadness in his eyes. Like any father, all he wanted was happiness for his son and perhaps a grandchild or two to dandle on his knee before he was too old to enjoy the event.

Inside their barracks, Hawkins rebuilt the fire. "I don't see any point in going back to bed, do you, guys?" he asked. The others agreed as they curled up by the fire.

"So, what should we talk about?" Zoe asked. "Or, do we pretend this is a campfire and tell ghost stories?"

"I have a better idea. Why don't you guys tell me about *Mr. Rainford* and what really brought all of you here? It boggles my mind that you're all friends," Hawkins said as he moved a little closer to Slick. Probably for extra warmth.

Sam's predecessors looked at her. She shrugged.

"There's four more of us," Olivia chirped.

Hawkins digested that information. "That makes eight!"

"Yep. Our ex was a honeymoon junkie," Zoe said.

"It was a hell of a honeymoon." Kayla laughed. "Six weeks to the day, three for the courtship, three for the honeymoon before the jerk divorced each of us. We assume he operated the same way with the other four, but we don't know that for sure."

"I hacked into the FBI computer when we were at Quantico," Sam said. "I didn't exactly hack, but I did what I wasn't supposed to do by accessing certain files. I think that's another reason I washed out. I knew I wasn't going to pass the physical part, so I threw caution to the wind and did it. I'm not sorry. Hey, if I hadn't, the five of us wouldn't be here right now discussing this unsavory subject. You'd probably be here, though, Hawkins, and you'd probably be paired up with Team Five. Admit it, we're the best of the best. That's not a *real* compliment if you consider our competition," Sam said.

Hawkins stretched out his long legs. "What's your game plan? I know you have one. I'm volunteering my services. Hey, you might need a guy to shill for you." The others burst out laughing.

Sam threw another log on the fire. "We go on R&R for thirty days when we're finished here. We're going to go after him as a group and give him a taste of his own medicine. We don't have a plan yet, but we'll come up with something during the next six months. And we'll definitely consider your offer, Hawkins," Sam said.

"I brought my laptop," Hawkins volunteered. "Nobody said I couldn't," he said defensively, as five pairs of eyes bored into him. "Look, I'm just as sly as the next guy so think about this. . . . I know how men do things!"

Olivia sniffed. "I wouldn't go around bragging about that if I were you, but we'll keep it in mind. Now, in your spare time, see if you can find out who those other four Mrs. Rainfords are." She gave him a high five to seal the deal.

"Hey, guys, let's get dressed again and go play in the

snow. When was the last time any of you made snow angels or a snowman?" Olivia asked.

The others needed no second urging as they pulled
on their thermal winter gear.

Outside, they pelted one another with snowballs,
squealing and shouting like ten-year-olds. They carried
their exuberance to the Omega Five building and
started to taunt their adversaries. "Come on out, you
wusses!" Hawkins shouted. Olivia and Kayla took their
exuberance to Pappy's quarters, while Zoe attacked the
staff building with wild shrieks and catcalls. Sam started
to roll a ball into what would be the base for a snowman.

Within minutes it was instant bedlam as Team Five
and the staff hit the compound running, scooping up
snow as they went along. Somehow or other, the group
broke up into pairs. To her chagrin, Sam saw she was
partnered with Pappy. *Is this good or what?* she thought.

The instant Pappy bent over to scoop snow into his
hands, Sam's foot shot out, hooking around his ankle.
He went down, face forward into the snow. He was on
his feet within seconds. Head back, mouth wide open,
he roared like a lion. Unable to resist what she was seeing, Sam took careful aim and scored a perfect hit with
a small snowball. Pappy ate snow.

Pappy roared again as he started after her, his intent
clear. He tackled her and she went down. Sam struggled, but his body weight was impossible to topple. After
several seconds of furious struggle, she allowed herself
to go limp. Then, with one mighty upward thrust of her

rear end, she flipped him over. Quicker than lightning, she had him straddled and pinned to the ground.

Sam stared down at the man she was straddling. In the blink of an eye, she lowered her head and kissed him until his teeth rattled. Either with fear or shock she wasn't sure. Was she out of her mind? Obviously. Like a jack-in-the-box, she jumped up and looked down at the man in the snow. She gurgled with laughter. "For a mountain hillbilly, you kiss pretty good. You also need to stop being such a *stiff*." She was off, running to join her teammates, her lips on fire. *Oh, God, I think I'm in love*.

"Awk!" Pappy squawked as he rolled over to see Alpha at eye level, glaring at him. "Yeah, yeah, yeah, are you happy now?" The wolf-dog looked at him, his yellow eyes blazing through the snow. "Okay, if my boots weren't laced up, she would have blown them off. Satisfied?" The dog ran off to join the others as Pappy got to his feet, the faint scent of strawberries tweaking his nostrils. He needed to *think* about what had just happened. *Really* think. She'd called him a *stiff*. Stiffs were dead people in his vernacular.

Normally, he was never at a loss for words, or actions for that matter. He was so befuddled right then he couldn't think straight. If someone were to ask him his name, he'd probably not be able to come up with it. In one breath she'd called him a hillbilly and a *stiff*. That hurt. But she'd also said he was *a pretty good kisser*. He bent over and finished rolling the ball that would be the base for the snowman. Out of the corner of his eye, he could see the others making snow angels in the far section of the compound. They were having *fun*. They weren't acting like a team or the raw recruits they were. They were just a bunch of young people enjoying the first real snowfall of the season. *Fun*. When was the last time he'd had fun? Did he even remember what fun was? He looked again at the laughing group and almost fell over when he saw Sam coax Alpha into lying down in the snow next to her. It looked to him like the wolfdog was trying to do what she wanted. Pappy literally fell over when he saw her hug the big dog. Alpha never allowed anyone but his master to touch him in any way. Adrian had, more or less at one time, been able to tickle him behind the ears; but even his father couldn't fondle the big dog these days. Pappy wasn't sure how he felt about *that*.

He kept working on the snowman. He finished just as the hard-driving snow turned to sleet, stinging his face like thousands of bee stings. He removed his wool ski cap and settled it rakishly on the snowman. He turned to leave when Slick handed him a carrot and a bunch of raisins smashed into little dark balls for the eyes and mouth. He grinned. Slick grinned back.

The dinner bell started to ring. The gang looked at one another as they all ran to the dining hall.

Breakfast!

It was a feast with waffles, scrambled eggs, pancakes, French toast, bacon, and sausage. The huge coffee urn was full and fragrant. Platters of thick, buttered toast with bowls of homemade jam sat in the middle of each table.

They ate heartily, friends for the moment. Tomorrow it would be a different story, Pappy knew. They were still high on the excitement of what had just transpired.

Pappy shook the snow from his clothing as he made his way through the dining hall. He stopped at the table where Team Five sat, and said, "We'll reschedule your run for Thanksgiving morning." He ignored the groans and moans as he ambled back to the kitchen, where his father was sipping coffee.

Pappy eyeballed his father. His voice came out in a tortured hiss when he said, "She kissed me, then she called me a mountain hillbilly and a *stiff*. A stiff takes me out of the human category. *She* actually had the gall to stand there and tell me I kissed pretty good for a hill-billy. She kissed me. She initiated it, Pop. And," he continued to hiss, "she's stealing my dog's affection. Alpha adores her. He lets her hug him. He *frolicked* in the snow with her. Are you listening to me, Pop?"

Kyros did his best not to laugh. "What part bothers you the most, the kiss, the name-calling, or that she's stealing your dog's affections?"

Alpha, lying in front of the kitchen fireplace with his big head between his paws, looked up and whined, as if knowing the two men were discussing him. It was a piti-ful sound, Pappy thought. "He's fallen for her," he said to his father. "Damn traitor. Look at him, just look at him! He's lovesick!"

"You're jealous, Kollar. Get over it. Dogs are shrewd judges of character, and we both know it. We also both know that we can learn a lot from animals. When we aren't acting stupid, that is. And you are being stupid." Then he rattled off a long string of Greek that made Pappy flush.

"Shouldn't you be cooking or something?" Pappy snapped.

"Or something." Kyros grinned, as Pappy let himself out the back door, Alpha on his heels.

Back in his quarters, Alpha raced over to Sam's flight suit and flopped down. Pappy stripped down and headed for another shower. He looked longingly at the bed and wondered if he'd ever sleep again. Something long dead in him had risen, and he didn't know what to do about it. Maybe ten years on this damn mountain was a few too many. How many more years could he stay up here, battened down in his cocoon? Maybe it was time to move to another mountain, desert, or maybe even another country.

For a long time he'd never thought he could ever fall in love again. That wasn't to say he was in love or falling in love with Samantha Rainford. But he had *felt* something. He'd returned her kiss. Big-time. And here he was taking a damn *cold* shower when it was twenty-eight degrees outside.

Women!

You couldn't live with them, and you couldn't live without them.

Five minutes later, Pappy's head hit the pillow. He was asleep within seconds, but his restless sleep was invaded by dreams featuring Sam Rainford, and his dog Alpha following beside her.

He called out, but she didn't seem to hear him. He called again, and Alpha barked. Loudly and ferociously. She turned, smiled, and waved.

"No!" he shouted. "No! Don't go there, it isn't safe. Alpha, bring her back!"

The wolf-dog ran to where Sam was standing. She looked so beautiful in her white ski suit, her long, dark hair swirling around her face. Alpha skidded to a stop and barked, shrilly. Sam reached down to tickle the dog behind his ears.

The red spot confused him at first. Then, his eyes widened in shock as the spot grew bigger and bigger until the whole front of the white suit was splashed with red. *Strawberry jam*, he thought crazily. He dropped down until he was crawling toward the dog and the woman. Popping sounds were everywhere. Balloons? Guns? "Help me, Kollar. Please, help me," Sam pleaded.

The smile was gone, the summer blue eyes closed, never to open again. He cradled her in his arms, his own ski suit smeared with the strawberry jam that wasn't strawberry jam. He struggled to pick her up but realized he couldn't lift his right arm.

Somehow, with his left hand and Alpha's superb strength, they managed to pull Sam to safety, at which point the wolf-dog raced off for help.

Pappy woke, his body drenched in sweat. He threw off the covers and swung his legs over the side of the bed. He was gasping for breath.

Alpha lifted his head, eyed his master. Satisfied that he was all right, he dropped his head between his paws and closed his eyes.

Pappy dropped his head into his hands, his own eyes burning unbearably.

Chapter Ten

The cold front that socked the mountain continued for the next four weeks with daily snowfalls, sometimes an inch, sometimes as much as six inches at a time. The bitter cold stayed around, too, the temperature dropping to the low twenties, frequently to single digits.

Pappy was forced to call an indefinite halt to the outdoor routine, concentrating on workouts in the gym and additional classroom studies. No one complained. Like Slick said, you could get frostbite just walking from the dining hall to the classroom. Thanksgiving had come and gone in a blur. There had been the traditional turkey, the plum pudding, and everything that went with a traditional Thanksgiving dinner. Even the staff and teams ate together to save Kyros work. With so many people in the dining room, all talking at once, it should have been a lively dinner and evening, but it didn't work out that way.

For some reason there was no camaraderie, no jocularity. It was a solemn dinner, with Pappy saying grace. There was barely any conversation, and what conversation there was was hushed or whispered for some reason. Hours later, back in their quarters, Sam explained it away by saying everyone was thinking of home and family, and the bottom line was they were all just a little homesick. The others nodded in agreement.

"And we all ate way too much," Hawkins said.

Slick had the last word when she said, just before lights out, "I wonder where we'll all be at this time next year."

It was a week before Christmas at Sunday night dinner when Pappy entered the dining hall just as dessert was being served. He got their attention when he said he had an announcement to make.

"In the spirit of the holidays and the unusual weather we've been having, I've decided to reward you all with a trip off the mountain, courtesy of your employer. You leave in the morning and will have five days to Christmas shop or just relax in a hotel. You'll be met at the airport by some of our people. It's not mandatory that you go. This trip is my Christmas present to you. You will return Christmas Eve morning. The week between Christmas and New Year's will be free time for all of you here on the mountain. There will be a New Year's Eve party to usher in the New Year. Finish your dessert and have your team leaders see me later in my quarters for last-minute details."

The recruits looked at one another when Pappy marched into the kitchen and closed the door.

Pappy waited for what he knew would be an earsplitting crescendo of sound. He didn't have long to wait. He grinned at his father as he shrugged elaborately.

Kyros eyed his son, his dark eyes sparkling. "I guess that means the minute the helicopter lifts off, you're going to go into decorator mode, eh?"

Pappy shrugged again. "You're supposed to have a Christmas tree on Christmas. You're supposed to have a wreath on the door. You can't ignore Christmas. They worked hard. They deserve this two-week respite."

Kyros clucked his tongue as he pretended to be upset. "You ignored it nine years out of ten. You were so big on bah humbug you were hateful. You also slept through Christmas right up through New Year's for nine of those years."

"That was then, this is now. Christmas is a time of joy. Let's be joyful. That's an order, Pop!"

"Yes, sir," Kyros said, saluting smartly.

"I'm thinking of a New Year's Eve party. What do you think of that, Pop?"

What Kyros thought was that it sounded wonderful to his ears. His son was finally coming out of his self-imposed darkness. "You mean the kind of party with drinks, good food, music, and everyone gets dressed up? Your suit is full of moth holes. When was the last time you wore a white shirt and tie? You plan on attending in your olive greens?"

Pappy smiled. "For your information, Pop, I ordered a suit from Brooks Brothers. It came in the last mail delivery. It fits, too. And, I got a shirt and a tie. Furthermore, they match! You gonna beat this to death or what?"

"I wouldn't think of it. You made those young people out there very happy, son. Where are you sending them?"

"New York City, where else? DC is out of the question. First-class all the way, Pop. I checked with the . . . what I mean is I got full approval for this little venture. They want the teams to be happy. I'm thinking this is happy with a capital H. I'll see you later to say good night. It was a great dinner, Pop," Pappy said, referring to the five-cheese, three-meat lasagna that was one of his father's specialties. "I'll take a slice of that praline pie with me if you don't mind. Wrap up something special for Alpha. He's off his feed a little."

While Kyros sliced and wrapped, Pappy watched the recruits through the glass window in the kitchen door. The happy smile on Sam's face did strange things to his heart. They were jabbering like magpies, especially the women. He felt pleased with himself. Pappy let himself out the back door, Alpha at his side. He was halfway to his quarters when he realized none of the recruits had asked where they were going. All they seemed to care about was leaving the mountain. He supposed that was probably a good thing.

In his quarters, Pappy tossed three logs on the fire,

slipped his favorite Frank Sinatra CD into the CD player, and kicked back with his feet on the coffee table. Eventually, he dozed off, the fire warming him through to his bones, his dog on the sofa next to him. *What more could a man desire? A hell of a lot*, he answered himself.

In the Omega Three building, excitement ran high, with the women babbling and jabbering to one another as they packed their duffel bags.

Slick, hands on her hips, surveyed the group. "Hold it! Just hold it a minute! We aren't taking any of *this stuff*. Think about it, do you really want to wear long underwear, sports bras, fleece-lined sweat suits, and combat boots? Or do you want to *shop*? We can hit the ground running the minute the helicopter lands. Our mission will be to shop till we drop. I don't know about you, Hawkins, but I'd love to see you in a tux." Hawkins grinned.

"Slick's right," Sam said, as she dumped everything but her makeup kit back into her footlocker. The others followed suit, even Hawkins. "I wonder where we're going," Kayla said. "And if we plan to shop till we drop, where are we getting the money? Lordy, Lordy, I can hardly wait to have my own bedroom with my very own bath with plush towels, room service, and a minibar. There is a God!"

"I can't believe we're having a New Year's Eve party! That means glitter and glitz! Do you think everything in the stores will be picked over by now?" Olivia asked, a worried look on her face.

"Listen, I have contacts," Slick said. "My home base was Manhattan for many years. I can get us anything we want within"—she snapped her fingers—"minutes. You know, samples, one of a kinds. Designer duds. We might have to return them after the party but, what the heck, where would we wear them a second time anyway? As soon as we get to where we're going, I'll call my friends and have them FedEx the outfits to wherever we end up. That will free us up to just shop. I can't wait to go to Victoria's Secret. They have this feather and lace . . ."

Hawkins just listened. He couldn't wait either.

"Oooh, I love the way that sounds. I'm not going to be able to sleep tonight," Zoe said.

Sam, for the most part, had been quiet in the dining hall and even here in their quarters as she tried to make sense out of this little gift from Pappy. A whole week of free time with a shopping trip thrown in. Not to mention Christmas and a New Year's Eve party. *What's wrong with this picture?* she wondered. She finally decided to blame it on the weather and let it go at that. She did wonder, though, if the hotel they would be staying at would have a gym. Well, she would demand one.

"Shouldn't you be going over to Pappy's for the details? Do it quick, Sam, just in case he changes his mind," Slick said.

Sam looked at her little group. "Will you all please stop and think about this for a moment? Don't you think it's a little odd how this just came out of the blue?"

"No," they chorused as one.

"It's Christmas. There's a foot of snow out there. We all have cabin fever, and Pappy knows it. Don't look a gift horse in the mouth, Sam. We've worked like Trojans the past five months. We haven't failed anything yet. We deserve this outing and the party. Try to be happy and stop being such a worrywart," Slick said.

Sam shrugged as she pulled on her jacket. "Is there anything any of you want in case I have to negotiate? Speak up now. I do know how to drive a hard bargain."

"Just get us everything you can. Lots of money, five-star hotel, five-star dinner reservations, silk sheets. Six-hundred-thread-count will do nicely. Make sure the hotels have a spa, so we can get massages, facials, manicures, and pedicures. I think that should do it," Slick said happily.

"Got it." Sam let herself out the door. It was snowing again, but lightly. She shivered inside her down jacket.

She heard Alpha bark long before she got to Pappy's quarters. She was starting to love the big wolf-dog. Every chance he got he would appear at her side, nuzzle her leg, and bark happily. Once, he'd even tussled with her out in the snow as they played with one of her gloves. Alpha would leap up, catch it daintily, and bring it back. She hugged him, and he allowed it. From time to time she'd slip a goodie from the dinner table into her pocket to give him at some point. He loved the gingerbread cookies that were full of raisins.

Sam knocked on the door of Pappy's quarters. She

could hear Alpha whining on the other side. She expected to see Pappy open the door, but it was Lukash, Team Five's leader. He nodded curtly to Sam and left, a manila folder in his hands. Sam stepped into the room. She didn't know what she expected to see, but this wasn't it. She thought of these off-limits quarters as Pappy's Lair. She took a minute to drop to her knees and play with Alpha. She slipped him one of the gingerbread cookies, trying to hide the act. Pappy pretended not to see what she was doing.

It was definitely a man's room, but it was also a home-and-hearth kind of room with deep, earth-tone furniture. The kind of furniture you sat down in and never wanted to get out of. Her kind of room. The fieldstone fireplace took up one entire wall, with almost a cord of wood piled on the side. On one side of the fireplace a huge copper tub held dry mountain flowers. *That's a woman's thing*. On the mantel were pictures she couldn't see clearly. Probably Pappy's parents. *Is that a woman's thing, too?* Bookshelves held classics, best sellers, books on nutrition, and one that read *Modern Combat*. Two pictures sat on the top shelf. Pappy with two different U.S. presidents. *That is definitely a guy thing.*

An entertainment unit built into the third wall held a VCR, TV, DVD player, along with stacks and stacks of CDs and DVDs.

As Sam walked across the room, she was aware of the soft music playing in the background. Frank Sinatra singing about a summer wind blowing. Pappy's choice of music surprised her. She herself was a Bon Jovi fan. But she liked Old Blue Eyes, especially when it came to dancing or just mellow listening. Douglas Cosmo Rainford, III, had liked the Grateful Dead. When he wasn't being romantic. Go figure that one.

"Nice place you have here," Sam said curtly. She felt uncomfortable and knew it showed. She wondered if Pappy was thinking about that kiss out in the snow or if he had just glossed over it. She thought about it a hundred times a day. Well, maybe not a hundred, but she did think about it, and she dreamed about it, too.

"Take a seat, Rainford," Pappy said, motioning to a deep comfortable chair across from him. Sam perched on the end of the cushion. She looked like she was poised for flight. Pappy looked like he recognized the position. He reached for a manila envelope and tossed it to her. She caught it.

"My team wants to know where we're going."

"New York. You'll leave at first light. Each team is on a different flight. You'll return Christmas Eve morning. Poke Donovan will meet you on your arrival and take you to the Ritz-Carlton. There are six credit cards inside the envelope. You may all shop till you drop, courtesy of your new employers. You can either bring your purchases back with you or have them shipped by FedEx for next-day delivery. There is $3,000 in cash for incidentals, five hundred each, again, courtesy of your new employers. Charge everything else. Do you have any questions?"

"Does the hotel have a gym?"

"Yes, and a pool. It's convenient to all the stores you'll want to shop at. Anything else?"

"The girls want six-hundred-thread-count sheets."

"Not a problem," Pappy said.

"Can we make telephone calls?"

"No. At the hotel you can receive incoming, but you cannot make calls. There will be people around you, so don't any of you try it. Don't make me sorry I agreed to this outing. Is there anything else?"

"Massages, facials, manicures, pedicures. Waited on hand and foot."

"Not a problem."

Sam's eyes narrowed. She wondered what he would do if she jumped his bones. The only problem was they were both wearing too many clothes.

She smiled.

He smiled.

Pappy's smile slowly faded. Was she laughing at him? "Something funny?" The minute the words were out of his mouth, he regretted them. A lawyer once told him never ask a question unless you already know the answer.

Sam winked roguishly. For some wild crazy reason she felt the need to get under Pappy's skin the way he was under her skin. Since the kiss in the snow, he was all she could think about. How could he not react to that kiss that had sizzled and smoked? Well, there was only one way to find out. "Sort of. I was wondering what you'd do if I jumped your bones right there on your comfortable couch." She shook her head, clucked her tongue, and moved toward the door. "The only problem is," she called over her shoulder, "you're wearing too damn many clothes, and it's against the rules. Your loss!" She tossed a cookie from her pocket to Alpha, who caught it in midair.

"AWK!" was the sound Sam heard when she closed the door behind her. She giggled all the way back to the barracks.

"Son of a bitch!" Pappy marched back to the bathroom to take yet another shower. Alpha barked and barked at these strange goings-on.

"Go eat your damn cookie, Alpha!" Pappy snarled as he turned on the cold water tap.

It was snowing the following morning when Teams Three and Five trudged out to the helicopter pad. The women were all chattering, except for Sam. The men talked among themselves in low voices, just as excited but in a more subdued way.

In one respect, Sam couldn't wait to board the helicopter, but in another way she longed to stay and didn't know why. Off in the distance she could hear Alpha howling. The sound was somber and mournful. She shivered. She did her best to stare through the swirling snow that had just started to fall.

Sam was last in line to board. Four others were ahead of her when she heard the sound. The others stopped in their tracks. And then the wind kicked up but it wasn't a wind, it was Alpha who created the noise and the breeze. The wolf-dog skidded to a stop at Sam's feet and started to whine. Sam dropped down to cuddle the big dog just as Pappy came on the run. She looked at him curiously.

"He doesn't want you to go," Pappy shouted to be heard over the whirling rotors. "He thinks you aren't going to come back." He now looked helplessly at Sam, who wasn't understanding any of this.

Sam took off her gloves and dropped to her knees. She whispered in the big dog's ear. She hugged him, then got up. She bent over one last time to rub noses with the dog. The dog looked up at her with his strange yellow eyes. Whatever he saw satisfied him. He trotted off, Sam's gloves between his teeth.

His eyes wide as saucers, his voice sounding strangled, Pappy said, "He crashed through the front window to get to you."

"What do you want me to do?" Sam shouted at the top of her lungs.

"Get on the damn helicopter. Now!" Pappy roared.

Sam climbed in, buckled up, and the helo lifted off. She strained to see if the huge dog would do an encore.

"What the hell was that all about?" Lukash barked.

"The dog loves me. Watch it, Lukash, or I'll have him bite your ass when you aren't looking. From now on when you talk to me, use a little respect."

Team Five's leader glared at Sam, but he closed his mouth.

Sam settled back, trying to make sense out of what

had just happened. It was easier to think about the dog than it was to think about Pappy. Loved by a dog. *It doesn't get any better than that*, she thought glumly.

It took all of thirty minutes for everyone to settle into their new rooms at the Ritz-Carlton. Another thirty minutes were used up making reservations for massages, facials, manicures, and pedicures. Slick was permitted to make a phone call to her designer friend requesting outfits for the New Year's Eve gala with no explanation of why she needed them or where she'd been. Donovan not only listened but taped the call. This was all done in the lobby.

Then they separated. "I don't want to see any of you till it's time to leave," Kayla said as she peeled out of the lobby, the others right behind her. Hawkins held back, as did Slick. He motioned her to the side.

"Ah, Sam, I . . ."

"The rules on the mountain don't apply here, Hawkins. I don't care what you or Slick do. Go! Hey, can I borrow your laptop?"

Hawkins handed over his small duffel. "Sure. It's probably going to need a charge."

Then Slick and Hawkins were gone, holding hands as they swished through the revolving door.

Left to her own devices, Sam took the elevator to the eighth floor and her room. She set out her toiletries, charged the laptop, drank a Coke, then left her room to go to Bergdorf Goodman.

Sam was back at the hotel two hours later with her purchases—flannel pajamas, underwear, shoes, slacks, sweaters, and a navy blue pea coat. Before she'd left the store she stopped for bath salts, bubble bath, scented soap, shampoo, and conditioner. At the last second she'd bought a bottle of perfume and some scented body lotion.

A nice hot bubble bath, a glass of wine, some television, room service, and a soft bed. A real bed—not a cot—with silk sheets. She almost swooned at the thought. Tomorrow she would shop and work on the laptop. Tomorrow would be soon enough to tighten the noose around Douglas Rainford's neck. *If* that was even possible.

Back on the mountain, Pappy walked around aimlessly in the snow, Alpha at his side. His front window was being boarded up as he made his rounds. Never in his life had he seen Alpha in such a frenzy. The bigger question was, how had it happened? It really couldn't be something as simple as Samantha Rainford's smelling like Adrian. That was almost too stupid even to consider. Alpha had liked Adrian, but he'd never crashed through a window when she left on the helo. He'd never let Adrian do anything but scratch him behind his ears.

Pappy wondered what Samantha was doing right that moment. *Jump my bones! Yeah, right. She must be a sadist of some kind.*

Then there was that sly wink. She was playing with him, *toying* with him. He didn't know what to think about *that*.

Alpha barked, alerting him that someone else was in the compound. Pappy looked around to see his father walking toward him. He stopped and waited.

"It's a little unnerving to realize there's no one else on this entire mountain but you, me, and the dogs. I was a little sorry to see the staff leave on the cable car," Kyros said as he hunched his thick neck deeper into his down jacket.

"It is a little quiet on the mountain, isn't it? Snow, on the other hand, muffles all sound. Do you remember Christmases when I was little, Pop?"

"Every single one. You used to get sick the night before because you were so excited about St. Nicholas. It was a long time ago, Kollar. Are you trying to go back in time? Do you want to talk to me about something?"

Yes, he did want to talk to his father. Pappy knew whatever he told his father would go no further. He led the way over to the bench where he always sat with Alpha before he turned in for the night.

"*They* want to . . . *sanction* one of their own," Pappy said when he blew his first smoke ring. "For some reason, it's bothering me. I wasn't told what it was he did to warrant such an action. I know the man's background. There's nothing in that background to justify such strong measures. They want Team Three to orchestrate it." Pappy took a long drag on his coveted cigarette before he continued. "That's bothering me, too, because I can't figure out why. Missions have always been left up to my discretion. I have a real bad feeling."

"Son, if you want to pull the plug, I'll not think twice about canceling the lease on this mountain. Now you know why I fought tooth and nail to put that clause in the lease contract. Is it getting out of hand, son?"

"No. Right now I'm out of the loop, and I don't like it. I'm not at all comfortable with Team Three taking on the mission. I don't care how good they are, how fit, how qualified, they aren't *seasoned*. If my feet were to the fire, I'd say they could handle it, but I'd rather send the agents from year two. I'm missing something here. Maybe I'm slipping, Pop. Maybe it is time to get out. I just don't know."

Pappy tossed his cigarette into the snow. His father puffed on his pipe.

"I think I'll take a trip to Greece in the spring," Kyros said.

"Good idea. Make sure you lay in a supply of TV dinners for me. Those Hungry Man meals."

Both men laughed. Both knew Kyros wasn't going back to Greece. His life was there on the mountain with his son. Besides, everyone knew those prepared dinners would kill you with their fat content.

"What's for dinner?" Pappy asked.

"Tomato soup and grilled cheese sandwiches. Two hamburgers for Alpha," Kyros said as he led the way back to the dining hall and his kitchen.

His father wasn't kidding. When it was just the two of them, they always had tomato soup and grilled cheese. It was a father-son kind of thing, with Pappy doing the cleanup. They usually followed up dinner with a couple of videos and a few ice-cold beers.

Outside, the snow continued to fall, covering the mountain with a pristine whiteness.

It was midnight when the father-son evening came to an end. As was his custom, Alpha walked Kyros back to his quarters. He returned immediately to take up his place on Sam's flight suit. Her gloves were laid out side by side. For some reason, a lump formed in Pappy's throat.

Pappy stripped down, pulled on pajamas, and sat on the edge of his bed. He hoped he would be able to sleep and not have any dreams. He had enough problems at the moment without adding bad dreams to the list. He crawled under the covers, pulled them up to his chin. It would be nice if he had someone to share his bed with. Maybe that was never going to happen again.

Pappy closed his eyes and was asleep within minutes. When he woke again it was still dark. He looked at the clock. Another few minutes, and it would be dawn. What the hell was he going to do with the new day?

Chapter Eleven

Sam strolled along Fifth Avenue, stopping from time to time to gaze into the beautiful Christmas display windows. She wasn't sure if she fell into the category of people who *loved* New York or not. A crazy idea hit her suddenly. She would buy Pappy a Christmas present. A Frank Sinatra CD, the one with the song about New York being his kind of place. Yes, that's exactly what she would do. A giddy feeling settled over her at the thought.

She only had two shopping bags in her hands while those who hurried past her were loaded down with boxes and gaily colored shopping bags. With just a few more days left to shop, she could understand the fury and the bustle. She continued to walk, crossing streets, zigzagging as she searched for a Starbucks so she could get out of the biting cold and wind to warm up. A *cappuccino would*

*taste so good right now. And a couple of cookies to satisfy
my sweet tooth.*

Sam looked at her watch. It was barely noon. While
she waited in line, she looked around, wondering who it
was that was tailing her. So far, she hadn't come up with
a face that looked like it had been with her since her arrival. No one looked familiar. Whoever he or she was
was good at this tailing business.

When it was her turn, Sam ordered her drink and
carried it to a table, where she sat down and munched
on cinnamon–macadamia nut cookies. They weren't
half as good as the ones Kyros made. The cappuccino
wasn't as good as his either, but it did warm her up.

While she sipped and munched, she thought about
the gifts she'd bought for her teammates. For Slick it was
a pair of amber earrings. For Kayla, Olivia, and Zoe it
was Chanel wallets along with one of the Chanel fra-
grances. For all of them, pairs of faux mink earmuffs.
Hawkins posed a problem until she found just the right
picture frame with a man pumping iron stenciled into
the border. She had just the right picture of Slick to put
into it. For Kyros, she found a meerschaum pipe and
some fragrant tobacco.

The gifts that gave her the most pleasure to shop for
were Alpha's. She bought him a Gucci collar and a tar-
tan bed that was soft and comfortable. The array of dog
toys fascinated her, and she bought a bagful. There
were pull toys, toys that squeaked, toys that sounded like
birds chirping, cats meowing. There was even one that

roared like a lion. A very old, tired lion. And, of course, the treats. There were doggie candy canes that looked like they were frosted, cookies in the shape of Christmas trees and snowmen. She had all of Alpha's presents shipped via FedEx.

Sam mentally counted the cash she had left. She needed something to wear Christmas Eve and Christmas Day. Something festive, something feminine as opposed to her usually preppy attire. She absolutely would not think about the kind of outfit Slick's friend was sending to the mountain. Maybe she should buy something just in case. Yes, yes, that's what she would do.

Sam gathered her packages and left the store. No one followed her. At least no one she was aware of. She shrugged. Let them watch her shop. Like she cared.

"Bloomingdales, here I come," she muttered to herself.

It was four o'clock when Sam headed for the hotel, her arms full. She sailed through the door and raced up to her room. Inside, she shed her clothes and ripped at her purchases. For Christmas Eve, she'd chosen a long, black, silk skirt, slit to midthigh, with a white silk top and black shoes—with three-inch heels. A push-up bra that did unbelievable things to her bosom and fishnet stockings completed that particular outfit. For Christmas Day she'd bought a bright red silk dress with a Mandarin collar that flirted with her ankles. It, too, was slit to midthigh. It was the New Year's Eve dress that made her nervous. It was gold lamé and clung to her body as if it was painted on. Actually, it *slithered* against her skin. It was off the shoulder with a drape in front and cap sleeves. In all her life, she'd never owned, much less worn, anything so stunningly sexy. Before she left the store, she bought an extra push-up bra and string bikini underwear. She was going to blow the fur right off Alpha's back. What it would do to Pappy she wasn't sure.

The last thing she bought before heading back to the hotel had been a pair of diamond earrings. *Big* diamond earrings. *Expensive* diamond earrings. *Magnificent* diamond earrings. *Real* diamond earrings. They would go with all three outfits. It gave her great pleasure to say the words, *"Charge it!"*

Sam looked at the shiny silver wrapping paper, the bright red satin bows, and the suitcase she'd purchased to take back to the mountain. She danced around the room in her underwear before she packed everything neatly. The chair by the round table called her name. The minibar offered a nice bottle of wine that she sipped at for over an hour as she watched an inane talk show on television.

She had an early dinner of coconut shrimp, wild rice, and a crisp garden salad, with two delectable éclairs to complete her meal. She followed up with another bubble bath and more wine before she wrapped herself in one of the hotel's thick robes. Then she settled herself in bed between the silk sheets to pound away at Hawkins's laptop.

In her travels about the city she'd passed a cybercafe

where she would be anonymous, and for a price, she could log on to the Net and hopefully get the information she needed on Douglas Cosmo Rainford, III. Of course, if she had struck out with the FBI database, the chances of finding anything on the Net were next to nil. Reluctantly, she closed the laptop. Tomorrow would be soon enough. And the day after. Surely in forty-eight hours she could do what was needed. She wondered belatedly if Pappy knew about the laptop and Hawkins's email account. She shrugged. Probably, since he seemed to know everything. Then she grimaced. Maybe not everything.

Down in the lobby, Poke Donovan took up his position in a comfortable chair, his eyes on the elevator, his BlackBerry in hand. In his disguise, he looked like a chubby Woody Allen. Messages flew like a blizzard to the mountain. The first read, **These women give new meaning to the word** *shop*. The return spate of messages was just as fast and furious.

The following morning, dressed in new cranberry-colored wool slacks, one of her new matching sweaters, and her pea coat, Sam left the hotel and started to walk to a storefront cybercafe, where she parted with her money, paying extra for a "Spy" program that guaranteed finding anyone, anywhere, and was advertised as simple as one, two, three. She chose a terminal at the far end of the room, one that gave her a perfect view of the front door. She listened intently as the office manager explained the system and how to send and receive emails. She nodded from time to time. All she cared about was that no one else would be able to access what she'd done once she left the terminal. She was the first customer of the day, which gave her an edge as far as someone spying on her. She settled herself and her Starbucks coffee cup and started to work.

Three hours later Sam demanded a refund for the "Spy" program. The manager cheerfully returned her money. It was almost as though Douglas Cosmo Rainford, III, did not exist. She tried a global search with no results. Now what? *I was married to the man for God's sake. I must have had a brain freeze for the entire six weeks I was with him. Either that, or I'm the stupidest woman walking the face of the earth.*

Sam pushed the swivel chair away from the terminal as she contemplated her problem. She watched as the manager refilled her Starbucks cup. He grinned. "We use their coffee. Are you having a problem?"

Sam nodded. "I'm trying to find someone, and I'm not having any luck."

"Bureau of Vital Statistics. Everyone is born somewhere. If you can't find a person through the bureau, that should tell you the person might be using an alias. Motor Vehicles is another good source."

Sam shook her head. "I already tried that." The manager shrugged and walked away with his coffeepot.

Two students came in, paid for time, and logged on to terminals. No threat there, Sam decided. She continued to mull over her problem. *Credit cards!* Douglas had used a credit card to pay for their honeymoon. Maybe . . . She turned around, logged on again, and started to type. She was able to email the accounts receivable department at the hotel where she'd honeymooned. Her message to someone named Harrison Rollins was simple.

> *My credit card company has billed me twice for my stay. Can you fax me a copy of the paid bill?*

Sam turned to wave at the manager. "What's your fax number?" He rattled it off, and Sam typed in the number. *Where are you, you bastard?* Ten minutes later the fax came through. The manager ripped it off the machine without bothering to look at it and handed it over along with a slip of paper showing her the charge amount for the use of the fax machine. She paid it willingly.

The name on the bill was Douglas C. Rainford, III. The address was that of the Prizzi law firm. "Shit!" Sam said under her breath. Another dead end.

Now she was getting mad. Damn mad.

Paper trails. Always follow the money. That had been one of the answers on one of the FBI tests at Quantico. Another answer to a multiple choice question had been C; ignore no possibility, no matter how remote or ridiculous it might appear.

Lawyers. Scum of the earth. Even Shakespeare

agreed, saying, first, kill all the lawyers. Prizzi. The pompous little weasel. Lawyer-client confidentiality. No help there either.

Three more people entered the cafe. One ordered coffee and a Danish and sat in the restaurant section. He looked like a sanitation worker. The other two were businessmen wearing overcoats and carrying briefcases. She watched as they paid their fee and took up positions at their assigned terminals. Neither man so much as looked at her. Businessmen who conducted their business from telephone booths and cybercafes, she decided. She'd seen a ton of them when she lived in Washington. As a CPA she'd had to call phone booths at designated times during tax season to track down clients.

Tracking down . . . Kayla's half brother was a police detective. God, where did she say he worked? Sam closed her eyes tight, her facial features crunched as she tried to recall everything Kayla had told the group almost six months ago. She felt like she hit the mother lode when the brother's name and his precinct came to mind.

Sam took a deep breath and started to type and search. The next time she looked up at the clock hanging over the front door it was one o'clock. She'd missed lunch, and with nothing but three cups of coffee, her stomach started to protest. She looked around. Every terminal was occupied, but no one person looked like anything but what they were, a person working the computers because they didn't own one.

Sam turned off the computer, slipped into her coat, paid her overtime charges, and reserved the same terminal for two o'clock. She left the cafe and turned left. She could hardly wait to get to one of the hot dog vendors. Just the thought made her mouth water.

It was cold, Sam thought, as a raw wind whipped her forward until she came to what in Washington she referred to as the umbrella cart. She ordered two hot dogs with the works, meaning sauerkraut, onions, mustard, and relish. She leaned against the nearest building and devoured them. The hot dogs were almost as good as one of Kyros's five-star meals.

Sam walked crossed the street, then backtracked to the cybercafe, which again was empty of computer users. The tables in the restaurant section were full. The manager nodded toward the terminal she'd reserved, and she paid for three more hours in cash.

She typed diligently for the next two hours as she tried to locate Kayla's brother. When she finally made contact she felt like she should stand up and cheer. She sucked in her breath as she typed a carefully worded message. The return message was just as carefully worded. When both parties were eventually satisfied that each was who they said they were, they got down to business.

> *We have a six-month window here, so take your time. I think Prizzi is the way to go.*

The return message agreed. Satisfied that she'd accomplished what she set out to do, Sam logged off, more than pleased with herself. If there was a way to locate Douglas Cosmo Rainford, III, Kayla's brother would find it.

Sam held up her hand, a signal for a cup of coffee. Now it was time to hit the Bureau of Vital Statistics again to see exactly how many other ex-wives Douglas Cosmo Rainford, III, had. She started her search state by state, a daunting task she knew but she was grimly determined.

At seven forty-five, eleven hours since her arrival, Sam leaned back and rubbed at her gritty eyes. She scanned the printouts in front of her. Seven more wives, four of whom she knew of from her FBI search. But the real bummer was that Douglas had applied for a marriage license in Las Vegas two days ago. An even dozen! Unbelievable!

Sam got up, used the rest room, splashed cold water on her face, and returned to the restaurant section of the cafe, where she ordered a cold soft drink. She was surprised to see a new manager, a young woman wearing tight leather pants and a vest and earrings that dropped all the way to her shoulder. Minutes later, she was back at her terminal, where she initiated an email search for the other seven wives and soon-to-be number twelve.

Close to midnight, Sam turned off the computer. She stuffed the printouts into her shoulder bag. Even though the cybercafe was open twenty-four/seven, she was too weary to continue. She had one more day to work at it. She had one email address out of the seven to show for her four hours' work. *One is better than none,* she told herself as she walked briskly back to the hotel.

The minute she locked the door behind her, Sam rang Olivia's room. "I'm sorry to wake you up, Olivia, but I need you to walk down to my room. Do not take the elevator. I have something I want you to show Kayla and Zoe. Now, Olivia. I'm tired, and I want to go to sleep."

Sam was at the door when Olivia appeared wearing a robe and slippers. Sam shoved the papers into her hands. "I think it might be a good idea to go to Kayla's and Zoe's rooms. Again, don't take the elevator, walk to their rooms. I'll call you tomorrow when I finish up. You got all this?"

"Yep. Are we having dinner together tomorrow evening?"

"Sure, leave me a message, time and place. Night, Olivia."

The minute the hotel room door closed behind Sam, Donovan had his BlackBerry in hand. He felt stupid when he typed in the message. **The bird's back in the nest. Cybercafe beyond my computer capabilities. Johansen is on it but he won't get zip. That's why those cybercafes flourish. Further instructions?**

The reply was almost instantaneous. **Printouts?**

Donovan replied. **Dozens.**

Pappy's reply. **Get them.**

Donovan snorted, dreading what he knew he had to do. He shivered as he went back to his copy of the *Wall Street Journal*.

Sam, sans her carry-on bag, was back at the cybercafe at seven in the morning. She greeted the day manager as though he were an old friend. She even sat down at the counter for her coffee and bagel. They talked about the weather, Christmas, and his girlfriend, and what he was going to buy her for Christmas. "Just as soon as my shift is over, I'm going shopping." He grinned.

"If you can afford it, you can't go wrong with diamond earrings. Diamond chips are good, too," she said at the look of dismay on the young man's face. "A diamond is a diamond."

Sam paid for an extra coffee and for her computer time. She settled herself into the same chair as yesterday and turned on the computer. She was up and running within seconds, searching with a vengeance. When she finally found a Martina Crystal, a Bally showgirl and Douglas's soon-to-be new bride, she almost fell off the chair. She calculated the time difference as she typed in her message to the next Mrs. Rainford.

The message was long but detailed, with particulars, and provided links to the Bureau of Vital Statistics along with a list of all of Douglas's previous wives, herself included. She used words like gigolo, honeymoon junkie, and marrying fool. The last thing she added was a curt sentence that read,

Beware of the law firm of Prizzi, Prizzi, Prizzi, and Prizzi.

She signed it simply,

One of Douglas's ex-wives.

Sam sent off the email, then dusted her hands dramatically.

She leaned back in the chair and laced her hands behind her head. She closed her eyes and let her mind roam. When it all came together in her mind, she sent off another email to Kayla's brother informing him of Martina Crystal along with a link that would take him to the marriage license bureau. If Joe could get someone to Vegas to talk to Martina, she might be able to lead him to Douglas. If she didn't kill him first. The thought made Sam smile.

By midafternoon she had five more email addresses. She sent off five emails before she broke for lunch to get another hot dog. She ate only one since she was going out to dinner with her team members. It was just as good as the two she'd eaten the day before.

It was a gray, depressing day, with the threat of snow in the air as she walked along, her eyes searching the crowds for someone who might be watching or following her. He or she was out there, she just couldn't spot the tail.

Back at her reserved terminal, Sam clicked on the special email assigned to her compliments of the undetectable cyber fairies. She was stunned to find three emails, two from ex-wives and one from Martina Crystal. She read them and laughed as they printed out. Then she forwarded all the emails to Kayla's brother.

Sam was turning off the computer when, out of the corner of her eye, she saw movement to her right. Someone else was turning off a computer. She made a production out of slipping on her coat and making her way to the restroom. Inside, after she shut the door, she cracked it to see the man dressed in casual clothes walk out the door. Her tail. She'd finally spotted him.

She took a moment to wish the day manager a Merry Christmas before she left. Outside, she crossed the street in the middle of the block when there was a break in traffic. She ran then, all the way to the hotel.

She knew even before she entered her room that someone had been in it. Call it woman's intuition, gut instinct, whatever, and she was right. She felt smug when she looked down at the carry-on that she'd thrown on one of the chairs. It was off a centimeter. The contents were the same but had been jostled from one place to the other. Someone had gone through it. *Detection 101*, she thought in disgust. Well, there was nothing to find since she'd given her printouts to Olivia. She jammed the new printouts into her carry-on.

There was a message from Zoe saying dinner was at an Italian restaurant around the corner at seven. She ended the message with, "No need to dress up, it's casual. Be in the lobby at six forty-five."

"Works for me," Sam said, heading for the bathroom. When she returned to the sitting area, she opened a small bottle of wine, poured it into a glass, sat down, kicked off her shoes, and propped her feet up on the bed. "Ahhh," she sighed as she shifted her mental gears to the neutral zone.

Sam came mentally aware at precisely 6:40. She put on her shoes and her coat and reached for her bag. She took a minute to wonder if she needed the bag or not. She decided she didn't. She removed the printouts, folded them into a tight square, and jammed them into the pocket of her slacks. It felt like the right thing to do.

It was like old home week in the lobby, with the girls laughing and jostling one another. Sam eyed Slick and Hawkins, who both wore sappy expressions. She grinned as she led the way out to the street. It was a brisk five-minute walk to the restaurant. It smelled heavenly to Sam, who loved Italian food.

It was a mom-and-pop restaurant and looked like any other Italian restaurant, with Chianti bottles and burgundy furnishings. The checkered curtains on the windows were clean and starched. The windows sparkled. But it was the fragrance that welcomed customers. There were nine tables, and all were full with people in various stages of their meals. No one entered behind them, and there was no one waiting to be seated. Sam relaxed when frosty bottles of beer arrived, along with two huge baskets of crunchy breadsticks and a red-hot Diablo sauce.

Sam fished out the printouts from her pocket and passed them to Zoe, who read them and passed them on.

"Damn, you do good work, Sam," Olivia said. "We owe you big-time. While we were out there shopping you were working your butt off. This is . . . fantastic."

Kayla read slowly, a wide grin stretching across her face. "Joey will find the jerk. Trust me. He's better than a hound dog. Oh, God, I can't wait to get my hands around his neck."

No one asked whose neck she was talking about. They all knew because they all felt the same way.

"I guess we need to flush this stuff, right?" Zoe asked. She volunteered to do it. Slick followed her to the ladies' room and waited outside while she did what she had to do. They walked back to the table together.

"All gone," Kayla whispered.

"Are we good or what?" Olivia chortled, holding her beer bottle aloft.

"We're *goooood*," the others chorused.

Then the conversation switched to what they'd done with their time in New York, what they'd bought, what they thought of the city, then the relief that they were actually returning to the mountain in the morning.

They all looked at Sam, in awe, when she described the outfits she'd purchased. She flushed when they asked if she was trying to impress Pappy, Lukash, or Vandameer.

"Alpha," she said. Then she told them what she'd bought for the big dog. The others laughed as they, too, admitted they'd all bought something for the wolf-dog with the yellow eyes.

"Anyone buy Pappy and Kyros a present?" Slick queried.

They all admitted they had, even Hawkins.

"Do you think they'll have a tree?" Zoe asked fretfully. "It isn't Christmas without a tree. Or do you think we're supposed to go out and chop one down?"

"I guess we won't know till we get there. I'm actually looking forward to going back," Sam said.

The others agreed as they clinked their bottles together. "Merry Christmas, everyone," Hawkins said.

Chapter Twelve

Sam could hear Alpha's shrill bark over the rotors as the copter began its descent to the helipad, which had been cleared of snow. She felt excited, giddy, actually. She looked forward to seeing the big wolf-dog and . . . Pappy again. In more ways than one she felt like she was coming home. She knew the others felt the same way because while she pretended to sleep, she'd heard them talking. How strange. Yet, it wasn't strange at all that they had bonded. She supposed living with a group of your peers twenty-four/seven would account for the feelings. What was even stranger was that she liked, really liked, the first three Rainford wives. If anything bothered her, it was that there were seven other wives out there. Clearly she wasn't really number four. She was more like number eleven, possibly number ten. She should know which one. Why hadn't she paid attention to the dates on the marriage licenses? How many women had Douglas married after he dumped her? In the scheme of things, did she really care?

They were on the ground, and everyone was unbuckling, checking to make sure they had everything they'd boarded with. Her heart was thumping in her chest.

Christmas Eve.

And it was snowing.

They would truly have a white Christmas.

Sam was third to hop off the helicopter. The others stood back when Alpha let out a ferocious, earsplitting bark and raced toward her. He slammed against her, his huge paws circling her neck. He licked at her cheeks, her hair, anyplace he could get his tongue. Stunned at the dog's greeting, Sam dropped to the ground and rolled in the snow with him while the others watched.

Alpha was *playing*.

From the kitchen window, Pappy and his father watched what was going on. "The dog is playing," Kyros said, awe ringing in his voice. "I find this very strange, son. The dog doesn't love you, but he obeys you. He respects you, but he has never shown feelings like that toward you. Can you explain that to me?"

"She's a woman." It was more a question than an answer. Pappy continued to watch Samantha Rainford and *his* dog. How in the hell had that happened?

"There are other women here, son," Kyros said slyly. "I'm thinking this one is special. At least Alpha thinks so." He watched the conflicting emotions on his son's face as he struggled to form a reply.

"She feeds him. Gives him cookies. He likes sweets," Pappy said inanely.

"So do the others. You just don't see them doing it. No, this one is special. I think you might have a problem, son."

Pappy stomped back to the coffeepot. He struggled with his emotions, trying to understand what it was he was feeling. He'd awakened feeling wonderful. Really wonderful. Why? Because people were returning to the mountain. One person in particular, or just people? He lifted the lid on a large kettle and was going to give the bean soup a stir until his father whacked his hand with a wooden spoon.

Kyros wasn't finished yet. "The other one, she wasn't for you. She belonged to that dangerous time in your life when you lived on your adrenaline and your wits. You had it all mixed up in your mind, Kollar. You thought the stolen moments were love. Perhaps for a time it was. It would never have gone beyond that. When you were compromised, did she come here to you? No. Yes, she visited twice. She didn't like the solitude. What you do here wasn't dangerous or thrilling enough for her. She wanted no part of it. She no longer saw you as the rakish, daring, covert spy you were. Admit it, and get on with your life. Stop sniffing that scarf. Throw it away. Burn the memories."

Pappy sat down on a stool and hooked his legs on the

rungs. "She saved my life, Pop. I wouldn't be alive if it wasn't for her."

"And how many times did you save her life? You were compromised because of her, you said so yourself. That's the part you refuse to believe or accept. Even then, she was getting sloppy. She lost her edge, and she died. She should have left the organization when you did. The second—and the last—time she was here, she told you she was thinking of leaving, settling into an office. Alpha sensed something even then. He wouldn't go near her. When she left on the cable car, he didn't go near it either. I think I've given you enough to think about for a while. You can ring the lunch bell anytime you feel like it."

Pappy stared at his father for a long time without speaking. Finally, his vision blurry, he hugged the old man and walked out to the main room. Alpha was nowhere to be seen or heard. There were no wet dog tracks underneath the doggie door. He opened the door and rang the bell. He backtracked through the dining hall and out to the kitchen, where he didn't even look at his father. He walked through the snow to his house.

His house. A two-story log cabin. It wasn't just a log cabin, it was a palatial log cabin with fifty-six hundred square feet. When he built it, he knew he'd be there forever, so he didn't stint in any way because money was no object.

Right then his palatial log cabin looked like a fairy house in a fairyland setting. A giant evergreen wreath with a monstrous red bow covered the huge arched door. Inside, it was breathtaking, with a Christmas tree that reached all the way to the ceiling. He still didn't know how he and his father had gotten the tree in the stand without the use of hydraulics, but they had. It held a million tiny, colored lights, hundreds of exquisite handblown ornaments from all over the world that had been collected by his mother and father. The mantel was decorated with artificial boughs of evergreen and family treasures his father had unearthed from somewhere. Piles of presents, all wrapped with silver paper and huge red bows, sat beneath the tree. The entire house smelled wonderful.

A fire blazed in the fireplace.

For his family. That was how he thought of them. The staff, the recruits, his father, and, of course, Alpha.

Pappy walked through his family room to the dining room, where the table was already set. It could seat twenty-four and had been custom-made, and would seat his employers and associates when they came to visit. It was set with fine china, silver, and exquisite crystal from Bavaria, which matched the shimmering Bavarian chandelier.

It was said among his employers that he set a good table.

He had no idea what the dinner menu was. His father hadn't shared that with him.

He knew he had put it off long enough. He walked back to his bedroom, dropped to his knees, and opened his dresser drawer. He took a deep breath before he reached down for the framed picture. He pulled the picture out of the frame, carried it out to the fireplace, and dropped it into the flames. Good-byes were always so hard. Adrian had said her own good-bye the day she left the mountain. He'd refused to accept those final words, convinced somehow that she would come back. Two weeks later she was dead, the victim of a deadly hit-and-run accident on an icy road in Austria. "Good-bye," he whispered.

In the kitchen, he popped a bottle of beer and carried it back to his favorite chair. He reached down automatically to scratch Alpha behind the ears, but the dog wasn't there. He clenched his teeth so hard he thought his jaw would crack.

Pappy let his eyes go to the tall, fragrant Christmas tree. The mound of presents beneath it showed that, for someone who hadn't seen the inside of a store in over ten years, he'd done rather well. He'd simply emailed Harrods in London, asked for a personal shopper, given instructions along with his *black* American Express card, and everything was taken care of. You could only get a black American Express card if you were willing to deposit a million dollars. He'd been willing. He'd been told he was one of only fifteen or so people who had a black card. His packages had arrived within six days, all gift-wrapped and tagged. It was cheating, he knew, but that was okay. He wasn't good at tucking in ends and tying ribbons. He didn't think his little family would mind.

He'd really gotten into the spirit when he went through the recruits' files to see their likes and dislikes. He'd made his Christmas list from that information. As he sipped at his beer, he wondered if any of the team members would buy him a present. Not that he expected any.

He shrugged, then, startled, he looked up when Alpha appeared. "Nice to see you, big guy," Pappy said quietly. The dog padded toward the chair, looked up at him, and nuzzled his leg. Pappy smiled. "You don't have to apologize. It is what it is." The wolf-dog settled himself at the side of the chair. Pappy, obligingly, scratched him behind the ears. When the dog drifted into sleep, Pappy reached for the pile of folders on the table near his chair. The recruits' charge slips from their trip to New York. He could hardly wait to read them; but before he started, he glanced at the totals on their individual cards. He rifled through the slips looking for Samantha Rainford's charges. He was stunned to see a note attached by Poke Donovan that read, "Ms. Rainford would like the earrings charge to be deducted from her personal bank account even though she charged them on the company card." Other than the earrings, her charges were in the lowball range. A few clothes, some toiletries. Not so the other recruits with the top amount going to Kayla for sixty-six thousand dollars. The woman did love clothes. Still, a forty-four-thousand-dollar pair of earrings was right up there. He wondered if the earrings would look like headlights.

In the end, he admitted to himself, grudgingly, that the only file he was really interested in was Sam's. Now, if he could just figure out what she was doing at the cybercafe, he would feel a lot better. One thing he was almost certain of was that Sam would never compromise the mountain or any of the people on it. He didn't know how he knew, he just knew. That meant whatever she was doing was personal. So personal, she didn't want anyone else to know.

Back in the old days, he would have gotten it out of her. Because knowing what she was up to would keep her alive. He knew if he asked her, she'd say it was NTK. Need-to-know, and no, he did not need to know her personal business was exactly what she would say. To a point, she was right.

Pappy closed the folder. There were still a lot of hours to get through until the evening's dinner and festivities. Until that precise moment, he hadn't realized how very lonely he was. His father, bless his heart, had for years been telling him that no man is an island unto himself. He finally understood what the old man had meant.

The Omega Three building buzzed with sound and music. Christmas carols blasted forth from Hawkins's new Bose radio and CD combo. Because the women needed *hours* of time in the bathroom, Hawkins had gone first.

Hawkins stood by the window, watching the snow fall outside. He felt melancholy, as he always did during the holidays, with no immediate family at his side. He hoped that would change soon. He sighed when he remembered the five days in New York. He knew in his heart they had been every bit as good for Slick as they had for been him. But he and Slick would both have to shelve their feelings until July, when their lives would begin anew. Would they go their separate ways or would they honor their contract and give Pappy the three years he was expecting? If they honored the contract they would be separated, seeing each other once a year if they were lucky. What the hell kind of life was that? His gut churned as he struggled with his feelings. He loved Slick. He knew that now, and he was certain she loved him as well. And yet they had shied away from discussing this very thing. Where was it all going to end? Would he be able to handle it? "I hope to God, I can," he muttered to himself. He looked up to realize what was going on around him. He had to get with the program. He forced a smile to his lips.

He listened as the women laughed and spoke a language only another female would understand. What he was getting out of the whole thing was each was jealous of the other's outfit and yet happy that their teammate looked *ravishing, darling*. He grinned to himself. They were lookers, that was for sure. They were also nice, warm, compassionate, and, at the same time, competitive, as well as being know-it-alls. He continued to grin as he listened to whose socks were going to blow off. Then he heard the whispered name that was as shrill as a whistle — Pappy. They all knew Sam had a *thing* for Pappy even though she wouldn't admit it. Hawkins thought Pappy had a thing for her, too, going back to that infamous episode at the wall, when Sam gave him her single-digit salute.

Perfume wafted out of the bedroom, delicious and intoxicating. Hawkins's eyes glazed over as he studied his reflection in the front window. He thought he looked pretty decent in the Brooks Brothers suit that Slick had helped him pick out. She said he could have posed as a male model. He'd preened like a peacock at her flattering words. He even smelled good. Slick had helped him pick out a new aftershave that she said smelled like a woody glen and did wonderful things to her senses. He could feel his body heat ratchet up a notch. He'd probably have to take a cold shower later that night. Probably from there on in he'd be taking cold showers on a daily basis. Come July, if he wasn't dead from being waterlogged, things would be different. The word *marriage* suddenly popped into his mind. If he didn't cut it out, he was going to have a brain freeze that very minute.

"Yoo-hoo, Hawkins, what do you think?" Olivia trilled, as the five women whirled and twirled for his benefit.

He was speechless as well as thunderstruck at what he was seeing. Now, he really did feel proud as a peacock as he gazed at all of them, his eyes coming to rest, finally, on Slick, who wore a long, skintight sheath made out of some kind of clingy material. She wore a single strand of pearls and no other jewelry. Her hair was smoothed back, accentuating her sharply chiseled features. She looked like the model she was, and she smelled like a flower garden.

He knew the women were expecting him to say something. He whistled approvingly. His teammates looked ravishing. Olivia was draped in something silver that hugged every curve and sparkled when she moved. Zoe wore a vivid scarlet sheath. Then there was Sam, who looked mouthwateringly delicious in a high-necked white blouse and a long black skirt, slit to midthigh. She was so covered up, except for when she moved a certain way and her skirt parted that it made her look even sexier. Everyone at the dinner would re-member what she looked like in her bikini. All the more tantalizing, which proved what Slick always told him, less is sometimes more. He couldn't help but notice the diamond earrings in Sam's ears, her only jewelry.

No doubt about it, his teammates were going to blow off a lot of socks this night. They all laughed as they returned the compliment. Kayla said, "You look good enough to eat, honey." Slick blushed furiously.

More laughter ensued as everyone donned their coats and scarves before slipping out of their spike-heeled shoes and into their combat boots. They all car-ried shopping bags full of presents. When they reached the center of the compound, they could hear the Christmas carols.

Sam felt tears gather in her eyes when she heard

Bing Crosby singing, "I'll Be Home for Christmas."
Was this home? For the next six months it was.

Team Five was already at the party. Lukash opened
the door, dressed quite nattily, Sam thought. They lined
up their boots next to the others by the front door and
slipped on their dress shoes.

Sam looked around. The room Lukash led them to
was unbelievably festive, a long room that ran the entire width of the house. A fragrant balsam tree twinkled
merrily in the corner. Pots and pots of bright red poin-
settias, hundreds, Sam thought, were placed all over
the room, adding to the Christmas decor. As one, Team
Three gasped as they handed over their shopping bags
to Vandameer to place under the tree. Seconds later,
flutes of champagne were offered.

Where is our host? Sam wondered as she looked
around. Then she saw him, and her legs turned to jelly.
The last time a man turned her legs to jelly was . . . was . . .
never. Even Douglas, with whom she'd thought she was in
love, had never turned her legs to jelly. She felt jumpy at
the realization.

Pappy's gaze found hers, and he smiled. Sam smiled
back as she made her way across the room behind the
others. All of a sudden she felt like singing. When it was
her turn, she thanked him for the trip, complimented
him on the tree, and started to apologize about Alpha.
Pappy held up his hand to stop her apology. "Alpha has
a mind of his own." He smiled before he moved off. At
least Sam thought it was a smile. Maybe it was more like

a grimace. She was left standing alone, feeling foolish. She turned around and bumped into Vandameer. She started to flirt outrageously with him. He ate it up and wanted more. Sam obliged.

Kyros was walking around with a tray of canapés and making small talk. When he reached his son, he hissed in his ear, "If they were giving a prize for jackass this Christmas, you'd win it, son. Do you think that young woman got dressed up like that for these people? You are a fool if you do. It's obvious you've been out of the game too long," he added.

Pappy felt a ring of warmth start to build around his neck, and he suddenly felt like he was going to suffocate in his own body heat. He'd probably be the only man who lived on a mountain who died of heatstroke while having a hard-on at the same time. Obviously, he was supposed to do something. Or, at the very least, *say* something to Sam. Something meaningful, according to the look on his father's face. Kyros was right, Pappy had been out of the game too long. His life for so long had been full of one-night stands, no commitments, no promises. Just plain old sex. Until Adrian. Even with Adrian there had been no promises, no commitments. His gaze swept the room as he searched for Sam. She was in profile, talking animatedly to Vandameer. Vandameer was ten years his junior. *Shit*. He was definitely the kind to make promises and commitments.

"So, what do you think, Pappy?"

Shit all over again. Hawkins had just asked him a

question. For the life of him he had no clue what it was. He tried to look interested. "Say again."

"The new GPS. What do you think of it?"

"We couldn't operate without global positioning systems. I like it. How about you?" His erection was shriveling fast. He wondered if he looked as miserable as he felt.

Apparently, he was fooling no one. "She looks pretty hot, doesn't she?" Hawkins said.

Son of a bitch! Does everyone in the room know my business? Am I wearing some kind of invisible sign or something? Well, he was in charge. He could do a number of things. Pretend to be confused. Pretend Hawkins meant someone else. He could ignore the comment and squelch him with one look, or he could ignore the comment entirely. Yes, sirree, he could do all those things. "Yes, she does. Everyone looks beautiful. You guys surprised me. You all look great."

Hawkins laughed knowingly and moved off. Now Pappy was the one standing alone. He didn't like the feeling. Not one little bit because he felt exposed, vulnerable. Sam was still laughing at something Vandameer was saying. Suddenly, she linked her arm in Vandameer's and led him to the bar. When she turned around, Pappy got an eyeful of one long slender leg, which seemed to go all the way up to . . . The hard-on was back. He turned on his heel and went in search of his father. Surely it was time to eat.

Pappy felt desperate. The last time he felt like this he

was in deep cover in Afghanistan, and his exit route had been cut off. The only way to the kitchen was past the bar, where Sam and Vandameer were standing, laughing and touching one another's arms. He pasted something that could have passed for a sickly smile on his face and shouldered his way to the kitchen, apologizing as he went along.

The matter was taken out of his hands when the tall blonde named Kate whirled around, jostling his arm so that he did a pirouette and in doing so bumped Sam's arm, spilling her drink down the front of her blouse. He started to apologize when Sam rendered him mute. "You did that on purpose, didn't you?" she whispered in a choked voice. He was shocked at her words, more shocked at the tears glistening in her eyes. "Stop making this personal. I don't give a good rat's ass if you like me or not. Let's be professional. This is Christmas after all," she hissed, the words sounding dangerous in his ears.

Pappy imagined that everyone in the room heard Sam's whispered words while in truth no one but Vandameer and Pappy heard what she'd said. All he could do was shrug, but it was an arrogant shrug, one that brought sparks to Sam's eyes to match the shooting sparks wafting off the diamonds in her ears.

In the kitchen, Kyros threw his hands in the air in disgust. He opened the refrigerator and withdrew a bottle of club soda. He grabbed a white linen napkin at the last second. He headed toward Sam, passing his son on the way. "Buffoon. Do I have to write you out a script?" he said sourly.

Thirty minutes later, dinner was served while Christmas music played in the background. The meal itself was perfection. Kyros and the kitchen staff served the traditional Christmas goose with all the trimmings. Plum pudding, fine wine, and coffee finished off the meal. The conversation was cheerful, with all the recruits recounting their days in New York.

Pappy listened to the tales, thinking back to the last time he'd been in New York. It sounded to him like nothing had changed except maybe the merchandise in the stores. When the staff started to clear the tables, he stood and led the way back to the lovely room he'd decorated with such enthusiasm. It was almost nine o'clock and time to gather around the tree to sing "Silent Night" before opening the Christmas presents.

"Silent Night" segued into "White Christmas," then to a rousing rendition of "Jingle Bells." Surprisingly, the loudest, most off-key voice was Pappy's. Everyone, including Sam, applauded long and loud. Pappy bowed.

Kyros looked at his son. It had to be the triple shot of ouzo he'd given Pappy. Anything to loosen him up. Well, his son was suddenly as loose as the goose Kyros had cooked for dinner. *Maybe I've created a monster,* Kyros thought as he started to arrange the chairs around the tree with Hawkins's help.

Fresh flutes of champagne were passed around by the kitchen staff as Kyros acted like Santa and handed out the gifts from under the tree. When everyone had their designated pile of gifts, Kyros started to take pictures. "Smile everyone." Everyone smiled. "For posterity," Kyros said.

Ribbon and brightly colored paper formed mini-mountains in the huge family room. Sam wondered who was going to clean it all up. She felt woozy with all the wine she'd consumed. Before she left she was going to need several cups of black coffee.

Whether it was deliberate or not, the last presents to be opened were from Pappy. They weren't ritzy presents, nor were they expensive, but they were thoughtful gifts. Each of them ooohed and aaahed over his or her gift, appreciating the originality, especially the three Rainford wives who got toy guns painted in their favorite colors. Sam looked down at her Bon Jovi CD and smiled at Pappy. "Thank you. I don't have this one."

Damn, did that mean he'd finally done something right? "My pleasure," he said gallantly. "Thank you for the Sinatra CD. It's a reissue, and I don't have it."

Alpha plowed his way through the debris to where his pile of gifts were. The group started to help him until he growled. They backed off. The dog looked at Sam, who dropped to her knees and started to undo the ribbons. One by one, Alpha carted off his gifts.

Pappy watched, feeling like a benevolent grandfather when he realized the big dog was taking his gifts to the bedroom, which had to mean he was still his dog. When Sam opened the biggest and last package, which was the down bed, Alpha looked at it, then at Sam, then back to Pappy. He dragged it to the door. His meaning obvious. He wanted to take it to where Sam slept.

Sam, a stricken look on her face, stared at Pappy. "It's all right, don't worry about it," was all Pappy could think of to say.

Maybe it was the wine, maybe it was Christmas, maybe it was a lot of things. "I'm not trying to steal your dog's affections," Sam said, a break in her voice. "I don't know why he's taken such a fancy to me."

Pappy's intention was to shrug and remain mute. "Maybe it's because you're easy to like, and he senses that."

Sam blinked as she tried to absorb Pappy's words. *That* was really personal.

Kyros almost stood on his head, his arms flapping every which way. At last, his son was *getting it*.

The others smiled slyly, some openly. Pappy gulped at the ouzo his father handed him.

He could feel it, he was on a roll.

Finally.

Chapter Thirteen

Christmas Day!

The recruits arrived at Pappy's promptly at four o'clock, dressed in their Christmas outfits. Outside, the snow fell in big fat flakes. It was as near a perfect Christmas as anyone could wish for. Even Pappy was happy, as he stood at the door and greeted everyone. He thought they all looked like high-powered business executives attending their boss's Christmas party. And they all appeared to be in a cheery mood. Even Sam, who smiled. She looked better than a million dollars, in a long red dress. At least in his eyes. And she was again wearing the diamond earrings. Then he wondered what kind of woman would spend a whole year's salary on a pair of diamond earrings. His know-it-all father would probably know. He made a mental note to ask. What he didn't like was the way Vandameer was at her side. Almost as though they'd partnered off, just the way Slick and Hawkins were partnered off even though they tried to pretend they weren't. His father would have an opinion on that, too.

Sam accepted her flute of champagne as she listened with rapt attention to something Vandameer was saying. What they were actually discussing was how tidy the room was after the wild disarray of the night before. "Pappy probably just burned everything in the fireplace," Sam said.

Pappy circulated, playing host, hoping to get close enough to the couple to hear what they were saying. He just *knew* they were talking about him. Eavesdroppers never heard anything good about themselves, but he didn't care.

Out of the corner of her eye, Sam watched Pappy's maneuvering. She moved, leaving Vandameer standing alone. She wasn't going to give Pappy another chance to insult her or continue whatever game he was playing. She wished she knew what there was about Pappy that attracted her to him when obviously the feelings weren't being returned.

"Ms. Rainford," Kyros said, holding out a tray of delectable-looking shrimp, "I would like to thank you again for the pipe and the tobacco. I tried it out last night, and the pipe is exquisite. It draws perfectly. Thank you."

"It was my pleasure. Everything looks so beautiful. I've always loved Christmas. When I was a child I always spent Christmas with my grandparents, my father's

mother and father. My parents were never big on holidays. They were usually out of the country, vacationing.
They especially liked to go to the Greek Isles. Of course,
they always had someone put presents under the tree at
Grandma's. I'm sorry, that sounds like I'm saying, oh,
poor me." Her voice was firm, even defensive-sounding,
when she said, "I think I like grown-up Christmases better. I so looked forward to this day."

"And where is your family now?" Kyros asked.

"Who knows? My father is an ambassador to some
foreign country. Paraguay, I think. My mother social-
izes. I haven't seen them in a few years. They send cards
once in a while. I guess you could say we aren't a warm,
cuddly family. Do you have family, Kyros?"

Kyros blinked. Didn't she know Kollar was his son?
"Yes." He pointed to where Pappy was talking to Kayla
and Olivia. "Pappy's my son."

Sam's face went from white to red and back to white.
She bit down on her lip. She knew she was supposed to
say something. What? Why was it that in times of acute
stress, and she was experiencing acute stress right now,
one could never think of just the right cutting remark
until later? "I didn't know that. I don't think any of . . .
us knew that," she stammered, caught off guard at the
remark. "I think your son is an *obnoxious . . . oaf.* I'm
sorry if that hurts your feelings, you being his father and
all." *God, did I just say that?*

"It's no problem. Just last evening I myself called him
a buffoon. I still love him because I have high hopes

that he will turn into a warm, fuzzy person." The old man chuckled at his own joke. Sam laughed, too, before she moved off to talk to Kate, the long-legged blonde from Team Five.

It's like playing dodgeball, Sam thought as she watched Pappy out of the corner of her eye. As soon as he moved, she moved . . . in the other direction. It was all so silly, like something she would have done when she was in high school. At the same time, she couldn't help herself. She'd been rebuffed once in college, then her husband dumped her. She had no intention of going for the charm the third time around. Plus, she hated herself for dressing up *for him.*

Dinner was finally announced, to Sam's relief. Her plan, which she'd just formed on the fly, was to eat, socialize for another hour or so, then plead a headache and leave. The day was entirely too stressful for her liking.

Alpha, apparently sensing her mood, walked alongside her to the dining room. Sam was sure he intended to lie at her feet the way he'd done last night. A sharp command from Pappy made the wolf-dog stop in his tracks. Pappy pointed to the door. The dog raised his big head, his yellow eyes fixed on his master. Sam sucked in her breath when the dog didn't move. Her hand dropped to Alpha's head. "It's okay, he isn't bothering me," she said quietly.

Kyros stood in the doorway, a platter of prime ribs in his hands. He, too, sucked in his breath as he waited for his son's reply.

"The dog doesn't belong in the dining room, and he knows it."

Sam's hand started to shake when she saw everyone staring at her. She squared her shoulders. "He was here last night. You can't give a dog mixed signals, even I know that, stupid as you seem to think I am. You know what, I'm suddenly not very hungry. Enjoy your dinner, everyone, and . . . Merry Christmas!" She turned on her heel and marched out of the dining room, Alpha sprinting ahead of her. In the foyer, Sam reached for her jacket, not bothering with her boots as she raced outside and across the compound. Somewhere along the way, she lost the slingbacks.

Racing into the barracks, Sam collapsed in front of the fire, tears streaming down her cheeks. Alpha approached tentatively and licked them away. Sam didn't think, didn't even consider that the dog was part wolf when she wrapped her arms around him and howled into his thick fur.

Back in the dining room, the assembled guests looked at one another, not sure what was going on. Pappy glared at everyone as he took his seat at the head of the table. Kyros, the prime rib still in his hands, leaned over and dumped the prime rib, by accident, everyone said later, into Pappy's lap. "Not only are you a buffoon, you are a *schmuck*."

"I don't think I'm very hungry either," Slick said.

"Me either," Kayla, Olivia, and Zoe said in unison.

Hawkins took his hands off the chair he was holding out for Slick. He didn't bother to say anything but just followed his teammates out to the foyer, where they dressed and left.

Outside, the snow continued to fall. "What the hell was that all about?" Hawkins demanded.

"If you're too stupid to know, then you aren't the person I thought you were," Slick snapped.

"Yeah," the others said as they trudged across the compound.

"We're supposed to be a team, so start acting like you're an active member. It's one for all and all for one," Zoe snarled.

And the war was on.

The score was one for Team Three.

Zero for the Establishment.

And it was just round one.

At eight o'clock, the last of the staff departed for their quarters. Kyros had the kitchen cleaned and the leftover food stored in the refrigerator. He'd made up dinners that two of his staff had delivered to Team Three unbeknownst to Pappy. He was sitting on one of the kitchen stools enjoying his cup of coffee and his new pipe.

Another Christmas had come to a close, no happier than those that had come before it. He'd had such high hopes this year, but it wasn't meant to be. He thought about his wife then, how happy they'd been during the holidays. How he'd loved the dark-haired, dark-eyed woman who was Kollar's mother. He knew what he felt for his wife was pure, true love because no other woman had come close to her. She was always in his thoughts. Always. Because . . . Kollar looked just like her.

He needed to go back to his own little cabin, back to his memories and his pictures. The big question for him was, did he walk through the house and use the front door? If he did that, he'd have to go past his son, and he wasn't in the mood for any more verbal fisticuffs. Or, should he leave by the back door and avoid his son entirely? Because he was a father and well able to handle the verbal fallout he imagined, he decided to leave by the front door.

Kyros stood in the doorway of the dining room, which gave him a clear view of his son in his recliner. He watched him for a few minutes. The jacket to Kollar's suit was on the floor, his shirt cuffs unbuttoned but not rolled up. His new tie was hanging drunkenly over the end of the coffee table. His left shoe was on the hearth, his right shoe under an end table. A whiskey bottle was clutched in one hand, one of Alpha's new Christmas toys in the other.

"Good night, Kollar. Merry Christmas."

"Night, Pop. It's really not our Christmas. Ours isn't until January 7. Why are we pretending? Merry Christmas anyway. It was a good dinner."

"How would you know if it was good or not? You didn't eat anything. We'll talk another time."

"No, we won't, Pop. We'll never talk about this again. That's an order."

"Whatever you say, son."

THE MARRIAGE GAME 237

"You're humoring me, Pop. I don't like that."

"Whatever you say, son. I'm tired. The girl was right, Kollar. Now sleep off that drunk you're on. Tomorrow is another day."

"So it is."

At six o'clock the day after Christmas, Pappy woke with a glorious hangover that was so bad he didn't bother to get out of bed. He closed his eyes and went back to his hateful nightmares. When he woke two hours later, he felt even worse when he opened his eyes to see his father standing over him. He had a tall glass of tomato juice and a cup of dark, black coffee on a tray. Pappy groaned. "Go away, Pop, let me die here in peace."

Kyros laughed. "To my knowledge, the last time you were in this condition was when you turned twenty-one. At which point, if my memory serves me correctly, you swore you would never, ever drink like that again. Drink the tomato juice. I put a little hair of the dog that bit you in it. If you don't want to drink it, don't. I'm ashamed of you, Kollar."

Pappy swung his legs over the side of the bed. He thought his head was going to pound right off his shoulders. He staggered to the bathroom. Kyros winced at the retching sounds he could hear through the closed door. "Did you hear what I said, I'm ashamed of you!" Kyros shouted.

"Yeah, I heard you!" Pappy snarled. "You're right, okay."

When Pappy returned to the bedroom, Kyros thought he looked like death warmed over. "I was working on this plan. I had it down pat. Then she started to avoid me. And she was . . . *glued* to Vandameer. That ticked me off. I blew it. I know that. The thing with Alpha . . . I saw red. I reacted like a fool. Look, I'm no Romeo, that's a given. What I am is a spook. I dream up and put into action covert operations. It's what I do best. It's the *only* thing I do. I was never into the small talk, dating game. I don't like it that I have no skills in that area. I was trying, Pop, and I'm not a *schmuck*. Where in the hell did you learn that word anyway?"

Kyros watched his son down the glass of tomato juice. He almost laughed aloud when he bolted for the bathroom a second time. "From Olivia. She says it all the time." He shouted to be heard through the closed door. "What's next in that crazy plan of yours?"

Kyros listened to his son gargling in the bathroom. He tried to stifle his laughter when he heard his son say, "I'm going to fall back and regroup."

"Now that sounds like a plan to me, a workable plan. You might want to run it by me before you implement a new one."

Pappy opened the door and stared at his father. His eyes narrowed. "Are you really ashamed of me?"

"Yes," Kyros said. He turned on his heel and left the room.

Pappy sat down on the edge of the bed and groaned. He wondered if he was going to die. Probably not. A pity. He squinted to see through the shutters on his window. It looked gray outside, but it wasn't snowing. He needed to teach himself a lesson. He dressed, albeit with some difficulty. When he bent over to lace up his boots he thought his head was going to split wide open. He almost called out to Alpha until he remembered the dog was with Sam, who seemed to love Alpha nearly as much as he did.

He'd found Alpha as a pup, half-starved because his mother and the rest of her litter had died. He'd been so weak he couldn't stand. For five days and nights he and his father had sat up with him, feeding him first with an eye-dropper, then with a baby bottle that Kyros had fashioned out of an empty syrup container and a latex glove. When Alpha grew stronger, Kyros cooked for him. Neither he nor his father was certain if their old shepherd had mated with the female wolf or not. In the end, it didn't matter. He grew attached to the dog, and the dog seemed to have an uncanny instinct when it came to him.

Alpha had never been affectionate, maybe because his mother had died. He was, however, devoted. He'd liked Adrian, almost right up to the end, then he'd turned against her, as if he knew something everyone else was too stupid to figure out. And now Samantha Rainford had somehow reached Alpha's inner core. It was easy to see that the dog loved her, and she loved the dog. Something tore at Pappy's heart. He felt like he'd lost his best friend.

His front door slammed behind him. He crossed the

compound, his tracks the only ones to be seen in the fresh snowfall. He sniffed the air, which was rich with the scent of balsam. He ran then until he could no longer make his legs work. When he collapsed on a fallen log, he wanted to die. His respiration was ragged, tortured as he struggled to breathe. He turned when he heard a noise, and found himself staring into a pair of yellow eyes. "Hi, there, big guy. I'm not mad. I'm jealous. Jesus, do you understand what I'm saying, Alpha?" The dog whined as he approached. Pappy reached out to stroke his big head. "How did you know I was out here? Never mind, it's enough that you're here." He talked then, for a long time, the wolf-dog standing quietly but listening intently. He made no sound as Pappy bared his soul.

The run back was as tortuous as the outward leg. By the time he returned to the compound, his headache was almost gone. Maybe his stomach would tolerate some toast and tea.

Man and dog entered the kitchen off the dining hall. Pappy got the bread and popped it into the toaster. While it toasted, he made himself a cup of tea, careful to stay out of his father's way. On the gas range he could see a huge pot bubbling. His father must be making soup. Gallons of soup. Maybe as much as twenty gallons of soup. It smelled good, and it wasn't upsetting his stomach.

"I'm not making this soup for you, Kollar. One of the recruits is sick."

"Oh."

"It happens when you wade through snow in nylons.

How many times have I told you that if you get your feet cold and wet, you get sick. That's why your mother and I always insisted you wear your galoshes in bad weather. Well, how many times?"

Pappy stared at his father, wondering where this new information was going. "A hundred at least." He bit down on the buttered toast. It tasted good. "Who's sick? Who would be dumb enough to walk through snow without shoes or boots?"

Kyros turned so he was facing the stove and the huge soup pot. He dumped in a bowl of chopped carrots. "Samantha Rainford. When she left last night, she ran out in those silly shoes women wear to parties. She left her boots behind."

Pappy stopped chewing; the toast in his mouth suddenly tasted like sawdust. "Just how sick is she?"

"I don't know. Zoe came to the kitchen and asked if I'd make some chicken soup. All she said was Sam had a fever and chills. A cold is a cold. You weather it; isn't that what you always say to the recruits when they come down with a winter cold, Kollar?"

"Yes, I always say that. Do you think she should be in the infirmary? It's warmer in there. Maybe you should suggest that to Zoe."

"Maybe I shouldn't. In case you haven't noticed, I'm making soup. Chicken soup needs to be watched." Kyros lied with a straight face. "I also plan on making a chocolate cake. I can't be two places at one time. You aren't doing anything."

Pappy shrugged. "They're all grown-ups. They know where the infirmary is. There's a nurse on duty twenty-four/seven, and they know that, too. We have a cabinet-ful of medicines."

"Thank you for pointing that out, son."

"You know, if you weren't my father, I'd bop you right on the nose."

Kyros banged a few pots to show what he thought of that comment. A moment later, his son stormed out of the kitchen.

Pappy went straight to his office and turned on the computer. It was time to do some work. Just because it was the holiday season didn't mean operations came to a standstill. And he had just a week to compile the year-end reports his employers expected on January 1.

Pappy worked steadily, stopping every so often to check in with his field operatives via his BlackBerry. Things in the world for the moment were on an even keel. It usually happened that way during the holidays.

It was midafternoon when one of the kitchen staff knocked on his door with a thick, robust ham sandwich along with a bowl of soup. He devoured both, happy that his stomach was more or less back to normal. Alpha padded in once or twice to check on him, staying just long enough to nuzzle his leg. On his second trip, he dropped one of his new toys and picked up another one before he trotted out.

Pappy was still working when the dinner hour came

and went. He looked up when his father appeared with a tray. Crispy fried chicken, mashed potatoes, snow peas, and carrots, and another bowl of chicken soup. Chocolate cake and coffee completed the meal. Pappy thanked his father and went back to what he was doing.

The night loomed ahead of him. Pappy decided to punish himself by sitting in front of the Christmas tree, knowing he'd ruined Christmas Day for his recruits. He *would* apologize. When, he didn't know.

In the Omega Three building, Sam's teammates clustered in a circle in the living room. Everyone but Slick was in favor of bundling Sam up and taking her to the infirmary.

"Slick, 103 fever is not a good thing. Sam needs some real medical treatment. Cold tablets aren't going to help her," Hawkins said.

"She doesn't want to go to the infirmary, Eric. She said she gets a cold every winter, and she felt this one coming on while we were in New York. She says she'll be fine by morning. She wants a hot toddy. A strong one."

"I'll get it," Olivia said. "I can stop in the infirmary and get some medicine."

"Go," Slick ordered.

Forty minutes later, over Sam's raspy protests, Hawkins bundled her up and carried her across the compound to the infirmary, where the nurse took over and ordered the others back to their barracks.

Alpha watched these strange goings-on, his yellow

eyes glowing in the darkness before he sprinted inside the house to where Pappy was dozing on his chair. He tugged on his pant leg, gently at first, then barking to get his master's attention. Pappy bounded out of the chair. "What?" Alpha raced to the door.

Pappy slipped into his boots before he pulled on his jacket to follow the big dog. Halfway across the compound, his heart started to thud in his chest when he saw where Alpha was going. He entered the building quietly, sought out the nurse, and had a whispered conversation. Alpha whined at his feet. He reached down to stroke the big dog's head.

Sam looked ashen, and she was shivering despite the mound of blankets on top of her. Her eyes were closed, but they opened when she heard Alpha whining.

"Under the weather, eh?" Pappy said in what he hoped was a neutral, upbeat voice.

"It's just a cold. I get one every year around this time," Sam said, her voice raspy and strained.

"I get one, too. Actually, I'm late this year. What I mean is, I usually get a bad cold around Thanksgiving. I used to get one in September, like a late-summer cold, then it switched up. I was never able to figure it out." Pappy was babbling, but he couldn't seem to stop himself. "Sleep is good. Hot tea and Pop's chicken soup. You'll be right as rain in a day or so. At least that's how it works for me. The hot toddy the nurse said you had makes you sweat out all the toxins." *Shut up already, Pappy,* he cautioned himself.

Her teeth chattering, Sam said, "I'm so cold. I can't get warm. I lost my shoes last night when I walked back to the barracks."

"Alpha will find them. Lie still. It's when you move that you get the chill. I'm sorry about last night. I don't have a problem sharing Alpha with you even though it sounded like I did. Would you like to hear Alpha's story?" Why did his voice sound so desperate?

"Well, sure, like I can refuse, right?" Sam grumbled.

Alpha barked as he backed toward the door, advanced, backed up again. Pappy watched him and knew what the big dog was going to do even before he did it. He nodded slightly. It was all Alpha needed as he ran and leaped neatly onto the bed, where he scratched around until he had the covers where he wanted them. He stretched out alongside Sam, warmth radiating from his huge body.

Pappy started to babble again. "I don't know how he knows things. He just does. He appears out of nowhere when someone needs help, like that time your team was in the woods and came across the snake. It's uncanny. There is nothing like an animal's warmth next to a human. I've seen documentaries where, by doing just that, an animal saved a human life. Lie still and let it work for you."

"Okay. Oh, he is soooo warm. I'd like to hear Alpha's story now, please," Sam said sleepily.

Pappy settled himself on a hard chair at the side of the bed. He started to talk until he realized that Sam was asleep. He stood up and looked down at her. What was it about this woman that made him so nuts? She wasn't model beautiful, more of a natural beauty who didn't need makeup or fancy potions to enhance her looks. He peered closer at the smattering of freckles across the bridge of her nose. She had two freckles on her chin. He hadn't noticed them before. Even in the dim light of the infirmary, he could see how glossy her hair was. He wondered what it would be like to wind his fingers through it.

"Stay, Alpha. Come get me if . . . if you need me." The wolf-dog raised his head, his eyes glowing in the dimness. Pappy knew he was leaving Sam in good hands. Not that it was easy to convince the nurse, but in the end he prevailed when he very blithely said it was the law of the mountain. She looked skeptical, but she didn't contradict him. Sometimes it paid to be the boss.

Pappy stopped at the Omega Three building and informed Sam's team about her condition. "She was concerned that she lost her shoes last night. I imagine we'll find them in the spring thaw." If he was hoping for a smile or a chuckle, he didn't get it. So much for being witty. *Sam was right, I am a stiff.*

When no one asked him to sit down or stay, he left the building and walked back to his own cabin, where he sat up all night watching the twinkling lights of the Christmas tree, leaving hourly to visit the infirmary.

Each time he stepped over the threshold, he saw that the patient and dog were both sleeping soundly.

Chapter Fourteen

By the time New Year's Eve arrived on the mountain, the snow had finally stopped, and the infirmary was full to capacity. Sam had returned semirecovered to her barracks, with only Zoe for companionship. What everyone thought was winter colds had turned into the flu. Even Pappy and Kyros were under the weather and stayed inside their own quarters. The New Year's Eve party had been canceled and each inhabitant on the mountain slept through the countdown to a bright new year.

It was almost three weeks to the day before everyone was back to normal. Not willing to risk any chances with the recruits' health, Pappy ordered all outside activities to be put on hold and tightened up the classroom work.

The Christmas decorations were gone, the compound had been cleared of snow. Sam's elegant sparkly shoes had been found by Alpha. She immediately tossed them in the trash, and the sun came out for days at a time. The air was fragrant with the smell of wet balsam that permeated everything for miles.

The days wore on, one after the other, until a late spring finally arrived in early May, along with the spring rains. Unfortunately, just as the rain arrived, so did the date for the last of the physical trials.

Sam felt confident as did Hawkins as they prepared for the daylong ordeal. They had mastered the wall and the rope months before. Slick, with hours of firearms classes under her belt and more hours of hand and finger exercises, was able to fire the Uzi, the very thing the FBI Academy had failed her for.

Team Three was in a tense but jovial mood as they made their way to the training field. The word *performance* was said over and over in hushed whispers among the team.

In the days and weeks since Christmas, relationships that were tense and unpredictable had turned to careful respect for one another. While Sam and Pappy weren't best buddies, they were at least civil to each other.

Sam led her team to the starting point for the ten-mile run. How was it possible, she wondered, for the weather to be almost identical to what it had been during the first trials months ago? She thought about the slippery rope, the muddy wall she hadn't been able to master, her humiliation, Pappy's arrogant attitude.

"C'mon, Sam, I know exactly what you're thinking. That was months ago. This is now. You worked hard,

Sam. You proved you can do it. Don't start off with negative thoughts. We've all come a long way. If it rains, it
rains, there's nothing we can do about it. These trials
were scheduled months ago, so don't go thinking Pappy
is out to get you. Okay?" Slick said as she playfully
punched Sam's arm.

Sam switched topics. "We're on the countdown. Six
more weeks, and we're outta here. Bet you can't wait.
What are you and Hawkins going to do, Slick?"

Slick laughed as she scuffed at the wet pine needles
at her feet. "Get married. At some point. I want you to
be my maid of honor. Kayla, Olivia, and Zoe will be my
bridesmaids. Not right now but soon. First we have to
see how things go once we're away from the mountain.
I decided to stick it out, Sam. I'm not going to pack it in.
I'll honor my three years. I learned a lot living up here,
and I want the opportunity to put all that hard learning
to good use. I'm not sure, but I think the others feel the
same way. I think I'd feel like a cheat if I packed it in
after the year. As to Hawkins . . . if it's meant to be, it's
meant to be."

Sam held out her hand. Raindrops fell into her palm.
An uneasy feeling settled itself between her shoulder
blades. "You really love him, don't you?"

"Yeah, Sam, I really do love him. I loved him back
at the Academy, but he had this thing about washing
out and needing to prove himself. I am so grateful to
you, Sam, for working all those nights with him. Together, you two did it. He's a different person. Of

course, if we get separated with each of us drawing different assignments, we'll have to deal with it. I know it's unlikely that we'll be partnered with each other. I've accepted the fact that this organization isn't concerned with our feelings for each other. I think it's safe to say it's a given that we'll be given different assignments and sent to different posts. I'm okay with it, Sam. I really am. I think Hawkins is, too. We all have something to prove to ourselves, and what better way than by working to defend our country?"

Sam settled her rain hat more firmly on her head. Something wasn't quite right, but she couldn't put her finger on what it was. "If there's a will, there's a way. If you love each other, you'll work around the obstacles. Look, we got Spinally again as our running leader."

Pappy moved to what Sam called center stage. He blew the whistle that he never seemed to be without. "You all know the drill. Take off on the count of three. Keep in mind that the weather is not going to get any better. One, two, three!" The flare gun went off, and the recruits spread out and headed for the forest, Spinally in the lead.

Pappy stood alone in the rain for a long time. Alpha finally nudged his leg, reminding him that it was raining. He moved off and headed for the dining hall, where his father was making him ham and eggs. He wondered if he'd be able to eat the meal. He hadn't slept at all as he sat at his computer watching the weather patterns across the state. He knew if he canceled the trials, they would all think it was because of Sam and Hawkins.

It was going to be a very long day.

Pappy prepared himself for his father's input when he sat down to eat his breakfast. When he didn't hear any comments, he looked up, his eyes full of questions. By the time he finished his second cup of coffee, his father still had not offered any type of conversation.

"Well, say it, Pop," he finally said.

"It's raining outside," Kyros said as he banged pots together. "It's going to rain all day. It might rain tomorrow and the day after tomorrow."

Pappy rolled his eyes. "Thanks for sharing that, Pop. See you at lunchtime. By the way, what's for lunch?"

Kyros banged his pots again. "I haven't decided yet."

"All right, Pop. Spit it out, what's your problem?"

Kyros squinted at a dent he'd just made in one of the pots. "You could have postponed the trials. It's not like it's life and death to do it today."

Pappy sighed. "I thought about it. The trials have been on the schedule from day one. Weather doesn't enter into it. Yes, we had to make an exception with all the early snow we had at the beginning of the year, and that damn flu that felled us all. But because of those delays we fell behind. We have to make up that time. I can't be viewed as showing any kind of partiality. Everything will be taken into consideration on the final report. This is about stamina, endurance, and skill. If those recruits can't give me that, then I don't need them. That's the bottom line. I'll see you at lunch, Pop."

Kyros put another dent in the pot as his son left the room. Lunch. He needed to think about lunch. He didn't feel like cooking. As he set about preparing a lunch he didn't want to cook, he thought about all the nights Samantha Rainford had come to the kitchen late at night for hot cocoa. They'd talked, sometimes for hours, with Alpha sitting at their side. He felt at times like she was the daughter he never had as they shared a few confidences, with Sam always saying, "This is just between us, Kyros," which meant he wasn't supposed to tell Pappy. He was a Greek. Like Zorba. A man of his word. All he wanted was for the young woman to feel like she had an ally there on the mountain. If he had visions of dandling little ones on his knee, he kept them to himself.

Kyros chopped peppers and onions for the sausage and peppers he was making for lunch. He felt sad suddenly, knowing his son was never going to leave the mountain, just as he himself was never going to leave it. What kind of person would commit to a life like this? Not Samantha Rainford. When it came to women, his kid simply wasn't cooperating. He put another dent in one of his pots.

Life would take care of itself without any help from him. Hopefully.

The recruits marched to the wall. So far, they had aced everything. They looked, as one, at the wall and the dangling rope. Pappy had expected chatter, even some grumbling, but they were silent. The silence bothered him, and he didn't know why. He held out the coffee can his father had provided. "Take a number."

Sam stepped forward, looked him in the eye with steely determination. She drew the number four. She felt jumpy and irritable. Being number four in anything didn't please her. She'd lived for a while being the fourth Mrs. Rainford, and she didn't like it. She didn't like being the eleventh Mrs. Rainford any better. Then there was the lawyer Prizzi, who was number four in the legal offices. She looked at Hawkins, and he mouthed that he was number nine.

Kate, the leggy blonde, went first, and was up and over in record time. She rappelled down on the other side, walked around, and went up the rope so fast, Sam almost gasped aloud. She could see that Pappy was impressed.

Lukash and Vandameer went next. Their timing wasn't as good as their teammate Kate's, but timing didn't count. Then it was Sam's turn. She struggled with every hand- and toehold, but she made it to the top and back down. She grinned when Hawkins and her teammates pounded her on the back and congratulated her. A deep sigh escaped her lips as she dried her hands on her pant legs before she reached for the rope. Again, it was a struggle but she inched her way up to the top. Her fist shot in the air as her teammates went wild.

Vandameer blew her a kiss. She laughed so loud

when she dropped to the ground she needed help getting up. It was Vandameer who pulled her to her feet. Sam continued to laugh. She would not look at Pappy. Nothing in the world could make her look at him.

She'd done it. She'd persevered, and she'd prevailed. Hot damn.

Sam stood next to Hawkins, whispering to him, offering encouragement. "You can do it, Hawkins. Just be glad timing doesn't count. Hey, you're up," she said, twenty minutes later.

Hawkins stepped forward and started the climb. He'd done it hundreds of times with Sam. She'd offered encouragement while she jeered at the same time. Now, though, when it counted, she was silent, and he wished she'd shout something to him. He was three-quarters of the way up when his foot slipped, and he went down two toeholds.

"C'mon, c'mon, you can do it." He couldn't believe his ears when he heard Sam shout her favorite phrase, "Pretend I have a blowtorch aimed at your butt. Go! Go!" He did, and he was up and over, laughing all the way down. Team Three burst into applause when he marched around to the dangling rope. He offered up a lopsided grin as he reached for the rope.

Sam sucked in her breath. This time it was Slick who bellowed at him, promising him all kinds of things if he made it. Hawkins took her at her word and made it to the top of the rope. He swung one leg over until he was standing on top of the wall. He flapped his arms before he tucked in his legs and dropped to the ground. Even Team Five applauded him this time.

Pappy made notes on his chart.

Sam walked away, Hawkins behind her. "We did it," he whispered. "Sam, we actually did it! I can't help but wonder if we'll ever use those two particular skills in whatever comes next but at least we did it. All those nights out here in the rain, in the cold, in the killer humidity. I have nightmares sometimes about it. Hey, by the way, thanks for the lamb's wool. Wrapping my feet in that stuff worked wonders. They feel really good, no blisters. How'd you hear about that stuff anyway?"

"Kyros told me they used to use it in the old country. I bought out the drugstore when we were in New York. Glad it worked. See you later," she said, walking away.

Inside the barracks, Sam stripped down. She hit the shower and let the steaming water soothe her weary body. As she poured shampoo onto her hair and lathered up, she wondered why she wasn't feeling more elated. She'd just successfully accomplished the very thing she'd washed out of the FBI for. But it had taken her ten months to do it when she only had five and a half months at Quantico. On the other hand, she and Hawkins had mastered the wall and rope before the holidays, so that wasn't a fair comparison.

She'd done it!

Sam stepped out of the shower and slipped into her robe just as her team barreled inside, whooping, hollering, and high-fiving each other. She joined her teammates and accepted a glass of wine Hawkins produced from somewhere. It was not the time to ask questions as to where he got it. They clinked their glasses and downed the contents.

"Six more weeks, and we're outta here," Olivia chortled.

"A piece of cake," Zoe said.

"I, for one, am not going to miss this place," Kayla said.

"I heard that once you leave here, you never come back. I heard Lukash telling Kate that a while back," Slick said fretfully. "I wonder how he knows that, or if he was just talking to appear like he knows what's going on."

Hawkins looked at Slick, his tone curious when he said, "Who cares? Or are you saying you want to come back here?"

Slick bent over to untie her boots. "I don't know. I might want to come back someday. Think about it. It's really nice up here. It's self-contained. It's peaceful. You can commune with nature twenty-four/seven. The food is better than what you get at a five-star restaurant. For the most part, everyone is nice. If we weren't in training, I think we'd all admit this is like a mountain Shangri-la. I'm not ashamed to admit I like it here, and yeah, damn straight I'd want to come back." Her voice was so defiant the others stared at her before she stomped off to the bathroom.

Sam felt nonplussed as she followed her friend to the bathroom. "Want to talk about it, Slick?"

"No. Yes. Oh, I don't know. I don't think I want to get married. This line of work isn't conducive to any kind of a relationship. All you have to do is look at Pappy. What man who looks like him isn't married? There haven't been any women on this mountain but us. Is he celibate? What's the story with him? I'll tell you what the story is," she ran on. "In this line of work, you don't have relationships. Here today, gone tomorrow. Don't you remember all that bullshit Donovan spouted when he recruited us? What sane woman would sign up for a life up here, never to leave? Don't pay any attention to me, Sam, I'm venting. I think I'm scared of marriage even though I love Eric."

Sam blinked when the shower door slammed shut behind Slick. "Uh-huh," was all she could think of to say.

Pappy turned his computer off, looked at the clock, and wondered where the last four hours had gone. He slid his chair away from the desk, laced his hands behind his head, then propped his feet on the desk. He eyed the printer, which was spitting out thirty-three pages per minute. The calendar said it was June 20. Five days remained with this group of recruits, then it was time to turn them loose. He hated these final reports. This was the first year out of the last ten where all the recruits who were still there at Christmastime made it to the finish line. They weren't just good, they were exceptional, and he knew it. Still, he had a few hard decisions to make. One in particular that he didn't want to dwell on, but he knew he had to.

When the printer finally came to a stop, Pappy swung around, picked up the pile of reports, and started to staple them together. He was getting company in two days, and they expected the reports. As usual, he would make recommendations, but his employers would make the final decision. His scalp started to prickle. He knew exactly what that decision would be. Unless he beat them to the punch and did what he really didn't want to do. He wondered if they would see through his actions. And if they did, what could they do? Fire him? The mountain belonged to his father.

His stapling done, Pappy reached for his windbreaker and headed outdoors. He needed to think. It was two o'clock in the morning. He also needed to clear his head. He looked around for Alpha, but he couldn't see the big dog anywhere. He would have to walk alone. That was okay, he supposed. He'd been alone for so long he felt like a hermit. He reached inside his pocket for a cigarette.

He saw her then, sitting on *his* bench with Alpha next to her. He felt like his heart was skipping every other beat. He walked over to her, intending to chastise her for being outdoors after lights out. Rules were meant to be obeyed.

Overhead, the sky was black, with a million pinpoints of light. Trees rustled in the warm spring breeze. He was standing over her and the dog. "Can't sleep?"

"No. I gave up after an hour of tossing and turning. I guess I broke the rules by coming out here. Maybe I just have cabin fever or maybe . . . It's almost time to leave. I think I'm feeling a little sad."

Pappy took a step backward as he digested her words. It was the most she'd ever said to him at one time. "I was just going to go for a walk. Sometimes stretching your legs before you go to bed helps. Would you care to join me?"

"Sure. It's a beautiful night, isn't it?" Sam said.

"Most nights are beautiful up here. It's a shame we have to sleep through them."

"Do you miss . . . what I mean is, do you ever . . ."

He knew what she meant. "Sometimes. Lately, I seem to miss it more, and I'm not sure why that is," Pappy said.

"What would happen to you if you did leave here? We've all heard stories about you. Did you really have something to do with all that stuff that went on in the Golden Triangle? They say you were the most famous spook of all time."

Pappy chuckled. Sam thought it a sad sound. "Every year the stories get better and better. There are *people* who know I'm here. People who shouldn't know. They just can't get to me. It's a life I chose way back when. I knew the consequences."

They were walking behind the firing range. "You're a good shot, Sam, the best of the group. You surprised me, being a woman and all."

Sam didn't take offense. Pappy didn't exactly have a way with words. "Having a target in mind really helped my arm," she said. "Well, not a target so much as a face."

Pappy wanted to ask her if it was his face when she turned and said, "I imagine you think it was your face, but it wasn't," she lied.

"Oh," was all he could think of to say.

They continued to walk in silence until they were at the wall. "Tell me, in this line of work, how often will any of us be required to scale a wall like this or climb that damn rope?"

Pappy grinned in the darkness. "Probably never. I told you all, it's about endurance, stamina, and skill. The wall is just a wall, and the rope is just a rope. Do you want me to apologize for that first time at this wall?"

"No."

The answer surprised him. "Do you think you could kill someone, Samantha?"

"I suppose if that someone was bent on harming me, I could."

"What if you were ordered to kill someone? As an assignment?" Pappy asked carefully.

Sam thought about the question. She looked up at the man standing next to her in the moonlight. She wanted to kiss him so badly, her lips tingled. He was looking at her so intently, she felt like he was reading her mind. She felt flustered. In the time it took her heart to beat twice, she was in his arms, and he was kissing her. Her world spun, righted itself, then went out of control as she grappled with her emotions. When he released her, she was so shook-up, he had to hold her upright. "What . . . what was the . . . the question again?"

Pappy's voice sounded so gruff, Sam could barely make out the words. It sounded to her like he said, "I don't remember." He was gone a second later, sprinting across the field.

Sam let her knees fold as she slipped to the ground. She cried then because she knew she'd just found the love of her life. In five days she would leave this place and that love. Her shoulders shook with pain and anguish.

"I think he needs you, Alpha, go to him," Sam blubbered. The wolf-dog paced and whined. "Go!" she cried brokenly. The dog sprinted off.

Sam walked back to the barracks and let herself in. She knew she'd never sleep, so she curled up on the couch and cried until she couldn't cry anymore.

Pappy was breathless when he reached his father's cabin. He was a wild man when he burst through the door and woke his father. "I need to talk to you, Pop. I want you to listen to me, but I don't want you to say anything," at which point he switched to Greek and rattled off a monologue that caused Kyros's hair to stand on end. When he wound down, he stared at his father. "Now you can say something."

In his life, Kyros had never seen his son in such a state of agitation. He understood it, though. "It should be her decision, not yours. You aren't God, Kollar. You make your own decisions, no one else's."

"I don't want to turn her into a killer. I don't want her to be like Adrian or me. She needs a life outside this . . . this . . ." Pappy waved his arm toward the window, his eyes glazed when he couldn't come up with a suitable term to explain what he was talking about.

"If you fail her, the others might walk with her. Is that what you want?"

"Hell, no, it's not what I want. It's not what *they* want either. I fell in love with her, Pop."

"You could ask her to stay up here. If she loves you, she would."

"Pop, that's crazy. I could no more ask her to do that than I could ask her to fly to the moon. She has her whole life ahead of her. I know what I have to do. Tell me you understand."

"I can't tell you that, son. I think you're wrong."

Pappy was already out the door, Alpha at his side. Kyros noted that the wolf-dog's tail was between his legs. That wasn't good. He shivered. The dog understood everything, he'd bet his life on it.

Back in his quarters, Pappy was like a robot as he did what he thought he had to do. His eyes burned unbearably as he stuffed papers into a manila envelope and sealed it. He would do what he had to do the moment breakfast was over. It wouldn't make a difference to the others if he posted the notice a day ahead of time.

It would only matter to Sam.

Chapter Fifteen

Sam was showered and dressed before anyone else. As she waited for her teammates, she gazed out the window. She didn't know what she felt other than depressed. She also didn't like the way Alpha was glued to her leg. He'd been whining for the past hour, making her wonder if the big dog was getting sick. She bent over to tickle him behind the ears. "I'm going to miss you when I leave here," she whispered. Suddenly she was on her knees, hugging the big dog. "I'll probably never see you again." Her voice dropped even lower. "I think I love you as much as Pappy does."

"Ready?" Zoe asked. "Damn, it's raining again. I want sun. I *need* sun!" she cried dramatically.

"Just think, in two days we leave here for thirty, count 'em, thirty full days of R&R. Not that we'll be using the time to rest. God, I can't wait to call my brother Joey to see how things are going with his search for Douglas. Where are we going to meet up? Did we even decide?" Kayla asked as she donned her poncho.

"Back where it all started, Washington, DC. We'll stay at the Airport Marriott. Isn't that what we agreed on?" Sam responded vaguely.

"Yes," Slick said. Her eyes looked worried as she stared at Sam. Something was wrong. The others sensed it, too.

"I can't wait to nail that bastard to the wall," Kayla said, referring—of course—to Douglas Cosmo Rainford, III.

Hawkins held the door for the others. "Yeah, well, from everything you've said, I have the feeling it's going to be like trying to nail Jell-O to the wall. Damn, I'm starved! Let's go, guys!"

They followed him, running across the compound to the dining hall. Inside there were no tantalizing smells. There was no food on the sideboard. They looked at one another as one of the kitchen staff appeared with a platter of toast, most of which looked burned and cold. The coffee in the pot was hot, the juice cold.

More cold, burned toast arrived with the entrance of Team Five. Everyone looked at it and opted for the coffee, hopeful that something other than the toast would magically appear. No one said a word. They were aware that something was going on, they just didn't know what it was.

Thirty minutes into the breakfast hour, Lukash stood

up and peered out the window. "The cable car just arrived."

"Maybe we're getting company," Kate said. The others ignored her. In the nearly twelve months they'd been on the mountain there had never been company during the daylight hours.

Alpha paced the dining hall. That alone bothered Sam more than the burned, cold toast and the cable car. A sick feeling settled in the pit of her stomach. She looked around. Everyone wore worried looks, even the affable Vandameer.

All of a sudden, Sam knew what was coming. She stood up and was about to leave when Pappy entered the hall. She sat back down and waited.

Pappy cleared his throat as he shuffled the stack of envelopes in his hand. "There's a bad front coming in during the next few days, so I thought I'd give you all a head start on your R&R. I would like to take this time to tell all of you how proud I am of you. You worked hard this past year. I hope you all have long distinguished careers ahead of you. They will be whatever you make of them. In these folders, you will find instructions. Obey them to the letter. Your financial records are also in there and are returned to you. Read everything carefully. Everyone made the cut except for Samantha Rainford."

Sam sat motionless, her eyes dark and steady. She heard Hawkins start to bluster but she *shooshed* him with a touch to his arm. She waited, knowing there was more to come.

"Your bags are inside the cable car, Rainford. Go now!"

Sam bit down on her lower lip, her eyes burning with unshed tears. She got up as if in slow motion and walked toward the door, trying desperately not to look at anyone. She ran across the compound and down the incline to where the cable car was waiting, Alpha on her heels. She was crying as she stepped on board. Alpha was barking and howling so loud the hair on the back of her neck stood on end. In the distance she could see the others running toward the cable car, Pappy in the lead. Just as the operator was about to close the gate, Alpha let out an earsplitting bark that chilled her to the bone and ricocheted off the mountain. When she saw the wolf-dog's intent, she screamed, NO, GO BACK! Just as the dog leaped on board, the gate closed, and the car started its descent.

Sam struggled to find her voice. "You have to stop and go back up and let him out."

"No, Miss. Pappy said he was to go with you."

Sam cried harder, her shoulders shaking. Alpha squeezed next to her on the narrow seat.

Up above, on the mountain, what was left of Team Three glared at Pappy.

"Screw you, Pappy. You can take this job and shove it. I want to go down the minute that cable car gets back up here," Slick said, tossing her envelope on the ground. The three Rainford wives followed suit.

Hawkins debated all of one second before he, too,

tossed his envelope on the ground. "You know, until this moment, I had the utmost respect for you. I hope you rot on this frigging mountain." His declaration over, he ran after his team members.

Team Five looked undecided.

"She was the best of all of us. How could you do that? Because she's a woman? I'm with them," Vandameer said, throwing his envelope over the side of the mountain.

"If this is how you judge your recruits, I don't exactly feel safe," Lukash growled. "I thought there was something screwy about this outfit from day one." His envelope followed Vandameer's. In the end, only Kate, the leggy blonde, remained. "I'm on your side," she said coyly to Pappy. She clutched her envelope and waved it in the air, to Pappy's disgust.

Pappy was on his way back to the dining hall when Kayla ran up to him, squared off, and socked him full in the eye with her clenched fist. "That's for Sam, you son of a bitch! Hawkins is right, I hope you rot on this damn mountain."

Pappy felt like the devil in disguise when he walked to the kitchen. He pulled up short when he saw his father throwing his pots and pans in every direction. He watched as coffee grounds, flour, and sugar sailed through the air. Silverware and crockery followed until the shelves were bare. "I quit!" Kyros yelled hysterically, and dramatically stalked out of the kitchen. At the doorway, he turned. "Even your dog deserted you. That should tell you something, Kollar. *Schmuck*," he said, using his new favorite word to sum up his feelings.

Pappy felt numb. He backed away to the main room and sat down on one of the chairs. He heard the cable car and voices outside as the recruits ran toward it shouting and cursing. For his benefit, he was sure.

Kayla was right, he was a stupid son of a bitch. He looked around, then pinched his arm. No, this wasn't a dream, he was wide-awake, and he was alone.

Pappy walked over to the coffee urn and poured himself a cup of coffee. He carried it back to the table and sat down again. *Now what the hell am I supposed to do?*

He looked up when the door opened. Kate entered the room. She walked over to where he was sitting. "I think I was a bit hasty earlier. I'll be leaving, too." She threw her manila folder on the table and left.

Pappy, his voice a hoarse croak, said, "Why?"

Kate walked back to the table. "Why? In the past you might have been Superman, Captain Marvel, and Batman all rolled into one. Up here on this mountain you played God with all of us. We let you because we came here willingly, wanting to do what you trained us to do. We worked our asses off for you, *Mr.* Havapopulas. As women, all six of us had to work harder than the men, but we did it. Sam was the best of the best, and you damn well know it. We all know it. That's why we're all leaving. How could any of us work for you knowing you blew Sam off for personal reasons? It had to be personal because nothing else makes sense. You're supposed to be the man in charge, above such nonsense. I wouldn't feel safe with my life in your hands. Neither would any of the others. The funny thing is, you really didn't surprise me. I actually expected something of the sort. *You're a man*," she said, as if that explained everything.

Stunned at the blonde's words, Pappy could only stare up at her. She looked like an angry goddess towering over him. And she looked like she had more to say. He realized that he was right when she continued.

"Somehow or other, Sam fell in love with you. We all saw it and knew. I guess you were so busy making her life miserable you failed to notice. Which doesn't say much for you in my opinion."

Kate turned on her heel. "You have a good life up here on this little ol' mountain of yours. Maybe your next batch of fools will be able to deal with you better than we could."

The words came out of nowhere, words Pappy didn't expect to flow from his mouth. "I thought you didn't like her."

"I was jealous of her—we all were—but that doesn't mean I didn't like or respect her. She was more centered, more dedicated. She gave you a hundred ten percent. You still don't get it, do you?" The door closed behind Kate with a loud bang. Minutes later he heard the cable car start up.

Pappy got up, looked around for Alpha, remembered that he wasn't there, would never be there again. His eyes burned as he made his way back to his house.

He had to reach out to his employers. He rehearsed in his mind how he would write out his resignation.

Sam settled herself on a bench at the base of the mountain. Alpha sat with her, licking her hand. Anger, hot and scorching, raced through her veins. When Alpha jerked to attention, she looked up. The cable car was coming back down. Alpha barked. When the car ground to a stop, her team barreled out and rushed to her.

"No, no, you have to go back. Don't give it all up for me. I don't want you throwing it all away, you worked too damn hard," Sam said as she wiped at her tears.

"Yeah, and you worked even harder. Did it make a difference? Nope," Slick said.

"We're on your side, and that's final," Kayla said.

"So, what do we do now?" Zoe asked.

"Where are your envelopes?"

The others shrugged.

"Well, inside are instructions. What mine says is my bank accounts are active now. My condo is mine again, as are my credit cards. So for now, I can foot the bill to get us back to Washington if you really want to go with me. Supposedly, Donovan is going to come and take me to the airport. We can all go to my house and decide what our next move is. You guys okay with that?" The others nodded.

"Here comes the cable car again. Oh, jeez, it's Team Five, and it looks like Kate is missing," Hawkins said, his eyes almost popping out of his head. They watched as Team Five hit the ground. The car started back up.

Sam started to cry again when Team Five gathered around her. She couldn't believe they were so solidly behind her. If anything, it made her feel worse.

Off in the distance they could hear the sound of a car approaching.

The white van came to a stop next to the little group. Donovan hopped out with a clipboard in one hand, a stack of white envelopes in the other. His face expressionless, his voice neutral-sounding, he said, "I'm to pick up twelve passengers and one dog and take all of you to the airport where a helicopter will return you to Washington, DC."

"Eleven passengers and one dog," Olivia said coldly.

"Twelve," Donovan said, as he pointed to the cable car. They all watched as Kate hopped out. She ran to Sam and hugged her. Stunned, Sam cried harder.

"Full house," Hawkins whispered in her ear. "That should make you feel good, Sam."

Donovan walked around to the driver's side of the van. He carefully avoided Sam's gaze when she climbed on board with Alpha and walked to the back, where she sat down next to Slick, Alpha at her feet. For obvious reasons, no one spoke a word on the way to the airport.

It was four thirty in the afternoon when Sam led her team to the rental car agency, where she signed up for a Ford Explorer. While they waited for their vehicle, they shook hands all around with Team Five. They were about to separate when the woman who had originally taken them to the helicopter almost a year ago appeared, her hands full of folders. She waited a moment until she had their attention. One by one, she called their names and handed each of them an envelope. "The short version is, you all signed a contract, and you will be held to that contract. Twenty-eight days from now, you are all to appear right here at the entrance to this airport at 0800. Except for Samantha Rainford. If you do not appear, you will be hunted down. Is that clear? Enjoy your R&R, ladies and gentlemen."

A lot of blustering and cursing followed, but in the end they had to accept the outcome. Sam allowed herself to be hugged again before Team Five set off to go their separate ways.

"Joey can help us all disappear," Kayla said. "He knows people who know people if you know what I mean."

"Not the kind of people who are associated with the mountain, Kayla," Sam said quietly. "You have to go back, that's the bottom line. Come on, let's go to my house and call your brother. First, though, we have to stop at the grocery store so I can buy Alpha some food."

At six o'clock, they were eating Chinese, pizza, and hoagies—food that Sam liked but only played with now—and swigging on beer as Alpha sniffed every inch of his new home.

When they were done eating, and the cleanup was over, Slick took charge. "We're going to go to a hotel, Sam. You need some time for yourself to come to terms with everything. We'll be back in the morning bright and early with a game plan. Try and get some sleep if that's possible. We're here for you."

Sam watched them go, grateful to Slick for giving her some private time. The tears started to flow the moment she shut and locked the door. Alpha was immediately at her side as she curled up on the sofa and turned on the TV.

It was so weird, everything looked exactly the same as it had almost twelve months ago when she left. There was no dust anywhere. The carpets had been vacuumed, fresh towels hung in the bathroom. Even the refrigerator had what she thought was the exact same food, but fresh. Even the windows looked like they had been washed. How weird was *that*?

Sam mumbled and muttered as she tried to make sense out of what had just happened to her. Her failing to make the cut was personal, she felt it in her gut. There was no other explanation. The kiss the previous night wasn't something she'd initiated even though she'd responded. With gusto. She'd been kissed hundreds of times but never like that. Even Douglas Cosmo Rainford, III, who had been a superb kisser, couldn't come close to evoking the kind of response Pappy had evoked. Did Pappy use that kiss as proof of her breaking the rules? One slip, that he'd initiated, on the eve of departure, was reason enough to bounce her from the program. She started to cry again. Alpha snuggled against her. "And then he lets me keep *youuuu*." Sam sobbed as she led Alpha to the door and walked him around the complex until he was ready to go back indoors.

Sam slept then, curled up on the couch, because she was too tired to do anything else.

At the Airport Marriott, the remaining members of Team Three gathered in the lounge. It was relatively quiet, most of the cocktail-hour patrons on their way home. Hawkins eyed two young guys who were jabbering on cell phones. He was off his chair in an instant and motioning to the two yuppies. When he had their attention, he said, "I'll give you a hundred bucks if you let me make one or two long-distance calls on your cell phone. The airline lost my luggage, and my phone was inside. What do you say?"

"Sure, I have free long-distance. Wait, you're not calling out of the country, are you?"

"Nope. California. They'll be short calls, so your minutes won't add up." The yuppie nodded. Money changed hands.

Hawkins walked back to his table and hissed. "Give me your brother's number again." Kayla repeated the number, Hawkins punched it in the phone, then handed the phone to Kayla. She spoke quietly and intently for a full five minutes. It was obvious to the others that she did most of the talking. The yuppies watched but didn't interfere.

Kayla clicked off the phone and handed it back to Hawkins, who in turn took it back to the yuppies. The one who owned the phone jammed it in his pocket. They left the bar, waving airily, a hundred dollars richer.

"Joey will be here tomorrow. He said he has news. I thought it best not to go into anything on a strange phone. At least he knows where we are. I gave him Sam's address, too. He'll catch up with us. I wonder what his news is. God, I hope it's good. I could really use some good news," Kayla said.

Slick ordered a new round of drinks just as the piano player started to play. They pretty much had the lounge to themselves, so they called out favorite songs for the pianist.

At ten o'clock, they left the lounge on wobbly legs, all of them hopeful that the coming day would be better.

Team Three wasn't the only one walking around on wobbly legs. On Big Pine Mountain, Kollar Havapopulas walked in circles until he was dizzy. Angry with himself, he walked out to the compound and sat down on the bench to light up a cigarette. The rain had let up, but it was still damp and clammy.

Pappy smelled his father's pipe before he saw him. Father and son at odds with each other. It wasn't right, and it was all his fault. Now he had to make it right.

Kyros walked over to the bench. He puffed furiously on his pipe. He'd never seen his son look so miserable. He sat down and continued to puff.

"I'm sorry, Pop. I did what I thought was best. It was right, yet it was wrong. What else can I say? I wrote out my resignation. I'll give it to *them* when they arrive the day after tomorrow. We'll have to give them a refund. It will be sizable, Pop. Are you okay with that?"

"Of course. If you're serious, that is. We can always use this mountain for a campground for kids. A free camp for city kids and handicapped kids. I could see that happening up here. Fresh air, good food, all kinds of activities for youngsters. What will happen to the others?"

"I don't know, Pop. Look, *they* don't own me. We aren't the only training camp, you know that. We're just the best, and they know it. I made some calls earlier."

Kyros stretched out his legs as he continued to puff on his new pipe. "I really like this pipe. It draws perfectly. I see some stars overhead. Guess it's going to be a nice day tomorrow. What will we do?"

Pappy made a sound that was supposed to be a laugh. "I guess you're going to clean up the kitchen. Me, I'm going to burn my files. I have to pay off the staff and make sure they understand what's going on. I'll be busy, too."

"Do you miss Alpha?" Kyros asked.

"What the hell kind of question is that, Pop? Of course I miss him. But I had to give her something."

Kyros blew smoke. "The first thing you have to do is start being honest with yourself and stop lying. You did not *give* the dog to Samantha. The dog chose to go with her. That dog's love was not yours to give. He may not have loved you, but you and he were partners. You understood each other perfectly. That's what is confusing me. I guess he loved Samantha," he said slyly, hoping to get a rise out of his son.

Pappy fired up a fresh cigarette. He squinted when the smoke made his eyes water. "You know, Pop, I used to watch her. I was always there on the periphery with my notebook and scorecard. Inwardly, I cheered her on. Sometimes I think she knew I was there, but she never let on. In the beginning I wanted her to be the best, better than all the others. I guess I thought I could turn her into another Adrian. I know now it was all mixed up in my mind. The thing was, Pop, I think she was better than Adrian ever was. Maybe I'm not being fair to Adrian, but she lost her edge long before I did. This is a business for the young. Then, because you kept reminding me of what a fool I am, I realized I didn't want her to be like Adrian. I didn't want her to do this for a living, looking over her shoulder, not having a life, married to the job. I wanted her to have a life, friends, a home."

"Why didn't you tell her that?"

"I couldn't. She thought she needed to do this to prove something to herself. She did, and I blew her off the mountain. You were right about something else, too. It was her decision to make, not mine. She qualified. I fell in love with her, Pop. I think Alpha sensed it and, dammit, he was okay with it. I think that dog thought of us as *one*."

Kyros emptied his pipe. "I think you're right. You can still correct the situation, son."

Pappy fired up another cigarette. He was chain-smoking, but he didn't care. "In order to do that, Pop, I'd have to tell her my life history. How do you tell a woman the CIA gave me a license to kill? How do I tell her that only five people in the government, including the president, know about me? How do I tell her I was one of the good guys who killed people so people like her and you and all those other recruits can sleep peacefully in their beds at night?"

"You just tell her, son. Sam went through the FBI Academy. She knows how things are done. Anyone who can read a newspaper or the hundreds of spy novels out there in bookstores understands what the world is like. I'm sure she's pieced together a lot of things."

Pappy shook his head. "If I had been honest with you back in the beginning when the CIA recruited me, would you have okayed what I was getting into? Assuming you were told the truth."

Kyros filled his pipe again from a pouch of tobacco in his pocket. He tamped the tobacco down and fired up the pipe with a butane lighter that lit up the darkness. "Probably not, Kollar, probably not," he said grudgingly.

"Then I rest my case, Pop."

Chapter Sixteen

Sam waited for news from her team members the following morning. She felt angry and out of sorts at her situation. Any dreams she'd had in regard to Kollar Havapopulas had turned to dust just the way they had with Douglas. Yet there was no comparison because she had fallen in love with Kollar, whereas she'd been enamored and mesmerized by Douglas. She realized that she had not truly loved her ex-husband. She hadn't felt mortally wounded the way she felt when she thought about Pappy. Now, when she thought back to her brief marriage, she thought of it as an interlude in her life. A bad interlude, but one she'd moved beyond.

Sam wondered what Pappy was doing. Did he regret his decision? Did he miss Alpha? Of course he did. Did he miss her? She'd been happy on the mountain, happy to work at the challenges. She'd looked forward to each new day knowing she'd see Pappy. It had been enough on the mountain. At least it had seemed that way at the time.

Why, she wondered, was life always so difficult? Why did she have to fight extra hard, kick and scratch just to measure up? And when she did finally measure up, to have it all blow up in her face. She wasn't good enough for Douglas, not good enough for the FBI, not good enough for Pappy. Even back in high school and college she'd never aced anything, always either washing out or coming in after the top contenders. Maybe something was lacking in her gene pool.

Sam squared her shoulders. There were no more tears left. She just felt numb, resigned to whatever was in store for her. She started to pace, going from the living room to the kitchen, to the dining room and to the den, where she turned around and started all over again. She was in love. That was her problem. And she'd been rejected. She swore then that it would be the last time that something like this ever happened to her. Every damn time she stuck her neck out, got brave enough to mingle and join, someone blew her out of the water. Well, she was sick of it. She was also sick of her wimpy, little-girl attitude, too. She needed to toughen up, to give back as good as she got.

Sam stopped her frantic pacing when the phone rang. Her greeting was cautious. She listened when Slick rattled off a list of instructions. The only response from her was, "Okay, but I have to bring Alpha. I'll see you at six."

The adjoining rooms at the Marriott buzzed with activity as the women got ready for their six o'clock meeting at the Red Dragon restaurant. Kayla departed for the airport to pick up her brother while Olivia set out to buy phone cards and a digital cell phone. Slick and Hawkins headed for the library. With nothing to do, Zoe took a bubble bath, but she wasn't able to relax as she contemplated what Kayla's brother proposed.

Promptly at six o'clock, all the members of Team Three along with Kayla's brother, Joey, entered the Red Dragon, which Kayla had rented for the evening. Rented for the evening meant there would be no other customers entering the establishment. Sam Chu, the owner and manager, looked at Alpha and shook his head from side to side. Sam stepped forward and nodded her head up and down. "He'll stay by the door after you lock it." An extra hundred-dollar bill changed hands. Chu bowed low and withdrew to the kitchen.

Kayla introduced her brother and smiled as everyone shook hands. Joey smiled, showing magnificent white teeth. Sam thought he had the shrewdest eyes she'd ever seen. He looked down at his watch, and said in a lilting voice, "The rest of our guests will be here by the time dessert is served. I'm happy to report that I was successful in convincing the other Rainford wives to join us. Miss Martina Crystal will be here, too. She's most eager to help us since she escaped Mr. Rainford's clutches this past Christmas, thanks to Samantha. That's the good news. The bad news is the newest about-to-be Mrs. Rainford won't be joining us. I thought it best to let things rest in that regard. It made it easier for me to keep track of Dougie. The newest nuptials are set for the Fourth of July weekend. I know where Mr. Rainford is, and I know how we can *snatch* him if that's what you want, but I don't advise it."

"You actually found him?" Sam gasped. "How? He was like a phantom. I was actually beginning to believe he didn't exist except in our minds. The Prizzi law firm wouldn't tell us a thing." The others looked speechless.

"Yes, I found him. It wasn't easy either. Do you want to know why it wasn't easy?"

"Tell us," Slick said.

"Douglas Cosmo Rainford, III, is not the man's real name. I found him on LexisNexis. Miss Crystal just happened to have a bottle of champagne with the most beautiful set of fingerprints a detective could ever hope to find. He brought it to her apartment to celebrate their coming nuptials but she booted him out. She said she kept the bottle, thinking we might want the prints. She also said that old Dougie wanted it back when she told him to hit the road, but she was quicker than he was, and she called him a cheapskate. Then she hid it in a friend's apartment. Smart lady."

"If Douglas was using an alias, does that mean we weren't legally married?" Olivia sputtered.

Joey shrugged. "I'm no lawyer, but I did have an associate visit the law firm of Prizzi, Prizzi, Prizzi, and Prizzi. After hours." He winked slyly as he whipped his briefcase from under the table and opened it. "You all have a folder. Your ex rated all of you on a scale from one to ten. I don't know if this will make your day or not, but you all got a ten."

"I should hope so," Kayla snapped. "Okay, who were we married to?"

Joey's round face puckered up, his shrewd eyes sparkling. "I guess none of you follow Washington politics. If you did, you'd know. Then again, maybe you wouldn't. Dougie did try to disguise himself a little, not much, just a bit. But it was enough that he could circulate, and people would just think he looked like someone vaguely familiar. Plus, he took all of you to out-of-the-way places in the hope that he wouldn't be recognized."

The wonton soup arrived. The diners ignored it. They'd ignored the four dishes of sauce and the hard noodles, too. They were, however, gulping the green tea by the potful.

"Who is it, Joey?" Kayla demanded a second time.

"Senator Malcom Wyne. Heir on his father's side to a coffee fortune. Heir to a cereal fortune on his mother's side. He has no siblings. He's one of the five richest men in the country. He loves women. The guy lives to go on honeymoons. He looks normal, and he's a force on the Hill. His colleagues and constituents love him. He's never too busy to donate his money or his time except when he's honeymooning. He goes on an overnight trip twice a year on government business, but we weren't able to get much info on that."

"What state does Doug represent?" Sam asked.

Joey laughed. "The fine state of Kansas. That pretty much explains why none of you would have recognized him even if he didn't make attempts at a disguise. You pretty much have to follow politics, and senators aren't on television all that much. I bet if I asked you to close your eyes and try to picture your own U.S. senator, you'd come up dry."

The women nodded in agreement.

"If he's so damn generous," Slick said, "why did he welsh on the money he promised his 'wives'? I understand he filed divorce papers in order not to pay up, but why?"

"Paper trail," Joey said as he started to eat his soup.

Sam played with the spoon in her hand. She looked around at the painted dragons on the walls. All were belching fire. She felt like belching fire herself. She'd been married for all of three weeks to a billionaire United States senator, as had her predecessors. And yet he'd cheated all of them. Deliberately.

Zoe dipped her spoon in and out of her soup. She didn't eat it, though. "What would happen to him if all this came out?" she asked quietly.

Joey stopped eating long enough to respond. "For one thing, his career in the Senate would come to an abrupt end. I think the story would grow legs, and the media would have a feeding frenzy. If this is about money, I think the guy will pony up handsomely to all of you. If it's about stopping him, well, just the threat of going public would probably do that. If it's about both, I think you'd all end up being incredibly rich. Now, if you want him to pay for the humiliation, for snookering you, that's something else. Right now, the guy has no idea we're onto him. But you're going to have to decide what you want to do and do it quickly, before he marries his next victim. By the way, she's a socialite right here in DC. She's also a fine horsewoman and travels in equestrian circles."

Zoe reached for a handful of the hard noodles and proceeded to break them into little pieces. She had a small mountain in front of her when she said, "Do you have any ideas?"

"Well, I have an idea. I think we should tar and feather him," Kayla snapped. "I fell in love with that jerk. He said he loved me, too. He promised me the moon and the stars. He talked for hours and hours about what a wonderful life we were going to have. He told me he wanted six children, a big house with two dogs, and said I'd never have to lift a finger. I didn't care about any of that, not really. I just wanted him. Do you know how many nights I cried myself to sleep? I couldn't eat. I lost weight. It was all I could do to drag myself to work. I hated the pitying looks everyone gave me. He has to pay for that."

"Yeah," Olivia said.

"We should take him to some faraway island and leave him there forever," Zoe said.

They all looked at Sam for her input.

In a voice that was so hard it could have chipped ice, Sam said, "He needs to pay. I'll go along with whatever plan you all come up with."

"How much money is this guy worth?" Hawkins asked.

"He's a billionaire according to *Forbes*," Joey said.

As one, the women sighed, evil smiles on their faces.

The food arrived, huge platters and bowls of everything on the menu.

Hawkins, Slick, and Joey were the only ones who filled their plates.

Sam fished out chunks of beef, chicken, and soft noodles for Alpha. She carried the plate over to the doorway and dropped to her knees. "We'll be leaving here soon," she whispered. She watched as the dog wolfed down his food. She followed up with a bowl of water. Alpha drank, whined, and Sam opened the door and walked him down the street to an empty lot. They were back inside the Red Dragon within ten minutes.

She'd been married to a United States senator. How mind-boggling was *that*?

Forty-five minutes later a knock sounded on the restaurant door. Joey excused himself and opened the door to admit the other Rainford "wives."

Ten minutes of wild jabbering followed as introductions were made. Within minutes they were friends as only women can be when a crisis brings them together. As dessert was served, the newcomers made a toast, which brought forth gales of laughter. "We'll strip the honeymoon junkie down to his boxers and walk away with his fortune," was the resounding mantra of the women. The group upended the glasses of plum wine, then held them out for a refill. They made more toasts, each one more evil than the one before, which just went to prove the old ditty that hell hath no fury like a woman scorned.

Hawkins made a mental note never to get on the bad side of these women.

Toward the end of the evening, close to the witching hour, Joey clinked his glass with his spoon for everyone's attention. When he had it, he said, "An associate of mine, a fellow police officer who I met years ago at a gun show, is helping us with this situation." At the look of alarm on the women's faces, he quickly reassured them. "I have a job. Mike is retired now and works parttime as a security guard. He's got lots of free time on his hands, and he lives here in the District. He also has some excellent contacts inside the Beltway. Retired law enforcement officers tend to belong to the same clubs and organizations. He has friends in the Secret Service, the FBI, and the CIA, so I felt confident recruiting him. With me so far away, it was the only way to go. Plus, we're just a phone call or a fax away. He doesn't do anything until he clears it with me, so rest easy.

"When Sam emailed me before Christmas last year, I put the wheels in motion. We had a big window of time, and Mike used it to his advantage. Since 9/11, security here in DC is tough, as you might expect. But Mike prevailed, and I brought along copies of what he's found in the past six months. It seems Senator Malcom Wyne is a creature of habit. There is nothing ostentatious about him, even with his wealth. He has security out the kazoo, as is natural for someone with his money. For instance, every Thursday night the senator takes his elderly mother out to dinner at a small Italian restaurant named Panella's off Dupont Circle.

"The mother is frail and in a wheelchair. She suffers from crippling arthritis. The senator is a doting son. Every week, the senator orders chicken piccata and an arugula salad. The mother has a Caesar salad and lobster ravioli. Lots and lots of garlic bread. Between the two of them, they drink a large carafe of the house wine.

"The restaurant is small, with only eight tables. They turn the tables once, and that's it. The first seating is at five thirty, the second seating is seven thirty. The senator arrives promptly at 7:25. He has a standing reservation. His security stays outside. Any questions so far?" The women shook their heads, engrossed in what Joey was saying.

"I have to tell you, this is when the senator will be the most vulnerable, and it will work to your advantage. Security is outside. Whatever we come up with will have a narrow window of time. I think it can be done, ladies.

The only time he has deviated from his solid routine is when he's courting a lady. What he does is, once he gets into his limo, he adds a little Vandyke beard and a mustache. He fills in his eyebrows a little, and he has a little hairpiece that he tacks on the side; then he parts his hair differently. He also wears colored contact lenses that he changes from time to time. He is so ordinary-looking, you never take a second look. Of course, his attire once he gets out of the limo is different, too. The driver, by the way, has been with his family in one job or another for close to forty years. We assume he pays his security detail handsomely to keep his little secret. Any questions?" Again, the women shook their heads.

"His finances are an open book, and they're included in your folder. You did say you wanted to go after the ten million that jerk promised each of you. So, if you get it, Mike and I get ten percent. Without our efforts on your behalf, we wouldn't all be sitting here right now discussing the matter. We think that's fair. Tell me now by raising your hands if you're on board with that."

Hands shot in the air at the speed of light. Joey nodded happily.

Olivia moved a little closer to Joey and smiled up at him. "I for one recognize your value, Joey. This is all so exciting. I'd like to talk about your job a little more at length when you have time. Like this evening. I'm asking you for a date, big guy."

Joey flushed and then grinned. "I'd like that."

The others hooted with laughter.

"That's the good news," Joey continued. "The bad news is you cannot kidnap a United States senator unless you want a long life in the federal pen. We have to make him come to you of his own free will. Did I say that the man loves his privileged life? He does. Mike and I both think that the risk of exposure will be sufficient punishment. The senator was interviewed not too long ago, and he made the comment that he wanted to die in the Senate just the way his daddy and his granddaddy did. As you may know, they are a very political family."

The women started to mumble among themselves. Kayla's voice was the loudest. "Just taking his money doesn't seem enough for what he did to us." The others agreed. Joey looked at all of them and shrugged.

"Do you really want to run the risk of going to a federal prison?"

Sam spoke for the first time. Even though she'd listened with rapt attention, she wasn't sure how she felt about what she'd just heard. All she could think about was Pappy and Big Pine Mountain. "Obviously you have some kind of plan in mind. Would you like to share it with us?"

Joey leaned into the table, his voice dropping to a near whisper as he motioned the others to lean toward him. He started to outline the plan he and Mike had come up with.

"It's perfect," one of the "ex-wives" trilled. The others concurred.

Sam's eyebrows knitted together. "So he pays everyone off, walks away and with another name, another disguise, does it all over again. Sometimes money isn't the answer to everything. I thought we wanted him to suffer like we did. He's not going to miss the money."

"I don't want to go to jail; I just want to spend the creep's dough," a ravishing redhead said.

Sam thought she was "wife" number seven. Then again, maybe she was "wife" number eight. Or nine or ten. "Remember this, we'll all end up dealing with the Prizzi law firm. They won't go easy on any of us." She looked at her watch. It said 11:45. "I'm tired. We have two days until Douglas goes out with his mother for their weekly Thursday night dinner. Let's meet at my house tomorrow and spin this a little more before we make a final decision." For the newcomers, she wrote out her address on paper napkins and handed them around the table.

"Okay," Joey said, getting up from the table. "I made the reservation at Panella's last week, so if it's a go, we're set. If not, I cancel, and we fall back and regroup. I have ten days left on my leave, so I'm at your disposal." He winked at Olivia, who offered up a megawatt smile.

Sam moved toward the door. Alpha was on his feet in an instant.

An hour later, Sam was in bed. Sam cried then, for the would haves, the could haves, the should haves. Now she had to start her life all over again. Not because she failed but because someone else had made the decision to banish her for his own personal reasons. She cried harder, her tears drowning the image of Pappy's face behind her lids. Alpha, at the foot of the bed, whined softly.

Kollar Havapopulas scrolled through the messages stored in his BlackBerry at furious speed as he tried to make sense of what he was reading. In the end he threw his hands in the air and stalked to the kitchen, where his father was baking bread no one was going to eat. He waited patiently with a cup of coffee until his father slid the loaves of bread into the oven and washed his hands.

"Take a look at this, Pop. Tell me what you make of it."

Kyros read the blizzard of messages and shrugged. "Old friends meeting after a long time? They all went out to dinner, even Alpha. Apparently Kayla had a 'brother' of some kind, even if your folder on her had no record of his existence. So he came to see her. Happens sometimes, though it's usually the sister who arranges the meeting. So what if they rented the restaurant for the evening? People do that for reunions so they have privacy. Are you seeing something I'm not seeing, son?"

"I've graduated ten classes from this mountain, Pop. Nothing like this has happened in those ten years. You know we monitored those classes. None of them banded together like this. They all went their separate ways, not wanting to spend any more time with each other than was necessary. And notice that it's only Team

Three, not Team Five. My gut tells me they're cooking something up."

"None of them quit on you en masse during those ten years. You never had a Samantha Rainford before either. She's the glue that kept them all together. They're on her side. Furthermore, why do you care? You have your resignation ready to go," Kyros said.

"I'm still on the payroll until *they* get here tonight. I just received an email saying they moved up the meeting from tomorrow to tonight. All of this," Pappy said, pointing to the BlackBerry, "has to go on the final report. And my gut tells me Samantha Rainford is in it up to her ears."

Kyros chuckled. "Son, maybe, just maybe, you created a monster."

Pappy didn't think it was funny at all. He scowled at his father. Then he wondered if his father was right. If he was, there wasn't a damn thing Pappy could do about it.

Or was there?

Pappy felt naked without Alpha at his side. He tried to shrug off the feeling as he waited for the cable car to arrive. The sound of the car's ascent made his nerves twitch. He was not looking forward to this meeting.

The men shook hands, commented on the warm summer evening, then fell into step with Pappy as he led them to his quarters. Once inside, when everyone was comfortably seated, he handed out drinks. Somehow the immaculately dressed men looked even older than they were. They also looked arrogant, as only the truly rich could, in his opinion. Everything these men did in their lives was somehow involved with money. Back in the beginning, ten years ago, he realized that of the five men, four of them worshiped money. He didn't like them then, and he didn't like them now. But he'd accepted it because the espionage game was his life's blood.

Pappy handed out his final reports, then he handed the oldest of the four his resignation. He watched through narrowed eyes as the man passed the crackly sheet of paper to his colleagues.

The man dressed in a dove gray suit looked up at Pappy with expressionless eyes. "Why?" he asked curtly.

Pappy took his time as he let his gaze go from one man to the other. "Because I'm burned out. And because I don't believe in the sanction you want executed. Contrary to what you might want to believe, I take a sanction seriously. There is nothing in this man's record to warrant such drastic measures. We all agreed at the outset that I had the final say on a sanction. If this is some petty, internal vendetta among yourselves, get over it. I have nothing further to say on the matter."

A man with snow-white hair and a scrawny neck fixed his intent gaze on Pappy. "It's unacceptable, Kollar. Totally unacceptable. We can't allow you to . . . ah, desert us."

Pappy deliberately took a long, slow drink from his glass. "Yes, you can. You have no other choice. This is my father's mountain. We lease it to you. We just canceled your lease. Our refund check is in the folder. It's done, gentlemen."

"We have great power, Kollar. You've seen this, experienced that power. You can't throw away all that we've accomplished. We cannot allow that to happen."

Pappy wasn't surprised by the man's threat. "I'm burned out. I can't do this anymore. Don't you understand, I'm no longer any good to you. If you think you can retaliate, then do so by all means. Just remember, if you even think of retaliating, I'll go after you, one by one. I'll invade your security, and you'll never know. You'll never sleep again. Worst of all, you'll never write another check. You're here, gentlemen; that alone should cause you some worry. It's up to me if you leave. If that doesn't convince you, I've downloaded all the files from our ten-year association and burned them onto a CD. They're in safe hands. The only way they will ever see the light of day is if you retaliate against me, my father, or this mountain. Cut your losses, gentlemen, and move on. Do you still think my decision is unacceptable?"

The third man, who hadn't spoken, spoke now. "Is there anything any of us can say to make you change your mind?"

Pappy listened to the man's soft tone. He'd always been the most reasonable of the five. His response was succinct. "I wish there was but, no, sir, there isn't."

"What about the operatives out in the field? What about this last batch of recruits?" the fourth man asked.

Pappy thought about what he should say. Should he tell these old men about Teams Three and Five and the rebellion? No, the deal was, if they passed the trials and were good to go, they had to honor the contracts they signed. He knew all of them but Sam would report on the proper day to the Colorado office to await their orders. For now, he had to prevent the execution of the sanction.

"I haven't notified anyone of the sanction if that's what you mean. The sanction is a mistake. One that could have dire consequences where the four of you are concerned. I told you that on your last visit. You hired me for my expertise, then you chose to ignore it. That makes you all very vulnerable." Off in the distance, Pappy heard the dinner bell. "It's time for dinner. You can give me your decision over coffee and dessert." He looked closely at the men as they got to their feet. He saw what he hoped he would see—*fear*.

His heart thumping in his chest, Pappy headed for the door.

It was over.

At least for him it was over.

Chapter Seventeen

Pappy led the four visitors to the housing in which the cable car sat. He could see that all four men were wary about setting foot inside the car. "I can control the car from here. Step inside and buckle the belts," Pappy said coolly.

The man with the scrawny neck narrowed his eyes. "How do we know we'll arrive safely at the bottom?"

"You don't," Pappy said. A tired smile worked at the corners of his mouth when the man stepped back. "It's late, get aboard."

"Why should we trust you?" the oldest of the group asked with a hard edge in his voice. He, too, was wary. Even in the dark night, Pappy could see the fear in his eyes.

Pappy shrugged. "Why should I trust *you*? This is called a stalemate, gentlemen. You're wary of me, and I'm wary of you. You have money, I have expertise. If you were betting men, gentlemen, where would you put your money? By the way, that strange feeling you're experiencing is called *fear*. It's probably the first time in your lives you've felt the emotion. I, on the other hand, have lived with it all my life."

The men stepped into the cable car. "Ready, gentlemen?" When there was no response, Pappy threw the switch, and the cable car started its descent.

At last, it was truly over. Pappy straightened his shoulders as he headed toward the compound. He settled himself on the bench next to his father. The moment he sat down, he fired up a cigarette. He looked down, expecting to see Alpha. His stomach curled itself into a knot.

"Did they like my dinner?" Kyros asked.

"They didn't say. Do you care? It's over. Seeing fear on old men's faces is not a pleasant sight, Pop."

"No, I don't suppose it is. Are we safe here?"

"You know what, Pop, I don't know. I tend to think we are, but there are no guarantees, as you know." Pappy blew a perfect smoke ring and watched it sail off in the light evening breeze.

Father and son sat in comfortable silence, Kyros puffing on his pipe and Pappy chain-smoking.

Four cigarettes later, Pappy said, "I have to go off the mountain, Pop."

Kyros stared off into the dark night. The cloud cover appeared to be moving on. Stars winked in the black sky. "I know, son. I'll go with you. When?"

"By first light. I don't see any sense in giving those guys an edge of any kind. I'll need the rest of the evening to secure things here, then we'll leave. The kennel master will keep an eye on things. You okay with this, Pop?"

Kyros looked at his son. "I think the question is are you okay with leaving this mountain. It's been ten years, Kollar. Things have changed down there. How do you propose to go about seeing the man who's been sanctioned? Since 9/11 . . . well, I don't have to tell you the security that's in place in Washington."

Pappy laughed bitterly. "How? I'm going to call him on the phone like a normal person. Rest assured, he'll take my call. I'm stepping over the line here, but I've done that before and lived to tell about it. I can't worry about that now, Pop."

"In that case, Kollar, I'm going to step over the line myself, and I'll worry about it later. Does this decision have anything to do with Samantha Rainford and Alpha?"

Pappy looked at his father as though he'd just asked the most stupid question in the world. "Of course. I'm going to explain to her why I did what I did."

Kyros's eyes twinkled just like the stars overhead. "And . . ."

"There is no *and*, Pop," Pappy said curtly.

Overhead the trees rustled. The light breeze suddenly turned blustery. Both men shivered.

"I think I'll turn in, son. How long will we be gone? I need to know how much to pack."

"As long as it takes, Pop. Pack light would be my suggestion."

"Good night, son," Kyros said as he patted his son's arm.

Kyros was halfway across the compound when Pappy called out to him. "This is the right thing to do, isn't it, Pop?"

Kyros turned around and walked back to where his son was standing. The wind licked at his hair, making it stand on end. The old man placed his hand on his son's heart. "If it feels right here, then it's the right thing to do. Try to get a little sleep."

Sam poured coffee for her guests. The house seemed filled to overflowing with all the Rainford "wives," Joey, Slick, and Hawkins. She eyed the huge cartons sitting in the doorway and wondered what was in them. Alpha sniffed and sniffed before he trotted into the living room to get away from the shrill voices in the kitchen and dining room. Sam set the coffeepot down and looked over at Alpha. She walked over, bent down, and whispered, "I know you're out of your element here. You belong on the mountain with Pappy. When this is over, I'm going to find a way to take you back up there. He needs you, Alpha. I don't know how I know it, I just do. Just a few more days." The dog whined. Sam thought it was a pitiful sound. No one would ever be able to convince her that animals didn't have feelings. The bottom line was the dog was homesick for the mountain and his master.

Sam returned and took her seat at the dining room table. She listened intently as Joey outlined the same plan he'd told them about the night before, but in a little more detail. "Everything we need is in the boxes I brought with me. Knowing you were probably going to want to bring that wolf, I got a special harness for Seeing Eye dogs. One of you will have to pretend to be blind. Sam?" She nodded.

"Okay, that's taken care of. Mike rented a van that will seat all of you. Eric and I are going to pretend to be clerics, the rest of you will be nuns. We had to go to four costume shops to get enough habits. The clerical collars for Eric and me were easier to find. No one will question any of you, and no red flags will go up. We don't want to scare off the senator. Mike and his people will be outside all the time.

"It's my understanding the senator doesn't know Slick. He knows *of* her because Sam talked to him about her famous model friend. It's possible he's seen her on magazine covers, but he doesn't seem the type to read women's magazines, so we're winging this one. The plan is at some point during the dinner, preferably as the senator is waiting for dessert, Slick will leave the table to go to the restroom. She'll pass the senator's table. On her way back to the table she will stop and speak to him. She will call him by the name you all know him by. She will apologize for interrupting his dinner and ask him to come to your table to meet the other sisters, slash, 'wives,' and of course the two clerics.

Now, this is where it gets sticky. He's going to do one of two things. Either he'll bolt, or he'll try to bluff his way out of it. The ideal situation would be for his driver to take his mother home and for him to take a taxi back to his fancy digs at the Watergate. After he invites all of us to join him of course."

One of the "wives," a stunning blonde with inch-long eyelashes, started to sputter. "What if he just takes off and disappears?"

Joey clucked his tongue. "This is not a rinky-dink operation even though it has all come together in a short period of time. Mike and his people, as I said, will be stationed outside and will simply follow the senator if he bolts. That's not going to happen, so stop worrying."

Pride rang in Kayla's voice. "I think it's foolproof." She got up to hug her brother, then looked around at the others. "If my big brother says it's going to work, it's going to work."

Eric Hawkins looked around at the Rainford "wives," the one who got away, and Slick. "Assuming he invites you to his home. What then? Are you all going to sit around and wait for him to write out checks? There's something wrong with this picture," he grumbled.

Sam stepped up to the plate, and said, "I think, Eric, this is one of those meetings where we'll all wing it. Like Interrogation 101. You react to the person you're interrogating. You go with the moment. We certainly don't have anything to lose. As far as I know, there is no law against going out to dinner dressed as pretend nuns and priests. We can manage this if we all do our parts."

The others agreed.

Joey opened the box and started to pull out black outfits. "They're pretty much one size fits all." Two dark suits with white clerical collars were at the bottom of the last box. The two men were checking the size when Joey's BlackBerry came to life. He moved off to the side as he listened and spoke quietly.

The time was five forty-five.

Joey rejoined the group, a worried look on his face. "That was Mike. It seems we have a small glitch. Mr. Panella just called Mike to tell him the senator called and said two old friends would be joining him for dinner and to say his mother wouldn't be there. He ordered a dinner to be delivered to her home. Is this a problem? I don't know if it is or not. Like Sam says, we'll have to go forward and wing it. If it looks like there might be a problem, we'll simply call it off and fall back to regroup. For whatever this is worth, Mike told me Panella said the senator has never brought anyone but his mother to the restaurant before. Whoever his dinner companions are, he must like them. Constituents visiting the capital would be my guess. Politicians always want to look good for the hometown boys, get their pictures in the local papers, that kind of thing."

"Why is this guy Panella so cooperative with an ex-cop?" Slick asked suspiciously.

"Mike said Panella runs a small bookmaking operation out of his kitchen. Mike and his fellow officers looked the other way while they were on the force because Panella had six boys to put through college. He owes Mike." Joey shrugged. "It's not what you know, it's who. Every cop has sources and snitches. Don't you guys watch those crime shows on TV?" Joey groused.

Sam's mind wandered back to Big Pine Mountain. For months she'd been consumed with getting back at Douglas Rainford for divorcing her. Now, she couldn't care less what the man did or didn't do. He could marry a hundred women, divorce them, and she would wish him well. That part of her life was behind her. Still, she had to go through with the plan because she'd committed to the other Rainford "wives." But once it was over and she took Alpha back to the mountain, she would get on with her life. She'd call her old boss, beg him for her old job if necessary, and settle down to crunch numbers for the rest of her life. Tears burned her eyes at the life that lay ahead of her. Angrily, she brushed them away.

Slick rinsed the coffeepot and proceeded to make fresh coffee. Sam watched her and half listened to the other Rainford "wives" as they spent the money they thought Douglas was going to give them. *How shallow they are,* she couldn't help thinking, as she continued to listen as one described buying a chalet in Aspen, another debated Bentleys vs. Rolls-Royces. Everyone, it seemed, was going to go to Paris to the fashion shows and buy one of everything from every single designer. Diamonds, one of the "wives" said. You can never have enough diamonds. On and on it went. *They'll all be paupers within a year*, Sam thought. What would she do with her share? Assuming she accepted whatever it turned out to be. Did she even want it? What was six weeks of her life worth? What was a three-week courtship worth? What was a three-week honeymoon worth? She'd enjoyed the honeymoon. It was the months of humiliation and low self-esteem that followed Douglas's rejection and the subsequent divorce that should have a price tag. Not to mention Douglas's deceit.

Sam's mind continued to wander. If she accepted a large settlement, she wouldn't have to crunch numbers for the rest of her life. She could turn herself into a do-gooder, volunteer her time to worthy causes. And how rewarding would *that* be? On the other hand, she could open her own firm, hire other CPAs, and oversee the operation. She shook her head.

It was time to take Alpha outside. Besides, she needed some fresh air.

It was ten minutes to six when Pappy and Kyros entered the Russell Senate Office Building to find Senator Malcom Wyne waiting for them. They went through the new security checkpoints with the senator at their side.

The senator looked worried as he headed for the elevator. Though they had the car to themselves, he continued making small talk about the weather. Pappy answered in kind.

It's a comfortable office, Pappy thought when they got to the senator's suite of offices, *all nicely paneled in some kind of beautiful wood.* There was a host of luscious green plants, a rogue's gallery of pictures on the wall. Pappy recognized presidents, heads of state, prime ministers, and assorted senators and congressmen. The senator, he noticed, was decked out in a power suit and power tie. He was a big man, with a shy smile and warm eyes. He wondered how the senator had evaded the marriage game so long. He had to be at least forty-five, and it was a known fact that there were few if any bachelors in the Washington fishbowl because Washington socialite matchmakers simply wouldn't tolerate a bachelor in their midst.

The senator opened the door to his office. "I dismissed my staff earlier, so we're alone. Can I get either of you a drink, or would you prefer coffee? What the hell is going on, Pappy?" he asked irritably. "I was told you never leave the mountain. I was also told the reasons why you never leave the mountain. Isn't this dangerous for you?" His tone of voice suggested that he feared Pappy's appearance in his office might be dangerous for him as well. "As for your disguise, it leaves a lot to be desired—you just look like an old man."

"This is the first time I've left Big Pine Mountain in

over ten years. I left because your colleagues in the consortium ordered a sanction on you. I refused to go along with it. In fact, I tendered my resignation last night when the four of them came to the mountain to see me."

The senator turned white. "Me? Why?" He lowered himself onto a chair.

"I don't know, Senator. They wouldn't tell me. They came up the mountain several months ago to put me on alert, with specific details to follow. I just came here to warn you. I'll be returning to the mountain tomorrow. And don't bother telling me what this is all about because I don't want to know."

The senator jumped to his feet, his eyes wild. "I don't have a clue. All I know is our last two meetings here in DC were canceled. Once they said it was because of bad weather, the second time, because one of them had the flu. They did accept my quarterly check in April. I can't imagine what I could have done to warrant this. You actually resigned?" he asked, bafflement and fear ringing in his voice.

Pappy looked around the suite of offices. He wondered what it was like to sit in a place like this day after day, rushing to vote on one issue after another. It had to be boring as hell. "Yes. It got rather ugly, with threats on both sides. You might want to think about updating your private security, Senator."

"You took a great risk coming here, Pappy. I appreciate it. I don't suppose it would do any good to confront the others and demand an explanation. Will the sanction be passed on to the program in Colorado?"

Pappy shrugged. "That would be my guess. You need to take extra steps to protect yourself. No one knows I'm here, Senator."

The senator looked at his watch. "We should be leaving now. Traffic is heavy at this hour of the evening."

"Senator, dinner isn't really a good idea. I don't want to be out and about any more than is necessary," Pappy said.

The senator made a funny sound that was supposed to be a laugh. "I guess we can all hide out and turn into recluses. That's not my style. I can get us all out of here and into my car with no one seeing us. My security detail waits outside the restaurant while I dine. They're ex–Secret Service. Panella's is a family-style restaurant near Dupont Circle. I've been eating there for years and years. It's safe in case you're worried." He eyed Pappy's thin disguise, which consisted of a little padding under his clothes, a fisherman's cap, wire-rim glasses, and a little latex filler around his nose and chin. "The food is wonderful." He directed his last comment to Kyros, who smiled.

Pappy shrugged. Maybe this weak link in the consortium wasn't so weak after all. Just then he looked like he had the right mix of piss and vinegar. He shrugged again. He'd come here to do what he had to do, and he'd done it. The rest was up to the senator.

*　　*　　*

It was precisely 6:20 when the Rainford "wives" and Slick exited Sam's bedroom. They were all giggling and laughing, even Sam. "We look like a bunch of penguins. How do those nuns wear all this stuff? These habits weigh a ton. Is this material what they call black serge?" Sam asked.

"As far as I know, only Benedictine nuns still dress like this. The more modern nuns dress in civilian clothes these days," Kayla said knowledgeably. "Speaking strictly for myself, I like to see a nun in a habit. I don't know how they ever got used to the headpieces and this starched white thing around the face. It's a wimple. And it itches. I guess they get used to it. The outfit somehow makes it more . . . solemn as well as official."

The others solemnly concurred as they filed past Hawkins and Joey, who just as solemnly said, "Bless you, my children."

"I hope God doesn't punish us for impersonating nuns and priests," Kayla said, her voice ringing with worry.

"Too late now," Slick replied, as they headed through the door. She started to giggle. "We do look like a line of penguins." The others tried not to laugh in case any of Sam's neighbors were watching.

One by one, they climbed into the oversize van and buckled up. Joey started up the van, and off they went.

Sam stared through the window. It was a beautiful, warm, summer evening. It would be cool on the mountain. They'd probably be wearing sweatshirts or sweaters if they were still there. She looked down at her watch. They would have been waiting for Kyros to serve dessert right about then. Her eyes started to burn as she listened to the women chattering away.

Sam felt a gentle hand on her arm. It was Slick. "You okay, Sam?"

"I'm okay. No, that's a lie, Slick. I don't understand any of this. Do I wear some invisible sign that tells people to reject me? Do I smell? Am I offensive?"

"You're none of those things, Sam, and you know it. It's Pappy. He made it personal. You got under his skin, and he didn't know what to do about it, so he bounced you. It's that simple, and that's how you have to think of it so you can move on. Not right now because you're hurting. If there's anything any of us can do, all you have to do is ask. We're here for you."

"I know, Slick. Thanks." Sam turned back to the window and the gentle breeze wafting through. Exhaust fumes sifted through, too. Not pleasant. She closed the window and leaned her head back against the headrest. She thought about Alpha and how frightened he was when he saw all the women in the black habits. He'd run to the bathroom and hidden behind the door. No amount of coaxing could get him to come out either. They'd scratched the Seeing Eye dog part of the caper and left. She hoped he would be all right alone.

Ten minutes later, Joey shouted to be heard all the way in the back of the van. "Okay, ladies, we're here, and, as usual, there are no parking spaces. I'll drop you all off and ride around until I find a suitable space. We're early, and that's a good thing. It will allow us to set up and arrange the table to our satisfaction."

People stared at them as they stepped out of the van. Everyone smiled and said, "Good evening, Sisters, Father." Sam felt like a cheat and a fraud. She wondered if the others felt the same way. She thought then about what she was going to feel when she set eyes on the man she had been married to for three whole weeks.

"Showtime," Slick whispered in her ear. "You can do this, Sam. He's just someone you used to know. That's how you have to think about it. The others only see dollar signs. Come on, Sam, square those shoulders and remember what I said. You guys got him. That alone should satisfy you. Here comes Joey. Time to go in and . . . what's that saying, beard the lion or something like that."

Sam smiled. "Do you think this particular lion is going to roar?"

"Oh, honey, this particular lion is going to mew like a sick kitten. Trust me."

It was a small, sparkling-clean restaurant with delicious smells emanating from the kitchen. Starched red-and-white-checkered tablecloths were on all the tables. In the center of each table were containers of grated cheese and hot pepper flakes and baskets of crunchy breadsticks. Standard Italian fare.

Mr. and Mrs. Panella came out from the kitchen to greet their distinguished guests. Sam couldn't remember if they were in on the plan or they really thought the group was what they pretended to be. Everyone smiled, everyone nodded. Mrs. Panella, a rotund little lady with rosy cheeks and short gray hair, beamed her pleasure. She had a smudge of flour on one cheek, and her apron was as white and as crisp as the checkered tablecloths.

The long table was set and just waiting for the group to sit down. They did. Carafes of dark red wine appeared as if by magic. Baskets of piping hot garlic bread followed.

Sam was annoyed that her back and the backs of her whole team would be to Douglas. The newest group of Rainford "wives" and Joey would be facing Douglas's table. Joey said it would be best. The newest members wore round granny glasses, and Joey had altered their noses a little with latex putty, so they looked nothing like the exotic creatures they really were.

By the time Senator Wyne and his two guests arrived, Sam's party had consumed all the garlic bread and downed two glasses of wine each.

Sam looked around, the head covering she wore shielding her face in profile. All the other tables were filled with quiet couples intent on eating a good, filling meal. Conversation was subdued. Soft music could be heard in the kitchen; then again, maybe it was a television.

Joey ripped at a chunk of garlic bread. "They're here, ladies and gentleman. The senator's guests are two old geezers. One is wearing a fishing hat and the other one is wearing one of those Swiss Tyrol hats. I make them at around seventy or so. Sound like anyone you guys might know?" All the murmurings were in the negative.

"They're having a very earnest conversation, and whatever is being said is not to the senator's liking. In fact, he looks a little angry. Somehow, I don't think his dinner companions are constituents. They're arguing now. It seems like they want the senator to do something, and he's balking." Joey clucked his tongue. "Neither one of those old geezers has taken off his hat. Kind of strange, don't you think?"

Sam was dying to turn around for a look-see, but continued to sit quietly and try to figure out what was going on. Men always took their hats off in a restaurant. Kids might wear baseball caps, but nine times out of ten their parents made them take them off.

"Maybe they're bald and they're self-conscious about it," Slick said as she took a bite of garlic bread. "Can I turn around and take a look? You know, very casual-like. The senator doesn't really know me, and in this getup he won't put two and two together."

Joey poured more wine into his glass. "Okay, but only when I tell you. The senator will be facing you. You'll get the other two in profile. If you turn to the right, you can pretend you're looking at the two ladies in the corner." Five minutes went by before Joey nodded ever so slightly.

Sam didn't know why, but she took a deep breath. She saw that Slick's hands were shaking when she turned back to face the others at the table. "It's Kyros. He's the one wearing the Tyrol hat. I . . . I think the other one is . . . I think the other one is *Pappy*. They're in disguises. I think."

Sam almost fainted. She drained her wineglass in one gulp and poured another with shaky hands. There was no way she could make her tongue work to say anything. The others were stunned at what was happening.

"Now what are we going to do?" Slick hissed.

"I'm thinking, I'm thinking," Joey hissed in return.

"Well, think faster," Hawkins snarled. "Are you sure, Slick?"

"Yes, I'm sure. They're in disguise, just the way we are. Whatever is happening, it must really be important for Pappy to come down out of his ivory tower. Maybe we should pack this whole thing in and exit through the back door. This place does have a back door, doesn't it?" Slick dithered.

Sam tried to make sense out of what she was hearing. Pappy came down off the mountain. What did it mean? How did he know the senator? She felt like standing up and pitching the wine carafe directly at him, but her legs were too wobbly. She was a disgrace to every nun in the world. And if those nuns of the world knew she was wearing thong underwear under this scratchy outfit, they'd drum her off the face of the earth. She'd have to do penance for the rest of her life. She should have worn cotton briefs. Her ass was going to itch for a week. It was itching at that very moment. She said so. The others just looked at her. Zoe moved the wine carafe out of her reach.

Their food arrived just as Joey was about to speak. Since it was Thursday night, only two dinner specials were on the menu: chicken piccata and the lobster ravioli. Joey had taken the liberty of ordering half and half when he made the reservation. So far their salads of fresh greens were untouched. More garlic bread arrived. The carafes were refilled.

"Eat!" Joey ordered. "I'll think while you do. Make sure you clean your plates, or the Panellas will be insulted."

Sam tried to spear one of her raviolis but she missed the little square and it sailed across the table to land on wife number 9's plate. *Pappy is here.* Just a few feet away. She tried to spear another ravioli with the same result. She laid down her fork and reached for the wine carafe.

"Easy on the wine, Sam. It's a home brew and pretty potent," Slick said. She lowered her voice, and whispered in Sam's ear, "What the hell is he doing here? Do you have any ideas?" Sam shook her head.

As Joey shoveled food into his mouth, he mumbled his plan to get them out of there.

Hawkins leaned across the table. "What kind of diversion can you possibly create with the senator's protection detail out there?"

"I'll think of something," Joey said as he dabbed his

lips with his napkin. "I won't be long, so finish your dinners." He was as good as his word and was back in five minutes.

"Well?" Hawkins said.

Joey smiled. He held up his glass of wine. "To a diversion"—he looked at his watch—"in eighteen minutes."

Chapter Eighteen

Sam propped her elbows on the table so she could stare at her watch. She watched the second hand sweep around the face sixteen times before she lowered her hands to her lap. She started to count under her breath, feeling like she was going to jump right out of her skin. She almost did when the door blew open to admit a big burly man wearing a windbreaker with bold lettering on the back and waving an automatic weapon. He rushed to the middle of the floor, waving his weapon around the room. "FBI! Did anyone come through here in the last few minutes? Is there a back door?" he bellowed.

No one moved, no one said a word until Joey stood up and said, "No, my son, no one has come through here. I don't know if there's a back door or not. I've never been here before."

The senator's security detail was there in the blink of

an eye, surrounding the senator and his guests. More men, probably Mike's people, rushed in. One of them shouted, "We think we have him covered down by the corner." The room cleared as suddenly as it had filled, with the exception of the senator's security detail. It sounded like the security detail wanted the senator to leave, but he insisted on finishing his dessert.

"Heads down, ladies," Joey hissed, as Kyros and Pappy sprinted for the kitchen and the back door.

Sam looked up in time to see both men's backs. She felt light-headed. "I think I'm going to be sick," she mumbled.

"No, you are *not* going to be sick. Take a deep breath," Slick ordered. She turned around to see the senator banish his men to the doorway, where they stood guard. It was clear he wanted them to leave the restaurant for the comfort of the other diners. Finally, they did leave, but they stood right outside the door.

"Now what?" Sam asked as she looked around the table at the shocked expressions on everyone's faces.

Joey bit down on his lower lip. "We're here. I say we go through with what we were planning. Slick, head for the restroom."

A bit of confusion followed as the other diners were arranging to pay their checks and leave, allowing Slick to make her way to the restroom at the far end of the dining room. She scurried inside but peeked out through the narrow opening. She took a deep breath and counted to thirty to still her pounding heart. When she was breathing normally, she washed her hands, flushed the toilet, and counted to thirty again. Satisfied with her steady nerves, she exited the restroom and minced her way toward the senator, aware that all the eyes at the table were on her.

Folding her hands in front of her to make sure they were visible to the security detail outside the door, she approached the senator's table. She was careful to stand a good foot and a half away. "Good evening, Senator Wyne, or should I say, good evening Douglas Cosmo Rainford, III? My party over there," she said, pointing to her table, "wondered if you would like to join us for an espresso. That would be your former 'wives,' Senator. And even Martina Crystal, the one that got away, is here. People are watching, so I suggest that you smile, Senator, as if I just said something witty. It is witty, don't you think? Imagine the field day the *Post* will have with this. Or, if you don't care for that scenario, you could invite us to your palatial digs at the Watergate. We'd love to have an espresso there with you. In addition, Senator, be aware that we know who you were dining with this evening: Kollar, better known as Pappy, Havapopulas, and his father, Kyros. What's it going to be?"

Senator Wyne placed his spoon carefully in his dessert bowl, turned, and looked at the long table full of nuns and the two priests. The women waved and smiled. Even from this distance, Slick thought she could see dollar signs flashing in the ex-wives' eyes. Joey and Hawkins nodded as both made sloppy signs of the cross.

Struggling with his voice, the senator finally was able to manage, "I'd be honored if you and your . . . ah, fellow sisters would join me at my home for . . . espresso."

"Good choice, Dougie. Call your security detail in here and tell them we will be following you back to your home. Make sure you sound jovial and believable. On the ride home you can think about all of this. Any funny stuff, and you'll be seeing and reading about your exciting double life in all the papers tomorrow. Are we clear?"

"Crystal, *Sister.*"

The two old men shuffled down the street, their heads bowed. It was totally dark, the June evening warm, almost sultry.

"That was a bit nerve-wracking," Kyros said. "We need to get you back to the mountain, son."

"Not yet. I still have something to do. Pop, did you think there was anything peculiar about what just happened?"

Kyros sounded perplexed when he responded. "Peculiar, how?"

An ambulance, its siren screaming, roared down Connecticut Avenue, three patrol cars right behind, their red-and-blue lights flashing. Instinctively, Pappy slammed himself against a doorway. His father looked at him, his eyes sad. It was time to go back to the mountain.

His breathing back to normal, Pappy looked around for a taxi. Traffic was light at that hour of the evening but there was no sign of a taxi. "The whole thing, Pop.

All those religious people, the FBI guy bursting through the door. My first thought was it was a setup of some kind. The senator didn't seem disturbed at all. Either he lives for food, or he has a death wish. The man was going to finish his dessert, and that was all there was to it."

"And that means . . . what?"

"I don't know, Pop. It didn't *feel* right the whole time we were there. My instincts were on high alert."

Pappy stepped off the curb, whistled shrilly, and waved his arm. A yellow cab slid to the curb. Both men climbed in. Pappy rattled off Sam's address. Neither man spoke on the thirty-five-minute ride to Sam's condo. Pappy paid the driver and both men stepped out of the cab.

Kyros lowered his body to the top step on the stoop while Pappy marched over to the door and rang the bell. Inside he could hear Alpha bark. The bark turned to a pitiful whine as he hovered on the other side of the door. Pappy dropped to his haunches and spoke to the door. "Fetch her, Alpha." The dog continued to whine. Pappy knew instinctively that Sam wasn't inside. His shoulders slumped as he continued to talk to the dog on the other side of the door.

"The moon is riding high in the sky, son. We're going to attract attention soon. Two old men dressed like we are will be considered homeless, and someone will call the authorities. Make it quick," Kyros said in a harsh-sounding voice.

"She's not here, Pop. I'm talking to Alpha."

"Write her a note," Kyros shot back. "We have to leave."

Write her a note. With what? He didn't have a pen or a pencil, nor did he have any paper. For one wild, crazy moment he thought about pricking his finger and scratching his name on her door in blood. Instead, he pulled out his wallet and withdrew the driver's license that had expired eight years ago. He slid it under the door. It was all he could do.

Pappy joined his father, and, together, the two men walked up the street to use Pappy's prepaid cell phone to call a cab that would take them to the airport for their return to the mountain.

Kyros patted his son's shoulders. "You tried, son. It's time for us to go back where we belong."

"Yeah, Pop, you're right. It's time to go back where we belong."

The senator's security detail was respectful of the religious group as they climbed out of the van and followed the senator to the elevator that would take him to his palatial apartment.

Sam couldn't wait to yank off her headpiece, which was what she was going to do the minute she got inside the apartment. She itched from head to toe. It was all so surreal. Her "ex-husband" had been dining with Pappy and Kyros. She wondered if she was dreaming.

The spacious apartment was beautiful, professionally decorated with a quiet, understated English coun-

try home decor. The walls were painted in shades of
brown and tan. Thick ficus trees stood in the corners,
bowing to the light. The oversize living room looked
manly and comfortable. It also looked like it didn't get a
lot of use. There was no dust, no smudges on the glass-
topped tables. The plasma TV hanging on the wall had
to have cost a fortune. The Oriental rug covering the
beautiful parquet floor was clearly very expensive.
There was no doubt that the person who lived here was
very rich, Sam thought, as she yanked at the headpiece
and pulled off the wimple.

The cool air from the air conditioner felt good on her
face. Her hair was damp and plastered to her head.

When everyone was seated, the senator looked
around and tossed his hands in the air in disbelief. "I
guess my question is how did you figure it out and how
did you find me?" He sounded like he was asking if it
was going to rain.

The women all looked at Sam. "It wasn't that hard,
Dougie. What are you, some kind of honeymoon
junkie? We would all like some kind of explanation."

The women started to talk all at once. Sam leaned
back in a chair covered in some kind of nubby material. She continued to itch, and listened as the women
called him a liar and other uncomplimentary names.
They jabbered about honeymoons, sex, foreplay,
whispered words. And then came the final insult,
"*You creep!*"

"Well? Say something, *Dougie*!" Kayla spit out.

Sam listened in disbelief as the senator tried to justify what he had done. "What can I say? I love getting married. I love going on a honeymoon. I loved each of you at the time. I'm just not marriage material. I didn't know how to tell any of you that. I guess you could say I'm a short-term kind of person."

"*Short* is the right word," Kayla sputtered.

Zoe shook her head in disbelief, a sad smile on her face.

"What are you going to do to make amends?" Olivia demanded.

The senator rubbed his neck. "What would you like me to do? Do you want me to say I'm sorry? I'm not. I loved every minute of the time I spent with each of you. Every single minute."

The itch was unbearable. Sam stood up. "Look around you. You had sex—with each of us. You went on a honeymoon—with each of us. And since you used a false name and fraudulently entered into a contract using that false name, you never actually married any of us, meaning that you essentially treated us as low-priced call girls. Where else could you get three weeks of adoringly given sex for so little money. *You are a creep!*" Sam shrilled.

"You have to pay for breaking our hearts," the ravishing redhead said. Sam thought the redhead was the one who wanted to buy a Swiss chalet.

"Will money mend your broken hearts?" the senator asked.

"Damn straight it will, you creep," Olivia said. "Now, make us an offer. You should know, none of us have much patience."

"All right, a hundred thousand each," the senator said.

Sam frowned. No Swiss chalet there. She waited for the women to boo the senator. Instead, the women laughed. They continued to laugh as the offers escalated. The Swiss chalet was looking more and more likely.

Sam started to squirm in her chair. She wanted to go home and take a cold shower and put on some cotton underwear. "This is stupid. They want ten million each. Take it or leave it, *Dougie*," she said. "They're done negotiating. Get your checkbook. *Now!*"

"Yeah, now!" the women chorused as one. The Swiss chalet was a done deal, as were the Paris fashion shows.

Sam was on her feet twirling the wimple in her hand. Surreal wasn't cutting it.

The senator walked over to a cherrywood secretary and pulled out a hardbound check folder. As he wrote, he spoke. "I'm going to want a waiver from all of you in regard to your silence."

"Well, sure, we wouldn't have it any other way," Sam snapped. "Just so you know, these two nice gentlemen are going to stay with you until these checks are certified in the morning. We don't want you taking off on us again, or maybe even changing your mind.

"It's amazing that you remember our names," she snapped again.

"I remember everything about each one of you. For instance, Samantha, I remember how you liked me to . . ."

"That will be enough," Sam said shrilly. "No one cares."

When each woman, Martina Crystal included, was holding her check, Sam marched to the door. She plunked the headpiece back on her head haphazardly, the wimple askew. She turned around and walked back to where the senator was sitting. She bent over, her eyes full of menace. "Where did your friends go? Don't pretend you don't know what I'm talking about. I could kill you with one chop to the neck."

The senator, who was suddenly $120 million poorer, swallowed hard. "I think they went home."

"What did he want? It must have been something crucial for him to leave the mountain."

The senator raised his eyebrows. "It was important, and it was personal." Suddenly, the senator's eyes widened. "You were one of the recruits, weren't you? That's how you know about the mountain. I didn't realize, Samantha. In a million years I never would have guessed." He looked at her closely and lowering his voice, he said, "You love him, don't you?"

"None of your damn business, *Dougie*." Suddenly she knew the senator belonged to the consortium. Sam backed up and followed the others to the door. She looked back and waved to Joey and Hawkins.

Outside in the hallway, the women were so giddy they made Sam nervous. "Decorum, ladies," Sam admonished, as she led the penguin parade to the elevator, through the lobby, and out of the building to where the van was parked.

Slick drove to Sam's condo, dropped her off, and headed for the Airport Marriott. She called through the window, "Meet us at the United Bank in Quincy Plaza at nine in the morning, Sam."

"Okay."

Inside, Sam ripped at the nun's habit as she ran to the bathroom to look at her rear end in the mirror. She was right; she wasn't going to be able to sit for a week. Just as she started to take off the rest of the habit, Alpha appeared at her side.

"Oh, Alpha, I'm sorry. You okay? Look, I'll feed you in a minute. First though, I need to . . . never mind. Just wait for me."

The cool water on her rump felt so good she almost swooned.

Thirty minutes later she was walking around in a loose-fitting nightgown. She padded into the kitchen and pulled out food for the dog. She was about to set the plate on the floor when she noticed Alpha holding something in his teeth. He offered it up as he whined at her feet.

Sam reached for the small square of hard plastic. She looked at it, blinked, then blinked again. Pappy's driver's license. An expired driver's license. *Oh, God, he was here, and I wasn't home.* She sat down not caring that her rear end started to burn. Tears rolled down her cheeks. She was on her feet a moment later. She ran to the door and slid the card underneath. It slid easily. She opened the door and retrieved it.

What did it mean? Obviously, Pappy had no idea she'd been in the same restaurant where he'd been just hours ago. They'd fooled the senator and Pappy, too. Instead of feeling elated, she felt horrible. He'd come to see her at great risk to himself. She couldn't believe she was the reason for the visit, though. He'd come down off the mountain to see the senator. And as long as he was in the area, he'd stopped by. To see Alpha, of course. The visit had nothing to do with her. *Hope springs eternal*, she thought.

Sam whistled for Alpha, who came on the run. "Let's go for a walk," she blubbered. Alpha sniffed every inch of the stoop and the steps before he reluctantly walked over to the copse of trees on the other side of the street. In her bare feet, Sam followed. She waited patiently as Alpha sniffed everything in sight before he agreed to return to the house.

Tears continued to drip down Sam's cheeks as she tidied up the kitchen, made herself some coffee, and carried it back to the family room. She turned on the television and stared at it, not knowing what she was watching. She continued to cry, as Alpha crawled up on the sofa and put his big head in her lap. "I could sit here forever, Alpha. I have ten million dollars. I never have to do anything I don't want to do. What do you think about that? Hell, we could buy a Swiss chalet, too, if we wanted to.

You could eat sirloin steak every day, but I'm thinking that kind of life would get real old real quick for both of us. When I open my new office, if I do, I will be able to take you with me every day because I'll be the boss." Alpha just stared at her, his yellow eyes unblinking.

Sam stretched out on the sofa. Like she was really going to do any of those things. She wiggled until she was comfortable and was asleep within minutes, the tears she'd shed drying on her cheeks.

Senator Malcom Wyne picked up the phone, mumbled a greeting, then handed the phone to Joey, who listened intently to the voice on the other end of the line. He nodded, got up, and motioned for Hawkins to follow him. Neither man offered to shake hands. "For all intents and purposes, this never happened, right, Senator?"

The senator nodded as he ran his hands through his hair. He needed to shower and shave. And by God, he needed to think, to plan. But first he had to call his office and tell his aides he wouldn't be in. "Right, this never happened. I'm just $120 million poorer."

"You know what they say, Senator, you play, you pay."

"Well, *Father*, you know what they say about extortion, don't you?"

"Nasty word." Joey grinned. "Nobody twisted your arm to write those checks. You looked like you were happy to do it. Honeymoons are getting more expensive every year. See you around, Senator."

The senator slid the dead bolt on the door, a huge sigh of relief escaping his lips. He called his office first, then his housekeeper, and gave her the rest of the week off. Then he took a shower, shaved, and made himself a cup of coffee. When he was dressed for the day, he opened his briefcase, withdrew his BlackBerry, and sent a message to the only person he trusted to get him out of this mess.

Exhausted, the senator leaned back in his favorite chair and closed his eyes. This was a fine mess he'd gotten himself into. But he'd loved every minute of it. So what if he had to part with lots of money? So what? His "ex-wives" would have a veritable blast squandering it. Like the man of the cloth said, you play you pay. He laughed, a great belly laugh when he realized the lengths they'd gone to to track him down and get him to write those checks.

But he knew now he had to make his plans. Perhaps the Greek Isles. Mykonos. He'd been there twice, and the women were beautiful. Beautiful, lusty, and fiery. Uninhibited, too.

The BlackBerry came to life. The message was short and simple. **Bring what you need. I'll take care of it.** The senator smiled. How strange that the only person he trusted in the whole world was the man who had been hired to kill him. The only man who could make him disappear without a trace.

The senator looked around his apartment, knowing it was unlikely that he would ever see it again. Everything he needed was in his briefcase.

Downstairs, he looked at his security detail, and said, "There's been a sudden change of plans. Take me to Dulles. I'll call you when I plan to return, and no, none of you are going with me." The senator closed the door, ending whatever argument his people were about to give him.

In the Town Car with the dark windows, the senator leaned back and sighed. Life was full of new beginnings. One more in his ledger wasn't going to hurt a thing. In fact, he was rather looking forward to his stay on Mykonos.

As Senator Wyne contemplated his future, Pappy fired up his computer and his BlackBerry. It took him all of two hours to arrange for safe passage to Greece for the senator. His business taken care of, he, too, leaned back in his comfortable chair and sighed. And, like the senator, he was also forced to look at a new beginning. He wasn't sure if he liked what lay ahead of him, but he was out of options.

Chapter Nineteen

Pappy stared at the computer screen in front of him. He motioned to the senator, who was standing off to the side. "It's the *Wall Street Journal*. Washington seems to be buzzing with your sudden resignation, Senator. It seems you're going to be missed. Every social hostess in town is pulling out her hair. It appears your absence will upset their table arrangements. The rest of the article is a rehash of your family politics. They also have a graph of your voting record. The last line says that as the paper went to press you were still unavailable for comment."

The senator shrugged. "The chopper's late."

"Yes, bad weather's got them delayed by thirty minutes or so. It's not a problem. Do you want to go over the details one more time, Senator?"

The senator shrugged again. "The chopper is taking me to Pittsburgh, where I will take a flight to Kennedy.

From there I will fly to Switzerland with the brand-new passport that arrived this morning. From now until I arrive in Zurich I will be Gerhard Metzer. One of your people will meet me and take me to a private clinic, where I will undergo some facial surgery. When I'm healed, I will be taken by private jet to Athens, Greece. From there, I go to Mykonos, where I will stay indefinitely. Accommodations have been arranged as well as a car. My bank balances have all been transferred to numbered accounts. I will be given a new passport in Greece as soon as my face has healed. The name on that passport will be Peter Nicoli. Did I miss anything?"

"Only one thing. Tell me why."

The senator looked away. "Back in Washington you asked me how I had evaded marriage so long. No matter how I say this, I'm going to sound like a fool. I don't feel like a fool, but that's what you're going to think. I've been married eleven times. It would have been twelve, but one of my ex-wives tracked down all the others."

Pappy's jaw dropped. "Eleven times! You were married *eleven* times!"

"Yes."

Pappy closed his mouth, his eyes full of awe. "So that means you were divorced *eleven* times!" *Brilliant deduction.* "Do you fall in love . . . easily? How did you keep it all so quiet? You lived in a fishbowl, for God's sake. Did the consortium find out? Is that what this is all about?"

The senator laughed, a rueful sound. "Yes, I fall in love easily. I love the marriage ceremony. I love the honeymoon phase. I just don't want to be married. I'm not marriage material, but I am a very good honeymooner. What can I say? If I'd played the game a little straighter, I would have gotten away with it. I welshed on the prenup. Well, not really. I promised each wife ten million if we were still married after five years, when I knew damn well I'd be gone after the honeymoon. I was deceitful. I didn't want to pay up. Like I said, they found me, and I was forced to pay up. They were all at the restaurant last night dressed as nuns and priests. Samantha, your star operative, was there, too. She saw you and Kyros. That's why I'm here. I suppose it's possible my partners found out and were afraid I would be an embarrassment to the organization or worse yet, confide in one of my wives. We'll probably never know. The bottom line is they're only worried about saving their own skins."

For the first time in the whole of his life, Pappy was at a loss. He didn't know what to say or what to think. "Is that why . . ."

"I assume my, ah . . . my partners found out somehow. I used another name and a partial disguise. I honeymooned in exotic places, where no one knew me, so it's hard for me to imagine how they found out. Let's face it, if it got out, my political career was over. There's embarrassment, and then there's embarrassment. Not to mention that since I used a false name and required a basically fraudulent prenup agreement, I probably broke the law. Maybe the consortium thought I would babble about our . . . *arrangement*.

Then again, it could be something else entirely. I have to wonder why you weren't told, considering they wanted you to sanction me."

Pappy's head was reeling. "They wanted you done away with because you love to get married and go on honeymoons? I don't know what to say other than I'm glad I bowed out. I think I hear your ride," he said inanely as he tried to cope with what the senator had just divulged. He'd been just feet away from Sam and hadn't even known it. If Sam was at the restaurant, that had to mean she was one of Malcom's eleven brides. It all made sense now. She was the one who tracked down the senator. Probably when she was in New York at the cybercafe. And he'd missed it all. He hadn't lied to his father when he said he'd lost his edge. Years ago he would have been on it all like white on rice. Kayla, Olivia, and Zoe, all part of the eleven. He must have been blind not to have figured it all out.

The woman he loved had been married to the guy he was now aiding and abetting. He felt sick at the realization.

The steady *twump*, *twump* of the helicopter's rotor blades were getting louder and louder as the two men walked out the door to cross the compound to the helipad.

Pappy couldn't help himself when he shouted to be heard over the incoming helicopter, "Are you going to . . . you know . . . keep getting married?"

The senator threw back his head and laughed. "Absolutely!" His hand shot out. Pappy grasped it as he shook his head from side to side in disbelief.

Pappy, his hair blowing in the downdraft, stood rooted to the ground. The senator leaned out and shouted something to him that he couldn't hear. It sounded to Pappy like he was saying, "She . . . loves . . . you." He waved.

All the way back to his house he kept shaking his head, then he laughed and laughed till he started to choke.

When Pappy had his wits about him, he started to wonder what he was going to do with the rest of his life. Maybe he should take a page out of the senator's book. He started to laugh again.

Three days passed before Sam opened her front door to greet the gaggle of jabbering women who wanted only to kiss and hug her and to shake her hand.

The Rainford "wives," all ten of them, and the one who got away, had come to say good-bye.

Even though it was only nine-thirty in the morning, the women wanted to make a wine toast. Sam dutifully uncorked several bottles and poured generously. They clinked their glasses, downed the liquid, then looked at one another, their eyes sparkling with happiness.

"No, no, we aren't smashing my wineglasses," Sam said in mock horror. "Listen, all of you, have a good life and try to save some of that money for a rainy day." She actually laughed aloud when she was told she would have a standing invitation to the Swiss chalet.

Then they were gone. Sam looked around at what

was her old team. She felt misty-eyed because they, too, were leaving. It was suddenly an unbearably sad moment for her. "Stay in touch," she managed to say in a choked voice.

"Sam, I don't know what to say," Slick said, wrapping her arms about her best friend. "You didn't have to give Eric and me two million dollars. God, I'm going to miss you. I'm going to worry about you, too."

"Yeah, I did, Slick. You stuck with me. If there's one thing I prize more than honesty, it's loyalty. I'm a big girl, I can take care of myself, so don't worry about me. So, where are you going?"

"We're off to Hawaii. Kona Village to be precise. We might or might not get married. I wish you would consider coming along, Sam. I know, you have Alpha now, so I guess I understand you wanting to stay here for a while. We'll stay in touch. Promise you will keep your phone on."

"I promise," Sam said solemnly. "Where are you three going?" she asked the three Rainford exes.

"We're going to Greece to spend the rest of our R&R before we have to report to Colorado. The chick at the airport told us we would be hunted down if we didn't honor our contracts. So . . . we're going to honor them or find a legitimate way to break them. All on the up and up of course. The stickler is we passed all the trials and, like the contract says, we owe Pappy three more years. We are the best of the best and we're not going to opt out.

"But now, we're going to visit all the Greek Islands.

I've always wanted to visit Mykonos. All those hand-
some Greek men. Ahhhh. Thanks for everything, Sam.
I'm sorry it turned out this way. We'll stay in touch, and
I don't just mean sending a Christmas card every year,"
Kayla trilled.

Olivia dabbed at her eyes. "You're like the sister I
never had, Sam. Thanks for everything."

Zoe wiped her eyes on the sleeve of her shirt. "I don't
know what to say either, Sam, so I'm not going to say
anything. I'll send you a postcard from Greece. You take
care now."

They were all crying, even Hawkins, who swiped at
his eyes. All he could manage to say was, "It's been a
hell of a year."

"Go on, get out of here, all of you," Sam said, a sob
catching in her throat as she pushed the little group toward the front door.

When the door closed with a final click, sobs tore at
her throat. She cried until she was exhausted.

Finally, Sam was able to drag herself to her feet. She
squared her shoulders and marched down the hall to
her bedroom. From here on in, her life was going to be
whatever she made it.

It was a time of new beginnings.

The days and weeks crawled by for Sam, who seemed unable to make any kinds of concrete decisions. She looked
at properties that would be suitable for opening her own
offices, but at the end of the day couldn't bring herself to

sign a lease on any of them. She spent a lot of time reading the old postcards the Rainford "wives" sent her from time to time. Slick and Hawkins sent cards from Hawaii with pictures of girls in grass skirts. One from Zoe in particular caught her eye. She'd partied up a storm for three full weeks. A few days before she left she met a handsome Greek. She was going to go back to Mykonos on her next vacation to meet up with Peter Nicoli. She'd added a p.s. that read, you wouldn't believe how much he acts like our old "ex-husband."

Sam's days were uneventful. She cooked, cleaned her condo, walked Alpha, shopped for knickknacks, and sat on her front stoop talking to her neighbors. At night she lulled herself to sleep with too much wine.

By the time the end of August arrived, Sam was convinced that if she was going to stay in the Washington area, she needed to buy a cabin in the mountains in order to get out of the city's oppressive heat and humidity. She thought of the trips she'd have to make to look at different properties, the paperwork involved. *Maybe next year*, she told herself as she walked to her mailbox, hoping for a card or letter from one of her friends. Most days there was nothing but flyers addressed to Occupant, or a bill.

On a bright autumn day at the end of September, Sam looked at Alpha, who seemed listless to her. He hadn't eaten the night before either, and that morning he didn't want to go for their two-mile walk. Tears formed in the corners of her eyes. She'd known this day was going to come and thought she was prepared for it, but she wasn't. She dropped to her knees. "You want to go home, don't you? You want to see Pappy again. Okay, let me get my stuff together, and I'll take you back to the mountain." The wolf-dog's ears perked up as he followed Sam while she filled a backpack.

"This is probably a stupid thing I'm doing, but I'm betting you can get us to the top of the mountain. If not, oh, well!"

Sam checked the condo one last time; everything seemed to be in order. Three days to climb the mountain, if what Pappy had said was true. Surely he would let her take the cable car down after she delivered the dog. What could possibly happen to her condo in three or four days? Not much. Who cared anyway? She should move into a mansion and hire people to do everything for her.

Sam rummaged in the kitchen pantry for the special leash Joey had brought when they were going to take Alpha to Panella's. She was going to pretend to be blind so she could take Alpha on the plane with her. He would go berserk cooped up in the cargo hold. She called the airline and booked two first class seats. She told herself she was meant to do this when she was told the next flight to Raleigh-Durham was in two hours. Her lucky day.

With Alpha at her side, she waited on the stoop for the taxi that would take her to the airport.

It was a beautiful day, she noticed. A perfect Indian

summer day. Already the leaves were starting to change color. Big Pine Mountain would probably be alive with color. Overhead, the sun was bright and warm. Somewhere off in the distance someone was burning leaves. She thought then about her youth, football games, pep rallies, and pumpkins. It was all so long ago. She wondered if she'd ever been as young as she remembered. Young with no worries other than whether she would have a date for Saturday night. Most times there wasn't a date. She'd been too shy, too plain. Boys wanted bosoms, brash words, wicked promises, and tons of makeup.

Sam gripped Alpha's lead, making sure the sunglasses she was wearing were secure, and started down the steps. The taxi pulled to the curb.

Alpha howled either his pleasure or displeasure as Sam settled him in the cab.

They were on their way.

The minute Sam shut off the engine, Alpha leaped to the front seat to paw her shoulder. He knew they were close to home. She hadn't seen him this excited since the day they'd left the mountain. They both got out of the rental car, and Sam stood perfectly still as she struggled to make sure she got her bearings. She was glad she had paid attention to their descent on their departure. The first time they'd arrived by helicopter. When she'd left by cable car, Poke Donovan had been waiting for her. He'd led her by foot for two miles through heavy brush to where his car was parked. Then he'd driven a full mile and a half to get to the highway. She thought she was in the right place, but she couldn't be certain. Hopefully, Alpha would lead her in the right direction if she lost her bearings.

Sam checked her backpack. Two apples, two water bottles, crackers and cheese, granola bars, toilet paper, and beef jerky for Alpha. Her stun gun and her GPS were secure in side pockets, along with her BlackBerry and a new cell phone whose number she couldn't even remember. She pulled out a flashlight and hooked it onto her belt. It was a new type that didn't use batteries. All you had to do was shake it, and the beam of light would penetrate fifty feet. It was heavier than she liked and awkward to carry, but she needed it. It was called Forever Lite.

Sam wore jeans and a long-sleeved yellow shirt in case the nights got cold. Timberland boots covered her feet. Her hair was piled high on her head and covered with a baseball cap that said ATLANTA BRAVES on the bill. She needed the hat so that bugs and ticks wouldn't get in her hair. A lightweight windbreaker lined in flannel was tied around her waist. Again, in case the nights were colder than expected. Satisfied with her inventory, she looked down at the wolf-dog, and said, "Let's go, Alpha. Time to go home." Alpha sprinted off.

A light mist was falling when Sam and Alpha started up the mountain. Even if the mist turned to hard rain, the overhead canopy of trees would protect her. The time was three thirty.

For the next twenty-four hours, Sam and Alpha climbed steadily. Every hour they stopped for a ten-minute break and sips of water. They napped for thirty minutes every four hours or so. The flashlight was turning out to be invaluable.

Nighttime proved the most worrisome to Sam, but Alpha had no problem. She was tiring, though, and needed to rest more often. The spike of energy she got from the PowerBars she munched on helped a little. This was all about stamina — Pappy's favorite word.

Nine hours later, Sam tripped on a vine and went down on both knees. She winced but forced herself to get back on her feet. She gave the flashlight a violent twist and waited for the beam of light to appear. She ripped at the vine before she moved on. Her legs ached and so did her back. Sleep was something she longed for. A nice hot bubble bath, clean sheets, and sleep. Well, that wasn't going to happen for a while, so there was no point in even thinking about it.

Alpha prodded her, growling deep in his throat. Sam moved, understanding that Alpha wanted to go home. She knew she had shin splints, and her knees ached unbearably. They were also swollen from her tumble. *This too shall pass*, she told herself.

As she continued to climb, Sam wished she'd kept up with her physical training after returning home. She should have continued with her daily runs and weight lifting. But, no, she'd wanted no reminders of her time on the mountain. So she cooked, baked, and got addicted to pineapple-coconut ice cream. You didn't need to be in shape to crunch numbers or count your money in the bank.

More hours passed, with more frequent stops and sleep times. She knew she was seriously behind schedule, but she was okay with her delay. When she got to the top, if she got to the top, it would be okay. There was no one to chastise her for not moving fast enough. Even if there was, did she care? No, she did not. She didn't care about much of anything these days.

Sam clenched her teeth. Every time she started to think like this, she invariably thought about her old team and wondered where they were and what they were doing. Slick, in her last email from London, said she would try to make it to DC over the Christmas holidays. But, she'd added, don't hold your breath that it will happen. The last line of her letter said everything was on a need-to-know basis. It was all Sam had to look forward to.

Life back in Washington was going to be very boring when she returned without Alpha. As she climbed, she planned a cruise on a singles cruise line. And what would she find on a cruise line? Someone with baggage, someone who owed back child support, a nasty ex-wife in the background, someone else's reject. Maybe even a secret alcoholic who pretended he didn't have a problem. Sam grimaced. Olivia was the queen of cruises and informed her of what she'd found in her search for a suitable husband. Okay, scratch the cruise.

Suddenly, Sam was sitting on her rear end. She'd tripped over a log. She sat for what seemed like a long time. She was incredibly tired. All she wanted was to curl up and go to sleep, but she knew she couldn't do that. Alpha tugged at her muddy jeans, urging her to her feet. Sighing deeply, she struggled to her feet and staggered forward, Alpha in the lead.

Sam turned her thoughts inward, playing a game with herself that she'd played when she was a child and longed for a fairy godmother who would grant her three wishes. Back then her first wish was for unlimited wishes. She tried to recall what she'd wished for. Silly things to be sure. A new bike, a sparkly party dress, a pony, a best friend, a boyfriend who would tell her she was the prettiest girl in the world.

She'd given her fairy godmother a name—Anastasia—and she talked to her on a regular basis, mostly in times of stress. She hadn't played the game in a long time. Maybe she should give it a shot. Or was she too tired even to think of a wish? "Hey, Anastasia, it's me. You still in the wish business?" Alpha stopped and turned to look at her as he waited for her to catch up to him.

"I'm coming, I'm coming," Sam muttered to the dog. She turned her thoughts back to her wishes. With only three wishes she had to be extra careful. Maybe she needed to postpone something this serious. To a time when she wasn't so tired and could think coherently. *Nah, I need these wishes right now. I want everyone in*

*the world to be safe and happy and free of disease. I want
a cure for every disease known to man.*

Two down and one to go. The last wish was always
the most important. What did she want more than anything in the world? Should she make a selfish wish? If
she did that, it would be like trying to make a pact with
God. If You do this for me, I'll do that for You. No, selfish was out. "Help me here, Anastasia," Sam muttered.

Since there wasn't going to be a reply, Sam called to
Alpha, and said, "I need to sleep for a while. She isn't
going to answer me." She gave the dog a drink and two
beef jerkys. She was asleep within seconds, her windbreaker her pillow, the pine needles her bed. Alpha sat
guard.

Pappy looked at his father and back at the closed-circuit
television monitors. "I should go after her, Pop, but I think
she needs to do this on her own. To prove something to
me. What the hell did I do to her?" he asked miserably.

"You rejected her. Women don't like to be rejected,"
Kyros said sagely. "What I don't understand is why she's
coming back."

Pappy bit down on his lip and looked away. "She's
bringing Alpha back. Not because she wants to, but the
dog is unhappy. She thinks he belongs here. She wouldn't
take the risk of calling me to ask if she could come here. I
would have said yes, but she wouldn't take the chance
that I might say no. She has to do it this way for herself.
Depending on how long she sleeps, she should be here by

morning. In a million years, I never would have believed she'd climb at night. Shows determination, Pop."

Ever practical, Kyros said, "Find some clean clothes for her and lay them out. Do you have any *pretty* stuff for her? Women like pretty things, soaps, shampoos, and that froufrou underwear."

Pappy looked at his father in disgust. "I'm not even going to bother to answer that. Where in the hell am I going to get *pretty* things?"

"Well, maybe you could pick some flowers or something."

Pappy shot his father another look of disgust. He went back to watching Sam sleep in her bed of pine needles, his heart thumping in his chest at her nearness.

Sam bolted upright when Alpha tugged at her shirtsleeve and a bolt of thunder roared overhead. She felt disoriented, unable to focus for several seconds. It was going to storm, that was her final thought as she started to trudge behind Alpha, who now seemed to want to run. Stamina. It was all about stamina. Go beyond the pain and move. Every bone in her body was protesting, wanting her to stay put, but the wolf-dog had other ideas. They must be close to the top for the dog to run. If only it was true. She worried that lightning would follow the thunder. She'd seen hundreds of downed limbs, and lightning gouges on the trees during her climb. It was a crapshoot if she should stay put or move. Unsure of her own instincts at that moment she opted to go with Alpha's.

Sam did her best to breathe deeply and evenly as she forced her legs to move to keep up with the wolf-dog. Head down, she grunted and groaned, but she didn't stop. She'd get to the top of the damn mountain or she'd die trying. Move! Move! Move! Thunder continued to beat at her eardrums as she made her way through the carpet of wet pine needles. She saw lightning, but it seemed off in the distance, not overhead.

It was a hard, driving rain, slicing down through the thick pines, soaking her. Alpha was barking, louder, her signal to hurry. Why, she didn't know, but she picked up on his fear and forced her legs to pump faster.

Alpha stopped and barked. The sound jarred Sam's teeth. She forced her head up to stare at what lay ahead. She saw it then—the compound. She stood completely still for one long minute. Finally, Alpha pushed her forward. She was almost to the center of the compound when she saw Pappy rushing toward her with a large golf umbrella. She started to laugh. Maybe the umbrella was for him. She continued to laugh. Then he scooped her into his arms and started for his house. Alpha barked shrilly at these strange goings-on. Finally, he stopped when Pappy carried Sam into the house and straight back to his shower. He turned it on and pushed her inside, clothes, boots, and all. Alpha growled. He started to snarl when Pappy tried to towel him off, but in the end he allowed it.

Pappy had laid out a pair of his pajamas and a set of clothes the nurse had left behind. They were way too big, but they were clean and would do until his father could wash Sam's clothes and dry out her boots.

Inside Pappy's shower, Sam started to peel off her clothes. It took all her energy to lather up and wash her hair. The soap and shampoo had a minty smell and felt cool and refreshing. She sighed. She was here. She'd made it. Sam toweled off in slow motion, her arms protesting as she pulled on a pair of pajamas that smelled minty but woodsy, too. They must belong to Pappy. Like she cared. He'd said something about sleeping in his bed. It was turned down. She fell into it, but not before she hugged Alpha.

Sam was almost asleep when she remembered she hadn't made her last wish. No time like the present. "Anastasia, my last wish would be that I don't cry when it's time to leave here. I wish for strength and dignity. Don't let me cave in like I did the last time. That's my wish."

And then she was asleep.

Chapter Twenty

Pappy and his father were like two scalded cats as they took turns waiting for their guest to wake. Kyros outdid himself when he prepared a breakfast of Belgian waffles with fresh blueberries, macadamia-banana pancakes, and eggs Benedict, only to have to throw them down the garbage disposal when Sam slept through breakfast. Certain that she would be awake for lunch, he immediately prepared delectable crab cakes with a mango chutney, sweet potato curls, and a crisp green salad. That, too, went into the garbage disposal when Sam slept through lunch. Absolutely positive their guest would wake for dinner he prepared chicken Kiev with a melt-in-your-mouth potato-onion-cheese casserole, fresh peas, garden salad, and delectable yeast rolls with sweet butter drizzled all over them. When Sam was a no-show once again, he dumped it, too, muttering, "If I were you, I'd check to make sure our guest is *alive*." Alarmed, Pappy ran off to check on her. To his immense relief, he saw that Sam was sleeping peacefully.

With nothing but time on his hands, Pappy walked out to his bench in the compound, with Alpha at his side. He fired up a cigarette and gave Alpha one of his favorite rawhides to chew on. "It's like old times, Alpha," Pappy said, with a catch in his voice. "I missed you, big guy." Alpha stopped chewing long enough to lift up his head to stare at his master as if to say, "I missed you, too."

The hours crawled by, one after the other. Alpha was on his fourth rawhide chew when the clouds overhead gave way to a full moon that bathed the compound in a silvery glow. The trees rustled softly. Somewhere, deeper in the forest, he could hear the night birds talking to one another. It was so peaceful. Pappy sighed. Alpha dropped his head down between his paws, eventually closing his eyes. Pappy sighed again. He'd never been more miserable or as unhappy in his life as he was right then. His only consolation was that Sam was sleeping in *his* bed, under *his* covers, wearing *his* pajamas. Yet, just what the hell was that going to get him?

At four o'clock in the morning, Pappy stirred on the bench. He looked around, panic on his face. Something woke him. What? He looked for Alpha, who was on his feet, the hair on his back standing straight in the air. He appeared to be listening for something. Pappy turned and saw her. She looked like a ragamuffin, in his too-large pajamas and her hair standing on end. She was barefoot, clutching the bottom of his pajamas in her hand. He wanted his voice to sound professional and courteous, but it came out jittery and anxious. "Are you all right?"

"A little stiff and sore, but I'll be fine. I was wondering if I could get something to eat. A peanut butter and jelly sandwich will be fine. Maybe a Coke. My throat's kind of dry."

"Sure, sure. Come on, I'll make it for you. No point in waking up Pop. Are you sure you're okay?" He thought his voice sounded tender and compassionate.

"I'm fine. Thanks for the use of your bed. I'll be leaving as soon as it's light if you can see your way to letting me go down in the cable car. I brought your dog back. He missed you. He doesn't belong with me." Her voice was so cool it bordered on frosty. Whatever she might have hoped for, she wasn't seeing it. She felt like crying.

All Pappy heard was that she was leaving when the sun came up. That was in a few hours. Suddenly, he felt sick to his stomach.

They were standing at the back door leading to the kitchen. He wanted to say something profound, something meaningful, but the words stuck in his throat.

Sam mistook his silence. "And," she said, "I wanted to tell you to go to hell to your face. You are the most arrogant, the most infuriating, the most obnoxious man I've ever had the pleasure of knowing. You had no right to bounce me off this mountain the way you did. You have no couth. You have no *anything*. You humiliated me, you son of a bitch. I gave you a hundred ten percent! You want to go six rounds with me, let's do it. I'll have you flat on the ground in ten seconds. You . . . you . . . *has-been terrorist*. I wouldn't work for you or those people you work for if you paid me my weight in gold. I'll make my own sandwich, thank you very much."

Stunned, Pappy backed up one step, then another. He still couldn't find the words he wanted to say. *Has-been terrorist*. That one hurt. The kitchen door slammed in his face. *Has-been terrorist*. He'd never been a terrorist, much less a has-been terrorist.

Inside, Kyros held out a peanut butter and jelly sandwich and a bottle of Coca-Cola. "I heard. Weren't you kind of hard on my son, Samantha?"

"No," Sam snapped. She gobbled down the sandwich and asked for another one. Kyros made it for her.

Kyros sighed unhappily. As he prepared two sandwiches, one for Sam and one for himself, he spoke. "Sometimes my son gets tongue-tied. Especially around women he cares for. We went to see you in June, but you weren't there. Kollar was devastated. He wanted to explain what happened and why he did what he did. He left the mountain, Samantha. I never thought he would do that. Never!"

"I know. I saw you both at the restaurant. I was there. Actually, I just saw your backs when you rushed through the kitchen door. I saw that you had been to my house and assumed it was to see if Alpha was ready to go back to the mountain. Your son left the mountain to see Senator Wyne, so don't pretend it was to see me and apologize. He went to my house to see Alpha. Do you have any cake or pie, Kyros?"

Kyros stared at the young woman dressed in his son's pajamas. "You were at the restaurant? You recognized us? I didn't see you. I'm sure Kollar didn't see you either, or he would have said something. No cake or pie, but I have some peanut butter cookies."

"I'll take them. Three or four would be nice. Yes, the whole team was there. We were dressed up like nuns. Hawkins and Kayla's brother wore clerical collars. Like you two, we were in disguise. It sounds kind of silly now when I say it out loud. It doesn't matter if you know this now or not because it's over. We were there to confront the senator. It had nothing to do with Slick, Hawkins, or Joey, Kayla's brother. All the rest of us had at one time thought we were married to the playboy senator. We threatened to go public, so the senator resigned. *After* he paid each of us ten million dollars. That's probably more than you wanted to know, Kyros." Sam slid off the counter stool. "Thanks for the food. Do you know where my clothes are? It's going to be light soon, and I want to go home.

"Do you want to hear something funny, Kyros? I thought of this as home for a whole year. I couldn't acclimate once I left here. I missed the team, the mountain. I missed you, too. I cried myself to sleep every night for a month. You're a wonderful cook." Hot tears pricked Sam's eyelids, but she blinked them away.

"Did you miss my son?"

"About as much as I'd miss a bad itch. You're so nice, Kyros, how did you ever get such a son?"

Kyros laughed. "The luck of the draw. He had a no-return policy. In case you don't know it, my son is in love with you."

Sam laughed so hard the pajama bottom fell to her ankles. "Where are my clothes?" she managed to gasp as she pulled up the pajama bottom and clutched it in her hands.

"I put them in Kollar's house on the coffee table. I'm not sure if your boots are dry. He does love you. Ask him. Kollar has never, to my knowledge, told a lie."

Sam laughed bitterly. "Like I'm really going to do that."

Kyros reached for Sam's arm. He looked deep into her eyes, his own full of sadness. "If you don't ask him, you will always wonder. You'll never be sure. It's a simple question. That's why he sent you away. He didn't want to turn you into an operative. He lived that dangerous life far too long, and he didn't want it for you. He wanted you safe and sound because he loves you. I know that because I am a father, and a father knows such things," Kyros said, thumping himself on his head.

"Ever hear that expression, too much, too little, too late?" Sam snarled.

"Many times. Did you ever hear the one, you snooze you lose?"

"*Touché*," Sam said.

Sam walked back to Kollar's house. It was almost light out; Pappy and Alpha were nowhere to be seen. "It figures," she mumbled to herself as she opened the door. He was sitting in his chair, his legs draped over the arm. She sailed past him with all the dignity she could muster. *You snooze you lose, huh?* She called over her shoulder, "Do you love me?"

"Yeah," came the response.

Sam stopped in her tracks. He said yeah. Meaning yes, he loved her. She forgot about the pajama bottom as she whirled around and tripped, sprawling in the doorway. In a heartbeat Pappy was on the floor and they were eye to eye. "I said yes in case you didn't hear me."

"I heard you, that's why I tripped. You love me, but you kicked me out of here. You humiliated me. You made me think, *for months*, that I was inferior."

"Because I love you. I'm not good at this fancy word game. In fact, I stink at it. I didn't think you'd want to live on a mountain for the rest of your life. That's the way it would have to be. I couldn't ask you to give up your life. If it's any consolation to you, I knew it was a mistake the minute I did it. I'm still not sure it was the wrong thing to do. The way I *did it* was wrong. I haven't slept through the night since you left. I've lost fifteen pounds. I've thought about you every moment since that day."

He was *so* close. She'd never realized how truly beautiful his eyes were. She could see herself in them.

"If you want, I can tell you my life story. It might explain a few things. Maybe it will explain me. By the way, I'm not *in the business* anymore. If you really want to join your team, I can arrange it. It's your decision. It was wrong of me to make that decision for you. You were the best, you really were. I was jealous, too, of your capabilities and dedication. I know you gave me a hundred ten percent because I pushed you. In the beginning I thought you could hang the moon, then I realized my feelings for you were getting in the way of your training."

"I wasn't the one who broke the rules. You kissed me first. I did everything you asked of me plus more."

"I know. Why did you ask me if I loved you?"

"Because your father told me you would never tell me, and I wanted to hear the words myself. Women like to hear all the sweet words. I wasn't lying to you before when I said I could take you out in minutes."

Trying to save face, Pappy blustered, "Not even on your best day. That one I am not giving you."

Outside, peeping in the window, Kyros rolled his eyes. Was this some kind of new mating dance? Where were the soft lighting, the candles, the wine and music? His son was hopeless. He blinked when Sam wiggled forward, her rear end exposed in the overhead lighting. What was she *doing*? Alpha, who was standing at his side, must have wondered the same thing because he started to whine. "Shhh. Something's happening. It might be good. Then again, it might be bad. Shhh."

Sam let her eyes droop and her body relax. "Well," she purred, "are you going to kiss me or not?"

Pappy moved closer, so close she could smell the wine on his breath. She wiggled forward, a half inch, then another half inch, her arm moving slowly until she had him in a hammerlock. With one wild motion, and a flash of bare derriere, she jerked Pappy backward until she was straddling him. She relaxed her hold and pushed his face down into the thick carpet. Her hard-muscled legs held his sides in a vise. "Gotcha!" she said triumphantly. "You know this position, this hold, you taught it to me, Pappy. One little push, and I smash your nose and break your neck."

Pappy sneezed. Startled, Sam's hold instinctively re-laxed. Before she could blink, Pappy let out a roar and she was on her back and he was straddling her.

Outside, Kyros covered his mouth so he wouldn't laugh. "I think this is where you and I should leave, Alpha. I think my son has things under control. Maybe there's hope for him after all."

Pappy was breathing like a distance runner when he leaned down, and said, "This is the part you didn't pay attention to. You thought you would never find yourself in that position. I distinctly recall saying if you ever were in that position, pretend to sneeze and your adversary would instinctively relax their hold."

"Oh, I remember *that part* very well," Sam purred. "Now that we're even, what are you going to do about it?"

He told her.

Then he showed her.

Kyros did a wild pirouette to Alpha's amazement as he waved his spatula in the air. "A feast this morning, Alpha, for the lovebirds." He did another little dance as he imagined grandchildren sitting on his lap. Dark-eyed little boys, beautiful little girls who looked like their mother. Happiness at last on the mountain.

He banged pots, sliced, diced, and chopped for what he called the ultimate omelet. He continued to sing and hum under his breath. Many people thought an omelet was just eggs and vegetables. Not his omelets. People would kill to eat one of his creations. The secret wasn't in the vegetables or the salt and pepper, it was in the spices. Greek spices. The treasure trove that he kept under lock and key in his spice cabinet.

"It would be nice, Alpha, if you would show a little more enthusiasm." The wolf-dog eyed him, watching his every movement. Kyros tossed him a slice of crisp bacon, which the dog ate daintily.

At eight o'clock, Kyros placed the perfect omelet onto two plates, half for Alpha and half for him. "I guess they have other things to do besides eat," he muttered to the dog.

At noon, Kyros was back at the stove, hands on his

hips. He looked at the array of cooking utensils he had used to make lunch. He sniffed appreciatively as did Alpha. Everything would be ready by twelve thirty. He set the table in the dining room and added some fresh flowers from his garden. "Beautiful," he said, smacking his hands together. Kollar and Sam both loved his grape leaf rolls. Everyone loved his grape leaf rolls. They all loved his fried apple and cabbage, too. His little new potatoes with the red skin glistened with the herbed oil he'd rubbed on them. They were to die for, or so his son said every time he ate them.

At one thirty, Kyros filled Alpha's plate and his own. He had to force the food down his throat. He thought about sending Alpha with a message but changed his mind. Maybe he should go over and knock on the door. He nixed that idea almost immediately. Instead, he cleaned off the table and tidied up the kitchen.

"All right, Alpha, let's go outside and sit in the warm sunshine. I think we both ate too much. A little nap might do us both some good," he said sourly as he led the dog out to the little wooden deck off the kitchen where he had a lounging chair and an umbrella. His pipe and his tobacco were waiting for him. At the last second, he reached into one of his cookie jars for a rawhide chew for Alpha.

They looked at one another, wonderment on both their faces. Neither said a word for a long time. Finally, Pappy found his voice. "What now, Sam?"

What now indeed. She'd woken a good thirty minutes before Pappy and had stayed quiet, thinking. She took a deep breath and told him what was in her heart. "This whole year can't have been for nothing. You have to let me have my time just like the others. I earned it, and deserve it. A year, Kollar. Then I'll come back. You need to understand something. All my life I was never quite good enough, didn't quite measure up, didn't quite make the cut, no matter how hard I tried. This time I did. Maybe this isn't for me. Then again, maybe it is. If I give it up, I want it to be my choice. For once in my life I want to finish what I start and come out on top. This is something I *need* to do. If you love me as much as you say you do, you'll help me."

Pappy closed his eyes. He'd found her, and now he was going to lose her. He was about to voice the thought aloud when Sam said, "I will come back because I love you. I love this mountain. I love Alpha and your father."

Pappy struggled with the question he was afraid to ask. "But will you come back to stay?"

Sam looked deep into his eyes and was as honest as she could be. "I don't know. I want to think I will. I love you. If I don't do this, I will always wonder if it was the world I was meant to work in. I would grow discontented here, I think we both know that. I'm asking you to wait, to give me a chance."

"All right. A year is a very long time, Sam."

"I know. It's 365 days. It could be an eternity if you want to think about it like that. I will come back, I promise."

Pappy smiled and reached for her. "If I told you my love for you was measured by the sands in the desert, would you believe me?"

"Yes. Would you believe me if I told you my love for you was measured by the depth of the ocean?"

Pappy laughed as he pulled her under the covers.

It was six o'clock when Sam headed for the shower, and Pappy headed for his computer. At seven o'clock, both were fully dressed and headed for the dining room.

"Damn, Pop, I thought you might have cooked something," Pappy grumbled. "I guess it's peanut butter and jelly again."

"I love peanut butter and jelly," Sam said as she tussled with Alpha.

"Like I have nothing better to do than cook. I'm retiring," Kyros said, stomping out of the kitchen. Outside, he clapped his hands gleefully. Never, since the day his son was born, had he seen such love on his face. He would have danced a jig, but his wobbly old legs would have protested too much.

Inside, as they munched on their sandwiches, Pappy talked earnestly. "Poke Donovan will meet you at the bottom of the mountain. He'll take you to the airport and escort you to the location in Colorado. You won't be working with your team, they've all been assigned to other projects. Everything you need to know is inside that envelope. Poke has other information for you. From here on in, I'm out of it. You're on your own, Sam."

Sam took a deep breath. "I need to get out of here before I change my mind. Let's go."

Pappy's heart lurched in his chest when he saw the woman he loved pull on her backpack. He held the door for her. Standing outside, the hair on his back bristling, Alpha blocked the way. Sam dropped to her knees and whispered in the big dog's ears. Then she removed the backpack and laid it at the big dog's feet. He looked up at her, then at Pappy, before he picked up the straps of the backpack and trotted off.

Pappy unlocked the gates to the cable car. Sam looked at him, her heart in her eyes. She didn't kiss him, she didn't have to. She touched his arm and smiled before she strapped herself into the skinny seat.

Kollar's heartrending shout ricocheted around and down the mountain. "Come backkkkkk."

Alpha howled, the sound crashing against Kollar's words.

Kyros dabbed at the corners of his eyes.

Epilogue

Almost a year to the day since leaving the mountain, Sam let herself into her condo. How strange it all looked. And how quiet and lonely. She looked around as she walked about, opening the blinds and windows to get rid of the musty, closed-up-house smell. She realized she'd never really had a chance to live there, to enjoy her little nest. She felt rootless, homeless.

She'd stopped to pick up some lunch and her mail, but she had jet lag and was too tired to eat or go through the mail. All she wanted to do was sleep, but she wanted to go to the mountain more. She'd finished up her project two weeks ago. It took a week to convince her superiors to accept her resignation. She'd been pleased with how hard they'd tried to convince her to stay, saying things like she was a natural for this line of work, she had keen instincts, a razor-sharp edge. In the end, she'd promised to be available for special projects suited to her particular talents.

Sam thought about the missions, the projects she'd worked on. A smile tugged at the corners of her lips as she thought about the last case she'd worked on. She remembered how stunned she'd been when her case supervisor told her they were taking on a middle-of-the-road HMO with thousands of dissatisfied members. Too many court cases where the customers lost their claims, their life savings, and, in some cases, their loved ones when medical care was denied. The legal system hadn't worked for them. Three months of intense work with her new team, and the HMO had not only paid up, they'd paid up retroactively. It was amazing what the fat cats in charge of the bottom line were willing to give up when they looked down the barrel of a SIG Sauer. The kidnappings had gone off without a hitch. Men who were used to two-thousand-dollar suits, private Gulf-streams, three-hundred-dollar dinners, private schools for their children while others suffered or died were stripped to their skivvies, held prisoner, and denied even the basics of life. Because she was a CPA and knew how to crunch numbers, she'd been in charge of the distributions to the members of the HMO once the fat cats folded their tents. The best part, though, had been giving the fat cats back their expensive suits and handmade shoes, then leaving them in the jungles of Brazil to make their own way back to civilization.

Barbaric. *Damn right*, she thought. But wasn't it

more barbaric of those same men to deny a six-year-old girl the ability to live by denying her a bone marrow transplant? Someone had to make those people accountable, and Sam had been the one to do it.

Sam leaned her head back on the chair and closed her eyes. A minute later, she was asleep, her dreams full of Pappy and her return to the mountain. She woke twelve hours later with a crick in her neck and a mouth that tasted like sawdust and glue.

Suddenly, Sam was more alert than she'd ever been in her life. Today was the day she was going back to the mountain.

Where she now knew she belonged.

Back to her love, to Alpha, to Kyros.

Home to the mountain to surprise Pappy a week ahead of schedule.

Since she'd returned sooner than expected, she had to make her own reservations, which she did even before she brushed her teeth. A one o'clock flight gave her five hours to shower, dress, eat, and go through her mail.

She was a whirling dervish as she raced around, chomping on the cold take-out food she'd bought the day before.

She chose a lemon-colored sundress with matching sandals, and her diamond earrings. They sparkled against her still-tanned skin. At the last minute she splashed on some sinful perfume made from lotus flowers. She sighed nervously. What would Pappy say when he saw her? Or would he just reach for her and kiss her till her teeth rattled? She hoped it was the latter.

With hours to go, Sam started to go through her mail. She tossed everything aside except the assortment of cards and letters from her old team. Everyone had annual leave coming up in ten days, and all five members of Team Three wanted to know if a vacation on the mountain was a possibility.

She was delirious with the thought of seeing all her old friends. Pappy could take care of the arrangements.

Sam gathered up all the cards and letters and put them in her purse to read and reread later on. All she could think of was how surprised Pappy was going to be when she contacted him on her BlackBerry from the foot of the mountain. She already had her message all planned out. "I'm waiting. Send the cable car."

Sam was so giddy with anticipation, she gathered up her purse and her overnight bag. She would feel closer to Pappy if she waited at the airport, plus she could get some hot food there. It would be a while before Kyros could prepare one of his gourmet meals for her.

She'd never been happier in her life.

Never.

At ten minutes to six, in her bare feet, her shoes in hand, her carry-on strapped to her shoulder, Sam took a break and sat down on a stump off the beaten path. She rummaged around in her backpack, her heart thundering in her chest as she yanked out her BlackBerry. She struggled to take a deep breath as she punched in her message, then turned it off. If she ran like the demons of hell were after her, she could get to the cable pad just as it made contact. She ran then, her hair flying in all directions, her heart singing.

At the top of the mountain, Alpha howled, the sound ricocheting down the mountain. Pappy pulled the BlackBerry out of his pocket, read the message once, then once again. He ran faster than he had ever run in his life, and arrived at the cable pad at the same time Alpha did. He unlocked it, turned it on, and climbed inside, Alpha half-on his lap and half-off. The wolf-dog howled all the way to the bottom.

He looked at her.

She looked at him.

Unable to wait, Alpha leaped out of the car and slammed his powerful body against Sam. He lavished kisses all over her. She hugged and squeezed him until he yelped. "I told you I was coming back."

And then she was in Pappy's arms. His lips never left hers as he backed her into the cable car and turned it on blindly. They were still in a lip lock when the cable car stopped and Kyros greeted them both, peanut butter and jelly sandwiches in hand. There was no way he was cooking that day. This time he knew better. When it was apparent neither his son nor his about-to-be daughter-in-law was interested in his food, he tossed the sandwiches off the mountain.

Sam hugged him, too, tears streaming down her

face. "Are you visiting, or are you here to stay?" he whispered.

"What do you think, Kyros? I'm here to stay. Forever and ever." The old man beamed.

Pappy and Sam were glued together as they moved about the compound. They talked about their year apart, their hopes and dreams, and about the right day to get married. "The sooner the better," Pappy said.

"We have to wait for my old team. Slick is going to be my maid of honor. Kayla and Olivia my bridesmaids. I think Hawkins would be honored to be your best man. Zoe won't be able to make it. She's leaving the organization and going to Greece. She said a year and a half was enough. She said Mykonos can use a plumber like her because the plumbing there is appalling. Plus, she met some guy while the girls were there last year on R&R. She's going to look him up again," Sam babbled happily.

Pappy's eyes almost bugged out of his head. "Mykonos?"

"Is it a nice place, Pappy? You being Greek and all, you must know the area well."

"It's wonderful," Pappy managed to say, his mind racing. Surely it wasn't possible. A coincidence. Never in a million years could . . .

Tuned to his mood, Sam asked, "What's wrong? Are you upset that Zoe won't be here?"

"Nothing's wrong. Of course I would like Zoe to be here for you. Did she tell you the name of the man she was interested in? Maybe I know him."

Sam's brow furrowed. "She did tell me his name in a postcard she sent. I think I have it in my carry bag. Let me look." She ran across the compound and returned with her carry-on. She dug around until she had the stack of old postcards in her hand. "Here it is." She quickly read the message on the postcard. "His name is Peter Nicoli. Do you know him, Pappy?"

Pappy started to laugh. "Yes, I know him, and so do you. It's Senator Wyne, a.k.a. Douglas Cosmo Rainford, III. I gave him a new identity, and he will live there the rest of his life, or at least for a good long time."

Sam stared at the man she was going to marry, her eyes full of questions.

"I can't talk about it, Sam. It all belongs to that old part of my life that I gave up. I'm sorry, but I can't say more."

Sam's head buzzed. "Well, we need to warn her. Don't we?"

"Zoe's a big girl. The senator's appearance has been altered but I'm sure she's going to figure it out sooner or later. He did tell me she was the only one he regretted divorcing. He really liked the way she could take apart a drainpipe. Even with her long fingernails."

Sam started to laugh, and Pappy joined in. They laughed so hard they fell off the bench they were sitting on. Glued together, they rolled around until they found a soft patch of freshly mowed grass.

"I love you so much it hurts," Pappy said. "I wasn't sure you would come back. Every night I prayed. I counted the hours and the minutes."

"I did, too. I'm here now, and I'm not going anywhere. At least not anytime soon. I explained my departure agreement. You're still okay with it, aren't you?"

"I'm okay with anything you want," Pappy said softly. "I'll always be okay with anything you want to do."

Sam kissed him to seal their bargain, and it was a bargain. A bargain of love.

Fantasy.
Temptation.
Adventure.

Visit PocketAfterDark.com, an all-new website just for Urban Fantasy and Romance Readers!

- Exclusive access to the hottest urban fantasy and romance titles!
- Read and share reviews on the latest books!
- Live chats with your favorite romance authors!
- Vote in online polls!

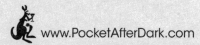 www.PocketAfterDark.com

26119